DANGEROUS TRADE-IN

RAY SCOTT

SILVERBIRD
PUBLISHING

Publisher: Silverbird Publishing
Ray Scott
website: www.raycwscottwriting.com.au

First published in Australia 2025
This edition published 2025

Cover design, typesetting: WorkingType (www.workingtype.com.au)

Scott, Ray
Dangerous Trade-In
ISBN: 978-1-7640421-7-8 (paperback)
978-1-7641394-8-9(ebook)

ABOUT THE AUTHOR

Ray Scott was born in Kent in England and lived and worked for over 30 years in the Midlands near Birmingham. After National service in the Royal Navy he joined the insurance industry and was employed for many years in Birmingham and Wolverhampton. He and his wife Mary and their two boys immigrated to Australia in 1970 and have lived since then near Melbourne where he again joined the insurance industry, while Mary rejoined the nursing profession.

Ray has been writing for many years. This is his sixth venture into publishing, the others being *The Fifth Identity, Cut to the Chase* (also a paperback) *The Wimmera Shoot, Double Dutch, Line of Dissent* and *Doubt of the Benefit*, all thrillers.

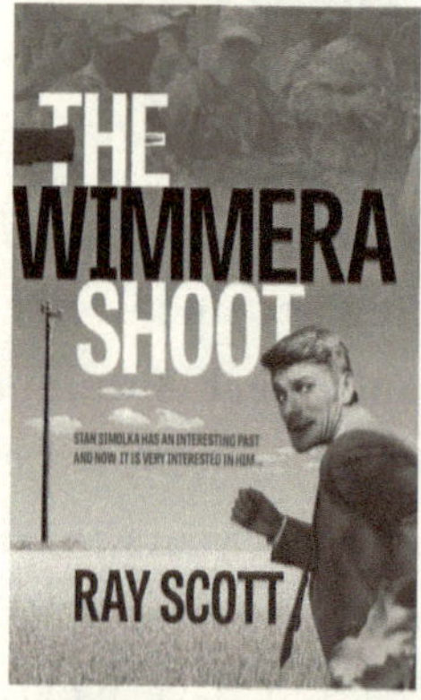

www.raycwscottwriting.com.au

To the regrettably late David Blackford, an enthusiastic follower and critic of my writings. We crossed paths at secondary school, cricket club and later family, his sister became my wife. A headmaster of traditional 'old school' values, and a skilled tweaker of a cricket ball.

CHAPTER 1

I f he was ever going to break out, it would have to be now! Whatever plan they had in mind, it appeared to be near fruition. There had been considerable activity in the house that day, whilst in the driveway below two vans were drawn up outside the shed. He could make out figures moving in front of and behind the two vehicles, loading items that looked like backpacks aboard them.

He still had the table knife in his possession, useless as a weapon but certainly useful for unscrewing the lock handle from the door. He cast his mind back over the past ten days or so, still puzzled why he had been kidnapped and incarcerated.

Roughly ten days ago, he had lost count, he had left his Melbourne suburban apartment in the early morning and climbed into his company vehicle. He had been heading for his place of work when he had been hemmed in by two cars that cut across him, forced him to the side of the road and onto the footpath. He had angrily jumped out to remonstrate but had been baled up against the side of his van by three armed men.

They had seized and forced him into one of their cars, which had then driven from the scene at high speed. He had seen a fourth man enter the driving seat of his van before a piece of sacking was thrust over his head. Thereafter it had been a case of trying to breathe, as the sack was musty and had previously contained something that irritated his nose. He sneezed violently a couple of times before his nostrils settled.

Not a word had been spoken by his captors, he had ascertained before being bundled into the car that all bar one were Asian, the exception being of European appearance.

As the car journey progressed, he had begun to feel queasy, fear of vomiting superseded fears of his impending fate. It was clearly a case of mistaken identity, he had little or no money, was not an heir to a vast estate, had no rich relatives and knew no vital state secrets. What the hell was going on?

He tried to ask the question, as well as he could from the confines of the sacking, but received a blow across his head in response which hurt. Thereafter he held his tongue, it was pointless asking questions when nobody was going to answer them.

The journey had seemed interminable, but in time fewer corners were turned, while fewer stoppages indicated they were likely on a freeway. The speed of the car was constant, with little variation.

That changed eventually after an hour or so, although time wasn't easy to assess. The overall speed declined and there were a few stoppages, the road appeared to have changed from a freeway to a highway, stoppages could be traffic lights, he could hear other cars and trucks revving up as the car moved forward after each stoppage. He tried to sit up straight, so he could listen but was pushed back into the corner seat. His head hit the back corner of the car's roof.

'Sit still!' a voice hissed, he wasn't disposed to argue.

After further travelling there was an abrupt left-hand turn, the car bumping up and down which indicated a country track. This continued for a short spell before he felt the car describe a 'U' turn and come to rest.

'Out Mr Samson,' was the order, despite the mispronunciation of his name he assumed the directive was for him. He scrambled out, was frog marched onto gravel; then stumbled over what could have been a low step. He clearly passed through a doorway, his foot hit an obstruction and again he stumbled forward but was prevented from falling by a hand on his left shoulder.

'Ten stairs, Samson,' the same voice hissed. 'Count as you go.'

He did so, reached a landing and was frogmarched forward again. He passed through another doorway and was pushed so he fell onto what felt like a bed. He heard footsteps, a door slamming and the sound of a key turning in a lock.

His hands were free, he seized the suffocating sack and wrenched it from his head. He was in a room 4 or 5 metres square, with a window at one end and could see the drive. A car was moving away towards the road, wherever that was, leaving a cloud of dust behind it. In the room was a single bed, a dressing table in which he could see his red and perspiring reflection, and a bedside table on which stood a small lamp, another small table and chair. On the wall was a picture of an obviously Australian scene.

The use of the name 'Samson' was puzzling, could this be a case of mistaken identity? He decided to ask, assuming he had an opportunity.

He had been incarcerated for about three hours before the door was unlocked and a man entered. It was the European he had seen before.

'What the hell's going on?' he stormed.

'You'll find out,' said the other. Any thoughts of assaulting the other evaporated as two Asians entered the room. 'But you'll do as you're told… understand?'

'No, I don't bloody understand, you can't just kidnap me off the street. Who the hell do you think I am? And by the way my name's…!'

That was as far as he got, a backhander caught him a glancing blow across the cheek, which he saw coming and managed to partially avoid, but dodging it caused him to overbalance and fall to the floor. He was dragged to his feet, ushered over to the small table and thrust into the chair.

'You have a letter to write, this is what you are to write to your employer. You have received another job offer; you are resigning now. Don't argue, just write.'

*

That had been several days ago, twice he had attempted to tell them they must have the wrong man as they had his name wrong, but to no avail. Thereafter his meals had been delivered with some adherence to a time table, his watch taken from him but whether this was to confuse him or was outright theft he had no idea.

He had spent the first few days trying to ascertain why he was there, nobody bothered to answer his questions. After the fourth day, his mind began to work on plans of escape, but with bars on the window this seemed a forlorn hope.

He tried to assess how many people were in the house. He'd seen an elderly couple in the garden from time to time. The man wore shirt and denims while the woman consistently had a scarf over her head, by which he assumed they were Muslims. They merely pottered around in the garden. There was also a younger woman, dressed from head to toe in black while her head was covered.

As for the rest, there was the single European who stood out, the rest were Asian. After a few days he calculated there were eight altogether, difficult to be certain. There were at least five bearded ones who were fairly slim, and two heavier in build, one very much so. The upstairs of the house was only occupied at night; he heard footsteps on the stairs, opening and closing of doors and once or twice the creaking of bed springs.

During the day, he appeared to have the top deck to himself except for toilet breaks. Nobody else appeared to use that toilet regularly, presumably there was a bathroom somewhere downstairs, although occasionally someone climbed the stairs to use it, maybe when internal pressures became unbearable and the downstairs bathroom was in use.

He had examined the lock on the door, which gave some hope. It was a very old rim type lock, being screwed onto the inside of the door on his side. The striking plate was also fitted onto the door jamb with screws. This gave him food for thought, he eyed the screws and noticed distinct screw heads on them. When he had meals, they supplied him with a knife and fork, the utensils were metal. After pondering this, on the fifth day he appropriated a table knife from the tray, collected by one of his Asian captors who picked up the tray without checking it.

He was then escorted to the toilet on the same floor, a daily routine. He took the knife with him and hid it behind the toilet bowl. He reasoned that if they discovered the missing utensil it would be soon and the first place searched would be the bedroom.

He was right on both counts, later that evening three men had suddenly burst in and baled him up against the wall while they grimly searched everywhere, stripping the bed and feeling all along the mattress. They frisked him and hunted all over the room, leaving nothing unturned, they even opened the window and looked out onto the window sill.

'What's going on? What are you looking for?' he asked but they ignored him.

'Nothing here,' said the European and they trooped out.

As they reached the door he asked. 'How long are you going to keep me here?' but nobody answered.

As they shut the door behind them and stood outside on the landing, he heard the European say: 'Nothing...it must have been mislaid in the kitchen or dropped off on the way, but check the bloody things after every meal from now on.'

*

That was how matters stood for the next few days. He had recovered the knife from the toilet on his next visit and thrust it into his sock. His one fear was that it may fall out as he was pushed back to his prison, but was sent sprawling onto the floor and the door locked behind him. He had already noticed a shaky board near the foot of the bed, he prised it up and placed the knife under it. He also levered out one of the nails with the knife blade so he could lift the board again with bare fingers.

The next two days passed uneventfully, the routine hardly changed, meals were delivered, he had regular trips to the toilet at the end of the landing and was escorted back to his prison room. His guards were mainly Asians, occasionally the European. Again, he asked why he was there and what was going on but received silence and the usual push back into the bedroom.

Each day he had noticed activity around one of the sheds, to the left of his vantage point and about 70 metres from the house. Two men exited the house early each morning and headed for the shed, one dressed in flowing robes who looked like a Middle Eastern religious figure. Mid-morning there were usually signs of activity, several men emerged, puffed on cigarettes and chatted before returning to the shed. He assumed the shed acted as a bunk house in which they slept. The same two men returned to the house each evening.

One day there was a change in routine. Two vans arrived and there was much coming and going from the main shed. One of the vans parked near it, the rear doors were opened and they started loading backpacks from the shed into the van.

Four men piled into the van which took off down the track. That meant four men less in the house, he estimated there could be four left, plus the elderly couple, and the younger woman or girl. The other van, having moved up, was similarly loaded.

If he was going to break out, surely now was the time. He procured the table knife from under the floorboard and attacked the screws on the old rim lock. The first screw turned grudgingly, then more easily and fell onto the floor. He then attacked the next screw, this gave at once and followed the first. The third wouldn't budge at all. He nearly wept with frustration as it refused to give even a quarter of a turn.

He stood for a moment, then had a thought and attacked the striking box. If he removed that, the locked door would have nothing to lock into. Its two screws unscrewed easily and the striking box fell into his hand. He turned the door handle, the door opened with the lock still in locked mode. The wood on the door jamb was old and splintered easily as the protruding lock tongue scraped against it, now the striking box had been removed there was little resistance.

He had no choice now, unless he replaced the screw and striking plate. He had to make a run for it and soon. His meal would be due up in...how long? Since losing his watch he had become adept in assessing time by the position of the sun. Maybe two hours.

He heard an engine start up and went to the window. The

second van was moving out with two men aboard. That left two men plus the older couple. He crept onto the landing, listened hard, then descended the stairs. So far so good, there was silence, everyone was either still outside or in the shed.

He headed on tiptoe for the rear of the house, found the rear door to the property, opened it, looked from side to side, crept out and closed it behind him. He ran at the crouch to the nearest bush, checked behind him, then, keeping the house in line with the shed, ran in a straight line. He reached a line of bushes, swung to the left, continued turning left until he was heading for the distant road by running parallel to the driveway.

He continued to run at the crouch, but nearer the road the line of bushes ceased and he had to cross open ground. He paused and considered, but there was no way around it. He emerged from the bushes and attempted to keep them in line with the house as he crossed the paddock. He looked back and his heart sank. Two men had emerged from the house and were running around the back.

He stumbled on, cursing angrily as he put his foot in a rabbit hole or undulation that sent him staggering, and realised he would have to watch it, if he ricked an ankle he was gone. Or maybe he was gone already, the road seemed a long way off as a vehicle came around the corner of the house and bumped down the track.

He had to reach the road first, that way he stood a chance. He was running away from the drive at an angle, he resisted the temptation to watch the progress of the vehicle and concentrated on looking ahead, watching where he placed his feet. The road wasn't far away now, he could see vehicles travelling on it and caught sight of a large truck heading from left to right. With a gasp of despair, he thrust into the roadside bushes, emerged on the other side with leaves and twigs adhering to his clothing, hit the roadside verge and ran.

He could see cars in the distance moving towards him from both directions, while the truck had passed by and was now moving away from him. Two vehicles were parked under a tree roughly 400 metres behind him, on the far side of the driveway, he could just make out a woman leaning over talking to the driver of the second vehicle. He pondered whether to run for that, then the pursuers' car reached the road and turned towards him, it was between him and the two parked vehicles. To reach them he would have to run towards his pursuers. He turned, ran away from them and from the other two cars.

As he turned and sprinted along the verge, he realised the hopelessness of his situation, the car's engine became louder as it overhauled him. It screeched to a halt alongside him, the two men leapt out and headed for him. The traffic ahead was still too far away to be of any assistance, so he headed off the road into the nearest paddock and managed to evade their grasp as he floundered through the undergrowth. As he twisted his head to see where they were, he tripped, fell face down in the mud, scrambled to his feet but it was too late, they were onto him.

'Game's up, Mr Samson!' one of them said, it could only be the European. He was dragged to his feet, pinioned by the Asian, was struck across the face by the European and fell back onto the turf again. He heard the sound of a car engine which presumably was the leading vehicle of an oncoming knot of traffic that had reached the spot and was now passing by. He was hauled to his feet and the European faced him, holding a gun.

'Just stand bloody still! Secure him Naji.'

As the Asian began to secure his wrists, there was movement behind him in the bushes.

'More of them!' their captive thought. 'What bloody chance did I have?!'

As he eyed the European, he slowly became aware the situation had undergone a change. The European's facial expression was changing from triumph to curiosity, then utter surprise and alarm. His mouth slowly dropped and his gun arm wavered. Simultaneously there was a chopping sound and the Asian behind him grunted and fell to the ground, clutching his head.

'Good afternoon,' said a strange voice. 'Would you mind dropping that gun...*now*... before we have a nasty accident!'

The European slowly lowered and dropped his gun. A fair-haired man moved from behind, picked it up and pushed the European backwards.

'Now lie face down and put your hands behind your head, there's a good chap,' the fair-haired man said quietly, with bad grace the European complied.

The fugitive regarded the two newcomers, both nearly six feet in height, both carrying firearms, one wearing a sports jacket while the other wore a leather jacket. The sports jacket wearer was fair haired, the other had dark hair that was nearly black. They both turned to him and the dark-haired man said:

'Who the hell are you?'

He looked at them, wondering if he had fallen from the frying pan into the fire, but had nothing to lose so supplied his name. The two men eyed each other.

'Bloody hell!' said the dark-haired man. 'You've no idea how long we've been looking for you.'

CHAPTER 2

The whole affair came to light by two fortuitous and entirely unrelated events, one was an argument over money, and the other a birthday dinner at a restaurant.

The money argument was acrimonious and was between Harold Henderson and his casual employee Donald Taylor. Henderson ran a small computer hardware and software computer business in Balaclava, an inner Melbourne suburb. Business generally was tight but had recently experienced a downturn, while Henderson's wife's spendthrift habits had not scaled down to match current circumstances, if anything her spending had increased.

Consequently, the business was in financial trouble. Henderson had little money to spare and had not replaced his full-time assistant, who had left him some months previously for a better job, but employed Donald Taylor, on a casual and part-time basis.

Don Taylor was a computer enthusiast, a fanatic who tended

to drift from casual job to casual job within the computer or allied industries, to supply money to feed his computer habit. He had been casually employed by Henderson for a few months but had begun to perceive that for the hours he was putting in, the money Henderson was paying failed to satisfy even Taylor's modest needs, so he had asked for more. This discussion had manifested itself a few times over a couple of weeks and degenerated into a festering sore. Another round of this argument or discussion was in progress when a computer technician staggered into the shop bearing a second-hand computer system he was off-loading.

Henderson broke off the discussion with Taylor to greet the new arrival.

'Hallo, Adam, what have you got for us this time?'

'A Pentium, not a bad one. I've got a monitor and keyboard in the van outside. What do you reckon?'

Adam the computer technician worked for a small company of computer technicians and mechanics. If anybody's computer needed updating, picked up a virus, crashed or would not respond he was one of those experts called on to sort it out.

He frequently installed new equipment, picked up monitors and computers from people who had updated their equipment and who didn't want old computers lying around. These replaced or outdated computers should then have been returned to his employer as trade-ins, to dispose of as his employer thought fit. In most cases, they were, but sometimes there was no record of trade-in equipment and this occasion was clearly one of them. Adam brought it into Harold Henderson's shop and after some haggling money changed hands.

As Adam exited, thumbing banknotes into his wallet, the argument between Taylor and Harold Henderson resumed.

Initially Taylor had been glad of the employment, being in

the computer industry he loved, but he couldn't subsist on what Henderson was paying him. He had come down from New South Wales about 12 months prior so needed the money primarily to pay rent for his apartment and for his computer enthusiasm.

Taylor was aware of the main reason for much of Henderson's parsimony, he knew Henderson's wife Florence was a spendthrift who had no idea of the value of money, where it came from and especially where it went.

Unfortunately, during the argument, Taylor mentioned this, he knew it was tactless and could have bitten his tongue after he'd said it, but once it was out it reverberated in the air. This stung Henderson into a bout of fury, mainly because it was true and he knew it, but baulked at challenging his wife, a formidable woman. Taylor knew he shouldn't have said it, the words just tumbled out, fuelled by his dislike of Mrs Henderson, a dislike that was mutual. Mrs Henderson had reached the point where she didn't even acknowledge Taylor when she entered the shop, usually to raid the till.

Finally, Taylor stormed out, vowing never to return and saying as much to Harold Henderson. He was still firing his parting shot as he exited the shop and brushed past Florence Henderson as she entered it, presumably on her usual till raiding expedition.

But overnight Henderson had time to reflect and reluctantly admit to himself that Taylor had a point about his wife's extravagance. After consideration, he reached a solution. He knew he was underpaying Taylor, but was so strapped for cash he had little or nothing to increase Taylor's wages. But he needed Taylor, and had a solution.

Next morning, he phoned Taylor and suggested Taylor took the traded in computer system, brought in by Adam, as an increment on his wages.

The equipment was not antiquated, but Henderson knew he may have trouble off-loading it immediately, most of his customers were interested in updating with brand new equipment, not second-hand stuff. Henderson usually updated traded-in equipment himself, by installing new hard drives and mother boards. However, Henderson was aware, from earlier conversations, that Taylor was after another system to run as a subsidiary in tandem with the one he already possessed. Therefore, it seemed a good idea to offload the computer system as it was to Taylor, which would act in lieu of extra wages and Taylor could do his own modifications.

'Seems OK to me,' responded Taylor, who had also cooled down after the previous day's row. He still needed the meagre wages he had been receiving to pay his way and knew he'd been out of line by mentioning Florence Henderson's profligacy. 'I'll take it.'

Despite the acrimony of the day before, he liked Henderson and appreciated his financial problems. He also knew how unyielding and vitriolic Florence Henderson was and how vicious she could be if roused or deprived of spending power. Further, business had been slack, so after sleeping on it, Taylor had sympathy with Henderson's plight.

The next day a slightly mollified Taylor came to work as usual, as a further olive branch Henderson agreed to lend him his car so Taylor could take the computer system, keyboard and monitor back to his apartment. It was loaded into the car boot and Taylor took it home before lunch. Business was still slack so there was no need to hurry back to the shop.

Accordingly, Taylor set up the traded in computer next to his other computer, he had decided to move certain programs from one to the other. He wanted his main computer to deal with software matter relating to a computer business he was thinking of starting up, and for personal use such as family correspondence, computer games and family ancestry he was researching. He was also pursuing stocks and shares transactions using the internet.

The second computer he wanted purely for internet and e-mails, he was fully aware unscrupulous people could gain unauthorised access to people's computers and data and wanted his proposed business data to be divorced from the internet and thus confidential. Further, if by mischance he imported a virus only the one computer would be contaminated.

At that point he realised the computer brought in the previous day by the computer technician, had not been cleared of data. He switched it on and was confronted by a request for a password. There seemed to be considerable data on the computer and he would have to delete it.

Taylor was no fool or novice with computers and decided to try to break in and bypass the password. Apart from curiosity, for him it was also an intellectual exercise to see whether his skills were still up to scratch by breaking through a system blocked by a password. He had nothing else to occupy his mind at present so set about searching for a 'back door' through which he could gain entry.

He worked at it for an hour before he hit the jackpot, cracked the system, and a series of directories and file names cascaded down the monitor. He keyed into one or two which were files relating to university courses, somebody was taking an engineering course, something to do with hydraulics.

While Taylor was working on it, he realised the hard drive within the computer had been partitioned, into a 'C' and a 'D' drive, with the university courses on the main 'C' drive. There were not many there, it looked as though Adam may have partially cleared the 'C' drive, so Taylor considered continuing the process. Before he did that, Taylor had a look at the 'D' drive, opened up files, found they had a chemical content and whilst looking at these became extremely puzzled.

One chemical encompassed in a chart was ammonium nitrate, which Taylor knew was something to do with fertilisers but the mix, together with aluminium powder that was being advocated in one of the files, appeared to be making up a form of explosive. Taylor knew this because he was a member of a group of computer fanatics, or 'nerds'. When having their private computer and beer sessions, usually in one of their houses, they compared notes on information and items they frequently downloaded from the internet.

One day one of his friends had keyed into and downloaded material on 'How to make a bomb'. For them it had only been for a lark and after joking references about what to blow up, the Taxation Office being one candidate, they had come out of the site and gone onto something else. Yet Taylor still remembered something of the various chemicals and the final ingredients.

He examined the file with some interest, but didn't take too much note of its contents. Since he and his friends had recently keyed into a similar site, he wasn't surprised the former user of this traded in computer had also keyed into the same type of site. He presumed the former owner's reaction would have been much the same as that of Taylor and his computer friends, make a few jokes about it and move on.

He was about to start deleting files when, by chance, he keyed into another file named 'Nemesis'. Mildly curious why a file should be named from Greek mythology, and knowing the connotations and use of the word, he opened it.

It opened up as a graphic drawing or floor plan of a two-storey building. What puzzled him were sets of escalators set in the middle of what appeared to be a foyer, and two sets of parallel lines that ran on each side of the foyer. These lines appeared to have cross ties.

He scrolled down the plan and referred to the text, the end of September was mentioned. There was another version of the floor plan with red crosses marked in various positions, with two letter initials of what he presumed were people against the various crosses. The cross tied parallel lines were shown again on each side of the floor or foyer.

At the foot of the text and the plans was a sentence which read: -

*'All will be timed to take place an hour after the end of the event,
and retribution shall fall upon those not of the true faith'*

Taylor scratched his head, read through it again, re-checked the floor plan then realised what it was. It was a plan of one of Melbourne's underground railway stations, probably Melbourne Central. The cross tied parallel lines must represent railway tracks running along each side of the platform.

'What the hell is this about?' he muttered, and noted the reference to the end of September. He sat back and thought about it while shaking his head in perplexity. He ran through it again from the top...then realisation dawned.

This was definitely a floor plan of two levels of the Melbourne Central underground railway station. There were four areas on each level marked with crosses and names.

There was the sentence at the end of the text. There was also the question of the other file which advocated the use of ammonium nitrate and other ingredients that Taylor knew, from the casual incursion he and his friends had previously made into the Internet site, related to bomb making.

'Good God!'

He reached for a CD box and thumbed a disc into the trap on the computer tower. He downloaded that file plus the explosives one, and others that appeared to relate to the same subject. As an afterthought, he printed a couple of hard copies, before he picked up his phone and rang Henderson.

'Harold...' he said: '...about that computer we took in from that technician.'

'Yes?' Henderson was terse, maybe suspecting Taylor was about to haggle about the quid pro quo regarding the computer and unpaid wages. 'It's all right, isn't it?'

'There's something odd on it.'

'Odd?' Henderson still sounded guarded. 'What do you mean... odd?'

'That technician who brought it in...what was his name... Adam? He didn't delete what was on it, and neither did we,' said Taylor. 'There was still data on it when I switched it on back here.'

'Well, just delete it and get rid of it.' Henderson responded somewhat irritably. 'Why bother me with it?'

'But it's a plan of Melbourne Central railway station and there's four spots marked on each level.'

'So?' Henderson sounded even more impatient. 'All right, so he was a railway enthusiast...,' and added with a trace of sarcasm. '...some people do like trains, you know!'

'There's another file on the drive dealing with bomb manufacture.'

There was a brief silence before Henderson spoke again.

'You what? What was that?'

Taylor repeated it.

'Let's get this straight,' said Henderson. 'You've found a plan of Melbourne Central railway station, points marked on it at both levels, and there's an allied file dealing with bomb making?'

'That's it!'

'Are you absolutely sure or are you misinterpreting something?'

'I'm sure, it's clear as a bell,' Taylor said sharply. 'I've run off a hard copy, I'll bring it with me when I bring your car back, see what you think.'

'All right, do that! I'll need the car shortly, Florence is coming in and wants to use it, her own is in dock today for a 40,000-kilometre service.'

'Right, I'll see you in about half an hour.'

Taylor folded one of the printed copies, picked up the copy disc he had just made and pocketed them. He was just leaving when he noticed the other printed copy still sitting on the bench top. He thought maybe he shouldn't leave it lying around, he looked at his bookcase, filled with computer, cricket and football volumes, reached up and inserted the paper into the hard-back edition of Wisdens Cricketers Almanack that was sitting there. Taylor had been born in Nottinghamshire, although he remembered little of it as his parents had emigrated when he was aged only two. But Nottinghamshire in that particular year had won the County Cricket Championship, their first for many years. Taylor had sufficient loyalty to his county of birth to invest $90 to keep a permanent record of the win.

'I watch too much television!' he muttered as he inserted the hard copy into the front of the volume, left it on the desk and went out through the door. He smiled to himself and wondered if he was being unduly melodramatic.

He entered Henderson's car and returned to the shop.

CHAPTER 3

Taylor parked in the small carpark behind the shop, left the copy disc in the glove box and pocketed the print out. He entered the rear door, which closed gently behind him, it had a spring arrangement which enabled the door to shut slowly and silently.

Taylor passed through the rear store-room, then entered the back end of the shop serving area, and commenced walking behind shelving at the rear towards its end, which would bring him out behind the counter. He was wearing rubber soled sports runners, the floor was concrete based, so he made little sound. Before he emerged from behind the packed shelving, he became aware of raised voices and Henderson's on a softer key.

'We were told this computer was brought in here.'

'Yes, it was, but it's not here now.'

'Where is it?'

'What is that to you, was this computer yours?'

'It belonged to a comrade...a colleague of ours. There is

information on it we need.'

'What information?'

'That is our business.'

'Oh really! You mean business to do with the Melbourne Central railway station and bomb making?'

There was a silence. Taylor, about to enter the shop area to give Harold Henderson moral support if nothing else, paused and peered through a gap between stacks of flat boxes, containing computer keyboards, in the shelving. He could just make out three men on the customer side of the counter at right angles to Taylor's line of vision, all Asian in appearance, two with jaw lines thinly covered with beards.

The trio exchanged glances, then two of them nodded to each other and came around opposite sides of the counter. One seized the telephone cable and ripped it from the wall, and. Henderson backed away in alarm. The other two men seized Henderson and thrust him up against the wall. Taylor was about to intervene but halted when one of them produced a knife. Taylor was no coward, but a knife altered the equation.

'You know about that, you have looked at the computer, where is it?'

Henderson literally went white with fright, obviously regretting his unguarded comment but it was too late. Taylor was surprised Henderson mentioned the bomb making and railway station aspect at all in the circumstances, but recalled his own outburst about Mrs Henderson the day before. In moments of stress, these things slipped out.

The knife was drawn across Henderson's face and blood drawn from a cut on his cheek. He gasped with pain.

'Please,' he cried out hoarsely. 'I'll tell you, please put that knife down.'

'Where is it?'

'My employee has it. He took it home with him.'

'Where does he live?'

Taylor's adrenalin ran as he heard Henderson spell out his address, but couldn't blame him for that. Taylor himself would never have argued with a knife at his throat.

'Write it down,' one of the men ordered and Henderson complied.

What happened next was something Taylor would never forget. Henderson meant to push the piece of paper with Taylor's details back across the counter, but it dropped from his nerveless fingers and fell slowly to the floor. One of the men behind the counter stooped to pick it up, creating a momentary gap in attention whereupon Henderson made a bolt for the street door. He never made it. The man in front of the counter, also armed with a knife, waylaid him. Henderson gave a strangled cry as he fell slowly to the floor, writhed briefly then became still, blood seeped from a wound in his chest and crept across the floor.

The trio stood as if paralysed, the one behind the counter furiously berated the man who had wielded the knife, whether in anger at the knifing itself or the position where Henderson had fallen, in full view of the street, Taylor didn't know. Then they bolted for the street door.

They reached it and rushed through it, the man with the knife was struck by the door stile as two of them collided in the doorway, the knife fell to the floor by Henderson's side. They reached the pavement and Taylor lost sight of them; all he could hear was their running footsteps.

Taylor emerged and rushed over to Henderson. He felt himself starting to pass out as he saw the extent of the blood seeping out of the wound, as he leant forward his one hand landed across the haft of the knife while the other landed in a pool of Henderson's blood. Furiously he shook off the impending faintness, now was not the time to pass out.

'Harold!' he cried out hoarsely.

Henderson's eyes flickered open.

'Donald,' he said. 'Donald...!'

'I'll ring the police, and an ambulance, hold on,' Taylor ran behind the counter to the phone, but the flex was disconnected from the point on the wall, he remembered one of the intruders had ripped it from the wall.

'Harold!' Taylor ran back to Henderson. 'Hold on Harold, I've got to get to a phone.'

'All right...Donald ...' Henderson muttered weakly. 'Hurry ... Donald...!'

Taylor rushed for the street door, and for the second time in two days ran into Mrs Henderson. She took in the scene and her eyes widened in horror.

'Oh! What's happened, who did this?' she screamed and fell onto her knees beside her husband.

'...Donald...Donald ...!' Henderson's voice became weaker and then his head fell to one side.

'You did this?' Florence Henderson screamed from her position on the floor. 'Why...why?'

'It wasn't me,' shouted Taylor. 'There were three men in here, I saw it happen...!'

'Monster,' she screamed. 'Just because of a little bit of money.'

Taylor walked back into the shop momentarily, still protesting his innocence, and she shrank away from him.

'Keep away...monster...!' she was screaming, whereupon Taylor panicked. He ran for the door and out into the street, falling foul of some passers-by who had paused as they heard the commotion.

Nobody tried to stop him as he ran from the shop. His first thought was to get as far from the scene as possible and head for his apartment. He continued running down the street until he realised that ahead of him were the three men who had been in the shop. They were walking at a brisk pace, not drawing attention to themselves by running, which Taylor realised he was doing.

He modified his pace to a fast walk, still some distance behind the three men as they boarded a parked vehicle and moved into the traffic stream. He broke into a trot to try to get close enough to read the registration, but only managed to read the letters as it joined the traffic stream.

'KGU...!' he muttered to himself. 'Dark blue Commodore, Victorian plates.'

Then it was gone. Taylor turned left and left again and walked back along the parallel street until he was back behind the shop. He still had the ignition keys for Harold Henderson's vehicle and decided to use it. He had no clear plan in mind, panic still ruled, but he had blood on his clothes and realised if he walked down the street the sight of it would jog people's memories when the police commenced enquiries.

He reached the carpark at the rear of the shop, entered the car, fired the engine and after a couple of turns to face the exit, drove out into the laneway. He nearly hit another car amidships as he drove out of the laneway into the main street, still in a panic. His mind was racing, which resulted in the momentary loss of road sense. He listened to the cacophony of horn blowing and the verbal assault before joining the traffic stream and heading homewards.

He nearly committed a faux pas when he arrived, being about to park in the street outside the apartments building when he spotted a blue Commodore outside, the one in which the three Asians had fled. This indicated they were inside the building, no prizes for guessing which apartment they were calling on. He drove past and parked in the side street opposite; after turning around so he faced the house, the blue car and its driver. This meant the other two were inside. He tried to check the registration, but the vehicle was side on to him.

Taylor waited about ten minutes, wondering what to do next, when the front door opened. Two men appeared, one carrying a computer tower, and they closed the door behind them. They loaded the computer tower into the car and roared off.

Taylor gave them time to clear, left the car and crossed the road to the front door. After a quick look around he entered, climbed the stairs and entered his apartment. The room was a shambles. His original computer was still there, the recently traded one had gone. All his desk drawers had been opened and contents scattered, his bookshelves were likewise ransacked and books lay all over the floor. He looked around, picked up the Wisdens Almanac from the floor, with countless other books and papers, and thumbed through the pages. The printed paper had gone. He felt in his pocket, the paper copy still reposed there. Many of his CDs had also gone, presumably the intruders were taking no chances and took the lot.

Taylor decided to get out quick, although where to go he had no idea. He entered his bedroom, which appeared untouched, changed into another 'T' shirt, discarded the bloodstained one and tucked it under his arm. He would have to ditch that, a pity as he liked that 'T' shirt. He'd have to go, the trio could return to maybe take his other computer as well, or the police could arrive and arrest him, in which case he would have difficulty getting the point across about the information he had found.

He could see in his mind's eye how a police interview would go.

'Listen, I have vital information about a bomb attack

on Melbourne Central Railway Station. I think it may be sometime during September ...!'

'Oh really sir. A bomb attack? Very interesting. Now let's talk about what you've done. Why did you murder your employer? Can you explain how your fingerprints come to be...!'

Fingerprints! Taylor clapped his hand to his head. His hand had touched the knife handle when he'd fallen to his knees to attend to Harold Henderson. Fingerprints! That was all Taylor needed to take off and quickly. He had a quick look around his apartment then headed for the door and stairs.

He ran across the street and scrambled into the car. After a quick look to the right and left, he turned right and headed off. As he reached the end of the street, he spotted distant flashing lights in the rear-view mirror, a police car. He saw it pull in opposite his apartment house, then lost sight of it as he turned left and entered the intersecting street.

Taylor drove to the centre of Melbourne, pocketed the CD and abandoned the car, there was no point keeping it. The registration would have been broadcast far and wide by now. He parked it by the River Yarra in an un-metered zone, it may be some time before a warden chanced on it.

There was a newspaper on the back seat where Henderson had thrown it, it was the Weekend Australian of the weekend just gone. Taylor appropriated it, deeming that walking along holding a newspaper looked more innocent than walking along carrying nothing. He ditched his bloodstained 'T' shirt into a garbage bin, then walked to the main business district.

He paused in Bourke Street, walked to the nearest ATM and drew out $500 on his credit card. After completing the transaction, he quickly walked away from it, he had watched sufficient police television series to know credit card transactions would be recorded, plus the likelihood he could have been filmed withdrawing that cash.

His next problem was...where next? He was on the run from the police, and also from the three men who had appropriated his computer. The police knew who he was, but probably at this stage didn't know what he looked like. That would soon be rectified as Henderson had a notice board in the shop on which he pinned various notices and occasional snap shots of the shop, his family and occasionally employees, while the ATM photo would also aid the police.

Henderson was a keen fisherman, or had been, there were several shots of him on that notice board with impressive catches. But Taylor knew there was also a snap of himself on that board, taken when Henderson had been experimenting with a new digital camera a few weeks back. Florence Henderson would no doubt point that out to the police, he hadn't thought to snatch it down before he ran out, but didn't know then he was going to be saddled with a murder accusation. In addition, the police were bound to contact his parents in New South Wales and could easily obtain whatever photographs they required.

He didn't like the idea of walking city streets, but had a brainwave. He went down into Parliament Station and purchased an all-day railway ticket for the inner part of the suburban rail system, then boarded a train. The all-day ticket meant he could ride around all day within the limits prescribed by the ticket. It would also give him time to think.

Taylor travelled in circles on the underground system until about 8.00 pm. When he felt in need of refreshment, he emerged at Flagstaff Station and went to a nearby café for a cup of coffee. Even after deep thought, while being whirled around the city railway loop, he still didn't know what to do. Should he give himself up? There was no doubt they'd catch him eventually, but what worried Taylor was the information in his possession. He had the feeling the police would pounce on him and whatever was in his pockets would finish up in a pigeon hole or evidence bag somewhere while they drew up the charge sheet. He had already run over the presumed course of the interview in his mind, and considered protestations regarding possible terrorism would be treated with utter scorn and derision, very likely considered by the police as a distraction or deviation to waste time while they totted up the evidence for Harold Henderson's murder.

But he had to stay off the streets, he couldn't go home. He had been sitting at the table for some time, trying to work out what to do next, when he realised sitting staring vacantly into space for about an hour was causing the proprietor to persistently cast glances in his direction. He was still carrying the Weekend Australian, so he opened it, held it up before his face and appeared to be engrossed.

He sat for another half hour and after exhausting the news items and editorials perused the various job advertisements. Some aroused his interest, especially those offering computer jobs. Whether he would ever be in a position to even think of a career for the next twenty years was a moot point, but he continued to scan the pages and his interest was aroused now and again.

Then a particular advertisement caught his eye.

Security Officers
Australian Security Intelligence Organisation
Intelligence Officers - Salary $90,000-$105,000

There was much more, a description of the people they

were looking for, qualifications and the like, and duties to be undertaken. It also described what the organisation did, gathering intelligence regarding terrorism, spies and illegal organisations.

Taylor looked at the advertisement, not only did it appear to be something he would like doing, it also presented a possible solution to his predicament. He looked at the bottom of the column at the phone numbers which were all Canberra based. He got hold of the bottom of the page and slowly tore out the phone numbers.

The television behind the counter had moved onto a news broadcast, to his horror he saw a full-size photograph of himself onscreen, wanted for questioning and assistance with police enquiries with regard to the murder of a computer shop owner. The photograph was a blown-up version of the one from the notice board in the shop. He rose to his feet, tucked the newspaper under his arm, and walked out into the street, now dark except for street lights and light cascading from shop fronts. He decided to look for a motel.

He found one after walking to the inner suburb of Carlton, entered reception and booked a room for the night. He was presented with a form to complete, which caused a few problems. He finally used a false name, a hotch potch of family names so he wouldn't forget what it was and gave a fictitious New South Wales address. The motor registration he left blank, since he was paying cash they might ask him for a driving licence for ID, as he had no car then he could legitimately say he wasn't carrying one. But they did ask for his driving licence, just for identification purposes.

'Sorry, I haven't got one,' he said.

'No driving licence?' the lady receptionist was surprised.

Taylor bit his lip. Saying one didn't possess a driving licence these days was like saying one didn't possess a phone. Then he had an inspiration.

'No, I have one but I don't carry it around at present,' he said. 'I've been suspended for drink driving.'

'Oh!' her face cleared. 'I see.' She seemed to accept that as a reasonable explanation which finished the request for ID. He took delivery of the key and headed down the corridor to his room.

He awoke early next morning and checked his watch, it was 5 o'clock. This was not the time he usually got up, but having woken up he couldn't sleep. He disliked lying around in bed so decided to get up. He washed and dressed; took advantage of the razor that was supplied and felt reasonably good. It was still fairly dark outside, and he weighed up the decision whether or not to have breakfast. The bed for the night would cost $90, being middle of the-week room charges were discounted, but he reasoned if he had a cooked breakfast as well this could knock a hole in his money. Maybe the best bet was to visit a grocery store and purchase some bread, butter and marmalade he could use again for a few days.

But, being famished, he decided to go and see when breakfast would be served. He strolled down the corridor, found the dining room on the left and peered around the door. There was a television high on the wall on a bracket, it was on and playing some quiz programme. A young girl was in the room behind a counter cleaning up. She looked up as he entered.

'What time do you start serving?' he asked.

'Serving what?' she answered.

'Well...coffee initially, then breakfast?'

'That coffee machine is ready at 6.30 am, breakfast commences at 7.00,' she said.

'OK, thanks,' he replied. 'I'll see you at 7 o'clock.'

'You can make tea or coffee in your room,' she said brightly, then looked at him quizzically. Taylor bit his lip; he wondered if she had recognised him. Bloody silly thing to do, wander around and draw attention to himself.

'Thank you,' he said. 'I'll go and boil a kettle.'

He wandered back to his room with adrenalin coursing through his system. The television had been on and it was likely a newscast would have been on every half hour; some cable television channels were on all night. He boiled the kettle, made himself a cup of coffee, poured in the milk and began to sip it.

Still sipping his coffee, he strolled to the window, looked out and was in time to see a police car drive into the car park and two constables alight. They paused by the car; one headed for reception and the other towards the rear of the building.

Taylor gathered up what few belongings he had and thrust them into his pockets. As he reached the door, he had a brainwave, headed for the bathroom, set the shower running and drew the curtain. Then he shut the bathroom door and exited the room in a hurry. He looked each way down the corridor, decided against approaching reception and walked the other way. He knew there was a door at the rear leading into the carpark, he heard the door open and shut and realised the second policeman could be entering it. There was a toilet for general use on his left in the corridor, after a quick look round he entered it.

He waited just inside the door, wondering what to do next. There was no guarantee it was him they were after, but it was likely. If he opened the door and stuck his head out, he would be easily seen, but his mind was made up for him. He heard banging on a door further up the corridor. It was his room, which confirmed he was the target.

He heard the sound of keys, one of the motel staff must be

with them, so he opened the door slightly to peer round the door jamb. The two police were just entering his room, a motel staff member stayed outside with his back towards Taylor. He slunk out of the toilet, trotted to the corner, thankful for the carpeted hallway, and was around it without the staff member seeing him. He was too interested in what was happening in the room, after all, it wasn't every day a murderer was apprehended in their motel by two brawny constables.

Taylor ran for the rear exit door and entered the carpark. He ran across it, jumped the low wall and landed on the pavement. He ran across the road into a side street opposite, turned into another street on his right, cantered down that and spotted tram tracks ahead. He reached the next street and looked left; a tram was approaching. Taylor saw the next stop just ahead of him, ran to it and waited with chest heaving. The tram drew up and he clambered aboard. Luckily, he had change so was able to use the ticket machine and sit on one of the seats. Being early morning, not many were aboard, mainly workmen.

He gave some thought as to how the police had locked onto him. Clearly someone from the motel, maybe the receptionist, had tipped them off. Maybe she had thought about it for some time, fearing to make a fool of herself, or else she had just seen his picture on television. That one on Henderson's notice board had been a good likeness, anybody seeing it should have no trouble remembering the man without a driving licence or any other ID when he booked in. Or perhaps the relieving staff had noticed his form was not correctly completed, but whatever it was, somebody had tipped them off. But, more than likely, noting the time the police had arrived, it could have been the girl in the breakfast room. He had another crime to his charge sheet, absconding without paying his bill.

He was now in a serious position. They must know by now he

had ditched the car, so he was limited to being on foot or public transport. Being caught by police was not the end of the world, Taylor had seen enough detective and police series on television to know forensics was very advanced these days, there must be other fingerprints on that knife apart from his own, and he reckoned he would have put a palm print on it, not finger tips.

What worried him was the text he was carrying, on paper and disc. He considered if arrested, anything he said would be submerged in the euphoria of catching a murderer. So far it was an open and shut case via forensics in the way of finger or palm prints and, no doubt after Florence Henderson had given her account of the proceedings, motive. The disc could just finish in an evidence bag, the paper printout could be tossed over a shoulder into a waste paper bin.

Taylor had no doubt the information he had was authentic, he had just seen Harold Henderson killed for it. Thinking of it made him search his pockets, thankfully both disc and paper were safe. His finger touched another piece of paper, he drew it out and realised it was the small piece of newsprint with the ASIO phone number.

Taylor took a southbound train on the Frankston line and disembarked at Cheltenham; deeming it best to be out of the city. He walked briskly towards the Southland Shopping centre, a vast shopping complex, keeping a watchful eye open for police or police cars. He crossed the main highway and entered the shopping centre. It was disconcerting to find there were a few police and security guards around, but this could be normal so they were not necessarily looking for him. There were also a few television shops with live sets in their windows, so Taylor gave them a wide berth. Inevitably there would be a newscast that any shopper or policeman could idly view while passing a television shop, to be standing alongside a television screen when his face appeared on it was asking for trouble.

Taylor was looking for a public phone, he had to, his mobile phone's battery was flat. He eventually found one, entered the cubicle, took out the piece torn from the newspaper and began dialling.

CHAPTER 4

I n Canberra, at the offices of the Australian Security &
Intelligence Organisation, Colin Attwood put down his
coffee cup and steeled himself to pick up the telephone.
He had taken many calls over the ASIO and ASIS Recruiting line
during the past week in response to two weeks advertisements
in the Weekend Australian. Some callers had been idiots who
thought it funny to play practical jokes on the national security
organisation, or left-wing cranks who believed the objectives
of ASIO were to hound ethnic citizens, with the ultimate aim
of herding them all into concentration camps, together with
union leaders and members of the Australian Labor Party. A
few calls had been genuine enquiries. He composed himself as
the phone rang a third time, paused to get in the right frame of
mind and answered it.

'Good morning, Colin Attwood speaking. ASIO recruitment,'
he managed to give a cheerful intonation to his voice.

A bustling background to the call indicated it was a phone in a public place.

'Here we go!' he muttered, a call from a public phone was usually some comedian and he waited expectantly for the farting noise or the abuse, he'd had plenty of those and had fielded two already this morning.

'Is that ASIO?' a husky voice asked.

'Yes, this is ASIO,' Attwood answered patiently. 'Can I help you?'

'Am I speaking to the Australian Security Intelligence Service?'

'That's ASIS, we are the Australian Security Intelligence Organisation and we deal with national internal security.'

'I need to speak with somebody,' said the voice. 'I have information and it could be important.'

Colin Attwood jerked upright. His colleague Mike Duval, also fielding calls arising from the advertisement, observed Attwood's reaction and cocked his head enquiringly. They were seated at separate desks that faced each other.

'Information?' Attwood asked. 'You have information regarding security or do you want information regarding a job interview?'

'No, it's about national security, it's vital I speak to somebody.'

Attwood had had a call like this the previous Monday. Somebody tried to tell him enemies of the state had been making small nuclear devices that could be carried by carrier pigeons. Long before the delivery of the punch line, Attwood had a hunch what was coming, but you always had to grit your teeth and listen, just in case.

There was always the danger of cutting someone off with real information. He remembered how the attack on the Twin Towers in New York, universally known as 9/11, had been a complete surprise because people who had information had failed to impart it to security services. Conversely, Attwood remembered reading how an FBI operative in Phoenix, Arizona in the USA had had suspicions regarding Arabs taking flying lessons which didn't involve learning to land the aircraft. His suspicions and warnings had fallen on deaf ears and been filed away, surfacing after the devastating events of 9/11.

'What's it about?' Attwood asked finally.

'There is to be a bomb attack on a Melbourne underground railway station at the end of September. I must speak to someone, please, I haven't much time.'

'Hold the line,' he eyed Duval who looked enquiringly at him and Attwood pursed his lips.

'Someone is saying he has information; I don't know, this could be for real.'

'Not bloody nuclear pigeons again?'

'No, it's about a possible bombing in a Melbourne railway station, he sounds agitated.'

'Then pass it on,' said Duval. 'If you do nothing and there's something in it...!'

Attwood thought again of the Phoenix FBI agent and nodded. He spoke to the caller.

'Are you still there?' he asked.

'Yes, I'm here, please hurry.'

'I'm transferring you, don't hang up. What number are you calling from, in case you get cut off.'

'I'm ringing from a call box in a Melbourne shopping centre.'

'Which one?'

There was a hesitation, and Attwood's doubts began to rise again. Then the voice spoke again.

'Cheltenham in Victoria.'

'You mean Southland?' Attwood was originally from

Melbourne.

There was another hesitation, then 'Yes!'

'Hold on, I'm transferring you.'

Attwood imparted what little information he had to his superior Robert Bramble. Bramble was in his office chatting to his friend and colleague Denis Shackleton when Attwood's call came through. Bramble absorbed what Attwood had to say.

'Put him on!'

He switched on a tape recorder to record the call and pressed a button to receive it. He heard the Southland bustle and activity in the background as the caller came through.

'Hello, my name is Robert Bramble. You say you have information?'

'Yes, it's about a possible raid or bombing attack in one of the Melbourne underground railway stations near the end of September.'

'Who are you, what is your name?'

'Donald Taylor, I found the information by accident when I was given a second-hand computer, I found some data on the hard drive that hadn't been deleted.'

'Where did you get this second-hand computer?'

'It was a trade in.'

'OK. My colleague tells me you're in Southland Shopping Centre. Where is that?'

'In Melbourne, that is, in Cheltenham. Your colleague seemed to know where it is.'

'OK! OK!' Bramble said soothingly. 'Listen, we have an operative in Melbourne now who can contact you within the hour.'

'Well, it will have to be quick. The police are after me.'

'What?' Bramble was startled. 'Who?'

'The police. The people who traded in the computer, they must have realised what was still on it and they murdered my boss. He ran a computer shop, where the computer was traded in. The police think I did it. I found the information when my boss, Harold Henderson, gave it to me, I downloaded it onto a disc and I have it with me.'

'Is there a coffee shop in Southland?'

'Yes, several.'

'Name one.'

'I...I don't know ...! Oh there's one near the entrance, it's called the...the....Maragogype Coffee House ...!'

'The what?'

'Maragogype ...' the voice at the other end spelt it out: '...I think it's a brand of coffee from Nicaragua or somewhere.'

'Yes, yes...I've got it ...our operative can meet you there. How will he recognise you?'

'I'm wearing a brown jacket over a white 'T' shirt. I'm aged 22. I'm medium height with dark hair.'

'Our man's name is David McKay, fair haired, blue eyes, about 5'11' or thereabouts.' Bramble said. 'He'll be carrying a...a...' Bramble thought desperately '...a copy of today's Sydney Morning Herald newspaper.'

'I understand, I'll go there now. You won't let me down?'

'No, he'll be there, give him half an hour to an hour, he'll be coming from South Melbourne, but he'll be there.'

'Thank you, thank you!' and the caller rang off.

Bramble turned to Shackleton.

'Have you heard the news this morning?'

'On and off, why?'

'Was there a murder in Melbourne yesterday of a computer shop owner?'

Shackleton shrugged, and reached for the Canberra Times.

'I didn't notice anything in today's paper.'

'It won't be in there, if it's outside the ACT the Times won't bother with it!' Bramble snorted. 'As far as the Canberra Times is concerned worlds outside Canberra don't exist!'

'I'll check and see we have a copy of a Melbourne newspaper?'

'Bound to be one somewhere, have a look around while I ring Dave McKay.'

Bramble was speaking to David McKay in Melbourne when Shackleton returned with a copy of that morning's 'Australian' newspaper.

'Something here,' he spread it on Bramble's desk. 'Chap named Harold Henderson, owner of a computer shop near St Kilda. Stabbed in the chest, so it says.'

'Hang on...did you hear that, Dave?' Bramble said into the phone. 'It's on page 7 of this morning's "Australian" newspaper. Computer shop owner murdered. Police looking for an employee, you know, the usual guff...to assist them with their enquiries. We think it might be Donald Taylor who rang us.'

He paused while listening to McKay at the other end.

'Yes, he's just phoned us, says he has news of a plot to blow up Melbourne Central Station about two weeks hence at the end of the month. He's at Southland Shopping Centre, in a coffee house near the western entrance named the Maragogype Coffee House.'

There was more from the other end.

'How the hell do I know whether it's a hoax or not, he sounded genuine, so far as one can tell. Colin Attwood, who passed it onto us, thought so too.'

Shackleton could hear McKay responding at the other end.

'I said you'd be carrying this morning's Sydney Morning Herald newspaper. All I could think of at the time. Someone's bound to sell it in Southland.' Bramble said. 'You can claim it back off your expenses! What?'

Bramble chuckled.

'Yes, and you can stick the coffee in the same place,' he said and rang off.

In the field office of ASIO in South Melbourne David McKay put down the phone and turned to his colleague Joseph Carter as he rose to his feet.

'Do we have a copy of The Sydney Morning Herald here?' he asked.

'Should have,' responded Carter. 'It's usually delivered together with The Age, the Brisbane Courier, the Australian and The Herald. We get most of the papers here.'

'Go and sort it out will you, I've got to get to Southland and quick.'

McKay slipped behind the wheel and drove out of the carpark. He had been seconded to the South Melbourne office of ASIO within the past two weeks, he was normally stationed at Canberra but the Melbourne No 2 was on leave and the No: 3 had been taken ill and wasn't expected back for three weeks, so McKay had been temporarily slotted in.

There hadn't been a lot happening in Melbourne over the two weeks McKay had been stationed there, but this sounded interesting. He was aware of the numerous hoaxes perpetrated on the security services, fire brigades and police were similar sufferers, but this one sounded different.

Normally hoaxers would ring up either with something outlandish, such as the nuclear pigeons, he had heard about that from Denis Shackleton, or else it was immediate, that is, there's a bomb at point 'X' and it's going to explode within the hour. The difference with this one was, the caller had indicated the event was about two weeks away. Hoaxers liked to see the panic they would cause and gave a short time frame. Then they hovered around the area to see the fun as all the emergency vehicles rolled up. Why should anyone give a date ten days or nearly two weeks hence yet not give a definite date? It might still be a hoax, but was worth investigating.

It took nearly forty-five minutes to reach Cheltenham, then he had to find Southland. McKay was not a Melburnian and had to check a couple of times to see where he was. Finally, he saw the shopping centre edifice before him, it was difficult to miss as it was on both sides of the highway with an overhead bridge connecting the two sections.

He drove into the carpark and strolled to the far end where he mounted the stairs. He walked into the bustle of the shopping centre and looked around for the Maragogype Coffee Shop. He eventually found it, but wasn't prepared for what he saw, police were around the entrance to the shop, and as he approached it two constables emerged with a man between them. McKay had time to note he was young, possibly early twenties, dark hair, wearing a brown jacket over a white 'T' shirt. His hands were handcuffed behind his back.

After a brief conference with their senior officer, their prisoner was manhandled away from the shop, heading in McKay's direction. McKay quickly took the newspaper from under his arm and stood at a point where the threesome would have to walk, or frogmarch, past. He unfurled it, turned it so he was looking at the back page, with the newspaper's banner facing the trio. The prisoner looked despondent with his eyes darting from left to right until his eyes settled on McKay's newspaper. He looked up and their eyes met, McKay briefly nodded and the prisoner's eyes flickered. Then they passed McKay, the prisoner cast an appealing glance behind him at McKay and was then ushered towards the escalator.

'Just my luck!' McKay muttered. 'I'm too late.'

The police by the café were dispersing and he decided to ascertain what had happened.

'What was all that about?' he asked one of the constables.

'Just some villain,' was the reply. 'What's it to you?'

And up yours too! McKay thought, but he uttered the words 'Sorry I asked!' with a fair degree of sarcasm and decided to enter the café, now returning to a state of normality. He went to the counter, where a knot of customers was asking the same question. A red-haired girl with freckles was behind the counter preening herself. She was the centre of attention and liked it. McKay waited until the others had dispersed, faced her, took out his ID and flashed it before her. He did it quickly so she couldn't read what it said.

'Herald Sun,' he whispered huskily and peered around in a conspiratorial manner. 'What happened?'

'Oh ...' she fluttered with pleasure: '...that man came in for a coffee and I recognised him.'

'Oh really, who was he?'

'He's the murderer,' she said proudly. 'I saw his picture on the TV screen over there and recognised him so I called the police.'

Blast you...thought McKay, so now the poor bugger is bailed up by police, still possibly holding vital information. He must have been apprehended a matter of minutes, maybe seconds, before McKay had found the café.

'The murderer, eh?' he said, she nodded and beamed with pleasure. 'How long had he been here?'

'Oh about ten or fifteen minutes,' she said. 'I recognised him when he walked in.'

Pigs Arse! McKay thought; she was beginning to embellish it.

'Where are the police from?' he asked.

'St Kilda Road, I think. I dialled the number they put on screen.'

'Oh well, we'll give you some footage in tomorrow's paper,' said McKay. 'What's your name?'

He garnered all her details and promised a photographer would attend within the hour.

'Better tidy your hair before he arrives,' he remarked cuttingly. He was far from pleased with her and found it difficult to restrain the comment. He was gratified as she touched her hair, and knocked over a bar of sugar as she cast an anxious sidelong glance at a nearby mirror.

'When will he be here?'

'Very soon,' McKay promised. 'You'd better clear that sugar up!' he added caustically, then left. He wasn't altogether being untruthful; no doubt somebody would arrive soon and plaster her features and the café all over the tabloids. He walked back to his car, seething with frustration. Now what?

He decided on the direct approach first, being inclined to agree with the red-haired girl's supposition the police had come from the St Kilda Road Police complex, the murder had been in Balaclava which was near their field of operations and the television screen was hardly likely to bear the number of Cheltenham Police station or any other minor establishment, they wouldn't have known where Taylor was likely to show up so it would have to be somewhere central.

He entered the St Kilda Police Complex and fronted up to the reception desk. There was a uniformed sergeant and a young constable on duty, McKay was momentarily thrown as he looked at the constable, his appearance was very similar to the man he wanted to see, Donald Taylor. McKay presented his ID, more slowly this time so the desk sergeant could read it.

'What can we do for you, Mr McKay?'

'You've just arrested a prisoner at the Southland Shopping Centre. We understand he's the suspect in that Balaclava computer shop murder.'

The sergeant tensed and eyed McKay narrowly.

'So?'

'Our organisation is also interested in this young man. We need to interview him urgently. Would that be possible?'

The sergeant laughed and shook his head.

'We're still processing him, the answer is no. He's suspected of having committed a savage murder and he's only just been brought in...to assist us with enquiries! Sorry mate!'

McKay pondered whether to pursue it any further but decided it wouldn't get him anywhere. As he walked out, he heard the desk sergeant tell one of his colleagues, at a desk behind the counter, that he'd just given the heave-ho to some spook. Seething with fury, McKay walked to where he'd parked his car and picked up his mobile phone. He'd have to go further up the line.

Alan Kelsey, Director of Intelligence, was closeted with Marcus Templeton, one of the Canberra computer operatives, when McKay's call came through.

'Kelsey!' he announced. 'Oh...hello Dave!'

McKay exchanged the greeting, then informed him of the problem. Kelsey turned to Templeton.

'We'll sort it out later, Marcus,' he said and as Templeton left, returned to his caller. 'What was that, Dave? What sort of problem?'

McKay expanded at length.

'This is the chap who spoke to Bob Bramble earlier on?'

'Oh...you know about that? Yes, that's the one, Alan, now he's been arrested,' said McKay. 'I can't get in to see him.'

'He's the chief murder suspect, isn't he?'

'He is and that's why he's in custody. But I reckon he could be telling the truth, so far as I can tell. If this is a hoax, why give an indeterminate date nearly two weeks away?' said McKay. 'If you're a hoaxer you'd give a time within the next hour or so and then hover around to see what happens.'

'I agree, that struck me as well. If you're going to play a hoax, you'd want to see the results,' said Kelsey. 'He may be trying to make a smoke screen to obscure his murder charge, but we can't ignore it. What do you want me to do?'

'I need authority from one of our top brass who has the ear of the high ups in the Victorian police force. Can you get that for me? Otherwise, I can't get in to see Donald Taylor. If he's got anything solid, we need to see it before it gets lost in police archives.'

'Yes, you're right,' Kelsey said thoughtfully. 'I'll have a word with Francis Burton. He knows all the top police brass. Get back to the South Melbourne field office, I'll contact you later.'

Taylor sat in an interview room with a police constable standing against the wall by the door. Outside, looking in through the one-way window was a Chief Inspector and two detectives. Chief Inspector Talintyre, a burly man of 15 stone, red faced with reddish hair, cast an eye over Taylor, fingered his chin and turned to Detective Sergeant Griffiths.

'Looks like an open and shut case to me, the wife caught him red-handed, literally, stooping over the victim, then he did a runner after ripping the telephone from the wall.'

'I agree it looks fairly conclusive,' replied Detective Sergeant Griffiths. 'But we've been interviewing for about an hour, he's sticking to his story.'

'Well, wrap it up quickly,' said Talintyre. 'We've got a hell of a heavy case load at present, at least this looks like one we can soon dispose of.'

'Will do, sir,' Griffiths picked up his file papers. 'Shouldn't take long,' he turned to the Detective Constable standing near the door. 'OK Stannington, let's have another go.'

They entered, took their seats and sat with their eyes boring into Taylor, then Griffiths dropped his eyes to the sheet in front of him.

'Tell us what happened yesterday in the computer shop,' he said.

'I've already told you,' Taylor said sourly. 'I borrowed Mr Henderson's car to take the computer away. Harold said I could take it in lieu of wages because he hadn't got much money to spare. We hammered out a deal and I took it home.'

'You've already told us that.'

'That's hardly surprising; since you asked the same question before. I'm giving you the same answer as before because you've asked me the same question.'

'Are you being funny with me?'

'No, why should I be?' Taylor responded with some spirit. 'You've already asked me that and I answered it. What is the point of me answering your questions if you want to believe something else?'

'Very well, what happened after that?'

'I started working on the computer and found the hard drive, the 'C' drive, hadn't been properly cleared. There was some engineering data on it which looked like a university or college course. I was about to delete it when I realised the drive had been partitioned, there was another drive, designated 'D' drive, that hadn't been cleared either.'

'So...you cleared it?'

'No, I didn't. Both drives were subject to a password but I know a bit about computers and tried bypassing it. I was intending to wipe them clean, but I guess I was curious to see what was on the hard drive and decided to see if I could get into it without the password.'

'And did you?'

'Yes, I did, I wish to God I hadn't now with the mess I'm in. Then I downloaded some of the stuff from the 'D' drive. There was a file called Nemesis, I had a look at that and found a plan of the Melbourne Central underground railway station.'

'You've already told us that, I feel we're getting off the point,' Sergeant Griffiths waved his hand dismissively. 'Now let's try another tack and get back to the subject in hand. Why did you kill Harold Henderson? Was it money?'

'No, it wasn't, and I didn't kill Harold.'

'His wife says you did.'

'She came in while I was trying to revive him, she didn't give me a chance to say anything before she jumped to the wrong conclusion. I wanted to phone the police and an ambulance but I couldn't because they'd ripped the phone from the wall.'

'Who had?'

'The three Asians who wanted their computer back, presumably because of the data still on it,' Taylor said testily. 'I've already told you that.'

'Oh...so there were three of them were there? Including you. Your hand and finger prints were on the knife handle.'

'I've already told you how my prints got on there. I want a lawyer.'

'Why should you want a lawyer if you're innocent?'

Taylor spread out his hands with exasperation, then clammed up and refused to say any more.

McKay's phone rang.

'Alan Kelsey here, Dave,' said Kelsey. 'Francis Burton has been in touch with the powers that be. Get your arse over to St Kilda Police Complex, call me again when you're about to go in. The Commissioners office should have rung the Police complex by then and you should be able to gain access.'

'How did Francis Burton do that? Does he have the ear of the Prime Minister?'

It was meant to be a joke.

'Yes,' said Kelsey. 'As a matter of fact, he does! This time he just tried the relevant minister. Just get over there and try again, but call me before you go in.'

McKay entered the police complex a second time, phoning Kelsey before he did so. He walked up to the desk sergeant, who had seen him off last time. The sergeant eyed him with some irritation.

'Yes, how can we help you?'

'I'm your favourite spook,' said McKay. 'The one you gave the old heave-ho to earlier!'

'Oh, it's you again, the answer's still no!' the desk sergeant said sourly. 'Taylor is under interrogation by two detectives and they are not to be disturbed. This is a murder investigation and they don't want any interruptions, if you don't mind.'

'Really?' McKay inclined his head, 'I'll just take a seat and wait then'

'You'll be wasting your time,' snapped the desk sergeant. 'I've told you; he's being interviewed by senior detectives and I'm not interrupting that. I suggest you come back tomorrow. All right?'

'Sure, I'll just sit here and watch the police force at work,' McKay sat in a chair near the window. 'Thank you for your kind assistance.'

'You're welcome,' the desk sergeant was clearly even more riled by McKay's sarcasm. 'If you want to waste your time it's up to you, but you won't waste mine. We've all got work to do and this damned job has been hanging around since last night... Oh...answer that will you, Cope?'

Constable Cope caught McKay's eye briefly as his gaze flickered over in his direction. He gave McKay a half smile as the sergeant muttered under his breath and bent his head towards something he was checking. Cope answered the phone, his amused expression gave way to one of puzzlement, then he asked who it was. He gave a double take and handed the instrument to the desk sergeant.

'It's for you,' he said.

'You take it, I'm busy right now, just take the name and number and I'll deal with it later. I don't want to break off now.'

'He wants to speak to you now.'

'Oh does he? Well he'll have to wait, I can't break off in the middle of this, not even for the bloody Commissioner!'

'It *is* the Commissioner!'

The questioning of Taylor had turned full circle. He had told Griffiths and Stannington yet again what was on the computer 'D' drive and it was quite clear they didn't believe him or else they weren't interested; all they wanted was a confession. Taylor could understand this, they had a murder enquiry, they had a Class A suspect identified by a witness, fingerprints and motive, kindly supplied by Florence Henderson, and this was their priority. Let's get the job finished, the confession signed, take him down to the cells and get stuck in to the next case.

Taylor was becoming increasingly irritated when he tried to tell them what was on the disc and couldn't get through to them; all he could detect was cynical disbelief. No matter how cynical police could become when interrogating suspects who may come up with a variety of fairy tales, surely with something like this they could at least listen.

'You didn't like Harold Henderson, did you?' said Griffiths.

'You're wrong, I liked Harold immensely; he was a good bloke.

More than I could say for his wife, she was the cause of most of his monetary problems,' Taylor hadn't meant to say that, despite the situation he was in, it was none of his business and had nothing to do with the case in hand, nevertheless it came out. 'But will you please listen to me, the information I downloaded from that computer could be serious...!'

Griffiths waved his hand impatiently

'Some other time, we'll deal with that later,' he said dismissively. 'She said you'd killed him, she saw you bending over him and when she asked Henderson who'd done it, he said 'Donald.''

'She didn't see anything. Harold was already on the floor bleeding to death from a knife wound when she entered. He uttered my name to me twice as she came in. He was trying to say something to me.'

'She said you ran out of the shop.'

'Yes, I did, but that was later. I intended to ring for an ambulance and the police and told her what I was doing.'

'Why didn't you use the shop phone?'

'I've already told you that, they ripped the phone cables out of the wall so it wouldn't work and I'd left my mobile behind.'

'Why didn't you ask Mrs Henderson if you could use hers?'

'Ask Mrs...! Bloody Hell! She was screaming her bloody head off and I doubt if she'd have given it me anyway.'

'Why not?'

Christ Almighty! Taylor thought to himself. We're going round in bloody circles!

'For Heavens Sake! This data I downloaded from that computer, I think you should pass it onto someone, possibly ASIO, it looked serious...!'

'For sure, we'll call out the troops from Victoria Barracks as well if you like...!' Griffiths said cuttingly. He thumped his fist on the table and Taylor and the Detective Constable jumped.

'Let's get back to the case in hand, shall we? Let's face it, Mr Taylor, she thought you were guilty, and as far as we can see right now, you're the only person with a motive. You were seen arguing with Mr Henderson the day before and the same day. Robbery wasn't involved; Mrs Henderson says nothing is missing from the shop.'

'She wouldn't know if anything was,' Taylor retorted bitterly.

There was a knock at the door and a uniformed constable entered. Griffiths muttered to himself and rose, said for the benefit of the tape 'Interview suspended 11.37. Detective Sergeant Griffiths is leaving the room.'

There was a whispered conversation outside then Griffiths briefly re-entered and said: 'I'll be back!' and stalked off in the direction of the front desk. He wasn't pleased, Talintyre was a hard man to please, and Taylor's resilience was making it difficult to wrap up the loose ends. Griffiths wanted to finalise the case quickly, he currently had a lot on his plate and needed an uninterrupted session to break Taylor down. This interruption, whatever it was about, didn't help as it upset his concentration.

He stalked down the passageway towards the reception desk, as he approached it, he saw a man, probably late twenties or early thirties, leaning against the counter, he had fair hair and piercing blue eyes which locked onto him as he approached.

'Who's this?' he brusquely asked the uniformed desk sergeant. Griffiths wasn't too happy at the way things were going, to add spice to the situation he and Sergeant Phillips, the desk sergeant, disliked each other intensely. In addition, Taylor appeared to be fielding questions well and his answers hadn't wavered from those previously given. Despite the overwhelming evidence that pointed in Taylor's direction, Griffiths was beginning to feel uneasy and entertain doubts, and knew he would have to accede to requests for a lawyer.

McKay inclined his head gravely to one side and didn't deign to respond to Griffiths' ill-tempered question, which wasn't addressed to him directly but went straight over his head and was clearly intended as a slight. He decided to let the desk sergeant do the talking.

'This gentleman wants to see Donald Taylor,' said Sergeant Phillips. His demeanour was one of almost pleasurable anticipation. He knew what Griffiths' reaction would be, the same as his own had been initially, and was looking forward to the next few minutes. There being no love lost between him and Griffiths, he wanted to savour the moment, having just suffered humiliation himself in front of Constable Cope by McKay's sudden elevation in status.

'He's from Canberra,' announced Phillips. 'National Security... ASIO!'

'So?'

'He wants to see Taylor.'

'Well...he can't, we're interviewing him as a murder suspect and he's off limits for anyone else. We've got a murder enquiry here and we're in the middle of questioning him,' Griffiths snapped, still ignoring McKay.

'He says he's conducting an enquiry which supersedes that.'

'Nothing can supersede that.'

'I'm afraid something can...!' McKay spoke for the first time. He had been an enthralled spectator as the confrontation between the two police officers had progressed, with him being referred to in the third person: '...and it will. We have a matter of national security involved here, which involves possibly hundreds of lives, not just one.'

'Well, it will have to wait,' snapped Griffiths.

'It won't,' said Sergeant Phillips.

'The hell it won't!' Griffiths snapped irritably.

'You're absolutely right, the hell …it won't', McKay cut in and there was a significant hardening of his tone. 'I'd like to see him now, if possible.'

'You can't …not even if you've got a direct line through to the Commissioner!'

'I have,' replied McKay. 'Ask your desk sergeant.'

Sergeant Phillips leant forward on the counter and placed his hand over his mouth to hide a smile. He'd been waiting for Griffiths to dig a hole for himself and this was a moment to be savoured as he fell into it, the same hole that he, Sergeant Phillips, had fallen into minutes before.

'What was that?'

'He said he has and he has,' said Sergeant Phillips. 'We've just had a call from the Commissioner's Office; from the Commissioner himself. They've had instructions from Canberra. The intelligence services want to interview Donald Taylor…now!'

CHAPTER 5

The door to the interview room opened and Detective Sergeant Griffiths re-entered. Taylor looked up dejectedly as his tormentor returned, then realised another man had entered as well, the same man he had briefly seen at the Southland Shopping Centre holding up that day's Sydney Morning Herald as he, Taylor, was being hustled away between two burly police constables. A thrill of hope ran through him.

'No Sam, don't re-start the tape,' said Griffiths. 'This gentleman will be asking Mr Taylor some questions. Can we clear the room please?'

The detective constable and the uniformed constable by the door looked surprised, but acquiesced and departed. McKay sat at the table, and looked at Griffiths.

'What I have to say now is strictly confidential...understand?' he said. 'Anything said in here now is not...repeat *not*...to be shared with your colleagues...nobody. Understood?'

He looked at Griffiths who didn't respond.

'Do you understand?' McKay repeated sharply. He considered he'd had a gutful of the Victorian Police Force.

'Yes,' Griffiths nodded sulkily. He had the feeling he was losing control and further, was discerning that his scornful dismissal of Taylor's protestations regarding the computer data he had discovered could have been unwise and was going to rebound.

'Can you put a fresh tape in please? We don't want what's in there to include anything from now on. You can replace yours after I'm done,' McKay said slowly.

Griffiths growled to himself as he removed the wrapping from a new tape and inserted it into the recorder. He was about to mutter something on the lines of 'these bloody tapes cost money' but McKay forestalled him, seeming to read Griffiths' mind from his demeanour. He added with a tinge of sarcasm. 'You can bill ASIO if you like, I'm sure we can run to it!'

Griffiths muttered again under his breath and McKay commenced.

'I am David McKay, from the Australian Security Intelligence Organisation and am interviewing Donald Taylor in the St Kilda Police Building in St Kilda Road. The date is... er....' he checked his watch face '...7th September, the time is...um ...11.48 am.'

He looked at Taylor.

'You are Donald Taylor, you telephoned ASIO Canberra this morning from the Southland Shopping Centre in Cheltenham saying you had information of national importance?' He placed some emphasis on the last three words and cast a sideways glance at Griffiths.

Taylor eyed McKay with something akin to disbelief, after all he had been through, especially in the latter stages in this interview room; it was like awakening from a bad dream.

'Yes?' McKay asked. Taylor realised he had allowed time to

elapse while experiencing euphoria.

'Yes, I did. It related to a possible bombing attack on Melbourne Central Station later this month.'

'How did you come across this information?'

'I took over a second-hand computer from my boss, Harold Henderson. He was giving it to me in lieu of wages. Harold had received it from a computer technician...!'

Taylor related his story again, from the moment the computer technician brought in the second-hand computer. He described how Henderson had offered it to him, how he had opened up the computer at his apartment, broken into it and what had been revealed.

He described events at the shop when he returned, how Mrs Henderson had assumed he had stabbed Harold, and subsequent events until his final arrest in the Southland Shopping Centre.

Throughout the whole story McKay said nothing, while Griffiths gave the occasional disbelieving snort.

'How long had you been working at Henderson's shop?' asked McKay.

'Not long, a few months.'

'Is there anything else you want to tell us?' asked McKay.

'Yes, two things,' responded Taylor. 'I left the motel without paying the bill, when I realised the police had arrived, I had to leave in a hurry...' a half smile crossed his features: '...I had over $500 in my wallet, the police have got that now, they took it from me when they arrested me. That money isn't stolen! It's mine. I presume they can trace the ATM in the city where I drew it out, and the cash withdrawal was exactly $500 in total. I want to pay that motel bill. I'm not having the police charge me for being a thief as well.'

'Very well,' McKay looked at Griffiths who nodded. 'What else?'

'The second hard copy was taken from me by the police when I came in here, as was the disc. If you want detail, it's all on there, or most of it anyway, assuming some idiot hasn't damaged it.'

The last aside was said with some bitterness, he looked at Griffiths as he said it. He felt the need to make some acid comment after Griffiths' scornful dismissal of his story. He saw Griffiths grit his teeth and felt he had scored a hit.

'Where's that disc now?' McKay asked Griffiths.

'It should be bagged with the rest of his personal effects,' Griffiths answered sourly.

'It had better be, that could be vital,' McKay said sharply. 'Tell me, has Mr Taylor's arrest been released to the press yet?'

'Not really my area,' replied Griffiths sulkily. 'I don't know.'

'Well, I need to have words with someone who *does* know, we don't want Taylor's name released. That girl in the Maragogype Café seemed to know who he was and the press will probably be all over her.'

'Why shouldn't Taylor's name be released?' Griffiths asked.

'Because if what Mr Taylor is saying is genuine, this could tip off anyone who had a bombing attack planned. Right now, we have a possible period when and where it could take place. If they change plans because they believe they've been sprung it could occur anywhere and anytime. Whether they know who Mr Taylor is by name I wouldn't know, but I don't think they've any reason, yet, to suspect the man whose apartment they ransacked is the one arrested at Southland.'

'What if it's a hoax?'

'By whom?' McKay spread out his hands. 'By Mr Taylor? If he'd committed a murder that resulted from a hoax. why would he ring the intelligence services, say where he was and ask us to pick him up?'

'Well maybe it's a hoax by the original owner of the computer,' persisted Griffiths.

'Possible, I concede that, but it would be a very long-winded hoax. But if it *was* a hoax, why were they so anxious to get the computer back?'

Griffiths looked discomforted, then tried another tack.

'We've only got his word his apartment was burgled.'

'Well, if the police attended, as Mr Taylor says they did, or alleges if you like, there should be a report somewhere, maybe here or the local police station. He says the police arrived at the apartment just after he'd left it. He saw a squad car arrive outside it.'

McKay turned to Taylor, who had been listening to the exchange with rapt attention, and hope. His relief that someone was taking him seriously shone through.

'That computer mechanic or technician, who is he?'

'I don't know, Harold knew him as Adam, he works for some company that specialises in repairing computers, or maybe fixing them if they pick up a virus. I'd say he was doing a deal under the radar, and the computer he brought in was part of a deal which should have been handed to his employer as a trade-in. I think Adam was pulling a swiftie!'

'You don't know who he is?'

'No. I've seen him a couple of times, same sort of deal, but never knew his second name nor his employer. I hadn't been working there long the first time I saw him but Henderson greeted him like an old friend, he's obviously been in before.'

'Hmm!' McKay sat back and considered. 'So nobody else would know either?'

Taylor shrugged.

'Guess only Harold would have known, maybe Mrs Henderson but I doubt it. She had very little to do with the workings of the shop, except to siphon money from it.'

'There were no other employees?'

'No,' Taylor shook his head. 'Not while I've been there. Money was tight and I doubt if he could afford it.'

McKay and Griffiths left the interview room and headed for the main foyer.

'Can we proceed with the murder enquiry now?'

There was an element of sarcasm in Griffiths' tone, which McKay ignored.

'Sure!' he replied. 'But we may have to see him again. Where can I see the report of the burglary at his apartment?'

'Can't help you, but Sergeant Phillips can probably steer you in the right direction. If we haven't got it then he can find out who has. Do you reckon there's anything in this, what he's saying, about a bomb plot?'

'I don't know,' McKay shrugged. 'You know as much as I do, but if there is and we ignore it, can you imagine the scream that would go up from the press and the public...and from State and Federal Parliaments...especially the Opposition?'

Griffiths looked pensive then nodded.

'Yes,' he said finally. 'Yes, you're right. I go along with that. OK, you want to see the disc we took from him, plus his print out. Sergeant Phillips is also the man for that.'

He pointed in the direction of the main reception desk, then on an impulse held out his hand. McKay took it and they both smiled.

'Will Taylor be released?' McKay asked.

'Not if I can help it,' said Griffiths. 'But magistrates will release anyone these days.'

'Yes, *we* know that, we've had Civil Libertarians screaming blue murder about people we've raided,' said McKay. 'But we're not anxious for Taylor to be released either. If these blokes are for real, if what he's saying is true, his life could be in danger the moment he steps outside this building.'

*

There was a protracted argument at the desk with Sergeant Phillips, who clung onto his shredded dignity and refused to release the disc or the printed copy from Taylor's effects without any authority from above. McKay merely took out his mobile phone and told Kelsey in Canberra what was happening.

'Hang on a minute,' said Kelsey. 'We have a contact at St Kilda, Superintendent Clucas, he's assisted us in the past with various cases. I'll give him a call.'

There was a phone call on the desk within ten minutes, Sergeant Phillips took the call, then put the receiver down. McKay gathered it was Clucas or somebody of equal rank judging by Phillips' obsequious manner and the numbers of times he said 'sir!'

Phillips made another call and after a few minutes an evidence bag was produced with bad grace, which had Taylor's possessions in it. McKay took out the disc and the printed copy, signed for both, then made his exit

CHAPTER 6

McKay phoned Marcus Templeton in Canberra.

'I have the disc, Marcus,' said McKay. 'I'll send it to you?'

'Get John Edmonds to transfer the data onto the hard drive down in Melbourne, then e-mail it here.,' said Templeton. 'When I tell you I've got it, send the disc up in the overnight bag. That way all bases are covered. I'll check it out when it arrives.'

'Will do,' McKay replied. 'Is Alan about?'

'I'll transfer you,' said Marcus Templeton. 'I'll be in touch.'

Kelsey came on line.

'What have you got?' he asked.

'The disc, I'm just sending the details to Marcus,' said McKay. 'But we seem to have struck a brick wall. Taylor only knows the computer technician's first name. This is the technician who brought the computer and monitor into Henderson's shop. He just knows him as Adam, which covers several thousand Melburnians.'

'Any record of him at the shop?'

'I'll go and check. It could be difficult as it's still a crime scene.'

'Have you found any friendly policemen?'

'Friendly!' McKay gave a hollow laugh. 'You wouldn't believe the hostility I encountered at St Kilda Road. The detective came round in the end, but the desk sergeant is an arrogant bastard with a chip on his shoulder the size of Ayers Rock.'

'I'll give Nick Clucas another call, see if something can be arranged about a visit to the shop,' answered Kelsey. 'Frankly I haven't much hope of finding anything, if this fellow Adam was doing an undercover deal, it may not appear in the books.'

'There could be a business card lying around somewhere, maybe on the notice board. Anyway, I'll wait until I hear from you.'

'Good! Incidentally, I'm sending you some help. Remember Catherine Parkinson?'

'Yes, I know her. She's at Sydney, isn't she?'

'She is. But I've already sent her down to you. You can either use her to assist in the field, or use Joe Carter. Either way, one of them can stay on station while the other is on the road with you.'

'Suits me,' said McKay. He remembered Catherine Parkinson, a first-class operative, intelligent, quick witted, and one of those women who seemed to prefer the company of men to her own sex. McKay judged Kelsey's move was to give her management experience, but McKay estimated she would be more valuable in the field.

*

McKay arrived at the Balaclava shop. It was still a crime scene. He walked up to the constable at the door.

'My name is Dave McKay,' he said. 'Is it possible to go in?'

'Who are you, sir...Oh sorry. You've just told me. What I really mean is, what are you, sir? Are you Press?'

'No, National Intelligence and Security from Canberra.'

'Canberra...National Security?' the constable looked impressed but shook his head. 'Sorry sir, not right now. Not even I could get in there. Forensics are still checking and will be there for a few hours yet.'

'Well, can I ask one question,' asked McKay. 'Not of you necessarily but from someone inside? Is there a business card on that board behind the counter from anyone named Adam?'

'I can find out that for you sir, hold on.'

McKay was left pondering the politeness shown by this particular constable, compared to the hostility shown by Sergeant Phillips and, initially, Detective Sergeant Griffiths. The constable called to someone inside and addressed a young woman dressed in a white plastic jump suit. She came to the doorway. McKay produced his identification.

'The notice board?' she asked. 'Why? We can't remove anything from it, not yet.'

'I don't want anything from it, I merely want to know if there's a card on there from anybody with the first name Adam.'

'We're rather busy in here.'

'All I'm asking is for you to look, that's all.'

'Look, we haven't time to...!'

'I'm from Canberra, it's to do with national security,' he nearly made an acid comment to the effect that he was busy as well but decided not to arouse further hostility from Victorian Police. He produced his ID again.

She studied it, hesitated, then nodded and vanished inside. After seven or eight minutes she re-appeared and shook her head.

'Nothing there for anybody named Adam,' she said.

'Thank you,' said McKay and returned to his car. 'Bugger it!'

When McKay re-entered the field office, Catherine Parkinson had already arrived from Sydney. She was with Joseph Carter who was at his desk and both were drinking coffee.

'Made yourself at home, I see,' McKay remarked as he entered. 'Good to see you Catherine, last time we met was that job at Wynyard Station, wasn't it?'

'Will I ever forget it?' responded Catherine. 'That was almost a bloody disaster!'

'We may have a similar one here,' said McKay. 'Somebody stumbled across a reference to a possible attack at a Melbourne underground railway station. If it's right with you, I'd suggest you accompany me in the field instead of sitting in here.'

'Suits me,' said Catherine. She was of average height, with short dark hair and was wearing a tight brown knee length skirt, and a white top, with a brown jacket that matched the skirt. She was sitting with her legs crossed, McKay swept his eyes over her briefly and ruminated she looked good. She also had a very astute brain to go with it, a quick wit, and a winning manner, invaluable when questioning people.

'You got here quickly,' McKay commented. 'Alan only told me you were coming about an hour ago.'

'I left early this morning, Alan said you probably needed back up, said he didn't like the look of this one.'

'He's not the only one,' said McKay. 'Taylor's story has the ring of truth. We've all been struck by one aspect, if a hoax, why say the alleged attack is two weeks away?'

'Where have we got?' asked Joe Carter.

'No bloody where,' growled McKay. 'Has Marcus acknowledged that e-mail yet.'

'Yes, he's got it. He's working on it.'

'What's the problem?' asked Catherine. 'A dead end?'

'Yes.' McKay answered. 'Do you know what's happened here, has Joe filled you in or do I start from scratch?'

'She knows some of it, not all,' said Joe.

'I'll give you a quick rundown,' McKay claimed the other chair in the room. 'They've arrested the fellow who tipped us off. He's bailed up in the St Kilda Road Police Complex on a murder charge.'

'Donald Taylor?' supplied Catherine.

'Ah...you know that already. Good. Well, they believe he may have murdered his boss, Harold Henderson. Taylor insists Henderson was murdered by three Asians who came in the shop and demanded their old computer back.'

'The one traded in?' asked Catherine.

'Yes, a technician brought it in, it wasn't a trade-in as far as Henderson was concerned, obviously an under the counter transaction for him and this man Adam. Henderson gave him cash for it.'

'Why did they want it back?'

'Well...' McKay pulled his chair nearer to the desk, and looked pointedly at the coffee pot. Carter hastily pushed an empty cup across and McKay poured himself a cup: '...as I read it, I'd say the technician replaced computer 'A' with computer 'B', and should have transferred all the data across from 'A' to 'B'. Looks to me as if the clients switched on their new computer, found much of their data was missing, and realised it hadn't been downloaded from the old computer.'

'How could that happen?' asked Joe Carter. 'Surely transferring data over should have been second nature for a computer technician when supplying a new system.'

'It should be,' said McKay. 'But Taylor said the hard drive on the old computer had been compartmentalised into two drives, 'C' and 'D'. It appears Adam, this technician, must have transferred over the 'C' drive data, and either forgot the 'D' drive or was unaware it was there. So...it failed to show up when our Asian friend booted up his new computer and there was only one place where the data could be, still on the old computer.'

'So they went looking for it and Adam,' Catherine suggested.

'Presumably, and persuaded Adam to tell them where it was'

'What happened with Taylor? How is he a murder suspect?'

'Mrs Henderson found him, Taylor that is, bending over Henderson who was bleeding to death on the shop floor. Taylor rushed from the shop; said he was going to ring the police as the attackers had disconnected the shop phone. The police have at least verified that.'

'What do we do now?' Catherine asked.

'We must isolate this computer technician, it looks as if he was doing a bit of moonlighting on his own account. The computer was a trade-in, technically it really belonged at that point to his employers, but he appropriated it for his own use... or to his own advantage.'

'So we go and see him?'

'Logically yes. Unfortunately, we don't know who he is,' said McKay. 'Taylor, who's been arrested, only knows him as Adam. I've been to the shop hoping there might be a card from Adam somewhere, but there's nothing.'

'Surely, if someone buys a new computer and there's a trade in value on the old, the employer would want to know where the old one was,' said Carter.

'You'd think so,' McKay shrugged.

'Unless ...!' Catherine said thoughtfully '...unless there was more than one transaction.'

'What do you mean?'

'Well, you say he was replacing computer 'A' with computer 'B', what if this replaced computer 'A' was then used to replace another, yet older model, say 'C', and it was 'C' that was brought into Harold Henderson's shop. Isn't it possible that Adam's employer's lines of communication might have become a little blurred?'

'What are you getting at?'

'Well, when a mechanic, or technician, replaces a computer, as you say they have to transfer all the data onto the new one, test it to make sure it's all there, and then delete it from the old before they trade it onwards.'

'Yes, I follow that. That's probably second nature.'

'But what if the replaced computer was then being used to replace a yet more inferior model elsewhere, isn't it possible the transfer of data and deletion could have been slip shod, or just not done properly at the second, or even a third transaction.'

McKay sat back and pondered.

'I see what you're getting at. The last process could have been hurried. In fact, Taylor said when he took delivery of the computer from Henderson in lieu of wages, it was an old model he wanted just as backup for use on the internet. When he opened it up, he found all its old data still present.'

'The old data related to what?'

'An engineering course, some of it.'

'Which means he maybe failed to completely delete the 'C' drive,' said Catherine. 'An engineering course could mean we're looking for a university student?'

'Very likely,' McKay agreed. 'But we'd be looking at several thousand students at any number of university campuses.'

'Not if we can trace Adam,' said Catherine. 'What about Mrs Henderson?'

'Taylor says she knew nothing about the business, except as a money tree.'

'She might know who Adam is.'

'She might,' agreed McKay. 'Interviewing her could be difficult at present though, remember her husband was killed a few days ago.'

'We're also in the month of September, if Taylor is right then the days are slipping past,' Catherine reminded him.

'Then we have to see her, but you can do the interview, she may relate better to you,' said McKay.' Our first hurdle is to find where Mrs Henderson is living. Anything in the phone book that gives a hint?'

Joe Carter reached for the phone book but shook his head.

'Any number of H. Hendersons,' he shook his head. 'The police would know.'

'And possibly Taylor,' said McKay. 'I'll try Detective Sergeant Griffiths. His demeanour seemed to improve as time went on.'

'Probably due to your personality and charm,' suggested Catherine.

'What else?' McKay reached for his mobile phone and called the St Kilda Road Police Complex. Detective Sergeant Griffiths was out so McKay left a message. He wasn't game to try Sergeant Phillips. He barely had time to make Catherine and himself a fresh cup of coffee when Griffiths rang back.

'Mr McKay?'

'Yes, the name's David,' answered McKay. 'Detective Sergeant Griffiths?'

'Call me Ted,' said Griffiths. 'You called?'

'Yes,' McKay was mildly amused at the exchange of first names as he recalled the initial hostility. Maybe mutual antagonism for Sergeant Phillips had made them friends... an enemy of my enemy etc! 'Ted, we're trying to track down Mrs Henderson. We need some information from her and think it's possible she may know who Adam is.'

'From what Donald Taylor told us I'm inclined to doubt it,' responded Griffiths. 'But it's worth a try. Henderson may have mentioned it at home. Hang on, I've got the address somewhere, and the phone number,' McKay heard the sound of rustling paper before the instrument was picked up again. 'Here we are ...' he gave an address and phone number and McKay checked them back. 'Best of luck, but be gentle with her David, she's been a widow for only a couple of days.'

'Will do, what's happening with Taylor?'

'We're holding onto him for the time being, normally we'd have to let him go if we can't charge him, but in view of what you said we decided to hold onto him, he doesn't seem anxious to be released either. If what he says is true, he's recently seen a man knifed to death and he's worried about the same happening to him. He's even withdrawn his request for a lawyer; just ordering bed and breakfast!'

McKay chuckled.

'We'll keep you informed,' he said. 'Incidentally, what happened about his motel bill?'

'Hell! I'd forgotten that. I'll deal with it.'

CHAPTER 7

They stood on the pavement outside the Henderson residence for some minutes and examined the house. It was an impressive double storey residence occupying a large block with a double garage.

'Nice house,' observed Catherine.

'Yes,' McKay said pensively. 'Over impressive when you consider the size of the business he was running. If that business was his only means of sustenance, then...!' McKay gestured with one hand at the house: 'Anyway, that's not why we're here. OK Catherine, lead the way, you can do the talking.'

'Thanks for nothing,' Catherine responded as they entered the drive and rang the bell. After a slight delay the door was opened by a young woman, clearly not Mrs Henderson.

Catherine did the introductions; she had already spoken on the phone to Henderson's daughter and assumed this was her. She made no bones about who they were and where they were from, identifying themselves as ASIO caused raised eyebrows and gained them admittance. The lady before them was tall, blonde, wore glasses, middle thirties at a guess.

'Moira Hammersley,' she said. 'I am Mrs Henderson's daughter. Why do you want to speak to my mother? How is national security involved?'

'We wish to say how sorry we are about the tragedy that has occurred, please accept our condolences.'

'Thank you,' Mrs Hammersley nodded and wiped a finger under her left eye. 'You said national security?'

'We have reason to believe your father's death could be related to national security, I can't tell you any more than that at this stage.'

'National security? But Donald Taylor killed my father...' she cut off a sob and recovered herself with an effort: '...my mother said she saw him do it, it was an argument over money. Are you saying it was something else?'

'We believe there could be an alternative explanation for your father's death,' Catherine said gently. 'The police are investigating. We're not the investigating officers, but are investigating another aspect that has arisen. We need information, which your mother could possibly supply, or you may be able to assist.'

'It depends what it is,' she led them into a sitting room and indicated a couple of armchairs.

'Last week your father accepted a computer as a trade-in,' Catherine said as she occupied one of them. 'Or a second-hand purchase, from a computer technician named Adam. We're trying to identify Adam. Would you have any idea?'

'What is this to do with...what has happened?'

'We don't know yet, but we believe it could be connected.'

'Are you saying it wasn't Donald Taylor who did it?'

'It's possible he may have arrived afterwards, we can't comment on that, the police are handling that aspect.'

'But Mummy said he'd ripped out the telephone and was running out of the shop.'

'We shouldn't comment on that, but I will say this,' McKay cut in. 'According to the police Taylor said he ran out of the shop to phone the police. Logically, if he had committed the attack, why should he bother to rip out the telephone, the shop at the time was devoid of anyone else, while Mr Henderson was in no position to use it.'

Mrs Hammersley pressed her hands to her cheeks and eyes and Catherine flashed a warning glance at McKay that plainly said: 'Shut up and leave it to me!'

'We're trying to trace Adam, who brought in this second-hand computer,' she continued. 'Would you, or your mother, have any idea who Adam is? We believe he's in the computer industry and that he and Mr Henderson may have done similar deals in the past.'

'I know nothing of the business,' Mrs Hammersley shook her head. 'But I can ask my mother. Excuse me for a moment?'

She rose and they heard her ascending the stairs. They heard the sound of voices up above, then Mrs Hammersley returned to the room shaking her head.

'She has no idea,' she said. 'She didn't know much about the business either.'

'She never served in the shop?' McKay asked.

'No, never.'

They rose to their feet, thoroughly dispirited. There was, understandably, a depressing pall over the house, it also appeared they had reached an impasse. As they walked into the hall McKay turned to Mrs Hammersley.

'Who was Mr Henderson's accountant?' he asked. 'Can you ask your mother that?'

'No need,' Mrs Hammersley opened the front door. 'I can tell you; he's my husband's accountant too. Arthur Shore, of Swain and Proctor, they have offices in St Kilda Road.'

They thanked her and the door closed behind them. As they walked down the drive Catherine turned to McKay.

'All sensible information,' she said. 'But you have something definite in mind?'

'Not sure what I'm thinking at present,' said McKay. 'But, as you say, all sensible information and we'll need the accountant eventually for more of that, and yes...I did have something in mind. Firstly, he does the books so Henderson might have dropped the name in conversation. Secondly, when I interviewed Taylor, he said he hadn't been working there long. I believe he was there on a casual basis, which accounted for the loose financial arrangement they had.'

'Where are you heading?'

'Taylor said Henderson's business was not going well and he was short of cash. He employed Taylor on a casual basis. This indicates there was possibly a previous employee, either off-loaded because Henderson couldn't afford him or was pissed off and left the business because he was underpaid, although very likely paid more than Taylor.'

'And he pissed off...literally!'

'As we both so eloquently put it, yes, he pissed off,' McKay replied. 'If Henderson was short of money, why put Taylor on at all? But he needed somebody there, an assistant. Taylor was a cheapie; he may have replaced someone else who wasn't.'

'You're thinking there could be a previous employee who could assist us?'

'Let's find out,' said McKay. 'Where's St Kilda Road from here?'

*

They found the building in St Kilda Road and parked in the side road. They entered the foyer and located the accountancy firm on the 5th floor. They took the lift and emerged into a vestibule on the 5th floor; it looked as if the firm occupied the whole floor. A young receptionist sat behind a curved desk, with the firm's name on a large board behind her head. They asked to speak to Arthur Shore.

'I'm afraid Mr Shore is very busy, have you got an appointment?' the receptionist asked with a shake of her head.

'No,' McKay said shortly. 'We are from national security. We shan't take up too much of Mr Shore's time, but can you tell him it relates to Harold Henderson.'

'He is very busy.'

'So are we,' said McKay curtly. 'Please tell him we are from Canberra and it relates to national security.'

'Did you say Harold Henderson?'

'We did,' said Catherine.

'But...Harold Henderson...wasn't he . . .?'

'Yes, he was. Now can we please see Mr Shore?'

She picked up the phone and dialled. There was a brief conversation and she replaced the phone.

'He'll see you, he's coming out,' she said.

'Thank you,' said McKay. He wandered over to the window that faced onto St Kilda Road and watched the ceaseless motor traffic and trams passing up and down. He heard footsteps and turned as Shore entered the reception area.

'Arthur Shore. You wanted to see me?'

'Yes,' said McKay. 'Is there somewhere we can talk? It shouldn't take long.'

Shore was short in stature, about 5'7" tall, with horn rimmed glasses, cavalry twill trousers and had a navy-coloured pullover over his shirt. He was balding on top, with a tuft of hair in the middle of his hair line that drifted back over the bald area. He looked about 45.

He showed them into an interview room, they sat at a table and he sat opposite. He looked at his watch.

'Will this take long?'

'No,' said McKay. 'But it relates to Harold Henderson.'

'Yes, so you told our receptionist. Terrible business, I'd known Harold for years. Who would have done this, was it that young man Taylor?'

'We can't answer that. That aspect is in the hands of the police.'

'Where are you from? What is National Security? Aren't you the police?'

'No, we're not,' McKay produced his ID. 'We are from ASIO, Australian Intelligence in Canberra.'

'ASIO?' Shore looked startled. 'Good God! Are you saying Harold was a spy or something? How are you involved in this?'

'No, he wasn't...and let's just say, for the present, that we are involved. We have some questions about Harold Henderson's business. You've been his accountant for some years, I believe?'

'Yes, and let me say that anything to do with his business is strictly confidential.'

'What we are investigating is far more serious than any confidentiality relating to the Henderson business,' said McKay. 'We can always obtain a court order, but it may not come to that. What we are after hardly comes within the sphere of confidentiality.'

'What is it exactly?' Shore seemed to unbend a little. 'Obviously if national security is involved ...!'

'Last week Harold Henderson took delivery of a second-hand computer from a computer mechanic or technician named Adam. We believe this computer could be the key to the chain of events that brought about Harold Henderson's death. We believe Adam was in the habit of calling at the shop, on an irregular basis, to bring in and off-load second-hand equipment. Do you have any idea who he could be?'

'Adam?' Shore scratched his chin. 'I can't recall any mention of any computer technician or contact. I take it you're saying this man was thought to be an outsider, and therefore not an employee or sub-contractor of Harold?'

'That is how it appears.'

'If it was purely cash there's no guarantee it would have been reflected in the books. It sounds to me like a backhander arrangement.'

'That's how it sounded to us, but we wondered if the name might have come up in conversation.'

'No, if it was anything like that, he would have had no reason to mention it to me. If there's anything remotely off-line going on, on a purely cash basis, even an insignificant thing like that, I'd sooner not know about it,' Shore gave a brief smile. 'Harold ran his business properly, but I guess...well we all do the occasional something or other under the counter for cash. In any case, I wouldn't think a second-hand computer coming in like that would have affected things very much.'

'Depends how often he did it,' commented McKay. 'But we're not from the Taxation Department so that aspect doesn't concern us. Did he ever mention anyone called Adam?'

'I'm afraid not.'

'Well can you answer my next question? You're obviously aware he was employing Donald Taylor, because you mentioned him just now.'

'Yes, I had Mrs Hammersley on the phone yesterday giving me the news,' Shore shook his head sadly. 'I didn't know about Taylor before, although his name and earnings would obviously have come up at the end of this current financial year.'

'Did Harold Henderson employ anybody else prior to Donald Taylor?'

'Yes, he did. He had two or three employees, not all at the same time, but things began to go downhill. I'm not sure why, but there seemed to be more outgoings than income.'

'Are we talking about Mrs Henderson?'

Shore inclined his head to one side.

'That's not for me to say ...' he began cautiously, then gave a resigned gesture: '...hell...yes, it is and it was! Her spending did not assist Harold. She had a job of her own until about three years ago, but she lost that and that's when Harold's troubles began.'

'We've been told already about Mrs Henderson's spending habits from another source so you're not betraying any confidences. Do you know who Harold Henderson employed? We need their names.'

'Yes, I think I can tell you that. Why do you ask?'

'Because they might know who this Adam character is. It's vital we find him, he may have information we can use, or...his life could be in danger as well.'

'What?' Shore abruptly sat up straight. 'His life! In danger?'

'The information he has is not only of use to us,' said McKay. 'Others are interested in what he knows, not so much the information itself but primarily the knowledge of where that computer came from.'

'Give me a minute, I'll consult the file,' Shore got up and left. He was away for about three to four minutes and returned with a couple of bulky files.

'Harold Henderson's computer business,' he placed the files on the table. 'We've had the shop account for years. As regards employees, we dealt with their taxation records as well. They were PAYE as far as the tax office was concerned, so we should have their details ...hmm ...let me see.'

He flicked through the pages, nodded, wrote down a name, did more searching, wrote down two more, then looked up.

'I've gone back five years. Will that be enough for your purposes?'

'Should be,' McKay stretched out his hand for the written notes. 'If we need more, we'll be in touch again. We're very grateful for your information, Mr Shore. You've given us much time, your receptionist told us you were very busy and couldn't see us initially, so thank you.'

'Your mention of poor Harold attracted my attention,' said Shore sadly. 'But there was another aspect. When you introduced yourselves, she thought you might be from an insurance company, we get quite a few in here selling Professional Indemnity cover, superannuation and trying to persuade us to give them names of clients so they can sell life assurance or superannuation policies to them.'

'Insurance?' McKay looked puzzled. 'Why should she think we were insurance?'

'You said national security,' Shore's expression cleared and he smiled. 'She thought it sounded like the name of an insurance company.'

Catherine began to giggle.

'She's right, it does,' she said. 'Maybe you should change your spiel, Dave.'

CHAPTER 8

They entered a nearby café, ordered coffee and studied the names and addresses.

'We have three previous employees here, we'll start with the most recent, Taylor's predecessor,' mused McKay.

Catherine Parkinson took the paper and smoothed it out.

'We have Andrew Dixon, Stanley Elverton and Piers Acland, plus their phone numbers,' she said. 'As you suggest, chronologically, we should start with Piers Acland.'

'Agreed, he finished in June, didn't he?' McKay ran his finger down the list. 'From what Shore said, Taylor didn't figure in the financial year just gone, he must have started some time from July onwards. OK, give Acland a call.'

She dialled the number and after a few moments shook her head.

'Number discontinued!'

'Bugger it...try the next one!'

She dialled Elverton's number, listened and shrugged.

'No reply! It just cut off short and I got an engaged tone.'

'Not our lucky day, is it? Call Dixon.'

'What did your last servant die of?'

'Sexual ecstasy!' McKay retorted and she went into peals of laughter. Other patrons turned briefly in their direction before they returned to their conversations, coffees and crosswords.

'This might be my lucky day then,' she keyed in the last number.

'Mr Dixon?' she looked at McKay and gave the thumbs up signal. 'My name is Catherine Parkinson, I am attached to the police and we wish to have a word with you about one of your previous employers.'

McKay could hear Dixon's voice at the other end as Catherine spoke again.

'Which one? I'm talking about Harold Henderson, the computer shop in Balaclava. We understand you had employment with him within the last eighteen months,' she said. 'You did? Yes, this is important ...oh you've heard. Yes, terrible business. We just need you to fill in details for us. Can we meet with you? Anytime that suits you.'

She snatched McKay's pen and notebook and began writing.

'That's marvellous, we can be with you in about ten to fifteen minutes. Which floor? Yes, that's fine. Thank you, Mr Dixon.'

She looked at McKay.

'A serviced office block in Collins Street, on the corner of King Street, seventh floor.'

'Where's King Street?'

'We head into the city and turn left. It's not far.'

*

They entered the foyer of the King Street building, checked the directory and looked for entries for the 7th floor.

'What firm did he work for?'

'I forgot to ask,' said Catherine. 'Sorry.'

'No matter, we'll find him if we have to go from door to door,' McKay responded. 'We'll try this one first.'

He pointed at an entry on the directory: "RRR Computers."

'Interesting name,' commented Catherine. 'What does that mean?'

'We'll soon find out, but I don't think it will be Arse Computers! Maybe he's running computer instruction classes…3 Rs?'

They emerged onto the 7th floor. A reception desk faced the lift, a large sign bore the words "Smith-Cheney Office Renting". Behind the desk was a blonde receptionist.

'We wanted Andrew Dixon,' said Catherine.

'Oh yes, he's expecting you. Fourth door on the right.'

'We were right about one thing,' McKay observed as they arrived outside the designated doorway. 'He *is* RRR Computers.'

They knocked, the door was opened promptly by an earnest looking young man with thin features, receding black hair, a hair line moustache and wearing glasses.

'Andrew Dixon,' he announced. 'You'll be Catherine?'

He shook hands with Catherine and she introduced McKay. Dixon indicated a couple of chairs opposite his desk. They looked around with interest, the room was mainly taken up with two long benches, on both of which there were four computers and monitors. There was a whiteboard in one corner with computer formulae on it. Apart from Dixon and themselves the room was devoid of personnel.

'What's this all about?' Dixon asked.

'We're investigating the murder of Harold Henderson,' said McKay. 'We understand you used to work for him.'

'Yes, in his shop, I left him about three years ago.'

'Why did you leave?'

'Various reasons, mainly lack of prospects and of cash, he didn't pay well,' said Dixon. 'The business wasn't exactly thriving.'

'What sort of a man was he?'

'Nice fellow, I liked him. But as a long-term career prospect it was zilch. I didn't like his wife, she used to come in and boss me around, yet had nothing to do with the business.'

'What about his daughter?'

'His daughter...hang on...what is this? Am I a suspect or something? Do I need a lawyer?'

'Sorry,' McKay shook his head. 'We should be more explicit. Although we are investigating the death of Harold Henderson, we're not from the police, we represent national sec ...' he caught Catherine's eye, gave a half smile and amended what he was going to say '...Australian Intelligence.'

He produced his ID and Catherine did the same. Dixon examined them and seemed mollified.

'Intelligence, you mean ASIO?'

'Yes,' said McKay.

'How is ASIO involved with this? Was Harold a spy or something?'

'No,' McKay shook his head. 'But we're after background information. If you answer our questions I'll explain later.'

'All right, go ahead.'

'Now...what's your opinion of his daughter?'

'Mrs Hammersley you mean? Nice type, I liked her, complete antithesis of her mother. She came in once or twice, nice lady.'

'She had no dealings with the business so she knew no people in the computer business?'

'Not to my knowledge, her husband is something in the city,

stock exchange or something like that. I never met him.'

'Next question. While you were employed by Henderson, did you ever come across a man named Adam? We believe he was a computer technician who worked either for himself or for a firm of computer technicians.'

'Adam?' Dixon pursed his lips. 'It doesn't ring a bell. Should it?'

'We believe this man Adam, whoever he is, traded in a second-hand computer system, one he'd replaced in his capacity as a technician and later supplied to Henderson either for cash or favours. Henderson, in turn, passed it to his employee, Donald Taylor, one of your successors, who wanted back up equipment, in lieu of salary.'

'Well, recalling Harold's financial parsimony, that sounds likely and logical. How does that bring ASIO into the frame?'

'I was coming to that,' said McKay. 'Taylor connected the computer to his own system at home and discovered neither Adam, nor Harold Henderson, had deleted existing data from it. What was still on it gave serious concern regarding national security. We believe the original owners subsequently realised this data could still be on the hard drive when they found it hadn't been transferred to their new computer, presumably installed by Adam.'

'So from Adam they found where it was?'

'Looks like it,' McKay agreed. 'At that point, in the light of subsequent events, they were prepared to go to any lengths to get that computer back. Adam himself might now be at risk. Any idea who he is?'

'No, none,' Dixon shook his head. 'Have you tried Stan Elverton?'

'You know him?'

'No...well...yes...not intimately. I knew he'd superseded me. I had to call in one day to collect something. I still dealt with Harold occasionally for computer gear. I use second-hand stuff here. It doesn't need to be too sophisticated for training purposes. Harold introduced us.'

'Do you know where he is?'

'No, but he's around, probably in the computer industry somewhere,' Dixon reached in his drawer, produced an address book and turned to the 'E' page. 'No, he's not here. But I can make enquiries for you. I've contacts around Melbourne, some of them may know where he is; possibly this Adam you're looking for as well.'

'Good,' McKay stood up. 'Here's my card. Give us a call if you find anything. I must stress...it's vital. Incidentally, if you do trace Adam, please don't elaborate on what we've told you, just call us straightaway. This is strictly confidential, you understand?'

'Understood,' Dixon took McKay's card and they shook hands. As they walked to the door, Catherine swept her hand around the benches.

'You do computer training here?'

'Yes,' Dixon said. 'I run classes in computers and computer programming. Many companies use us because it's easier for them to contract training out than employ full-time training staff they would only use occasionally, in addition it's so expensive to employ people these days. I learnt a lot from Harold and I'm using what I learnt at his shop to teach pupils here. I'm sorry to hear what happened to him. Nice fellow.'

'How's business?' asked McKay.

'Good... plenty of demand.'

*

'Another dead end,' commented McKay as they paused in the building's foyer. 'If that disc is referring to a genuine attack, time is drifting on.'

'Maybe we'd better give Marcus Templeton a call, find out what's on it.'

'Try that number for Elverton again.'

Catherine dialled on her mobile, listened and grimaced.

'Same as last time.'

'And Acland?'

She dialled again and shook her head.

'Same again.'

'Not our day,' McKay said ruefully. 'Let's get back to South Melbourne.'

*

McKay phoned Kelsey at Canberra.

'Stick on the trail of this man Adam,' said Kelsey. 'Marcus has been through the info you sent to him, I've got a full report here. I'm in touch with Superintendent Nick Clucas who will be dealing with the physical security angle in Melbourne, but we must find Adam. He's the key to the whole business. He must know who that computer belonged to.'

'We've followed some leads, we've found a past Henderson employee, but drew a blank.'

'Well done, keep at it. How are you making out with Catherine?'

'Fine, she's a smart operator.'

'Good, keep in touch.'

CHAPTER 9

'We could try searching through the various computer technicians and programmers,' Joe Carter suggested when they returned from lunch. 'Phone them all and see if anyone knows them.'

'Good idea,' McKay replied, but after they'd checked through the Yellow Pages, they all looked at each other.

'Bloody Hell!' said Carter. 'There's pages and pages of them!'

'Sign of the times,' commented Catherine. 'Thirty years ago, they wouldn't have occupied half a column. Now, if we call them all, the phone bill alone will take up ASIO's appropriation for the year.'

'Well, we'd best make a start; offhand I can't think of a better idea,' said McKay. 'Can you arrange that, Joe?'

'Case of having to,' Carter said resignedly. 'I'll have to get John Edmonds off his computer, and I'll draft Jim Waters, Dean Hateley and Gordon Anscombe onto it.'

'How about calling on any firms near St Kilda and Balaclava?'

suggested Catherine.

'That would make sense,' said Carter. 'Possibly more chance of a hit there.'

McKay's phone rang and he answered it.

'McKay.'

He listened intently and signalled to Carter to fling his notepad across. He wrote down an address and after a brief conversation snapped his phone shut.

'That was Andrew Dixon, he found Stanley Elverton,' he said. 'He rang round a few of his mates in the business world and struck gold.'

'Where is he?' asked Catherine.

'Not far away, he's working at Tullamarine Airport for one of the airlines.'

'What sort of work?'

'As far as Dixon could gather, computers, but he wasn't sure. Southern Airlines, he said.' McKay replaced his phone in his pocket. 'Let's take a trip to Tullamarine. You can start the phone calls, Joe. Get John, Jim and the others onto it.'

'Thanks very much, when do you go back permanently to Canberra?'

'Maybe never, I think I like it here.'

'So did I, until about fifteen minutes ago,' Carter said morosely.

*

They arrived at Tullamarine Airport, strolled into the main terminal building and looked around for Southern Airlines. They found a frontage on the top level of the concourse and paused outside it.

'Cross your fingers,' McKay said as they entered a small

reception area. A blonde girl greeted them. McKay asked for Stanley Elverton.

'Stanley Elverton!' she raised her eyebrows. 'He doesn't work here any more.'

'What? Since when? When did he leave you?'

'Last week,' she responded. 'He got a job in the city; he started there last Monday.'

'Do you know where he went?'

'Who wants to know?'

'We do,' Catherine gave a winning smile. 'We need to speak with him and it's important. Can I ask you a question, without you telling us the finer details?'

The girl nodded.

'Do you know where he went?'

After a brief hesitation, she nodded.

'All right, can you phone him and tell him we've been contacted by Andrew Dixon. Tell him it's about Harold Henderson. Ask him to ring on this number...' Catherine snapped her fingers at McKay who produced one of his cards. She handed it to the receptionist: '...and I'll just write this down ...can I borrow your pad?'

She wrote down the names of Andrew Dixon and Harold Henderson and handed the pad back.

'If you get hold of him, can you ask him to ring us immediately on that number on this card? It's vital we contact him today.'

'What were the names again?'

'They're on that pad that I gave you, Andrew Dixon and it's about Harold Henderson. You know where we are from, it's on the card. Just tell him it's urgent.'

The girl looked curiously at Catherine, then nodded. 'Take a seat, I'll see if I can get hold of him.'

Five minutes later she beckoned to them.

'He's at the Yarra Banking Corporation, merchant bankers at the Parliament end of Collins Street. He says he'll see you and suggests you come down now, he won't ring you. He's on the 9th floor,' she handed them a note with the address and a phone number.

'Thank you,' said Catherine. 'Tell him we're on our way.'

*

They found the offices of the Yarra Banking Corporation and entered. They were greeted by a receptionist. Catherine leant over the desk and asked for Stanley Elverton.

'Would you like to go into that interview room? He is expecting you,' the girl said. 'I'll give him a call and tell him you're here.'

'He seems to move around a bit,' commented McKay. 'This would be his third job within what...12 months?'

'Sign of the times,' said Catherine. 'My father worked for the same company for 40 years, nowadays people move around more frequently.'

McKay picked up a magazine and thumbed through it, then put it down as the door opened and a young man walked in. He was dark haired with a trace of a black beard, and was fairly short in stature. He wore light coloured trousers and a dark blazer.

'G'day!' and they responded in like vein.

'What's this all about? I heard about poor Harold, what a terrible thing.'

'That's why we're here,' said McKay. 'There are aspects about his death that are of interest to us. As mentioned, we are from Australian Intelligence.'

'Yes?' Elverton looked baffled. 'Why intelligence?'

'I'll explain in a minute, but firstly, we need background

information. How long were you employed by Harold Henderson?'

'Not long, but I wasn't actually employed, I was on a contract basis. I install, and design, computer packages. Harold wanted an accounting package because he wanted to account for incomings and outgoings; his existing system appeared to have flaws. He was right; money was creeping out through the back door and he wasn't accounting for it properly. I was working in conjunction with his accountant, Arthur Shore.'

'What was happening?'

'Shore wanted to make the system more foolproof. Frankly, Mrs Henderson was spending too much, when she ran short of funds she called in at the business and raided the till. That was the leak, a perfect system for Harold would have had to be wife-proof, but Harold was reluctant to pinpoint it. He was frightened to say boo to her, but he talked about it to Arthur Shore and Arthur introduced a new system that could curb it, and make it more difficult for money to be drawn out casually.'

'The best system could have been divorce,' Catherine commented cynically.

'My view entirely, but don't quote me on that,' said Elverton.

'Did it work?' asked McKay, Elverton grimaced and inclined his head on one side.

'Up to a point, we reduced the cash float and paid in more often to the bank. It made it more difficult for her as there was less for her to raid, but she is a formidable lady.' he said. 'No, I'd put it more strongly than that, she was an arrogant, selfish, ill-mannered bitch.'

'You were there purely on a temporary basis?'

'Yes, I wasn't the only one. My successor was brought in to manage and serve in the shop. We coincided for a couple of weeks.'

'That was Piers Acland?'

'That's right, nice bloke. I was in the back room most of the time working on the accounting system.'

'That's what you do for a living is it?'

'That's it, after that I had a short-term contract with Southern Airlines, which you know, and I'm on a contract basis here. This system has been in for years, and with the increased size of the company problems are cropping up. I'm working on a new package altogether, which will take some time, certainly a few months.'

'I see,' McKay said. 'The reason we're here is we need assistance regarding Harold Henderson's business. As you know his death wasn't accidental.'

'So I heard, police suspect his latest employee don't they?'

'That's true, but we suspect there's another reason for what happened to Harold Henderson.'

'Oh? What's that?'

McKay ignored the question.

'While you were working there, did you ever see any technicians come in who traded in systems they had replaced?'

'No, I was working in the rear of the shop most of the time, checking on the system. I spent some evenings there occasionally after the business closed for the day, easier that way when the system wasn't in use.'

'So, you never saw any customers or visiting computer people at all?'

'Not quite true, occasionally during lunch-hours I was drafted in to speak to people and just keep them occupied while Harold or Piers were dealing with other customers. I did meet one bloke who brought in a replaced computer, like you mention, he told me his name and I've forgotten it ...!'

'Was it Adam?'

'No!' Elverton shook his head. 'No, it wasn't Adam, I have a feeling it began with a 'C' I think it was ...hang on a minute, just let me think...!'

He raised his hands and pressed the heel of his hands to his temples, concentrating. McKay began to feel impatient as about 15 seconds elapsed, then Elverton pushed his hands out sideways with his palms pointing upwards.

'Got it...Chris! Chris Prescot. He worked for himself. I saw him once or twice. He sorted out computers that had attracted viruses, or kept crashing, and supplied new hard drives if the user needed more capacity. He also supplied new equipment but had his own sources of supply. He ran into problems disposing of old trade-in computers at times and Harold used to take them from him. Didn't pay much, but Chris was glad to have them off his hands. Better be rid of them for a few dollars so they could be used again sooner than finish on the Council tip.'

'You never came across anyone named Adam?'

'No.' Elverton shook his head. 'Doesn't strike a chord, if he was in the equation he must have been after my time.'

'Did Chris stop coming in ...I mean...could he have been dissatisfied with what Henderson gave him and stopped coming in?'

'Anything's possible, but up to the time I left, he still made occasional appearances. I don't think he was after money as such, as a computer man through and through he considered it criminal to throw stuff away, especially if it still worked. Plus, he liked to chat with other computer nerds, kept them all in touch with things.'

'Can we contact him?'

'Ah! Good question, I don't know where he came from, but if he's working on his own, he should be in the book. He'd been in the business for some time, he was in his early thirties I'd say.'

'How did you get onto Harold Henderson or how did he get onto you? Did he advertise for a technician or programmer?'

'Family,' said Elverton. 'Geoff Hammersley is my cousin, he suggested me to Moira, she's his wife and Harold Henderson's daughter, she gave my name to Harold. I'd already done work for Geoff's company in the city, so it wasn't entirely a case of nepotism.'

'Did you know Piers Acland at all?'

'Only in passing, he came in while I was still there, he replaced Andrew Dixon. Young chap. Dixon fell out with Mrs Henderson and decided to go, plus his bent was in another direction, which is what he's doing now; teaching computer systems and techniques. When Harold replaced Andrew, he decided on a fairly young bloke, he looked like a teenager to me, say 19 or 20.'

'Dixon never mentioned to us about problems with Mrs Henderson being the reason he left, not in those terms anyway.'

'Well maybe he was just being reticent. He's doing quite well running computer classes in the city now. Piers seemed a nice young fellow, I knew him slightly, keen on computers, as you'd expect, and an avid football fan. I remember he supported Hawthorn; he had a run in with Mrs Henderson one day because he'd put a Hawthorn sticker on the front of the till drawer ...trust her to notice anything stuck there. It was always her first port of call, before she said hallo. Harold sent for me on one occasion after I'd gone from the business. He wanted me to sort out glitches in the money system.'

'Well Andrew Dixon enabled us to trace you,' said McKay. 'Can you lead us to Piers Acland? Do you know where Piers Acland is now?'

'Acland?' Elverton scratched his head. 'No, I don't. He was there when I left the business and still there when I called in later to sort out a couple of problems in the accounting system.

Don't know where he is now, but he was temporary, or casual.'

'Could he have been a university student?'

'Could have been, but I don't know. Try Chris Prescot. As far as I know Chris was still around when I left, so he may have had conversations with Piers. He may even know who Adam is.'

McKay took out his notepad.

'Do you have a mobile number? We may need to contact you again.'

'Sure, but you haven't told me your interest in this.'

'No, I didn't. It's just that we need to trace the source of a computer Adam brought in as a trade-in. We need to find the previous owner and quickly.'

'Can you be more explicit?'

'No, not at this stage. But it is important. Now, do you have a mobile number?'

Elverton wrote down a number on McKay's pad and handed it back.

'We've tried to contact you on another number, all we got was the number unobtainable signal.'

'I replaced it because I had endless trouble with it,' said Elverton. 'I couldn't hear what people were saying on it, if I was in the car, in a tram, in the street or a crowded office I almost had to thrust it right into my ear or else find somewhere quiet. With this current one, callers come through clear as a bell, no problems.'

'We'll probably be in touch, thanks for your help.'

*

'Give Joe a ring, ask him to look up Chris Prescot in the computer pages, we might be able to track him down,' McKay said after they returned to their car. 'Maybe we can catch him before he knocks off for the day.'

'I think you've got a parking ticket,' Catherine said mildly, pointing to the windscreen.

'Bloody hell!'

McKay angrily snatched the ticket from the windscreen wiper and flung it onto the back seat. Catherine stood with her phone to her ear, then snapped it shut and clambered into the passenger seat.

'Any luck with Joe?'

'Answering machine, so I left a message. We'll have to chase Prescot tomorrow.'

CHAPTER 10

They arrived early next morning at South Melbourne, where Joe Carter handed McKay a note pad with a number on it.

'Easy task this time,' he said. 'We're still hunting through all the other computer technicians and mechanics for this fellow Adam, but we found this one straight away. He's trading on his own, not in his own name but there aren't many C. Prescots in the book and after a couple of false starts I got his home. I spoke to his wife and he's the right bloke for sure. He's trading as CP Computers.'

'OK!' McKay took the pad. 'We'll call him.'

McKay dialled the number and it was answered immediately.

'Mr Prescot, my name is David McKay. We are conducting enquiries relating to the death of Harold Henderson, and need to have a word with you.'

'Harold Henderson? I heard what happened to Harold, how can I help?'

'We need some information.'

'Hells bells, I'm not a suspect, am I? Are you from the police, or the Press?'

'I am from Australian Intelligence from Canberra, and no... we are not anything to do with the Press.'

'Intelligence! What is this? MI5?'

'Same thing,' McKay experienced irritation at the assumption of the parallel British organisation. Prescot was plainly English, his Lancashire accent stood out like a beacon. But at least he'd got the message. 'We must see you as soon as possible, where can we see you?'

'I'm doing a job at Glen Waverley right now. I'm just clearing a virus the lady of the house picked up two days ago. Usual story, she opened a suspect e-mail attachment and it let in the virus. My next job is at 2 o'clock, so when I'm finished here, say about 10.30, I should be clear for the rest of the morning.'

'Can you meet us at...hang on a minute,' he cupped the receiver and looked at Joe Carter. 'He's in Waverley, where's a good place to meet?'

'Try the Burvale,' suggested Carter. 'It's a large road-house style pub on the Burwood Highway, it shouldn't be crowded mid-morning. It has a large bar-room and makes good coffee. He should know it. Big car park, no risk of parking tickets.'

McKay took his hand off the mouthpiece and spoke again.

'What about the Burvale?'

'Suits me. Are you buying?'

'For sure,' McKay gave a low chuckle. 'There will be two of us, man and a woman. The lady is wearing...' he looked at Catherine '... blue top, fawn skirt, and she's dark haired. Me, dark trousers, sports jacket.'

'I'm wearing a Rugby shirt with CP Computers on it,' responded Prescot. 'Give me your number, I'll phone you when I'm on my way.'

*

McKay and Catherine were drinking cappuccino coffee in the corner of the bar-room when a burly young man dressed in denims and a green Rugby football style shirt strolled in through the main doorway. He cast his eye around, caught sight of them and came over. The 'CP Computers' wording on his shirt front was clear to see.

'At a rough guess, I'd say that's our man,' said McKay. Catherine looked suitably impressed.

'You're wasted in ASIO,' she said cynically. 'You should be a detective in the Police force. How *did* you find out?'

'Just deduction,' McKay replied modestly.

'Cute shirt design,' observed Catherine and McKay had another look. The message CP Computers was written across the chest, and in front of the 'CP' were the letters 'CP', but these were backwards so it was like a mirror image. They stood as Prescot came over.

'G'day,' he said. 'Chris Prescot.'

'David McKay and Catherine Parkinson,' McKay indicated a vacant chair to Prescot. 'What can I get you?'

'Make it a Pepsi,' said Prescot. 'I spend most of the day on the road so I keep off the turps.' Catherine rose and went to the bar while Prescot looked quizzically at McKay.

'You said this was to do with intelligence, are you ASIO?'

'Well, that's better, you said MI5 before.'

'Sorry, I watch too much television,' Prescot said ruefully.

McKay studied him. He was fair-haired, burly without being obese and he looked as if he spent considerable time in the gym. He had small lines around the edges of his eyes and the end of his mouth appeared to be permanently turned upwards. He looked a cheerful, good-humoured type. He had a tattoo on his forearm,

McKay squinted at it; it looked like a replica of a motor cycle.

'Are you a Harley-Davidson man?' he asked.

'How did you guess that? Oh ...the tattoo, it's been there so long I tend to forget it's there,' Prescot grinned. 'Yes, I'm a bit of a bikey, not as much as I was. Good fun, but it gets expensive these days.'

Catherine returned with drink can and glass. Prescot cracked it open, poured the liquid into the glass and took a deep draught.

'I really needed that,' he put down the glass. He looked as if he really wanted something else as well, his eyes wandered up and down Catherine and it seemed to McKay that in his mind he stripped her naked, dressed her again and then stripped her again slowly. He had another go at the glass and put it down again. Catherine was aware of the effect she was having; she seemed to like it. 'Now, what's this all about? How is Harold Henderson's murder involved with ASIO?'

'We're trying to track movements of people who went into Henderson's shop over the last few months,' said McKay. 'We've been investigating and your name came up.'

'Hell! You don't think I did it, do you?'

'No!' McKay shook his head. 'That's not why we've contacted you. It's a long story and much of the information we can't reveal at present. We understand from Andrew Dixon and Stanley Elverton you called in the shop to trade in, or off-load, second hand computer systems. Is that right?'

'Yes, I do, or did, if this hadn't happened I still would. I haven't been in the shop for a few weeks, maybe a couple of months, I've been away in New Zealand. My wife's a Kiwi and we usually spend a month or so over there.'

'I see,' McKay nodded. 'Now, we're trying to trace two people who either worked or called in there. Do the names Piers Acland or Adam mean anything to you?'

'Piers certainly does, he was employed there until a few months back, I think he left about July, then a young guy named Taylor replaced him. Never met him, Taylor that is, but I knew he was there because I called in one day and spoke to Harold. Piers wasn't there so I asked about Piers' replacement. Harold said he had one, meaning Taylor, he was working in the back of the shop at the time and I never made contact. He's been arrested, hasn't he?'

'Yes, but whether he did it or not is open to question,' said McKay. 'Did you ever come across a man named Adam? He would be the same as you, a technician who brought in second hand gear.'

'Adam?' Prescot held his chin between thumb and forefinger and considered. 'Adam...it does ring a bell, but I never met him, not to speak to anyway. Piers mentioned him once when I took in an old Pentium III, there was another one on the counter and a bloke came out of the shop while I was parking across the street. I remember I made some comment about it to Piers, I asked who he was because you like to meet fellow computer techos on your rounds so you can swap notes and contacts.'

'Did you know his second name and where he worked?'

Prescot shook his head.

'Not a clue, he was young, perhaps mid- twenties. Drove off in a blue van, had some writing on it but I didn't take much note of it.'

'Can you remember anything about the writing on the van?'

'No!' Prescot shook his head. 'I was too busy watching traffic so I could cross the road. I was carrying a monitor at the time so had to watch my feet. It had a 'P' in it, I noticed that because I've got the same letter in my trade name, but more than that I can't say.'

'And that's all?'

'Afraid so.'

'What about Piers, do you know where he is now?'

Prescot reached into his pocket and pulled out an address book. He thumbed into the letter 'A' and then handed the book to McKay.

'Got an address there, but don't know if he's still there,' he said. 'We had a drink or two, met him once at a weekend and we went to the football together. He was mad keen; I go occasionally and he talked me into a Friday night game. We were both members of the same footy club so when I went into Harold's shop after that we talked about last week's game most of the time, even more than we did about computers.'

'You think he's moved from this address here?'

'He said he was going to; he's from the bush and lived in lodgings. He complained the rent was too high.'

'Where was he from originally?'

'He was ...er...hmm...western Victoria somewhere, beyond Ballarat, maybe Hamilton or Horsham, somewhere like that.'

'Who do you barrack for?' Catherine suddenly asked. 'Which footy club?'

'There's only one club in Victoria,' he replied which made Catherine laugh.

'Yes, I realise that. It's just that I've been away and forgotten.'

Prescot chuckled and eyed her appreciatively.

'The mighty Hawks of course,' he said.

'Of course,' said Catherine. 'You say Acland, Piers that is, was a member?'

'Yes, he is. He's been a member for years, I understand, even though he's only a young bloke. And his father before him and probably his grandfather as well.'

'Is this his last phone number?' McKay asked.

'It's the only one I've got,' said Prescot. 'I used it on the football night, to tell him I wasn't far away ...think that was the only reason he asked me...because I had transport. But it was a great night, he was good company.'

'I take it they won.'

'Don't they always?' retorted Prescot.

'This number we already have,' Catherine was looking over McKay's shoulder. 'It's permanently engaged; we can't get a response.'

'I can't account for that; it was certainly valid when he gave it to me but that was months back.'

'You've no idea where he is now?'

'No.'

'What about Adam? Any idea who he is?'

'None, apart from being a computer tech, which I guess you know already.'

'OK,' McKay closed his notebook. 'Thanks for your help, Mr Prescot. We may be in touch again. As a matter of interest, where are you from?'

'Where was I born, you mean?'

McKay nodded.

'Prescot.'

'No...where were you were born?'

'I've just told you,' Prescot grinned. 'Prescot! It's a town in Lancashire. It's near Liverpool, between Liverpool and Manchester. Guess that's where my surname originated.'

'Who do you support, Liverpool or Manchester United?' McKay asked as he rose to his feet.

'Neither, hate 'em both,' Prescot finished his drink, rose and extended his hand to both of them. 'My father always supported Bolton Wanderers; in fact, he's still a member, even after he immigrated to Australia. It was the first thing he did when he moved here, renew his membership and notify them of his new address. He's kept it going ever since, over 35 years! I followed his lead and supported them. I left England when I was a kid, but I've seen them play a few times when I've visited England. Seen them on TV occasionally.'

They walked out to the car park.

'Good to meet you, Chris,' said McKay and meant it. 'If we need you again, we'll give you a call.'

As Prescot climbed into his van and drove off, McKay turned to Catherine.

'We're still no nearer,' he said. 'This bloody man Adam is an enigma, and we're no nearer to Piers, I have a feeling this address will be out of date.'

CHAPTER 11

It was! They drove to the given address in Gardenvale, an old house divided into separate units. McKay looked at the grid which had various names slipped into notches for the separate bell pushes, Acland wasn't one of them. He rang the first at random, from its position he assumed it was on the ground floor.

'You answer it if there's any response,' he said. 'People, especially womenfolk, feel less nervous if it's a female.'

A voice answered and Catherine introduced herself as police, but the occupier didn't open the door, saying she would be along in a minute.

'Being cautious,' observed McKay.

'Wouldn't you be?' replied Catherine.

'I would,' agreed McKay. 'I'll back off and stand in the drive. She'll be more inclined to open the door if she only sees you.'

A face appeared at an adjacent window, then vanished. A young woman, probably late twenties, opened the door.

Catherine greeted her and showed her ID. There was a brief conversation then Catherine beckoned to McKay. They entered the hallway and she motioned to them to enter the ground floor unit.

'How can I help you?' she asked.

McKay left Catherine to do the talking and settled himself in an armchair.

'My name is Catherine Parkinson. We're not from the police exactly but we are working in conjunction with them, we are Australian Intelligence from Canberra,' she produced her ID again and the woman studied it at close quarters.

'Australian Intelligence?' she queried. 'Why are you here... intelligence...is that ASIO?'

'It is. Can I ask who you are? The name label outside said Ellison, is that right?'

'Yes, Meriel Ellison.'

'We're trying to trace Piers Acland, who used to live in one of these units. Do you know anything about him?'

'Piers Acland?' she shook her head. 'Can't say I do. When was he living here?'

'We think within the last six months.'

'Well, there's quite a turnover in these units, what did he look like?'

'Young man, probably early to mid-twenties.'

'No, sorry...oh wait a minute...there was a youngish man I used to see in the hallway occasionally, usually in the mornings when we were going to work, about 8 o'clock. I never knew his name, but he always said 'Good Morning.' Now you mention it, I haven't seen him around for...let me think...must be some weeks now.'

'You had no idea where this young man worked?' Catherine asked.

'No idea, but he wasn't a manual worker. Whenever I saw

him, he was always dressed for an office, or possibly a shop. He usually wore sports jacket and flannels.'

'Who runs these apartments?' asked Catherine.

'Dalton & Newbury, real estate and managing agents in Sandringham.'

'All right, thank you,' said Catherine. 'You've been very helpful.'

'What has he done, this young man?'

'Nothing,' smiled Catherine. 'But we're hoping he can lead us onto someone we want to interview.'

*

They entered the estate agency and were greeted by a receptionist. Catherine opened the proceedings.

'The units, or apartments, at 42 East Street, Gardenvale,' she said. 'We understand you manage those apartments.'

'Oh yes. Are you and your husband interested in one of them, we have a couple of vacancies.'

Catherine's mouth quirked upwards and she shook her head.

'Not at this stage,' she said as McKay turned away to hide a smile. 'We understand a young man named Piers Acland used to live in one of those apartments. We wondered if you could tell us where he is now.'

'I don't think I can release that information. Who are you?'

Catherine and McKay flashed their IDs, the girl looked impressed. She rose to her feet. 'I'll ask one of the partners to speak with you,' she entered a nearby office cubicle and emerged within minutes. 'He'll be with you shortly.'

A man in his thirties with a florid complexion emerged and approached them.

'James Baxter,' he said. 'You are making enquiries about one of our tenants, or former tenants?'

'We're anxious to trace a young man named Piers Acland who used to occupy an apartment in East Street, Gardenvale. Can you tell us where he is now?'

'Our receptionist said you were from Canberra?'

'We are.'

'Australian Intelligence?'

'That is correct.'

'Come into my office, I'll see if we have any information on him. What's he done?'

'Nothing, as far as we know,' said McKay. 'But he may be able to give us information on somebody who has.'

Baxter led them into his office pen, consulted a ledger, keyed into a computer and scrolled down the screen. He shook his head.

'Don't know where he went, but he gave a previous address in Toorak Road. From the look of it I'd say it was another apartment block....' he wrote it down and handed it to Catherine; '...sorry we can't be of more assistance.'

*

Two hours later they returned to South Melbourne field office very dispirited. They had tried the former address and were led to another firm of managing real estate agents, this time in Brighton, but again drew a blank. They found a former address before that but the procedure was the same, and at that one they found no information regarding any previous address. They had struck a brick wall.

*

'So!' McKay said with exasperation. 'No trace of bloody Acland, and consequently, we're no nearer to Adam. Is it worth another go at Donald Taylor to jog his memory?'

'Probably worth a try,' agreed Catherine. 'Perhaps tomorrow.'

*

McKay awoke in the small hours, his mind was racing, trying to resolve the conundrum regarding Adam and Piers Acland. Unable to sleep he rose early and paced around the motel room, tempted to turn on the television but decided against it.

He sat at the table and drew a time line chart that related to Henderson's shop since Andrew Dixon left the business and the subsequent personnel made their entrances and exits. It reminded him of the Shakespearian quotation from "As You Like It". *"The world is like a stage, and all the men and women merely players, they all have their exits and entrances...etc etc!"*

He recalled those lines from his school days, in detention for misbehaviour he had to learn and recite 12 lines without reference to the book before being allowed to leave. He recalled there had been a servant named Adam in the play.

Chris Prescot had habitually traded in computers to Harold Henderson, and Henderson in turn sold them on to customers who wanted cheap equipment not too obsolete. This routine had persisted until about March or April, when Prescot went on leave for two months to New Zealand with his wife. During that time, Henderson continued to supplement his second-hand stocks from elsewhere, namely Adam. When Prescot returned from his overseas trip they had briefly coincided, Prescot catching sight of Adam when they both attended Henderson's shop on the same day.

Prescot reckoned Adam's van had had a 'P' in the name

on the side or rear, so could Adam's surname begin with a 'P'? That was a job for next morning. Prescot had mentioned another point which started a train of thought that had been interrupted, and once it was interrupted McKay couldn't reconnect it. It occurred to him again while he lay awake in bed but had again escaped him completely. He sat back in the armchair and wracked his brains; then fell asleep in the chair.

*

He was still puzzling over it when he arrived at South Melbourne, Joe Carter looked up as he entered.

'We're still ploughing through these computer guys,' he said. 'No joy as yet.'

'I lay awake half the night thinking over this damned thing,' said McKay.

'How you did you get on with Prescot?' asked Carter. 'Any joy there?'

'Not much, we got a couple of addresses but they led nowhere, both Acland and Adam are still untraced.' McKay replied. 'Piers Acland never gave a new address when he moved on from Gardenvale and ...Bloody Hell!'

McKay hit his forehead with his clenched fist as the point he had been attempting to remember, the comment made by Prescot, finally broke through.

'What?' asked Catherine.

'Prescot! Do you remember what he said...about his father?'

'His father!' she cupped her chin in her hand. 'Can't say I do... oh... didn't he support a soccer team in England? Blackburn Rovers?'

'No, it wasn't, although you're not far out geographically, it was Bolton Wanderers. The club itself is immaterial. Remember what he said? His father's first notification of his change of address when he emigrated here was to advise Bolton Wanderers.'

'Yes, I remember him saying that.'

'Well Piers Acland is a rabid Hawthorn supporter according to Prescot. Someone else did too, Elverton mentioned it. Didn't they say Acland was a member?' McKay raised his hands and clenched his fists in triumph. 'Would Acland have done the same and notified his club when he changed his address? He wouldn't want to miss out on club communications, would he?'

'Club communications?'

'These football clubs, or any sort of club, send out newsletters and promotional stuff all the time by e-mail and ordinary mail. Where is the Hawthorn club situated, far away or close at hand?'

'They're in the Melbourne general area somewhere,' said Joe Carter. 'Probably Glenferrie.'

'Where the hell is Glenferrie?'

'Not far out, in the eastern suburbs.'

'Well, let's take a trip out there.'

'Why don't you telephone?' asked Catherine.

'Telephone?' McKay shook his head vigorously. 'I'm tired of sitting around in here. Besides, Joe's got kids, they may want autographs!'

'How can I argue with that logic?'

*

They arrived at the football ground, walked through a gateway and found themselves on the terraces.

'Bit small isn't it?' asked McKay. 'I'm no expert on Australian Rules, but I reckon even I could kick a ball from one end to the other on this ground.'

'They don't play here anymore,' explained Catherine. 'I don't know much about the game either, but I do know that. All the clubs now play at one or two grounds owned by the League, most of the old club grounds are now defunct. It's a case of saving expenditure and safety. It all started with that disaster in England when terracing collapsed and all those people were killed. Remember?'

'I do,' said McKay. 'Hillsborough Stadium in Sheffield if memory serves me right. That would have cost their insurers heaps.'

'That was the problem here, they realised they could have a similar disaster. But it was cheaper to build central common grounds sooner than bring all the old ones up to scratch. And, as we can see here, this one is a bit small for Australian Rules.'

'Can I help you?' said a voice from behind them, a wizened man wearing overalls emerged from a doorway.

'Yes, we're looking for the secretary,' replied McKay. 'Where do we go?'

'Up there, through that glass door and then turn left.'

They entered the small stadium building; inside a girl was cleaning out the small foyer. McKay asked for the secretary, she indicated a door, they knocked and a voice bade them to enter. Four desks were in the room, all occupied. A young man greeted them, McKay explained who they were and why they were there.

'You'd best see my boss,' he said. 'Hang on, I'll ask him to come over.'

He went to the end of the room and returned with a middle-aged man, who looked carefully over their IDs when they flashed them. He shook them both by the hand and indicated to them to follow him.

'Jim Bain,' he said. 'What's this about?'

McKay explained they were trying to trace someone who

could assist with an enquiry they were pursuing.

'We've tracked him to two addresses so far, but drawn a blank each time. We believe he can point us in the direction of someone else we want to interview. We're working in conjunction with Detective Sergeant Griffiths of St Kilda Road Police.'

The other grunted and sat at a computer keyboard.

'What did you say his name was?'

'Acland, Piers Acland.'

'And you reckon he advised us of his new address after he moved?'

'It's possible, a question of priorities. We assumed this would be the first organisation he would advise.'

Bain chuckled and examined the screen.

'Of course,' he said. 'This *is* Victoria you know.'

He scrolled down a list of names on screen.

'Acland ...here we are, there's three of them. Hallo, they're all the same address, or two of them are, and the other isn't far away. They're all in Horsham.'

'Horsham?' McKay leant over to peer at the screen. 'Are you sure?'

'Yes, here's your man, Piers Acland and Samuel Acland, both of the same address. There's a Gene Acland living nearby, also in Horsham. Looks to me as if Samuel Acland is the father, hang on, let's see how long he's been a member...there it is...well over 30 years. The others, Piers and Gene, haven't been on the books so long. One is for seven years and the other for four.'

'So they're all one family, Horsham's a long way out isn't it?' asked Catherine.

'Distance means nothing with football support, we have supporters in Brisbane and Perth,' said Bain. 'This must be the family home address. I'd say the young man, Piers, if he moved to Melbourne, would have known he could be changing addresses quite frequently so he hasn't bothered to change it. If he's tended to move around a lot, as you say, that's a wise decision. Otherwise, he'd be notifying us every few months.'

'Thanks a lot,' said McKay. 'You've been a great help. Thank you very much.'

*

'Where does this get us?' Catherine asked as they motored back to Melbourne. 'That's his former address so we're still nowhere...ah! I see your reasoning. Of course, Samuel is his father, contact him and presumably he knows where Piers is now. Am I normally this thick?'

'No. Not normally, just now and again!'

'After that comment, you've confirmed who's paying tonight,' Catherine replied acidly. 'I presume we ring him, no point travelling to Horsham.'

'Where is it?'

'A long way, a good journey along the Western Highway,' said Catherine. 'But it's a long way and a long time. Do we ring him, or ask Sergeant Griffiths to send one of his local coppers around?'

'We'll call him, if a uniformed constable appears on Acland Senior's doorstep asking if he's the father of Piers, it will frighten the shit out of him, he'll think something has happened to him. I'll find a number and ring him.'

*

'Any joy?'

'He's out in the paddocks, looks as if he's a farmer,' McKay responded. 'I think I got hold of a housekeeper or a casual employee, it certainly wasn't his wife because I asked the question about Piers and she asked "Who?"'

'We'll have to ring later then?'

'Yes, not sure what time a farmer comes in from the paddocks, we'll try again tonight.'

*

McKay finally contacted Samuel Acland at about 8.00 pm while in his motel room in company with Catherine. They had both been waiting for the call back, and obtained and consumed take away food until it came. They had almost given up hope, McKay thought they would have to ring again, when the call came through.

'Mr McKay?'

'Yes, Mr Acland?'

'Who are you? I had a message you were making enquiries. Are you from the police? Is my son all right?'

'Have no fears about your son Piers,' McKay said soothingly. 'As far as we know he is all right, but this *is* about Piers. We have to contact him.'

'Why, is he in trouble? What's he done?'

'Mr Acland, I appreciate the reason for your questions, but there is nothing to worry about, your son is all right, he has committed no crime. We are pursuing enquiries and we believe your son may be able to assist us in a capacity as a witness.'

'A witness to what?'

'I can't tell you too much about it at present, but we're trying to trace a man who made regular visits to a shop in Balaclava, in Melbourne. We need to speak with your son to try and locate this man.'

'Is this anything to do with Harold Henderson?'

'Yes, it's everything to do with Harold Henderson,' McKay saw no point in denying it. 'Your son is not, repeat not, a suspect, nor is the man we are trying to trace, but we believe if Piers can guide us to this man, then he in turn can lead us further onwards with our enquiries. Have I made myself clear?'

'I think so, but why don't you speak to my son, why contact me?'

'We don't know where he is,' said McKay. 'He moved from Gardenvale recently and we don't know where he is now.'

'Oh yes, that's right, he has. How did you find me?'

'We tracked you via Hawthorn Football club, you've been a member for many years, we understand.'

'Oh, I see,' Samuel Acland gave a dry chuckle. 'Isn't Piers listed as a member?'

'Yes, he is, but he's still registered at your Horsham address.'

'Oh, is he?' Samuel Acland replied. 'I didn't realise that, but that makes sense, he's moved around a bit since trying his luck in Melbourne. I've got his new address somewhere, but how do I know you are who you say you are? How do I know you're not chasing him for money?'

'You don't,' replied McKay. 'But if you have any doubts, I suggest you ring the St Kilda Police Complex in St Kilda Road and ask for Detective Sergeant Griffiths. Or, you can ring the offices of ASIO in South Melbourne and ask either for myself, Catherine Parkinson or Joseph Carter. I leave that to you to decide, but I commend you for being cautious, I agree I could be anybody. Can you do that first thing tomorrow morning, please, I assure you the matter is urgent.'

'I can do that. Can you give me the telephone numbers?'

'I can, but if you're not absolutely sure about me now, it's best you find the numbers for yourself...you get my drift?'

'That makes sense, I'll do that. I'll give you a call tomorrow.

I'll ring Piers in the meantime. OK?'

'Yes,' said McKay. 'We'll hear from you tomorrow then?'

'What happened?' asked Catherine as McKay put down the phone.

'A cautious father, but a prudent one,' said McKay. 'It doesn't assist us immediately, but he's a sensible man. You heard what I said, he's uneasy about passing on his son's whereabouts to a stranger. Fair enough, I might be a bookie's bully boy. When in doubt, check it out! On reflection, it's what I'd do, and it's what I'd like to think my father, or your father come to that, would do in similar circumstances.'

'Why not get Ted Griffiths to arrange to send a police constable around?'

'Well...we could, now Acland Senior knows his son is all right, but we won't gain any time doing that because we'd still have to wait until tomorrow. So...we're making progress.'

'Hopefully,' said Catherine. 'Our next hurdle is Adam!'

CHAPTER 12

They compared notes with Joseph Carter the following morning, Carter with the Yellow Pages before him opened at the pages for computer engineers, technicians etc.

'An exhausting process,' he said dispiritedly. 'I had to stop Edmonds opening his enquiry with: 'How are you today?' Many of those he called initially thought he was selling something or conducting one of those damned surveys which means selling something in the long run, or trying to persuade you to switch suppliers.'

'Or a foreign accented scammer telling you there's something wrong with your computer,' said Catherine.

'Too right!' agreed Carter. 'That's why my home phone is ex-directory.'

'Makes no difference,' commented McKay. 'All the numbers they call are computer generated, so it doesn't matter if you're in the book or not. When you give them the brush off the computer just dials the next number in the sequence.'

'How far have you reached?' asked Catherine.

'We're up to 'L',' replied Carter.

His desk phone rang. He listened to the caller, then handed it to McKay.

'It's for you,' he grunted. 'It's that cop you spoke to the other day.'

McKay took it from him.

'Hello.'

'Griffiths here,' said the voice at the other end. 'I have some information for you.'

'Yes?'

'Samuel Acland phoned us this morning. I have an address for you and a phone number.'

'Piers Acland?'

'Right first time!' Griffiths chuckled. 'Got a pen and paper handy?'

'Go ahead,' McKay wrote down the information and checked it back. 'Good! I've got that. We'll contact him now, unless you want to do it…Oh OK! Yes, that's fine. We'll do it. How are things at your end, Ted?'

'We're still holding Taylor, but he could be in the clear, his story holds up. We checked, when a squad car went to arrest him, they found his place trashed and we don't think Taylor would have done it. Somebody was looking for something.'

'How long can you hold him?'

'We could let him go now, but he could be in the firing line?'

'Agreed, if what Taylor told us is correct, they killed Harold Henderson for what seems to have been an unguarded remark.'

'Could have been an over reaction by one of them, from what Taylor said, they seemed shaken by what they'd done. But I agree we should keep him here. He hasn't been lawyered up, but if he wants to go, we can't stop him. You've been busy?'

'Still trying to track Adam. We've been through Henderson's recent employees, we found Dixon and Elverton, but drew a blank with Acland.'

'How did you find his father?'

'They're all rabid Hawthorn supporters and members; Piers' brother is on the membership list too. Piers never altered his address from his original Horsham home, which makes sense when you consider he's changed addresses a few times.'

'Yes, it does,' Griffiths said. 'I'll leave you to follow this one up, keep us informed.'

'Will do,' McKay handed the phone back to Carter and turned to Catherine. 'Let's see if we can nail this young lad down at last'

*

They called the phone number given to them by Griffiths, McKay deemed it best if Catherine made the call and she managed to contact the elusive Piers Acland at last. He was working in the computer department of one of the larger insurance companies.

'Where did you say you were from?' he asked, the point didn't sink in until after he'd virtually agreed to meet them.

'Australian Intelligence,' she responded.

'Intelligence? You're not police?'

'No, but we're pursuing the same line of enquiry, it relates to Harold Henderson.'

'I heard about Harold, what happened?'

'That's what we're trying to find out. We need to see you urgently. We have to ask you some questions.'

'Look here, I don't know anything about that, you're not accusing me of being involved, are you?'

'No!' Catherine responded patiently. 'But we believe you may have knowledge that could lead us to who did. Can we meet you at lunch-time?'

There was a brief pause, Catherine registered that Acland had his hand over the mouthpiece, but the reason for that became clear when Acland spoke again.

'We can use an interview room on the ground floor. Do you know where we are?'

Catherine reeled off the address and Acland confirmed it, a large building in Collins Street in the Central Business District.

'See you at 12 o'clock,' she ended the call and turned to McKay. 'I didn't ask about Adam at this stage, it may be easier to jog his memory when we're facing him.'

'Makes sense,' agreed McKay. 'OK, let's take a trip into the city.'

'In the car?' asked Catherine.

'Not bloody likely!' snapped McKay. 'I'm not contributing any more cash to the Melbourne City Council. We'll take a tram!'

CHAPTER 13

Acland was awaiting them when they entered the foyer of the building just before noon. He was medium height, clean shaven, dark haired and wore black framed glasses, smartly dressed in sports jacket and grey trousers.

'Doesn't change his mode of dress, does he?' Catherine remarked. 'That's how Meriel Ellison described him when he was living in her building.'

McKay was unable to comment as Acland was approaching and was now within earshot. Acland extended his hand to Catherine.

'Catherine?' she nodded and indicated McKay.

'This is David,' she said. 'David McKay.'

With the introductions completed he ushered them towards an interview room which contained a table, four chairs and a computer terminal. He sat with his back to the window with the two ASIO operatives facing the busy Collins Street scene with motor vehicles, trams and pedestrians passing outside.

'Whatever happened to Harold?' Acland asked, momentarily putting McKay off his stroke as he was about to ask his questions. 'Was it really my successor who did it, what's his name, Donald Taylor?'

'We don't know why it happened, but we're fairly sure it wasn't Donald Taylor,' McKay said heavily. 'We need to ask you some questions, which may seem unrelated but they are relevant.'

'Go ahead, but I'd left the Henderson shop long before poor Harold was...was... murdered.'

Acland appeared to have trouble in saying the word, McKay could understand that, not easy when something like that happened to somebody you knew well.

'How long have you been here?' Catherine asked.

'A few months, thought it was time I got a proper job,' replied Acland. 'I enjoyed my time with Harold, apart from his wife. Harold taught me a lot about computers as did Stan Elverton while he was there, but it was hardly a career move. My father gave me hell one day when he asked what my prospects were. I had to say...zilch!'

'So you looked around.'

'Yes. Dad was right, but it was Mrs Henderson who supplied the trigger. I had a run in because I put a Hawthorn sticker on the till drawer. Bloody silly really! I guess I shouldn't have done it, but it wasn't on the customer side of the till, and Harold didn't seem to mind. She noticed it when she came in for her customary raid.'

'Her what?'

'Raid ...!' Acland grinned. 'I picked that up from Stan. Apparently, it was Andrew Dixon who first coined the expression. She used to come in and take money out. She ruled Harold completely. Don't know what she'll do now, I presume the shop is closed down now which will cut off her spending money.'

McKay heard Catherine giggle at that and smiled. Mrs Henderson had clearly not ingratiated herself with successive staff members.

'Now why does everyone we've spoken to say the same about her?' McKay said cynically, a question to which he didn't really expect an answer. He opened his notepad and turned to Acland. 'We need information from you, Piers, you don't mind me using your first name?'

'No, go ahead, how can I help?'

'Do you know a man named Adam, who called in the shop from time to time?'

'Sure do. That would be Adam Simmerson; he worked for a computer technician company. He used to, or still does; go around sorting out people's computer problems and replacing old equipment for new.'

'We've been trying to find out about Adam for a few days now, at last we have a surname,' commented McKay.

'I knew Adam well long before I went to Henderson's shop. I met him at one of those computer swap sessions held in Blackburn, he had some obsolete equipment he was trying to offload, and I bought it from him, it wasn't all that old as it turned out. After that we met fairly regularly at various swap meets, and one day Harold had an enquiry from some university students who wanted second-hand equipment fairly cheap. Harold used to get a lot from Chris Prescot, have you contacted Chris?'

'Yes, we've seen Chris Prescot,' said McKay.

'Well, Chris was away for a month or so, he went with his wife to stay with her family; they live in New Zealand. They stay there a few weeks every year. Anyway, Harold needed some equipment fairly quickly. I asked Adam about it and he turned up the next day with some older units. They were quite serviceable; there's some good second-hand stuff on the market when people and companies update. The next day he turned up with some more, and after that he supplied us on a fairly regular basis...or should I say...irregular basis. It depended on when he picked anything up.'

'Shouldn't this stuff have belonged to his employer?'

'Technically yes, I guess,' Acland nodded. 'How he avoided that aspect I don't know. He did mention once he couldn't supply every time because he had to hand in most of his trade-ins to his boss, I think as long as he didn't overdo it, it wasn't noticed. But that wasn't our worry.'

'What happened when Chris Prescot returned?'

'No problem,' said Acland. 'They rarely coincided; I don't think either of them would have worried if they had. They nearly clashed once, I remember Adam had just left when Chris came in through the door, I remember Chris looking at the old Pentium III Adam had left. He asked who he was, and I told him.'

'Who did Adam work for?'

'He used a blue van. Parking isn't allowed outside the shop. Adam had a couple of towers and monitors, and he'd spotted a traffic warden at the end of the street, so I gave him a hand. The company name was a play on words: "Above Parr Computer Technicians", Parr was spelt with two 'R's. Not sure where they were based, presumably in Melbourne somewhere.'

'Above Parr ...so the proprietor's name was, presumably Parr. You don't know their address?'

'I was going to look it up once, but got distracted, it was the day I had that run in with Florrie Henderson. I never did find out...hang on, I'll get hold of a phone book from the switchboard.'

He left the room and returned bearing the business telephone directory version of the white pages. He triumphantly pointed with his finger.

'There they are, in Moorabbin,' he said triumphantly. 'Nepean Highway, that's right, I remember now. I *did* look them up eventually. They're near the railway station.'

'Adam is still there?'

'As far as I know, I've lost touch since I left Hendersons and came here, but I still see Chris Prescot occasionally, we sometimes go to the football together.'

'We tried to contact you before, a few days back, your mobile phone didn't respond.'

'No, I know,' Acland smiled ruefully. 'It was nicked by some mongrel when I was at Gardenvale and I haven't got around to replacing it. Funnily enough, I was thinking today about a replacement, then you rang up.'

'Well, thanks, Piers, you've been most helpful,' said McKay. 'If we need you again, we'll give you a call.'

'A pleasure,' responded Acland. 'If it helps you find the people who killed Harold, all well and good. Hell of a nice bloke, a damned shame. Very sad.'

As they reached the pavement outside McKay turned to Catherine.

'Eureka!' he said. 'We've moved along a notch. We've identified the mysterious Adam. But why didn't Joe's boys find this firm. They said they were up to 'L'. This damned firm begins with 'A'.'

*

'You told us your lads had tried all entries up to 'L'.'

'Yes, so I was told. Why?'

'This bloody Adam character, he worked for a firm called Above Parr Computers.'

'What! Bloody hell…!' Carter shouted to his secretary outside the door. 'Amy, get John Edmonds to come in here…and tell him to bring the Yellow Pages.'

John Edmonds presented himself, looking suitably apprehensive, with a yellow phone book under his arm. Carter reached out his hand for the directory.

'You said you'd covered all bases up to 'L'.'

'We have, we're up to 'M' now.'

'Well you can stop, we've tracked this man down, but the firm he works for begins with an 'A'.'

'What? Oh God no!'

Carter thumbed through the directory and reached the computer area.

'Which section were you combing?'

'Computer Equipment Second Hand,' replied Edmonds.

Carter looked at the directory, flicked over some more pages, and uttered an exclamation.

'Damnation!' he said. 'We've got 'Computer Equipment Installations', 'Computer Equipment Hardware', 'Computer Systems Consultants', 'Computer On-Line Service Providers'… bugger it! Look, here it is! This bloody firm is under 'Computer Equipment Installations'.'

'Sorry Joe,' said Edmonds contritely.

'Don't apologise,' snapped Carter. 'If it's anybody's fault it's mine. I never realised there would be so many different headings, all under computers. OK! OK!' he handed the book back to Edmonds. 'Tell all the others to stop looking, we've found him. You've done well, thanks anyway John.'

He looked at Catherine and McKay.

'Lunch-time,' he announced. 'It's on me, for not using my

loaf. I accept full responsibility for this, but thank God! You've found him.'

*

But they hadn't!

McKay and Catherine Parkinson arrived at the workshop with the name "Above Parr Computer Technicians", proprietor Gerald Parr. Parked outside the workshop, which lay at the end of a small alleyway leading between two shops on the main road, was a blue van, also bearing the same motif.

They entered a door marked "Reception", a young woman looked up, a brunette this time.

'Can I help you?'

'We're looking for Adam Simmerson.'

'Adam? He doesn't work here any more.'

'What!' McKay felt his world fall about his ears.

'He resigned last week. You'd better speak to Mr Parr.'

She went to a door at the back of the reception area. McKay could see a workshop behind it, with many computers and monitor screens in evidence. He turned to Catherine, and said, 'I don't bloody believe it!'

A grey-haired man of about 45-50 appeared and came over to them looking quizzical.

'Gerry Parr,' he announced. 'You were asking about Adam?'

'We need to speak with him but your young lady said he wasn't here any more.'

'Who are you?'

'We're assisting the police, investigating the murder of Harold Henderson, who had a computer business ...!'

'Yes, I know all about Harold Henderson, our paths crossed occasionally,' said Parr. 'You'd better come into the office.'

Parr moved behind his desk and indicated a couple of vacant chairs to Catherine and McKay. Behind Parr there was a window in the wooden partition wall, through it they could see several young men working on computers, they seemed to be electrical mechanics as opposed to computer operators. At the far end another young man was sitting at a keyboard.

'Who did you say you were from?'

'We're assisting police with regard to Harold Henderson …!'

'You haven't answered my question,' Parr shook his head. 'I'm convinced something is wrong somewhere and I want to know who I'm talking to. I've been thinking about it for days now and today I was going to do something about it.'

'What did you think was wrong?'

'You still haven't answered my question, are you the police or not?'

'No, we're not,' McKay usually felt reticent about introducing himself as ASIO, if the press got wind of their interest in any matter it was enough to bring down a shoal of excited journalists, but Parr's demeanour intrigued him. 'We are from Australian Intelligence in Canberra, the Australian Security and Intelligence Organisation, ASIO.'

'You have ID?' asked Parr. He peered keenly at their badges as they produced them.

'Why is Australian Intelligence looking for Adam?'

'We believe he can assist with enquiries we're conducting into the death of Harold Henderson. For your information, we *are* working in conjunction with the police. You are free to contact Detective Sergeant Griffiths at St Kilda Road if you have concerns.'

'What has this to do with intelligence?'

McKay began to feel they were making little headway as both sides were asking questions. He cleared his throat, but Catherine intervened.

'Mr Parr, it's best if we stop asking each other questions and give explanations instead. Otherwise, we'll be firing questions at each other all day.'

She leant forward as she spoke and realised Parr's eyes had inadvertently dropped down a foot or so. She realised she was wearing a nylon top with a low front which exposed some cleavage. She hastily leant back, while flattered she didn't want to provide any distractions, they needed information.

'How about we start, then you tell us what's worrying you.'

'All right!' said Parr. 'That suits me, go ahead.'

Catherine eyed McKay, plainly deferring to him after she had cut the knot.

'I'll start from the beginning,' said McKay. He gave a sequence of events, starting from the point where Adam Simmerson brought in the traded in computer, the arrangement with Taylor and the subsequent murder of Harold Henderson. 'Clear so far?'

'Crystal,' Parr grunted. 'Adam shouldn't have done that. Any computers he replaced should have been brought back here.'

'We'd already reached that conclusion,' said McKay. 'But that's where the troubles began. Donald Taylor, Henderson's assistant, was alarmed at what he saw on the hard drive, he's no computer mug, he cracked the password and got in.'

'Taylor, isn't that the young man the police are holding?'

'Yes. According to Taylor, he rang Harold Henderson and told him what he'd found.'

'What did he find?'

'I'd sooner not say at this stage, but it affects Australian security.'

'OK...what then?'

McKay recounted Taylor's story about how he'd entered the shop and witnessed the scene with the three men, that they wanted their computer back and must have traced

Adam Simmerson who told them where it was. He mentioned Henderson foolishly let drop what Taylor had found and was consequently stabbed to death, an act Taylor claimed he had observed through shelving from the back of the shop. He mentioned Mrs Henderson's appearance, who jumped to the conclusion that Taylor was the miscreant, Taylor's panic and escape and subsequent arrival at his home flat.

'I saw Mrs Henderson being interviewed on television, no doubt in her mind about Taylor being the guilty party,' Parr commented.

'Taylor saw them carry this computer out of his apartment and they then took off.'

'Who were they?'

'We don't know, that's why we're trying to track down Adam. He must know who they are, he supplied them with a new computer, or rather a replacement. He transferred data from the hard drive, the 'C' drive, but there was a second hard drive, a partition, on the "C" drive, and Adam either missed it or was in a hurry and forgot to transfer the data.'

Parr sat back and digested what McKay had told him, thinking hard.

'You said you were going to ring someone...possibly the police?'

'Yes, I was,' Parr leant forward on his elbows. 'I was in a quandary, it was nebulous, but odd. It's a case of it being a semi-crisis if you like. Any bloody fool can do the right thing in a crisis, if your house is on fire or has been burgled, you ring someone, police or fire brigade straight away. If you're not sure or puzzled about something, what do you do?'

'The young lady out there told us Adam Simmerson had left your employ?'

'That's what puzzled me,' Parr replied. 'I didn't know whether to ring anyone or not.'

'Try us!'

'Adam has worked here for years, a good employee, valuable to me and we have a good relationship. He has an extensive knowledge of computers, how to take them apart and put them together again, and very knowledgeable from the software angle. Of late he's not been altogether satisfied, we've had talks about money, he has a regular girlfriend and is considering marriage. I didn't want to lose him so I gave him a boost in salary, I could just about afford it. We're not exactly BHP or Shell Oil, but business is going fairly well and could stand it. We had a long talk about it and he seemed satisfied.'

'When was this?'

'About three weeks back, maybe a month. I was aware some trade-ins weren't appearing, but turned a blind eye. If he was making a bob or two it didn't worry me if it helped keep him in the fold. It wasn't a big issue, in today's computer world things become obsolete quickly and everyone wants updated equipment. That doesn't just apply to computers, it's everything, cars, mobile phones, the lot!'

'So whatever problems you had with Adam had been resolved?' asked McKay.

'So I thought. But three days ago, or maybe four, I arrived here as usual in the morning at 8.30 and found the van Adam uses parked outside with the keys in the ignition. When I opened up the office there was the usual collection of mail inside, including a resignation letter from Adam.'

'Resignation...why was that?'

Parr spread out his hands in mystification.

'I have no idea, it was most odd, unexpected and, unlike him, most rude and cavalier,' Parr shook his head in perplexity. 'But that wasn't the issue, these days people resign and change jobs all the time, not like my father who had the same job from 16 until he retired! The manner was so unlike Adam. He is quite refined; was educated at a grammar school and I think he'll go far in life...that's the puzzle.'

'What is?'

Parr reached into his desk drawer and produced an envelope which he flipped across the desk to McKay.

'See what you make of that.'

McKay took the envelope, extracted a letter and smoothed it out.

Dear Gerard,

I very much regrett that I have fownd another job and I doan't need to work here any more. As you no we have not been in agreeance about things lately, especially about the mony I have been recieving.

I have another job, I may need a refrence cerstificate so will be in touch. It is not in Melburne so doan't try and contract me.

Yours truly

Adam Samson

'I thought you said he'd had a grammar school education,' said Catherine after McKay handed it to her.

'He has!' Parr said. 'That whole letter is out of kilter. Quite apart from being littered with spelling mistakes, which are completely out of character, his surname has been spelt incorrectly, and he used the word 'agreeance'. That was a standing joke between us, he detested people who mutilated the English language and one example was people who used the word agreeance instead of agreement, and the extra 's' in certificate is definitely not Adam, being another of his pet aversions. As for using 'no' when it should be 'know' and misspelling Melbourne, it is decidedly odd.'

McKay took the letter back from Catherine.

'Is it his handwriting?'

'It is, but it looks different, as if he's trying to change his style,' Parr replied. 'Another thing, he's addressed it to me and called me Gerard. My name is Gerald, but everyone calls me Gerry, including Adam.'

'And you were sufficiently worried about it to think of ringing the police?'

'Yes,' Parr nodded. 'After thinking about it for a few days I was going to call the local police. I did ring his girlfriend, she said she hadn't seen him for three or four days, that really made up my mind to do something.'

'Do they live together?'

'Not as far as I know. She lives with her parents, while Adam has an apartment. I've got the address here somewhere,' said Parr. 'But I believe they've been going out together for a long time now, it seemed so odd for him to just disappear and leave her high and dry.'

'Let's have the address, we'll check it out,' said McKay. 'Has anyone used the van since then?'

'No, it's still where he left it,' said Parr. 'I've locked it up and the keys are on the board over there.'

'Well don't move it, and don't let anyone near it,' said McKay. 'Can I use your phone? I'll ring the detective who's also on the case as he might want to examine it. You're right, there's something odd here, whatever else is strange about that letter, if he's a well-educated guy it's the misspelling of his own name and Melbourne that gets to me.'

Parr pushed the phone across and McKay dialled Griffiths' number. McKay told him where they were and about the mysterious disappearance of Adam Simmerson.

'The van is where he left it, Ted. Maybe your forensic people should look at it.'

Clearly Griffiths thought so too. McKay gave him the address and after a brief conversation put down the phone.

'He's on his way,' announced McKay. 'In the meantime, we'll go to Adam's apartment and have a look around. But make sure that van isn't touched until Ted Griffiths gets here.'

As they reached the yard outside, Catherine turned to Gerry Parr.

'What's his girlfriend's name and address, do you know?'

'No, I don't,' said Parr. 'No wait...I do know her name, it's Rhonda Muston. Hang on, Lilian, my receptionist might know where she is.'

He went back inside and returned within a few minutes. He handed Catherine a phone number.

'She works in a bookshop in Malvern,' he said. 'It's in High Street.'

'OK,' McKay turned to Catherine. 'Good thinking, it's possible she may have a key to his apartment.'

CHAPTER 14

The shop, like many buildings in Malvern, had been renovated with an impressive shop front that overlapped space formerly occupied by two shops. Through the glass they spotted a young woman serving a customer.

'That's probably her,' commented Catherine. 'You want me to handle it?'

'Best if you do,' said McKay. 'I'll hover modestly in the background.'

'That'll be a first,' Catherine said acidly as they entered. The sale was in the last stages as the assistant ran the payment through the system. A grey-haired man appeared from behind a screen and advanced towards them.

'Can I be of assistance?'

'We wanted to speak to Rhonda Muston,' said Catherine.

'Is this personal or have you ordered a book from her?'

'It's personal to Miss Muston, business to us, we are connected with the police.'

'The police?' he looked startled. 'For Rhonda?'

'We're making enquiries, it's nothing she's done. Can we interview her privately?'

'I have an office at the rear, you can use that. Can I have proof of who you are?'

McKay nodded to Catherine who produced her ID.

'You said police.'

'We are working with the police. This is an intelligence matter, relating to national security,' said McKay. 'She may have information on someone who can help us. It's urgent!'

The proprietor went over to Rhonda Muston, she had completed the sale. He had a brief conversation with her and indicated McKay and Catherine Parkinson. He put his hand on her arm and steered her over, she looked curious and apprehensive.

'These two officers wish to speak with you, Rhonda,' he said. 'Use my office.'

Rhonda removed her glasses, shook her head and her long dark hair swirled over her shoulders.

'What's all this about?' she asked. 'What has Intelligence to do with me?'

'You are associated with Adam Simmerson, Miss Muston?' asked Catherine.

'Adam? Is he all right? I'm so worried. I haven't heard from him for three or four days. He's just vanished.'

'We're worried too,' said Catherine. 'When did you last see him?'

'On my birthday, he took me out to dinner at a restaurant in Armadale,' said Rhonda. 'I hadn't seen him for a day or so, he'd been doing a job up country in Bacchus Marsh. After the meal we went back to his apartment...' she hesitated and blushed '... and we were quite late.'

'What happened after that?'

'We...um...we both left in the morning and went to work.'

'You stayed the night?'

'Well...yes.'

'Then you came to work that morning, but where did Adam go, any idea?'

'He was going to Balaclava, I remember him mentioning that, something about having to deliver a computer. After that he was going to his work at Gerry Parr's.'

'He always called him Gerry, did he?'

'Yes, I think his name is Gerald or Gerard but he doesn't like it,' she said.' I met him once when I called in the workshop to pick Adam up because the van was being serviced. Everyone there called him Gerry.'

'And you haven't seen Adam since that day?'

'No, he hasn't been in touch at all.'

'Hmm!' McKay intervened. 'Do you have a key to his apartment?'

'Yes,' she blushed again.

'We may need to get in there; there may be a clue as to where he's gone. Can you take time off from here for a couple of hours, we're trying to locate Adam and there may be something in there that could lead us to him.'

'What's happened to him? Are we talking criminals? Has he done anything wrong?'

'He's done nothing wrong that we know of...but can you do that?'

'Oh yes ...I think so. I'll ask Mr Jennings.'

She left and McKay turned to Catherine.

'You've proved one point; it confirms that letter of resignation is suspicious and Adam was trying to tell Gerry Parr and anyone else who read it that something was amiss. Using the name

Gerard indicates again a likely signal, plus the bad spelling and the use of 'agreeance'!'

'Looks like it,' agreed Catherine. 'We'll see what the apartment turns up.'

But the apartment didn't provide much, Rhonda produced the key after they entered the building and climbed to the first floor. It was a typical bachelor pad, computer equipment, football pictures on the wall, and plenty of beer in the fridge.

'Did he keep a diary?' McKay asked Rhonda.

'Diary?'

'Yes, I don't mean anything like Samuel Pepys! I mean a working diary, which would indicate what jobs he's been doing.'

'I've never seen one,' said Rhonda. 'But he must have one somewhere.'

'It's most likely in the van if it's anywhere,' commented Catherine.

'Let's look around, see if we can find anything.'

But nothing turned up and McKay bit his lip. He thought when they traced the elusive Adam, most of their worries would be over as far as tracing the owner of the computer was concerned. They had advanced another step, and hit another brick wall.

When there was nothing left to search, McKay raised his hands in resignation.

'Nothing of assistance here,' he said ruefully. 'Thanks for your help, Rhonda.'

They dropped Rhonda off at the bookshop and watched her enter the shop. McKay showed no inclination to move off, Catherine turned and looked at him.

'What?'

'Gerry Parr,' he replied.

'What about him?'

'All jobs would come through the office, that is, through Gerry Parr,' said McKay. 'Adam would have kept a work diary; most people on the road have to if only to justify fuel consumption. Let's face it, you and I have to do that if we take a car from the pool. But back to Gerry Parr, he should have an itinerary of Adam's jobs. Give Griffiths a call and see if he's found a work diary in the van.'

*

They parked in front of Above Parr Computers; the van was gone. They entered the reception area and Lilian greeted them like old friends.

'You want to see Gerry again?' she asked.

'If we could, please Lilian,' responded Catherine. Lilian buzzed Gerry Parr and he appeared immediately.

'Come on in,' he said. 'The police have removed the van.'

'We saw that,' said McKay. 'But we have further questions.'

'Go ahead!' Parr waved them to the same two chairs.

'We've been to Adam's flat, nothing of any value there, apart from a few computer odds and ends and his own computer system. Did the police find anything in his van?'

'Not that I'm aware, they haven't been long gone and weren't too communicative. They said they'll be in touch. I have a card here, Detective Sergeant Griffiths.'

'Do your lads keep a diary - a job diary?'

'They should do, detailing time spent on a certain task, we charge by the hour. There's also a mileage aspect; we keep a close check on fuel costs. We have to with petrol prices skyrocketing.'

'Did Adam have a job diary? We couldn't find one.'

'Yes, he would have kept it in the van. That would be the logical place. He'd take it wherever he's working; he'd make out a charge account after finishing a job. Adam and the others have to collect cash or credit card details for the work done on the spot. We don't give credit these days, been bitten once too often.'

'What happens next?'

'They carry out whatever jobs they have for the day, or week maybe, if we're busy we may not see them for a few days. For repair jobs or software problems we just give instructions over the phone. When they do come in, they hand in their job diary and take out another. They have two weekly diaries which they use alternatively. They hand one in when they come in, then take the other.'

He paused as Lilian arrived with a tray of coffee cups.

'You'll like this, it's percolated, not the instant rubbish you get from coffee making machines. Lilian has turned it into an art form. Thanks Lilian.'

Lilian distributed the cups and left with the tray.

'One of Adam's books should still be in here?'

'Yes, I keep a close check on them, every system is open to fiddling, the only way to prevent it is close and regular checking ...although it looks as if he appropriated a computer or two without me noticing!'

'Well, it's caught up with him,' McKay said soberly. 'It seems to have caused him huge problems.'

'Even worse for Harold Henderson,' commented Parr. 'Anyway, let's look at the weekly job diary we *do* have.'

He reached over to a shelf next to his desk and produced a work journal, muttered 'Wrong one!' ...and extracted another. He opened it and ran his finger down the pages.

'What date are we looking at? When did he take that computer into Henderson's shop?'

McKay consulted his notebook. It must have been the day

after Adam took Rhonda Muston out for her birthday, which had maybe caused him to knock off early that day and leave the task of transferring information from one computer to the other incomplete.'

'About 3rd September,' he said.

Parr examined the work book and shook his head.

'No go!' he said. 'This is the alternate work book, Adam has, or had, the other in his possession.'

'So we have no idea where he went that week?' McKay said.

'Wait,' said Parr. 'All is not lost. If we were supplying a new computer that day, or thereabouts, it would have to be booked out. We note all serial numbers of outgoing gear, plus any modifications we've made, so if anything goes wrong, we know what computer went where. Hang on a minute.'

He picked up his phone.

'Lilian, ask Colin Farrand to step in here a moment please,' he put down the phone and turned to them. 'We have an average of three or four computers going out in the course of a month, maybe more, maybe less. If we find where those computers went, we may be able to isolate where the trade-in came from.'

A young man entered. To McKay he seemed very young, yet this appeared to be the hallmark of newer industries such as the computer industry. He could recall going to a computer exhibition in Sydney a few months before and had been astonished at the number of schoolboys present who seemed to know as much if not more about the equipment as those demonstrating. This lad looked as if he should still be at school.

'Colin, give us a run down of the computers that went out on these dates,' Parr wrote on a pad and ripped off the top page. 'Especially any allocated to Adam.'

'Easily done, how soon do you want it?'

'Five minutes ago.'

'Leave it with me, Gerry, I'll be right back.'

Colin departed; Parr took a sip of coffee.

'He won't be long,' he said. 'His bench is a shambles, yet he always knows where everything is. Try your coffee. Lilian has surpassed herself this morning.'

They sipped the coffee and could only agree. It was as if Lilian had been making up her own blend of various types of coffee. Colin Farrand re-appeared.

'Adam was delivering three new computers in that time slot,' he said. 'There was Jean Alletson down in Frankston, Ken Dewberry at Glen Waverley, and Richardson & Gamble in Bourke Street in Melbourne,' he tore off the top sheet of his note pad and handed it to Gerry Parr. 'We had a few computers going out that week, but these three were handled by Adam.'

'Thanks Colin,' Parr dismissed him with a wave. 'You've done well.'

Parr studied the three names before him.

'Jean Alletson runs a small accountancy business, she's aged about 40, and has teenage sons at university. She's a regular customer, nice lady. There are three computers in the house, hers and her two sons.'

'Any idea what courses her two sons are taking?'

'One of them is something to do with engineering, the other, I'm not so sure.'

'Who or what is Ken Dewberry?'

'A marriage celebrant, keeps all his records on computer. Nice chap, he's called on us for some years too. I remember that one, he received an e-mail he thought was from a contact in England who was coming to Melbourne to get married here. He opened it and it was one of those virus jokers, it permeated his whole system and we had to clean it up for him. While we were at it, he decided to update his system.'

'What's Mrs Alletson's address?' McKay asked. 'The university connection could be relevant.'

'Frankston, I'll ask Lilian to get it for you.'

'What was the other one?' asked Catherine. 'Richardson & Gamble?'

'Architects, a top firm in Melbourne. They've been around for years, commenced about 1949. Both the present partners, Alex Richardson and Matthew Gamble, are sons of the original founders, they are well connected. We've obtained business through them by recommendation.'

'We'll have their address as well, but we'll make Jean Alletson a priority,' said McKay.

'I hope this is of some help, but please be gentle with Jean, and Alex Richardson, I'd hate to have good business relationships upset.'

'Have no worries,' McKay replied. 'I'll leave Catherine to do the talking. She's more tactful than I am.'

'We'll have Ken Dewberry's address as well,' said Catherine after withering McKay with a glance.

'No problem, but his old computer is still in here, Colin is still working on clearing it. That virus was particularly nasty. We had to strip the disc completely.'

'Does he have a computer at present?'

'Yes, we replaced it. Luckily, he kept back up files on an external hard drive. We took over his old one and we're still cleaning it up.'

CHAPTER 15

Jean Alletson operated a small accountancy business in Frankston that occupied a shop front and employed a young receptionist. Catherine had already made an appointment.

Jean Alletson was as Catherine had envisaged her, mid-forties, dark hair streaked with grey, dressed in a dark business suit. She was quite tall, slim and had the look of somebody who loved what she was doing. She could give McKay a few years but he eyed her appreciatively as they entered.

'You wanted to see me, something about my computer system?'

'Indirectly yes,' answered Catherine. 'We've been talking to Gerry Parr of Above Parr Computers. You've recently consulted one of his technicians, Adam Simmerson?'

'Yes, we know Adam fairly well, he's sorted out many problems for us,' said Jean Alletson. 'But you said something about internal security, what's that about?'

They had already settled on a course of action and decided there was no point beating about the bush. Catherine gave a brief synopsis of what had occurred, mentioned the tragedy with regard to Henderson and that they were trying to track a computer Adam Simmerson had collected.

'Did Adam take away a computer belonging to you? One that was superfluous?'

'Yes, that is he took it away from here...you say somebody has been murdered? Now you mention it I do recall it, some days ago wasn't it, in Balaclava...a computer shop?'

'That's the one.' Catherine nodded. 'You say he took it away?'

'Yes, he took it from here, he took it to my home and my son took it over, it's more up to date than the one he was using. He wiped all my data from it after transferring it, then did the same with my son's computer. After that, he took my son's computer away with him. My other son wasn't involved with the transaction, he purchased a new one earlier this year and he's up to date.'

'What courses is your second son taking?'

'Medicine.'

'I must ask another question, it's important bearing in mind the nature of our investigation, can you give an indication of your sons' politics?'

'Their politics?'

'It's important, if only to eliminate them from our enquiries.'

'My husband and I tend to be Liberal and have been for years,' she smiled. 'We're a little disappointed in them right now, but being in business I suppose we'll never change. Our sons are free to make up their own minds, we rarely discuss politics at home, but I'd say they're inclined to be...well...right of centre.'

'Do they have strong views on religion?'

'Definitely not,' Mrs Alletson shook her head. 'If you are talking extremists, they both become very angry at fanatics who destroy things and kill people.'

'Good!' McKay nodded. 'Can we ask one favour, again I stress this is vital.'

'Yes?'

'A man has been murdered because it was thought he'd accessed information still residing on a traded in computer,' said McKay. 'We believe this data belonged to somebody who intends to commit an act of sabotage on Australian soil. Is it possible to allow us to access your sons' computers?'

'You think my sons would contemplate an action like that?'

'These days, Mrs Alletson, we don't know what to think,' McKay shrugged. 'The London bombers were home grown, apparently model citizens and intelligent, as were the 9/11 airline hi-jackers. We have to cover all bases. We have to investigate three more similar lines of enquiry, if we can totally eliminate you and your sons it simplifies our task.'

'I'll have to ask them, and consult with my husband.'

'Please do,' said McKay. 'What's your husband's line of work?'

'He works for a commercial television channel.'

'Very well,' said McKay. 'We have another similar call to make, if you could do that for us it would be much appreciated. We'll be in touch.'

'What now?' Catherine queried when they were outside.

'We'll go for Ken Dewberry, then back here. This one looks a possible; we have the university element, a computer that replaced another and the next in line traded in. This was the scenario you suggested, remember? This could be our target, although we've established Jean Alletson is a true-blue conservative and maybe all her family.'

'Yes, but there's no accounting for the direction of politics of offspring, they often oppose parents just for the sake of it. I did,' mused Catherine.

'Another thing, is there anyone at South Melbourne who is a computer whiz kid, like Marcus Templeton at Canberra?'

'Ask Joe Carter.'

'I will,' McKay whipped out his mobile. 'We're going to need someone who knows his way around computers and can detect hidden files. Bit beyond me, I'm afraid.'

'John Edmonds is your man,' said Carter when McKay asked the question. 'He's no mug with computers; he can almost make them talk. You believe Alletson may be our key?'

'Possible,' agreed McKay. 'How do we go about it if they refuse?'

'Maybe a warrant,' Carter said pensively. 'Perhaps your friendly copper at St Kilda Road can assist. Alternatively, mention of the police might do more than intelligence and security.'

CHAPTER 16

Their next call was on Ken Dewberry, he looked puzzled when they stood on his doorstep, but invited them in, accompanied by John Edmonds who had just arrived.

'What exactly is this about?' he asked, McKay explained the circumstances.

'How on earth can I be involved in that?' Dewberry asked irritably. He was aged about 50, grey haired and overweight with a florid complexion.

'We don't think you will be,' McKay explained patiently. 'We are working on a process of elimination. You'll appreciate we have to examine all areas.'

'You say you're not from the police?'

'No, Australian intelligence, but the police are involved, and they should arrive here shortly.'

'They're here now,' said John Edmonds. 'Just arrived outside.'

McKay turned, Griffiths had just disembarked from a car outside and was walking up the drive.

'Detective Sergeant Griffiths, Victorian Police,' he announced as he entered and addressed himself to Dewberry. 'I gather you know what this is about?'

'Vaguely,' said Dewberry. 'Your colleagues have only just got here, and haven't fully explained matters yet, except that you want to examine my computer.'

'It would assist us greatly if we could.'

Dewberry hesitated, looked afresh at Griffiths' warrant card, then shrugged.

'Well, I've nothing to hide,' he said. 'Come aboard.'

He invited them into the hall, and indicated the front room of the house.

'There it is,' he said. 'What exactly is the connection?'

'It's to do with a traded in computer to Gerry Parr,' said Griffiths, which wasn't strictly true because it related to one that wasn't, but he didn't want to complicate the issue. 'It wasn't cleared before being traded in and information found on it could prejudice national security. That's all I can say, we've traced four or five transactions during the same period in similar circumstances, yours happens to be one of them.'

'This affects national security?'

'Yes,' said McKay. 'And it's a matter of urgency.'

Dewberry leant over and switched on the computer, which began to hum. Edmonds sat himself down and waited as it booted up.

'There's confidential information on this equipment, you know.'

'Yes, be assured of our discretion, it's our watchword at all times,' responded McKay which seemed to placate Dewberry.

'Go on then, get it over and done with.'

'How many drives do you have?' asked Edmonds.

'Drives? Just the one ...the hard drive...' C' drive.'

'No second hard drive?'

'No...yes,' Dewberry corrected himself. 'Several years ago, Gerry Parr supplied me with an external hard drive for backing up, that's the one on the top with the blue light. Just as well he did, it saved my bacon because everything I lost was still on it.'

Edmonds entered the "My Computer" file and cast around.

'Like some coffee while he's doing that?' Dewberry suggested.

'Why not?'

They trooped into the kitchen. Dewberry set the coffee machine going as they occupied chairs around the kitchen table.

'Do you live alone?' asked Catherine.

'No, my wife works at a dress shop in Waverley,' answered Dewberry. 'We're both retired, sort of. But we both needed something to keep us ticking over. Being a marriage celebrant is ideal, one or two weddings a week, and if we want to go on holiday, I just stop taking bookings. I've been doing this over ten years now.'

'Do you do religious ceremonies?' asked Catherine.

'Not unless I'm specifically asked,' Dewberry shook his head. 'The whole object of civil celebrants is to cater for people who don't want religious ceremonies, although there are some who want a religious flavour. If they do, it's up to them and I'll go along with it. It's their ceremony and their day; what they want they get.'

'Who would want religious connotations if they choose a civil celebrant?' asked Griffiths. 'If they want that, why don't they go to a church?'

'Some can't, such as divorced Catholics,' said Dewberry. 'The church won't allow divorcees to remarry in their churches, as they don't recognise divorce, which means a civil marriage. But some still cling to the religious aspect. Some religious ceremonies aren't recognised by Australia, so sometimes people have both, the religious then the civil, which is where I come in. That makes everything legal. But it's up to them, whatever they want they get. It doesn't worry me.'

They chatted for about twenty minutes, about the celebrant system in general; then Edmonds appeared in the doorway.

'All clear,' he said. 'This wasn't the one.'

McKay finished his coffee; stood and extended his hand to Dewberry.

'Thank you for your co-operation,' he said. 'It is much appreciated.'

'No problem,' said Dewberry. 'Everything on there relates to my business, plus some oddments on various hobbies like stamp collecting and family research, so there was no point in refusing. I hope you find what you're looking for.'

Outside they had a brief discussion.

'What was on it?' asked McKay.

'What he said, details of marriages he's conducted which went back some years. He keeps details and maintains touch with them from what I could see,' replied Edmonds.

'Wise man,' commented McKay. 'The best business is from old clientele. How does the saying go...new clients are silver, but old clients are gold?'

'I think the saying relates to friends, not clients, but I get your point,' Griffiths commented. 'But how could that help him? People don't marry twice.'

'These days they do,' said Catherine. 'But I doubt if he's thinking of that kind of repeat business. Married couples have children ...!'

'And children mean naming ceremonies,' Griffiths nodded. 'I stand corrected.'

'He had a few of those listed too,' said Edmonds. 'Catherine's right.'

'What about Mrs Alletson?' asked Griffiths.

'She said she'd be in touch later.'

'Not good enough,' Griffiths said briskly. 'Time is getting on, I believe you isolated a time period at the end of the month on that disc Taylor downloaded. We'll go down there now, I'll come with you this time. We can't afford to horse around.'

'We'd best go there at night time, there'll be nobody at home during the day,' suggested Catherine.

'Good thinking,' said Griffiths. 'What's the home address?'

McKay consulted his notebook.

'Good enough, we'll meet in Mornington in that road at when? Say 7 o'clock?' Griffiths suggested. 'All agreed?'

When they arrived that evening, the door was answered by Mrs Alletson, she looked askance when she saw the grouping on her doorstep.

'I said I'd give you a call,' she said, somewhat irritably.

'Yes, you did, but this can't wait,' Griffiths took control. 'We're investigating a problem that could result in hundreds of deaths, we need information quickly.'

'I haven't seen you before,' she said.

Griffiths showed her his warrant card, which she examined closely.

'Well, I don't know ...' she began but her husband appeared in the hallway.

'Hugh Alletson,' he announced. 'What's all this about?'

Griffiths introduced himself and produced his warrant card again. Mr Alletson viewed it and nodded.

'This is about Alistair's computer again, is it?'

'Yes, it is. We're running out of time. We found information on a traded in computer and we are trying to trace its source.'

'What sort of information?'

Griffiths hesitated, but McKay stepped into the breach.

'The matter affects Australian security and is highly confidential, suffice to say that the information described a possible bombing attack on Australian soil, and was timed for the end of this month,' he said. 'It's vital we isolate the source, by eliminating all other sources. It was discovered on a computer traded into Harold Henderson's shop in Balaclava, Henderson was recently murdered because of what he downloaded from that computer.'

Again, not strictly true, but near enough. A complete synopsis of events would have taken too long to explain.

'How do I know that's true?'

'What more do you want?' Griffiths persisted. 'You have Victorian Police and ASIO on your doorstep.'

'But Alistair wouldn't be mixed up in anything like that.'

'Maybe, but we have to examine it if only for elimination purposes. Further, it's possible somebody he knows may have had access to his computer.'

'Frankly, I doubt that...but...!'

Hugh Alletson hesitated, then made up his mind and invited them in.

'What will this entail?'

'We have a computer expert here,' McKay indicated John Edmonds. 'It is just a case of having a look through the files. What subject or subjects is your son taking?'

'Metallurgy,' said Jean Alletson. 'Our other son is taking medicine.'

'Can John Edmonds just have a quick run through, if your son *is* involved with anything off beat, you'd be better off knowing now, when you can nip it in the bud, sooner than later.'

'What is the information we're talking about?' Hugh Alletson asked.

McKay shook his head.

'I'm sorry, for the time being this is completely confidential,' he said. 'I understand you work for a commercial TV channel, it's vital that nothing of this current situation leaks out, not yet anyway.'

Alletson still hesitated but his mind was clearly clicking over.

'All right, I understand up to a point,' he said.

'I stress once more, this is strictly confidential, and it's preferable you say nothing at all about our presence here or that we are searching for information. This data originated from some undercover group, we have to locate them and if anything leaks out prematurely, they could take fright and disappear or change their attack plan. At present, we know what they are planning and secrecy will assist to apprehend them before they put their plan into operation.'

'Where?'

'That *must* stay confidential, I'm afraid.'

'Whatever it is, can our channel have an exclusive later?'

'There can be no pre-conditions, this is far too serious, we've already said too much. I can't make any promises. I don't have the authority for a start. It will have to be arranged through my superiors.'

'All right, you'd better go ahead.'

'John, follow Mr Alletson,' instructed McKay as Alletson headed for the stairs. 'I assume your son is out.'

'Yes, he is, but will be in later.'

John Edmonds went upstairs after Mr Alletson, followed by McKay. The others stayed below in the living room. In Alistair's bedroom Edmonds turned on the computer and it began to hum as it booted up.

'Does he have a password?'

'Don't think he's ever bothered,' answered Alletson. 'No doubt we'll soon find out.'

Edmonds made some key movements, then shook his head.

'Yes he has, have you any ideas?' he said. 'What's his birthday?'

'14th September.'

Edmonds did some key pressing and shook his head again.

'Girl friend?'

'Elizabeth.'

Again Edmonds drew a blank.

'Football team?'

'Essendon.'

Edmonds tried the name of the club, its nickname and several current players from the club and again drew blank.

'I'll try a back door,' Edmonds announced.

His hands wandered over the keys and he went into several screens.

'How long will it take?' asked McKay.

'How long's a piece of string?' answered Edmonds. 'I don't anticipate too long. This is a private computer and I gather he's not a computer expert; he just uses one like most people do for record keeping and details of his courses.'

They watched as Edmonds worked hard on the keyboard.

'We'll leave you to it,' said Alletson. 'My wife is making coffee, I suggest we go below and let your colleague do his work.'

An hour later, as they were drinking coffee and chatting, the front door opened and closed, and two young men entered the living room, and looked perplexed at the assembled gathering.

'Our two sons, Alistair and Ross,' announced Hugh Alletson. 'This is Sergeant Griffiths and Agents McKay and ...' he looked questioningly at Catherine.

'Parkinson,' she filled in for him.

'Police and agents?' the elder boy looked startled. 'Agents for what?'

'Intelligence,' said McKay.

'They needed to look at your computer,' said Alletson. 'There's someone up there now.'

'What?' Alistair Alletson blenched and went white. 'Someone on my computer?'

He looked around wildly, then made a dash for the door. The others exchanged glances. They heard the sound of his footsteps on the stairs, heavy footfalls upstairs which ceased, then there was the sound of a more measured tread descending the stairs. They heard more heavy footfalls up above, while Edmonds appeared in the sitting room doorway.

'What ...?' McKay began but Edmonds shook his head. As he turned to McKay he gave an almost imperceptible head movement.

'Nothing to report,' he said. 'All clear!'

He looked at the other son, Ross, who was also looking concerned.

'Can you let me into the car, Dave,' he asked McKay. 'I need something from it.'

'Car, why do you ...? Oh, yes. Sure,' McKay cottoned on and produced his keys. 'Yes, can you excuse us for a moment?'

They reached the drive outside and McKay turned to Edmonds.

'What ...?' he began but Edmonds pointed to the car as they headed for the front gate.

'You found something?' asked McKay.

'Yes, but not what we were after, from that point of view it was all clear.'

'What then? The lad seemed panicky.'

'With good reason,' said Edmonds. 'For a start, there's porn on it. Various poses, very acrobatic and some...er...let's say eccentricities! On the bright side there was definitely no child pornography. Nevertheless, hardly anything his parents would approve.'

'Pornographic movies?'

'Not on the computer itself, but yes, he has the capacity to download them and he has been doing so. There probably are some Swedish and Continental films there or brief scenes from them. Some of it's pretty hardcore stuff,' Edmonds said. 'But it's what was in his filing drawers that startled me, stuff he's downloaded and recorded on CDs. Guess I took a liberty, illegal search and all that, but I inserted a few into the computer and had a look, hot enough to burn your fingers.'

'Hmm!' McKay scratched his chin. 'Not really what we're after, but I agree, his parents wouldn't approve. Do you think he's downloading and selling it?'

'It's possible. He's got a drawerful in his cabinet.'

'Leave it with me, I'll make an oblique comment to Alletson and Ted will have to be informed.'

'Maybe if Sergeant Griffiths could pass the warning, it might come better from him. This lad could be caught sooner or later downloading this stuff,' said Edmonds.' And if he's supplying this sort of thing to his mates then it's all highly illegal, especially if it's going to minors.'

'They're tightening the noose on this sort of piracy now,' mused McKay. 'If he is caught, that would devastate his parents, especially if he finishes up in court.'

'Another point is, if he's downloading this stuff now at his age, he could go for more spicey stuff in time, if somebody wanted it and offered enough ...if you get my drift?'

'I get the message,' said McKay grimly. 'You stay here. I'll pass the word on.'

Edmonds was still outside when the others eventually came out. He looked quizzically at McKay.

'What happened?' he asked and McKay inclined his head towards Griffiths, who smiled and paused before making for his vehicle.

'We just passed it on,' he said.

'What will happen, will you run him in?'

Griffiths shook his head.

'I could do, I suppose, but I agree with your reticence about illegal searches, any defence counsel could give us a hard time. But I think at this stage his father will be able to do far more than I could, if he's a top executive at a TV channel this could hurt him too,' he added with a grin. 'I wouldn't be in that young man's shoes right now.'

'What about the other son's computer?' asked Catherine.

'Nothing, no password on that one,' said Edmonds. 'That was as clear as a bell.'

'Did the university stuff correspond with anything that Taylor downloaded? I understand there was engineering data on that apart from the Melbourne Central Station.'

'No,' Edmonds shook his head. 'Nothing that coincided.'

'That leaves us with Richardson & Gamble,' said McKay, 'You'll be in on that, will you Ted?'

'It's our last hope now,' grunted Griffiths. 'Maybe we'll find more porn, we need some new stuff for our Christmas party.'

They were still chuckling at that as they boarded their cars and drove away.

CHAPTER 17

'What have you found on that disc, Marcus?' McKay was on the phone to Marcus Templeton in Canberra. 'Nothing much else, Dave,' Templeton answered. 'I assume they're referring to arrangements to meet and then move to Melbourne Central. They refer to places and people but it's all code names. They refer to something called 'the event' which doesn't appear to be what they have planned, but which coincides with what they intend to do.'

'The event!' McKay scratched his chin thoughtfully.

'That's right.'

'In September?'

'Presumably so, the dating is vague but most definite in that it refers to the end of September. Any joy at your end?'

'All dead ends so far,' said McKay ruefully. 'We've interviewed three people and all we've found so far is some porn.'

'Not entirely wasted then!' observed Templeton.

'Whatever turns you on. Keep trying Marcus, something may

turn up,' he put down the phone and turned to Joseph Carter.

'Nothing from Marcus, he's still working on Taylor's disc.'

'No names or dates?'

McKay shook his head.

'Not a cracker, all we have is the back end of September, possibly Melbourne Central, and something referred to as 'the event''

'Hmmm!' Carter pondered for a moment. 'Not much to go on, but we do have the approximate date.'

'Any joy on sales of ammonium nitrate or aluminium powder?'

'Griffiths and his squad are working on that, they're contacting every agricultural fertiliser company in the vicinity,' said Carter. 'What's your next move?'

'Richardson & Gamble, Catherine's phoning them now. If we draw a blank there...we're stuck.'

*

'I'm not clear on this. How exactly can I help you, why are Victorian Police interested in our computers?' Alex Richardson waved Griffiths, McKay and John Edmonds to chairs before his desk. The offices of Richardson & Gamble were situated in Bourke Street, Melbourne on the top floor of a building near Parliament House.

The firm occupied the whole of the top floor apart from some offices near the back end tenanted by a firm of solicitors and another by insurance brokers. Alex Richardson himself was aged about 50, grey haired and sporting a well-trimmed beard. He was wearing a dark suit and a Melbourne Cricket Club tie. He was a big man, overweight but not excessively so.

As he sat facing them another thought occurred to him.

'Your female colleague mentioned Australian Intelligence, what is all this?'

Catherine wasn't present, McKay had deemed it advisable to limit their numbers otherwise they could have filled Richardson's office. She was at the South Melbourne field office collating information with Joseph Carter.

Griffiths indicated McKay.

'This gentleman will explain why we are here. It's something that could affect the security of the nation.'

'I'm listening, go ahead.'

McKay told the story from the beginning. He explained the link with the death of Harold Henderson and the vital information discovered on the traded in computer, although he didn't say what the information was. As he finished Richardson leant forward.

'I remember the news item about the murder of a shop-keeper named Harold Henderson...near St Kilda, wasn't it? We never had any dealings with him though. All our computer work is handled by Gerry Parr. We've had an arrangement with him for years. He supplies our computer gear and has always given good service. We have a number of computers here, although Gerry is small business, we always found his services and knowledge satisfactory.'

'What exactly was the work carried out recently?'

'We have several computers, as I said, nine in all. We were updating, but to avoid too much upheaval we were having them replaced one at a time. We started six months back and there's still two or three to go.'

'Who did the work?'

'Young chap named Adam Simmerson; he usually did the work. He seems a competent fellow.'

'We've heard he's a good operator. So, Simmerson took away your old computer?'

'He did. Although it was replaced here for a better model, the old one wasn't out of the ark. It was an effective unit so I offloaded it onto my son Roger.'

'Your son?'

'Yes, he needed more capacity so Adam offered to take it to our home and replace Roger's computer with the one he took from here.'

'What does your son do for a living?'

'Do? Sponge off me,' Richardson grinned. 'He's a university student.'

'Doing what? What subjects?'

'Architecture, I hope one day he can qualify and join the business. Matt Gamble already has his son working in the business, and I hope the firm can continue on with other Richardsons and Gambles running it.'

'Architecture? That's nothing to do with engineering?'

'Only insofar as building materials and equipment are concerned, we have to know much of building requirements, heavy machinery such as cranes and building safety procedures apart from the actual design of new buildings and structures.'

'We may need to see your son's computer,' Griffiths spoke for the first time. 'A traded in computer has started a train of events that led to the death of this man Harold Henderson. It had data on it prejudicial to Australian security. It was left on it by mistake. We believe Simmerson would, in the normal course of events, have erased all information before passing it on but it looks as he slipped up. We believe it was his fiancée's birthday and he was in a hurry and consequently omitted to transfer everything over from the replaced computer. He traded in, or off-loaded, the computer to a third party, Harold Henderson, with this information still intact.'

'Information...what information?'

'We can't tell you as yet, but we need to examine your son's computer. We thought we might have to examine yours, but it looks as if your son's is now the last in the line we are pursuing.'

'But what is this information?'

'Can we look at your son's computer?' Griffiths ignored the question. 'It is vital we do so.'

'But he isn't here.'

'Where is he?'

'He is in the States. He comes home next week.'

'We can't wait that long, we must see it now.'

*

Alex Richardson opened the front door, stood aside and waved them in. He didn't look too happy. He had mentioned more than once he had a pile of work to do in his office. But after they had impressed on him the urgency and importance of the matter in hand, he reluctantly acquiesced and took them to his home. He indicated the stairs and started to climb them, with John Edmonds in his wake, followed by McKay and Ted Griffiths. He paused on the landing and indicated a door on the right. John Edmonds pushed it open; it was a typical young man's bedroom; which closely resembled his own room at home.

Apart from the computer, two monitors and a printer, there were posters on the wall depicting North Melbourne Football Club, Chelsea F.C., The Wallabies and the Cleveland Guardians Baseball Club. There were various items of sporting equipment scattered around the room, tennis racquets and golf clubs.

'Active young man,' Griffiths commented as he regarded the various items and wall posters. He indicated the golf clubs. 'What's his handicap?'

'Twelve,' said Richardson with a smile. 'He got a hole in one the day before he left, cost him a packet at the bar, so I heard…' he pointed to the computer '…well there it is, there's another one over there in the corner.'

'Go ahead John,' McKay said to Edmonds. 'Do that one first.'

Edmonds sat down and began working on the keyboard. He switched it on and the screen lit up. Edmonds opened up a list of files.

'Have you found a password?' asked McKay.

'There isn't one, I'm straight in.'

'Well, that looks good for the lad straight away,' mused Griffiths. 'If he had anything untoward in there a password would have been his first priority.'

They were downstairs in the kitchen drinking coffee when McKay's mobile phone rang. After a brief exchange he snapped it shut.

'That was John Edmonds,' he said. 'He's been through the first computer and found nothing like we're looking for. He's opened up the second, there's no password on that either and he's in, which indicates …' he turned to Richardson '…your son isn't too bothered about hiding anything.'

'I hope he isn't doing anything illegal. What is it exactly?'

McKay and Griffiths exchanged glances and McKay cleared his throat.

'Let's just say what we found indicates there are malcontents within our society, who are not bothered what they do to satisfy their discontent with the way we live.'

Richardson momentarily looked puzzled, then light dawned.

'Are we talking terrorism?'

McKay hesitated, then nodded.

'Yes, we are. We believe something is planned for the end of this month, we think we know where, but not when.'

'Good God!' Richardson was startled. 'This could happen

here? In Australia?'

'It could, it happened in London,' said Griffiths. 'We've been chasing up any computers that Adam Simmerson touched within the last few weeks to trace who these people are and where they could be planning to strike.'

'You think Roger is one of them?'

'Frankly, from what I have seen of his bedroom, and you, his father, I'm inclined to doubt it. But this is the third lead we've followed up and we've drawn blanks each time. It looks as if Roger's computer was the last one Adam Simmerson serviced or exchanged before he appeared with a trade-in at Henderson's shop.'

There was another call from Edmonds. McKay answered it, made some comments and closed his phone.

'That's it,' he said. 'Edmonds has been through the second computer, another blank. There was nothing on the second one that looked remotely like the thesis data that Taylor downloaded, and certainly nothing about Melbourne Cent... about the possible attack.'

'What was that? Were you going to say Melbourne Central? Are we talking about the underground railway station in the city?' asked Richardson.

McKay cursed himself for his slip and reluctantly nodded.

'Yes, I was, and we are,' he said. 'I'm afraid I must ask you to keep that under your hat. We don't want that information leaking out, especially to the press. If these people know we're on to them they could change target, then we'll have no idea where they could strike.'

'Bit risky isn't it, keeping mum?'

'Even more so if we blurt out what we know up to now,' said McKay. 'If they alter their location plan, they could strike anywhere, then we'll be completely in the dark.'

They heard footsteps on the stairs, Edmonds made his way up the hall and appeared at the kitchen door. He looked desolate, but perked up when Richardson poured out a coffee and pushed it across the table.

'Seems to be in the clear,' he announced. 'Yes- milk thanks.'

They thanked Richardson for his co-operation and headed down the drive. They reached the car, standing by the kerb, and McKay turned to Edmonds.

'Nothing doing then?'

Edmonds shook his head.

'No, not what we were looking for,' he said. 'But there was something that may interest Sergeant Griffiths.'

'Not more pornography?'

'Not directly, no. This young fellow appears to be more wholesome in his tastes than the Alletson lad.'

'What are we talking about?' asked Griffiths. 'What's he up to?'

'It looks as if he's been downloading movies and transferring them onto DVDs, there's a drawer full of them in one of his filing cabinets, and he's been printing labels that are very like the real thing,' said Edmonds. 'It looks as if he's been downloading recently released movies, and others that haven't been released here yet. I'd say he's selling what he's downloading, all strictly illegal. His equipment is very sophisticated; maybe it's paid for out of his profits.'

'Piracy eh?' Griffiths pursed his lips. 'Another young lad into the same game. No wonder they're starting to tighten up on this type of thing now, he could find himself in trouble if he's selling what he's downloading and putting it on DVDs.'

'That seems to be your province again, Ted.'

'It does, I'll have a word now with Richardson Senior, before he goes back to his office. I'll tell him what we've found and tell him we're prepared to turn a blind eye, but suggest he has a word with Master Roger when he gets back. Leave that with me,' Griffiths took a couple of steps back up the drive, then turned and smiled. 'This is easier than telling the Alletsons about the hardcore stuff, I thought Mrs Alletson was going to pass out!'

*

'Anything else on Taylor's disc?' McKay asked Templeton the following morning. He was in a filthy temper, he had started the trail a few days ago full of high hopes and now these had been dashed, they were no nearer to finding the original owner of the computer and bomb making data than they were at the start. He was also furious with himself about his slip of the tongue, thereby revealing the possible target to Alex Richardson. He could only hope no lasting damage had been done.

He had arranged a meeting that morning with Griffiths and one of his colleagues, Detective Constable Sam Stannington. They intended to analyse their information to date, put it together again and hope something would turn up.

'Nothing new,' replied Templeton. 'All the information is vague, although the end of September appears to be the time slot, nothing definitive, no date can be isolated.'

'Right! Put me onto Alan Kelsey, Marcus, we seem to be having no luck and he'll no doubt blast us all to hell and back.'

'He may not, he's actually smiling today. He got tickets for one of the Rugby League preliminary finals this week end. First time his team has been in the finals for years.'

'Good!' McKay replied. 'I'll mention that first off then, see you later, Marcus.'

The phone rang once before Kelsey came on line.

'Kelsey!'

'Alan…Dave McKay here. Just a quick report on what's happening here.'

'It had better be good!'

McKay gave Kelsey a run down on developments so far, and that they seemed to have drawn another blank

'Well time's getting on,' said Kelsey. 'What have you got in mind now?'

'Carry out a recce of surveillance tapes at Melbourne Central station. If anything is planned there, they could carry out a rehearsal. That's what the London bombers did.'

'That's true. It's possible they'll do that here.'

They discussed the investigations of the previous few days, Kelsey laughed briefly when McKay told him about young Alletson's panic-stricken rush upstairs when he realised Edmonds could uncover his pornographic downloads.

'We also found Roger Richardson has been carrying out a lucrative business downloading modern movies and selling them. We left Griffiths to handle that. He had words in both fathers' ears.'

'Some of these kids today know more about computers than the experts. Keep at it, Dave, let me know when you find anything.'

'Will do,' McKay was about to hang up, then added. 'You're off to the football this weekend, according to Marcus.'

'A friend of mine got me into his company's private box; a meal goes with it and unlimited alcohol. Six of us are going. We'll all be pissed to our eyeballs.'

'Way to be,' responded McKay. 'Hope they win. First time they've been in a final for 15 years isn't it? The event of the decade, eh?'

'Too right,' Kelsey replied and hung up.

McKay sat back and looked at his watch. Nearly time to go. Then realisation of what he and Alan Kelsey had been discussing hit him forcibly. He jack-knifed forwards and hit his elbows onto the desk, clapping the palms of his hands to his forehead.

'Christ Almighty!' he shouted. 'How could we have been so stupid? The event! It's the Grand Final!'

CHAPTER 18

'The event, it must be Grand Final day,' McKay said to Griffiths. They were with Catherine Parkinson and Detective Constable Sam Stannington in the St Kilda Road Police complex. Stannington was young and just off the beat, he had been partnered with Griffiths to gain experience. McKay and Stannington had briefly crossed paths during the initial questioning of Donald Taylor. Stannington struck McKay as a quiet type, a thinker.

'Seems logical,' commented Griffiths.

'That disc bears references to an event at the end of September, what other event is there in Melbourne, or Sydney, in September?'

'Grand Finals...and crowds of people using Melbourne and Sydney main line stations near the football stadiums. You're right. We should have worked that out before?'

'How much closer does it bring us to finding these people?' asked Catherine.

'It doesn't...yet!' Griffiths replied. 'But the date is useful.'

'Any joy with investigating ammonium nitrate sales?' asked McKay.

'We've been calling on virtually everyone who deals in the stuff, we're following up a couple of leads, a store in Gippsland said they'd sold a quantity a couple of weeks back to some people they hadn't seen before, we're covering that later today,' said Griffiths.' We had another call north of Melbourne but it seemed genuine when we followed it up. Many farms up there lost top soil when those heavy winds blew up. The excess sold was to farming people they knew, old customers.'

'What's happened to Taylor?' asked Catherine.

'Still here, but he's due to be released today, no reason to hold him,' replied Griffiths. 'He doesn't seem too keen to go; he's scared stiff after what he saw at Balaclava.'

'Why don't we use him as bait?' asked Catherine.

'Bait?'

'Let him out, with a fanfare, and see if they try to nobble him.'

'You mean, tether him out like a goat to attract a tiger?' McKay was scandalized.

'Something like that,' said Catherine.

'Why should they attack him?'

'For a start, he's the only one to have seen Henderson's murderers,' said Catherine. 'They must be aware of that now. Let's face it, Adam Simmerson was in a similar position and he's disappeared.'

'It's worth thinking about,' Griffiths nodded pensively. 'It might have the desired effect. Right now, we've got nowhere.'

'I don't like it,' McKay shook his head.

'Well, it's all we've got,' said Catherine. 'If what was downloaded is for real, we'll have possible deaths of hundreds of people to contend with.'

'You're suggesting we let him out with a tail on him to see if anyone attacks him,' McKay said with distaste. 'What if they stab or shoot him?'

'We lose!'

'So does Taylor...Oh bugger it!' McKay leant forward and cupped his chin with his hands. 'I can't see any alternative.'

*

As anticipated, Taylor didn't view the plan with enthusiasm. He had one consideration about the proposed idea, which was his regard for the late Harold Henderson. He still had the image in his mind of the surprise and shock registered on Henderson's features as he was stabbed, and the gradual softening of that expression as he sank to the floor and slowly died.

He also had the images of Henderson's attackers in his mind, the details of the murder scene were still as fresh in his mind as the day he witnessed them. He had given thorough descriptions to the police artist and twice made modifications to a couple of likenesses.

He also had an uncompromising anger against Florence Henderson, he had never liked her and although he knew she had been under considerable stress at the time, her unquestioning initial, and maybe subsequent, assumption of his guilt still rankled.

He listened to the proposal as outlined by Griffiths and McKay and was clearly not enamoured of the prospect. Getting out of the building was another matter, there was a limit to how long he could be, or wanted to be, incarcerated before he succumbed to sheer boredom. He was itching to be seated before his computer again, that is, if there was anything left of his system after the trashing by Henderson's killers.

'What guarantee do I have you'll get them before they get me?' he asked, not unreasonably.

'You haven't,' said Griffiths. 'We'd have you under constant surveillance, providing you don't try and evade us or make any sudden decisions, like jumping on a train or tram. If anyone, approximating the descriptions of the men you gave us, comes anywhere near you we'll be onto them.'

Taylor was still not altogether convinced, but had to admit he was bored stiff where he was. Having been quite fond of Harold Henderson despite their money dispute, he had a burning desire to see Henderson's murderers brought to book. The thought also occurred to him that even if he went home, he wouldn't feel safe. They had been in there once and could easily break in again if they considered him a threat.

'What about my apartment, have there been any other break-ins there?' he asked.

'None,' said Griffiths. 'We've kept it under surveillance, so far nothing.'

'What priority will you give me?' asked Taylor. 'Will any police shadowing me be likely to be drawn off to other areas?'

'No!' Griffiths shook his head. 'Priority will be absolute. You know what's at stake, you know better than I do what's on that disc you copied.'

'I read about the events leading up to 9/11 in New York,' said Taylor. 'They had their suspicions because of the chatter over the ether, and then did bugger all about it. Can't your experts isolate these people from that?'

'There's been chatter from overseas, but nothing here,' McKay said. 'Any communication could be by hand; they could distribute instructions via disc which they hand to various people involved. That way there's no local ether chatter or e-mails.'

'Back to the days of carrier pigeons and mail drops,' Griffiths commented cynically. 'We need your help, Donald. We've struck blank walls everywhere else. Adam Simmerson replaced three computers shortly before he handed that trade-in to Henderson. None of the three have been of any assistance, except for discovering a possible pornography ring and piracy of the latest movies. We've failed to find any possible conspiracy candidate.'

'What about the engineering course?'

'That restricts it to about 300 or 400 people, and more than one university. That's assuming he *is* a university student. He could be researching stuff in libraries.'

'Let's face it, for the present we're stuck,' McKay broke in. 'And what we are proposing is a desperate measure, but something may come of it.'

'Yes...my damned funeral!' Taylor declared with heat. 'Christ! A few days ago I was leading a normal existence, since then I've seen somebody murdered, been arrested and accused of being a murderer, had my apartment wrecked, locked up in here and given the third degree, and read bloody newspapers that all assume I'm guilty and a knife toting thug!'

'Well, now you have the chance to prove otherwise,' said Griffiths soothingly. 'Look, you know what's on that disc. You could save the lives of hundreds of people.'

'And lose mine!' Taylor said dispiritedly.' Oh bugger it! All right, I'll do it!'

'How do we approach it?' asked McKay as they left the interview room.

'Let him out tomorrow morning, after we've given the Herald-Sun all the details of his release, and no doubt they'll print a picture of him leaving the building.'

'You mean you're giving them full details of when he's coming out?' asked McKay. 'Maybe you'd like to leave a loaded gun on the pavement.'

'If you don't like it you can register a protest,' said Griffiths mildly.

'Protest hell! I think it's a great idea!'

They chatted in the foyer before McKay took his leave. McKay cast his eyes around the reception area and noticed a different sergeant in charge of the main desk.

'Where's your friend?' he asked

'Rostered off, he's on tomorrow,' grunted Griffiths. 'That's Brett Grafton on duty now...he's a mate of mine...good bloke.'

'I'll remember to see who's on duty before I come in next time,' said McKay. 'Well, I'd best be away.'

Griffiths' mobile phone rang, he walked about ten feet away as he answered it to prevent being overhead, and then walked back to McKay.

'This affects you as well,' he said. 'We've been running that car registration through the system, the one Taylor noted after Henderson was killed. If you remember he only got the letters as it drove off, unfortunately he couldn't note the rest of it when it was outside his flat. Anyway, we've isolated 22 vehicles that come under letters KGU and a blue Commodore. I'll put Sam Stannington onto it, and suggest he isolates any with Arab sounding names.'

'I can hear the Woke brigade now...racist!'

'My bloody oath it is, it's also common sense,' said Griffiths. 'But we'll have to modify our plan for Taylor. If we're investigating these various vehicles, we'll need Taylor around so he can observe the people we're interviewing. If we have him out on the street acting as bait as well, this could delay matters,' said Griffiths.

'What about a substitute?' McKay suggested.

'How do you mean...a substitute?'

'It's possible Harold Henderson's killers don't know what Taylor looks like, they never saw him at the shop, they didn't know he was there. They raided his flat because they got his address from Harold Henderson but they never set eyes on him.'

'We put out pictures on television, don't forget,' said Griffiths. 'That's how we got hold of him in the first place, the girl at the Maragogype Café recognised him and the young woman at the motel.'

'True,' agreed McKay. 'But he hasn't been shown since and that was some days ago. They possibly didn't see the pictures and if they did, details may be hazy by now.'

'What are you suggesting?'

'Do what we planned to do, but use one of your blokes who resembles him, same height and features if possible, then release a picture to the papers, let him out and publicise the time he's hitting the pavement.'

'Hmm!' Griffiths rubbed his chin reflectively. 'A better bet in many ways, one of our blokes could handle himself better in an emergency. We may have to tell the papers though, to prevent any leak to an enterprising journo which could scupper the idea.'

'You've got leaks in your police complex, have you?'

'Fact of life I'm afraid, we blocked a couple a few months back, but news still leaks out. I know the editors at the The Age and Herald-Sun, we'll have to play it straight with them.'

*

McKay phoned Kelsey in Canberra, who referred to a note on his pad.

'This suspicious purchase of ammonium nitrate in Gippsland, I understand Ted Griffiths mentioned it.'

'Yes,' answered McKay. 'Some farming property near Flinders Creek, the dealers were curious because they were first time customers and the property turned out to be a fairly small holding. They supplied the stuff, but in accordance with regulations, they informed the local police, who in turn contacted Melbourne.'

'Have they investigated it yet?'

'No, a question of manpower at present, they'll get around to it.'

'We can't wait for that,' commented Kelsey. 'I'll call Griffiths and suggest we do it. I can send Bob Bramble and Denis Shackleton down there. We don't want chemicals like that floating around and us not knowing where they are.'

They discussed various other items, Kelsey re-iterated he would set up observation of the Flinders Creek property. McKay rang off and turned to Joseph Carter.

'Is that this morning's paper?' he asked.

'Feel free,' said Carter. 'What are you after, football scores?'

'Later,' said McKay. 'Has Ted Griffiths done what he said he was going to do?'

'What about? You mean Taylor?' asked Carter.

'I was wondering if it's been publicised.'

'Have a look,' Carter tossed the newspaper across.

McKay glanced at the front page. There was a note about an item on one of the inner pages headed 'Murder suspect released!' so he opened it up at the designated page. There was a picture of a young man leaving the police building in St Kilda Road taken at a distance, with a circular inset.

'Is that Taylor?'

'No,' said McKay. 'But it's a good likeness. I was taken in myself at first. I know who it is, I've seen him around ...ah...I've got it. He's the constable on that reception desk. I thought at the time he resembled our friend Taylor...Cope I think his name is...young constable...uniformed branch.'

'What about Taylor?'

'Griffiths is checking motor vehicles thrown up by that part registration Taylor supplied. There are over 20 vehicles, he's following them up and needs Taylor who says he can still identify those three Asians in Henderson's shop.'

'So Cope is the clay pigeon, I don't envy him.'

'He'll be under intensive observation, he's also on his guard and, although he's a rookie, if anything erupts, he's quite capable of handling himself...more so than a civilian like Taylor,' said McKay. 'Nevertheless, he's playing a dangerous role.'

'What will you and Catherine do now?'

McKay turned the newspaper pages and considered.

'Don't know right now, she isn't in yet. But we'll have to go over the calls we've made, we could have missed something somewhere.'

*

The next two days were frustrating, McKay and Catherine Parkinson went over old ground, initially they had a cool reception from Mrs Alletson but when her husband came in from the garden, he was more amenable. He was appreciative of being tipped off about the pornographic angle and had grimly superintended the deletion of all porno files from his son's computer. He had instituted a regular checking routine.

Catherine followed up the angle of there being an intermediary computer transaction, whether Alistair Alletson knew if Adam had made a further deal with his computer before taking a trade-in to Harold Henderson. Alistair was sulky and embarrassed, his current relationship with his father was not the best, but there was no doubt Alletson Senior appreciated his son's activities had been revealed and curtailed. He accompanied them to the front gate where they had a brief conversation.

'Not only was there the danger of police or Customs locking onto him, I reckon if he was reproducing it and providing it to his friends there was a real danger of becoming involved with the criminal fraternity,' Hugh Alletson said as he shook hands with them both. 'He's angry and resentful, but I can live with that. I've had words with Gerry Parr and he sent one of his lads down, the three computers are linked now and I can access both Alistair's and Ross's through mine. It won't happen again.'

'That's one satisfied customer,' Catherine commented as they drove away. 'Who do you want to see next?'

They decided not to visit Dewberry again, Catherine recalled that Gerry Parr had told them that his old computer, badly affected by a virus, was in their workshop being stripped. No chance of an ongoing transaction there.

They returned to South Melbourne feeling dispirited, a phone call to Griffiths indicated Constable Cope had made an ostentatious entry into Taylor's flat, and also walked up and down outside the now closed Henderson shop premises. He had two plain clothes police tailing him, but had not attracted undue attention. The car registration investigation had also not borne fruit, although 12 of the 22 vehicles had been eliminated.

'Guess that's progress, even if it's negative,' McKay put the phone down. 'Let's hope something comes from the remaining ten.'

They phoned Alex Richardson but he was out for the day, they left a number then went through all their notes again to see if they'd missed anything. They called Marcus Templeton in Canberra but although they now suspected the exact date,

Marcus had gleaned nothing more that assisted. Initials were used, which could indicate the plotters, but the bald letters were of little help. There were references to 'AM', 'MG', 'NJ', 'QR' and others, also noted on the Melbourne Central drawing, presumably referring to individuals.

The day passed slowly, they left the field office and went to a nearby restaurant. They compared notes again before they retired to their motel and eventually turned in for the night.

They phoned Rhonda Muston the next morning to see if she'd heard from Adam Simmerson. She hadn't, and was quite tearful during the conversation as she was now very worried. Adam's absence had been bad enough but subsequent visits by police and ASIO personnel had caused even more agitation. Catherine carried out a further interview in the bookshop, checking whether Adam had said anything on their last date to constitute a clue as to his whereabouts or intentions, but she could think of nothing, apart from the reference to Balaclava, which indicated the Henderson shop which they already knew about.

McKay had helped himself to a coffee from the drinks machine when the switchgirl told him there was a call for him. He assumed it was Catherine to say when she'd be back, but it was Alex Richardson.

'Hallo Alex,' he said. 'We called you yesterday as we wanted to check a few things.'

'You called me?' Richardson was surprised. 'I didn't know that, I've been in Perth for a couple of days and just got back, I haven't checked my messages yet.'

'We just wanted to see you again, we haven't made any progress and thought we'd go over a few things, see if we'd missed anything.'

'Well, I have news for you,' said Richardson. 'Roger is on his way back from the States, he should be in town tomorrow. I spoke with him just before he flew out from Los Angeles, I told him what had been going on and your interest in his computer. I also told him to watch what he was doing in future with his downloading.'

'Pity, I wanted a few movies that haven't been released yet,' said McKay.

'I'll tell him...' that obviously amused Richardson. '...he'll be ready to negotiate! But I have information for you. Roger told me Simmerson took his old computer, which was handed on to another student at the university, a young lad who had a very old machine and Roger's would have represented an update for him.'

'Did he by God?' McKay felt a rising excitement.

'Adam Simmerson took Roger's old one away with him and passed it to this other student, then presumably appropriated the one he replaced,' said Alex Richardson. 'Maybe that was the one that finished up at the Henderson shop. Does this help?'

'My bloody oath it does,' said McKay. 'Who was the other student?'

'A young lad taking an engineering degree. Roger knew him because he was in the same university cricket team. He's a Pakistani, named Asif Mahmoud.'

CHAPTER 19

McKay put down the phone, leapt to his feet, clasped hands over his head in a boxer's salute, and shouted 'Eureka!' John Edmonds, depositing computer sheets into an IN basket near the door, paused to eye him with mild surprise. McKay was in no mood for explanations. He clapped him on the shoulder as he left the room and entered Joe Carter's sanctum.

'We may have a break through!' he announced.

'Has somebody had a go at Constable Cope?'

'Nothing to do with that.'

'We've found that blue Commodore?'

'No, something entirely different. Catherine's theory was right. Roger Richardson's computer was in the middle of a transactional chain. His computer was used to replace one belonging to another student, and the next computer could have been the last in the line traded in to Harold Henderson.'

'In that case it's no wonder Gerry Parr lost track of it,' Carter responded. 'Who was the recipient of Roger Richardson's computer?'

'A young university student named Asif Mahmoud,' said McKay. 'He's a Pakistani who's taking an engineering degree. We don't know where he is...yet. We could probably track him through the university, but I'd prefer to see Roger Richardson first, he can help us lock onto him.'

*

Early next morning McKay arranged with Alex Richardson to see Roger. Roger was due to arrive at Tullamarine Airport late afternoon, but McKay decided to wait until he had settled in. Jet lag was a factor, he didn't want Roger Richardson dropping off to sleep during an interview and giving wrong or confused information. He asked Alex Richardson to make it clear to Roger they were not interested in his downloading activities nor whether he was earning cash from it, all they wanted was information.

'Make sure he doesn't make any phone calls,' he warned Alex Richardson. 'We don't want Roger tipping this guy off for friendship's sake. This is far too serious.'

'Understood.'

Catherine Parkinson was jubilant, after all the dead ends and disappointments the computer trail had moved up a notch which she considered could bear fruit. McKay was hopeful, but they'd hit so many brick walls his prevailing view was one of caution.

'We'll get there early, if possible while he's either still in bed or just getting up to avoid Roger making any warning phone calls to this Asif character from any mistaken sense of loyalty,' he said and added. 'I want words with him, Roger that is, before he's had time to gather his thoughts. It might be another false lead, but it looks good and we want to contact this Asif fellow or tail him without arousing suspicion.'

'Have you told Ted Griffiths?' asked Catherine.

'Not yet, but not for want of trying, I had to leave a message,' said McKay. 'He's probably on the road checking Holden Commodores and hasn't had time to ring back.'

But Griffiths rang within half an hour and McKay gave him the news.

'Good work!' commented Griffiths, 'We've news for you too, Constable Cope picked up a tail earlier today, so he went back to Taylor's apartment and settled in there. His follower stayed outside and was relieved after an hour or so. We're following the original tail to see where he goes. They are still watching Cope and the watcher is under surveillance.'

'What about the Commodore?'

'Some progress. We've eliminated another six, so we have about five left. I'll let you know if we make a hit. Taylor's with us to see if he can point the finger. When are you seeing Roger Richardson?'

'Early tomorrow,' said McKay. 'Before 9 o'clock if possible.'

'Good, keep in touch. Maybe we're getting somewhere at last.'

'Keep your fingers crossed. This could be another dead end.'

'Perhaps not this time,' said Griffiths. 'I think this young fellow Asif could be our man, or one of them.'

'I tend to agree,' said McKay. 'I'll be in touch.'

McKay and Catherine Parkinson arrived outside the Richardson household at 7.30 am. Alex Richardson answered the door, grimaced and let them in.

'By God! You buggers don't let a man finish his breakfast,' he grumbled. 'Come in. Coffee?'

They sat at the kitchen table and Mrs Richardson plied them with coffee.

'Percolated!' McKay exclaimed. 'Luxury indeed.'

'Nothing but the best for the Intelligence Services,' grunted Richardson. 'Roger knows you're coming; I've told him on no account to speak to this young man Asif. His mobile phone is on that shelf, I made doubly sure of that before he turned in. I was taking no chances, although the likelihood of him tipping anyone off in this type of situation is remote. He's been in New York on this trip and visited Ground Zero.'

'You've told him of the possible situation?'

'Had to, he's no bloody fool, and I couldn't fob him off with any fairy tales. He has cousins living in New York. Christine, my wife, is American, and after staying with them for several days, visiting the site of the former World Trade Centre at first hand and viewing the emotional aspect of the memorials there I can't see Roger tipping off a possible saboteur.'

'I hope you're right,' McKay sipped his coffee, looked at Mrs Richardson 'Whereabouts in America are you from, Mrs Richardson?'

'Cleveland,' she replied. 'We met when I was on holiday here, years ago now.'

'Ah! That accounts for the Cleveland Guardians regalia in his bedroom. This is good coffee, Mrs Richardson.'

'Glad you like it, and the name is Christine,' she turned to the doorway. 'This sounds like Roger on his way down.'

A young man entered, dressed in jeans and a Rugby shirt with "Wallabies" inscribed across the chest. He was a slimmer version of Alex Richardson, six feet in height with dark, close-cropped hair, probably a legacy of his stay in America. He looked enquiringly at his father, shook hands with McKay and cast his eyes approvingly over Catherine as he shook her hand.

'G'day,' he said. 'I could kill for a coffee.'

He sat at the table; his mother poured him a cup and he eyed the two visitors.

'You want to see me about Asif?'

'We do. How well do you know him?' asked McKay.

'Not that well, we play in the same cricket team. He's a good tweaker of the ball. We're taking different courses so we don't have much contact off the cricket field.'

'How did you become involved with him on the computer aspect?'

'It just came up in conversation during a cricket general meeting back in June. His computer equipment was, I gathered, antiquated with limited capacity. It was too slow for him and lacking in memory. He was talking about it to another Paki who's in one of the cricket elevens and I mentioned I was replacing mine. Dad was changing computers at work and it gave me a chance to update. Asif said he wanted to update his so I suggested my old one might be a good replacement, it had heaps more memory than his. Adam Simmerson came here before I left for the States and changed mine. He downloaded all my guff onto the new one and wiped mine clean.'

'Which he then took away.'

'Yes, all part of the deal, I wouldn't have minded selling it myself, but Adam knew how to switch data around and I didn't, plus I'd already received an updated one for free.'

'How long ago was this?'

'I think it was round about June or July, Asif was in Pakistan for a short spell, he wasn't around the university at the time, so presumably Adam couldn't switch them immediately.'

'Can you still download modern movies?' asked Catherine.

Roger gave his father a sidelong glance.

'Guess so, I don't know about that now.'

'Don't worry about us with regard to that,' McKay gave a brief smile. 'We're not into that, but the Victorian Police are involved in this case as well. The detective we're dealing with isn't that bothered either, but bear in mind there's probably a note on their file about it now. There's an added note that it's been dealt with so if a young ambitious constable gets hold of it...everything is covered! Our main concern is your friend Asif. Do you know where he lives?'

'Not a clue,' Roger shook his head. 'Somewhere in Prahran or Windsor I think, I'm not on intimate terms with him. We're merely in the same cricket team; I occasionally see him at the nets. This computer transaction was a one off, I had little to do with it after the initial contact. Adam was the main player in that.'

'We need your help to identify this young man. Your father has made you aware of the reason for our interest?'

'Yes, he has. Something to do with a possible terror attack.'

'You *must* keep this to yourself, this is vital. Tell nobody, not any friends, no relatives apart from those here who know already, and no girlfriends. You probably know by now that telling anyone anything in confidence is tantamount to telling the whole world. If these people get an inkling we're onto them and suspect what they intend to do, they'll switch plans and attack elsewhere.'

'I understand,' Roger nodded. 'What do you want me to do?'

'Are you likely to see this man soon?'

'The cricket season isn't far away and we're due for a preliminary meeting, a general meeting of the cricket teams this week. Just a guide for the coming season, checking what team members we've lost and any new blood. We don't start practice sessions yet, but it won't be long, the football season's nearly over and cricket starts soon. It's more than likely he'll be there.'

'We need you to point him out, then leave the rest to us.'

'You won't be arresting him, will you?' Roger looked

concerned. 'I'd hate him to be apprehended in the middle of a meeting.'

'No, that's the last thing we want to do. We need him to lead us to others. Have no fears on that score.'

'How will I point him out?' asked Roger. 'I can't guarantee to leave at the same time as he does. I was vice-captain last season and could be in line for the captaincy this coming year. If I'm elected, it could be difficult to get away, I may get held up and it's possible the coach will want words with me.'

'I've decided what we'll do. You point him out to us outside the meeting room before you go in.'

'It won't be easy for me to hang around outside.'

'We'll fix that ...have you got a regular girl-friend?'

'Er...no!' Roger grimaced. 'I did but we fell out!'

'Well, you have now. Sit or stand outside with Catherine while everyone goes in, look affectionate and stay with her...' McKay eyed Catherine and grinned '...well not too affectionate...! Being outside with a girlfriend before you go in shouldn't arouse suspicion. Let Catherine know which one he is and she'll do the rest.'

'OK!' Roger sipped his coffee. 'Sounds fine to me.'

'When is the meeting, and where?'

'Day after tomorrow, at the university.'

'OK!' said McKay. 'You settle the arrangement with Catherine here, when to meet and where.'

'A pleasure,' Roger's eyes wandered in Catherine's direction.

'Good,' McKay was aware of Roger's glance and rubbed his nose as he caught Catherine's eye. 'Catherine will give you a call tomorrow, unless you want to fix it now.'

'Now is as good a time as any,' said Catherine. 'What time is the meeting?'

*

'How should we play this?' Catherine asked when they were in McKay's car afterwards. 'Exactly what part do I play in your cunning master plan?'

'We could have Jim Waters or Dean Hateley outside the meeting with Roger, but I tend to think if Roger's inside the foyer with someone who could be his girlfriend it would look more normal. You'll need to shed a few years to make it convincing.'

'Damned cheek, I'm not that old!'

'Roger is what - maybe 19 or 20? I'm not casting aspersions upon your appearance, far from it. You dress well, maybe too well. You'll have to dress as you did 6 or 7 years back, very casual and eye catching, whatever 19year old female fatales wear these days.'

'Point taken, then what?'

'If he points him out to you, that is, if he can keep his eyes off your cleavage...!' McKay added cynically: '...see if you can get a snap of Asif with your mobile phone. I could arrange for Jim or Dean to give you a call at the right time so you can wave your phone about. If that's not an option, you may have to stay outside the meeting room until they emerge, I'll have Jim or Dean within easy reach and you can point the finger for them.'

'And after the meeting they'll follow Asif?'

'It will look odd if you start tailing him, having been introduced to him as Roger's girlfriend, he'll think it strange if he looks round and sees you following him without Roger. We need someone he won't have seen before, Hateley and Waters if possible, tailing him when he leaves, we can't risk losing him.'

'Then what will you want me to do?'

'I'll be outside,' said McKay. 'Join me in the car when you've done your bit.'

'The hell I will! I wouldn't trust you if I'm dressed to kill.'

'Neither would I!'

CHAPTER 20

'Is there a lock on the door?'

'I think so...yes there is,' Constable Dudley Cope held his mobile phone to his ear as he checked the entry door to Taylor's apartment. 'Not a very substantial one. He's got a chain as well.'

'Well settle yourself in, your sentry has left his post and is heading off. We're tracking him. They may have something in mind for tomorrow. Just make yourself at home. I'd say you'll be safe enough tonight but I'm posting two men outside, one in the front and the other at the rear. Don't contact them, certainly not physically,' said Griffiths. 'Maybe you could put something in front of the door when you turn in for the night.'

'I'll do that,' Cope said pointedly. 'I'll hear from you in the morning?'

'You bet,' Griffiths rang off.

Griffiths turned to Detective Constable Alec Oliver and indicated the man walking slowly up the street away from the vicinity of Taylor's apartment.

'He's all yours,' he said. 'Don't lose him.'

'It's raining,' Oliver complained.

'It's only a slight drizzle, it won't last.'

'It's all right for some,' Alec Oliver climbed out of the car.

Griffiths watched him go. He'd already had a tail on the previous watcher, the one who followed Cope to Taylor's apartment; he was awaiting a report on where he'd finished up. This second watcher was another youngish Asian casually dressed in jeans and a blue shirt. Maybe the slight rain had persuaded him to abandon his post, or perhaps being late it was decided that Cope (Taylor) was settling in for the night and to return the next day.

He wondered what they may have in mind. The date for the possible terror attack was less than two weeks away, presumably they feared Taylor may compromise their plan and were prepared to watch him, maybe with an ultimate aim to ensure his silence.

It was likely they were only concerned about the terror attack details; they shouldn't have any inkling that Taylor had witnessed the murder of Harold Henderson, but Griffiths didn't entirely discount that. They would know Taylor had discovered the plan of Melbourne Central, Henderson had told them that before meeting his demise and they must have found and digested Taylor's print out found in his apartment, but they didn't know Taylor had a disc containing a copy of the information, maybe that was a possibility they wanted to ascertain.

As for Taylor, he would spend another night in his cell, this time as a guest. He had been out on the road all that day as they'd checked various blue Commodores that matched the incomplete registration, they'd drawn blanks but there were more to check.

Griffiths picked up his radio and checked with the two police guarding Taylor's apartment. Both were in position and would be relieved after four hours. He didn't envy them, an evening of sheer boredom and rain showers.

He drove slowly down the street and headed for home. As Alec Oliver had said, it was all right for some, but Griffiths would be called out if anything happened. However, he should be able to have his dinner and crack a bottle of red.

*

Griffiths phoned Cope from outside Taylor's apartment early next morning. Both front and rear were still under police surveillance and Cope had had a restful night.

'Not too boring I hope,' said Griffiths.

'No Sarge. Taylor's got some Wisden cricket almanacs in here, I've been reading through them,' said Cope. 'I never realised there was so much information in them, I'd always thought they were Pommie based statistics and nothing else.'

'I know what you mean,' said Griffiths. 'Pick one up and you can't put it down. I gather there's nothing to report. Your two guardians have seen nothing?'

'Apparently not.'

'Well don't get careless, these bastards mean business, they've killed already and may not hesitate to kill again. Understand?'

'Right Boss!'

He dialled Alec Oliver.

'Where did he go?'

'To Prahran, an address just off Chapel Street. There's a squad car watching it, they're keeping it under observation from a side street.'

He dialled another number.

'Hallo Martin, where did your fellow end up?'

'Richmond,' answered Detective Constable Martin Southern. 'Near the railway station. Bill Dempsey is watching it now.'

'We seem to be getting somewhere with this case, at one stage I thought we'd never get anywhere.' Griffiths muttered as he dialled McKay to pass on what information he had.

'One from Richmond and another from Prahran, eh?' McKay mused. 'It could be relevant. Roger Richardson reckoned Asif came from Prahran or Windsor. That makes it imperative Catherine or one of the others obtain a photograph of Asif, Taylor may be able to identify him. We may strike lucky at tomorrow's university cricket meeting.'

CHAPTER 21

Roger Richardson stood in the foyer outside the meeting room chatting to cricket team mates. He had arrived early to check whether Asif had arrived, as yet there was no sign of him. He checked his watch, it was about 2.25 pm, he had arranged to meet Catherine outside at 2.30 as the meeting commenced at 3 o'clock. He felt a thrill of fear up and down his spine at the possibility of Asif being connected with a terrorist ring contemplating a terrorist act in Melbourne.

McKay had contacted him that morning to confirm arrangements and ensure he gave Asif no warning, but there was little likelihood of that. Roger, recently arrived from the United States and New York in particular, had been profoundly affected by Ground Zero where the World Trade Centre had formerly stood. He had seen at first hand the perpetual grief of the city and had met contacts of his cousins who had connections with people who'd been killed that fateful day. Any fears Roger experienced were tempered with anger at anyone who could perpetrate such an act. His main concern was the possibility he might say something in anger to Asif. He would have to watch his step.

He eyed his watch again, and made his apologies to Stephen Fellows, a team mate from the previous season.

'Back in a minute, Steve,' he said. 'If the doors open save me a seat?'

He wandered onto the porch, and looked down the steps. Still no sign of Asif, Roger looked around and spotted Catherine Parkinson, she had just crossed the road, heading towards the steps.

'Bloody hell!' he sucked in his breath as she approached. She was wearing a denim mini skirt, tight white blouse showing much cleavage, and sandals with raised heels. She had a blue bag slung over her shoulder and gave him a broad smile as she climbed the steps.

'Maybe I'll join ASIO instead of becoming an architect,' he muttered. He was aware Catherine must be a few years older than he was, probably middle or late twenties, but her choice of clothing made her look late teenage/early twenties vintage.

'Er...G'day!'

He couldn't prevent himself scanning her from head to toe. She gave him another flashing smile that sent tremors up and down his spine.

'Will I do?' she asked brightly.

'My oath!' he answered. 'I'm honoured.'

'Thank you,' she replied. 'Any developments? Is he here yet?'

'Not yet,' said Roger. 'Should we wait out here or inside?'

'We have a man posted out here...don't look around...' she cautioned: '...and one inside, he's in there now. He'll give me a phone call so I can wave my phone around in there. He will try to snap Asif too, as will our colleague out here when we know who he is.'

'Do you think he'll turn up?' asked Roger. 'In view of what they're planning ...!'

'Don't ever refer to that, not even obliquely or even to one of us,' warned Catherine. 'There's many a slip...! But in answer to your question, I'd say yes. Normality will probably be preserved.'

'Let's go in then.'

Catherine created a sensation when they walked into the foyer, she held Roger's hand, much to his pleasure, and some embarrassment. He was aware of heads turning as they entered.

'Steve! This is er...!'

'Catherine,' supplied Catherine. 'Pleased to meet you, Steve.'

Conversation ceased initially as two others, who had joined Stephen Fellows after Roger previously left him, were also shuffling their feet. Roger introduced them and Catherine took charge of the conversation. She had three brothers, was well versed in all sports and had much knowledge of racing cars as well so she was able to hold her own in mixed or male company. She began talking about cricket and Formula I racing and from then on conversation was easy. She had also had a crash course in American baseball from Joseph Carter, with emphasis on the Cleveland Guardians, and knew all about the current World Series currently entering its final stages.

Dean Hateley had surreptitiously entered the hallway and was hovering modestly near the doorway, wearing a polo shirt and denims and didn't look out of place. He was studying the racing page of the daily newspaper and avoided contact with anyone. Apart from a brief exchange of glances with Catherine they had no further eye contact. Nevertheless, he watched her, it had been arranged for Roger Richardson to tip off Catherine when Asif appeared, then she would give Dean Hateley the nod. Dean wore an earpiece and had a microphone attached to the inside of his polo shirt; he was in constant communication with Jim Waters outside.

The doors to the meeting room opened and people began to leave the hallway and drift in, a few remained chatting. Dean Hateley began to worry, if Asif didn't show up today's operation would be a waste of time. He looked out of the main door; two young Asians were climbing the steps.

'Two possibles approaching,' he muttered which was picked up by Jim Waters and Catherine, who had an earpiece in her left ear, well hidden by her hair.

''I see them,' was Waters' response. 'Already snapped them just in case.'

Roger and Catherine likewise had a problem, Stephen Fellows was itching to enter the meeting room and plainly expected Roger to follow suit. Catherine caught hold of Roger and administered a peck on his cheek, and hissed in his ear.

'You'll have to go, we'll think of something! There are two likely ones coming in... take a look.'

She took a side step to the left so Roger was facing the doorway. He saw the latecomers enter, passing by a young man in denims standing near the entrance with a newspaper in one hand and mobile phone in the other. After entering, the two Asians headed for the meeting room.

'That's him, the one on the left.'

Catherine's phone rang and she answered it, setting it into camera mode.

'Attract his attention! Say hallo or something,' she whispered as they parted.

'Hi Asif!' Roger called out. 'How are things?'

The young Asian paused, looked a little surprised but nodded and smiled at Roger.

'Hallo Roger, will you be captain after today?'

'We'll see,' answered Roger. 'I'll be in shortly.'

Asif nodded again and walked into the meeting room.

'He seemed a bit distant.'

'Not really, although we had this computer deal, apart from the cricket team we don't really know each other. Being more acquaintances than friends he was probably surprised at me calling across the foyer to him. Did you get a shot?'

'Don't know yet. I'll see you later, we'll be in touch. Hope you make captain!'

'Thanks, not so sure I want it, if games are won it's because of brilliant batting or bowling by someone else, if lost it's always the captain's fault.'

'That's life,' smiled Catherine. 'Prime Ministers have the same problem. Who was the other one?'

'Not sure, I've seen him before, he was in the second eleven last season.'

'See if you can find out.'

'Will do, but have to go now. I'll see you again I presume,' Roger made to shake her by the hand, but Catherine pulled him over to her.

'We're supposed to be an item, you idiot,' she hissed. 'Items don't shake hands. They kiss or at least give a peck!'

'A pleasure,' Roger chuckled and gave her a dutiful peck. 'How was that?'

'You need to practice,' Catherine commented and Roger chuckled.

'I'll take lessons.'

She gave his hand a squeeze and took her leave. Roger entered the meeting room but remembered to turn and give her a wave as he did so. Dean Hateley had already left and was sitting on a wall outside.

'Jim's over the road,' he said. 'In that café, head for it and I'll follow.'

Jim Waters was at a table next to the window, he smiled as Catherine entered and indicated a cup of coffee.

'Black, no sugar,' he said. 'Any joy?'

'I'll tell you in a minute,' she manipulated her phone, eyed the screen and bit her lip.

'The light wasn't brilliant in there, but he's probably recognisable on this,' she said.

Dean Hateley arrived and moved over to the table.

'How did you go?' he asked.

'It could have been better,' said Catherine.

'I got a shot as they came up the steps. I didn't know for certain but thought it a fair bet he was one of them,' Dean began pressing his keypad. 'How's this?'

Catherine looked at it and gave a brief nod.

'Brilliant,' she said. 'The light and angle of the sun was just right.'

'I used the camera to get a long distance shot of them. Which one is it?' Jim Waters held out his hand for Dean's mobile phone.

'The one on the left.'

'Let me have a look, maybe I can lock onto him and take another shot when he comes out. Who's the other one?'

'We don't know yet, Roger isn't sure either, but he recognised him as a second eleven player last season. Be useful if we can get another shot of the two of them.'

Catherine drank her coffee and stood up.

'I'll send my shot back to John Edmonds so he can get it into the system.'

'Take this as well, Catherine,' Jim Waters handed her the memory stick from his small digital camera. 'It's come out well. I've got another memory stick here, I'll see if I can snap him again when he comes out.'

*

Waters stationed himself outside the meeting building while Dean Hateley, after transmitting his photo to John Edmonds, stayed in the café across the street. The meeting had ended and participants were trickling out, a trickle that soon became a flood. Of Roger Richardson there was no sign, but Asif and his companion re-appeared, which enabled Waters to take three or four more shots of them as they descended the steps. They walked down the street together with Waters about 50 metres behind. Dean Hateley swallowed his coffee and followed suit on the other side of the street.

He activated his radio and gave Waters a test call.

'Are you receiving, Jim?'

'Loud and clear!'

'I have them and you in full view.'

'Over and out.'

*

Catherine reached the South Melbourne field office and was with John Edmonds, who had downloaded Dean's photograph of Asif onto the computer system. A call came through on her mobile, it was Roger Richardson.

'Just a quickie, Catherine,' he said. 'The name of his companion is Rafit Qadri, I'm trying to find out more about him, I'll be in touch.'

'How do you spell it?'

Roger did so and stressed there was a 'Q' in it.

'Thanks Roger, keep in touch.'

She had no sooner disconnected the call when another came through, this time from Dean Hateley.

Where are you now?' asked Catherine.

'Just about to board a 64 tram,' said Dean. 'Jim's already aboard the No: 6 tram in front. I missed it...couldn't cross the road in time. The two routes run together down St Kilda Road for part of the way.'

'Looks as if Roger was right, he thought Asif lived in Prahran or Windsor.'

'The tram's drawing up, I'll have to go. See you later.'

*

Griffiths was driving towards Richmond when his phone rang, it was Alec Oliver.

'Where are you, Alec?'

'Back outside the apartment house in Prahran,' answered Oliver. 'The squad car has just left, I have a good position in a laundrette across the street, I'm on the window seat.'

'Keep in touch,' ordered Griffiths. He turned to Martin Southern in the passenger seat. 'What cover have you got at Richmond?'

'Enough,' answered Southern. 'The house is a terraced type. God knows how many people are living there. There's a tram stop over the road, and a few shops nearby.'

'I'll drop you on the corner, see if you can find Bill Dempsey, I'll be in the side street.'

After Griffiths dropped him Martin Southern walked towards the house under observation. Griffiths sighted Bill Dempsey just before he pulled into the side street.

'We'll do that next vehicle address when Bill arrives,' he said to Donald Taylor in the back seat. 'What was the address?'

'Somewhere in Windsor, or Prahran,' Taylor thumbed through the street directory. 'It's off Chapel Street somewhere. Another bloody false alarm I suppose!'

'The joys of police work,' said Griffiths dryly. 'Excitement is about 2%, the rest is sheer boredom. You can't believe all you read in the papers or see on television.'

'When this caper's over, I'll also assume everyone who's arrested is innocent!' Taylor retorted with feeling and Griffiths chuckled. He opened the door for Bill Dempsey who clambered in.

'A fruitless day?' asked Griffiths.

'Fruitless and bloody boring,' growled Dempsey. 'What now?'

'We just make a quick call at Windsor then go back to St Kilda Road.'

'Good, I could do with a cuppa.'

*

Dean Hateley left the tram and watched the leading tram bearing Jim Waters and the two he was following recede in the distance. He had hoped he could jump out of his tram and run for the other when they both stopped, but the distance between them, before Jim's tram deviated onto a track on the left, was too great. He sighed and pulled out his mobile.

'I'm stranded on St Kilda Road,' he announced to Joseph Carter. 'What now? You want me to head for the office or stay put?'

'Where's Jim?'

'On a No: 6 tram. It turned off down High Street in the direction of Glen Iris.'

'Stay there, we'll pick you up. You're on the junction of St Kilda Road and High Street are you?'

'Yes.'

'Stay put,' ordered Carter, 'Don't worry about Jim, if they split he'll stick with Asif.'

*

'That's the address given,' said Griffiths. 'Any signs of the vehicle?'

He drove past the address and they all viewed it.

'There might be a garage round the back, let's have a look.'

Griffiths took the next right, and then right again. They parked in a narrow street, a fairly quiet backwater with bollards, a chicane and a few speed bumps installed by the local council to prevent speeding. They left the car and entered an alleyway between two houses, another alley crossed it at right angles.

'There's the house,' said Dempsey. 'I'd recognise that shit coloured paint anywhere.'

'Can you see over that fence, Bill?' Griffiths asked Dempsey, who was well over six feet tall. Dempsey shook his head.

'Nope!' he replied. 'But there's a gap in the fence just there, maybe dwarfs like you could see through it.'

Griffiths grinned as he sidled up to the fence and applied his eye to it.

'Eureka!' he said. 'There's a blue Commodore in the yard.'

He turned to Bill Dempsey.

'I'll take the car round to the front and park across the street opposite the front door. Bill, you stay in it with the camera on full zoom and take as many shots as you can while I'm on the doorstep,' he turned to Taylor. 'And you, Donald, use the field glasses and see if you recognise whoever comes to the door.'

Griffiths drove around to the front and parked across the street outside a laundrette.

'This is a no parking area,' commented Taylor.

'I'm shaking in my shoes!' Griffiths said sourly. 'Are we ready?'

*

Jim Waters left the tram and allowed the two men to get well ahead before he moved after them. They turned into a side street and Waters followed, taking cover in an alleyway at the rear of the houses. He saw them turn right into another street. Waters reached the corner and peered around it.

The two men were walking along slowly, they looked around and Waters, in full view, cursed his luck. He continued walking at a fast rate, but they took little interest in him, they merely checked for approaching traffic before crossing the street.

Waters continued on, he was catching up but dared not slacken pace or stop, which could attract attention. The other two continued walking and so did Waters. He paused as if unsure of his actual position, but didn't dare linger for long, a prolonged stoppage could arouse suspicion. Waters eyed Asif and his companion again and with rising excitement saw them turn into the front gate of a terraced house and walk up the short drive to the front door.

'Looks as if we're home!' he said to himself. 'Bloody Goodoh!'

Fortunately, there was a laundrette nearly opposite the house, Waters entered it, intending to use his mobile phone. The window seat was taken by a youngish man sitting looking out onto the street. He looked up as Waters came in, eyed him closely, then recommenced staring outside.

A car came up and drew to a halt outside the laundrette, the driver got out, leaving two men in the car. He had words with his two companions and crossed the street. The man on the window seat produced a mobile phone and began talking.

Waters decided this was as good a time as any, there were very few customers in the laundrette, a young woman sat reading a magazine near the back, while another was idly watching her washing go round and round. He dialled a number on his mobile and retreated to the rear end of the laundrette.

'Waters!' he said sotto voce. 'Joe?'

'Where are you?'

'In a laundrette opposite the house where they went in...' Waters answered and gave the address of both. 'There's a car outside, it looks as though they're calling on the house. I've got the rego.'

'Good man!' said Joe Carter. 'Dave McKay says to stay there and he'll give Ted Griffiths a bell. Have you got anything that needs washing?'

*

Jim Waters took a seat and picked up one of the magazines. Another two women entered with laundry baskets and commenced filling two of the washing machines, he felt better with newcomers than with the woman who was already there. She would know he'd just walked in, sat down and done nothing else but the newcomers would assume he had washing somewhere. He watched the house over the road, the driver of the car was at the front door talking with the occupant but he didn't look like either Asif or his companion.

The man on the window seat got up and left, walked a short distance up the street, one of the occupants of the car got out and walked in the same direction. Waters advanced to the window and looked up and down the street but couldn't see either of them.

He went back and picked up his magazine again, from his seat along the side of the laundrette he had a good view of the house. The driver of the car had left the house and was climbing back into the car. He sat in the driver's seat with a mobile phone to his ear. His erstwhile passenger returned, climbed into the front passenger seat and there was a brief conversation. The passenger then made a call on his mobile phone.

He was still talking when the driver finished his call and the car drove off, leaving Waters with a clearer view of the house opposite. He was mildly amused to see a traffic warden had started to cross the street towards the vehicle before it took off. The warden had just stepped off the pavement when the car moved away. He hesitated, shrugged and returned to the opposite side of the street.

'Hard luck mate!' muttered Waters. 'That's one that got away.'

He wondered who they could have been since they had called at the house he was watching. He heard the door to the laundrette open and close which caused a slight draught. The window seat man had returned, he looked around the laundrette, then slowly ambled around the opposite side of the laundrette, reached the back wall, then came over to Waters. Waters tensed, and slowly looked up from his magazine.

The other man nodded pleasantly and gave a half smile. Waters eyed him guardedly and wondered if trouble was in the vicinity. The other man spoke.

'Jim Waters?' he asked.

'Who's asking?'

'Alec Oliver, Victorian Police,' the other produced his warrant card. He inclined his head at the window overlooking the street and the house opposite. 'I've just had a call from my boss, who's been speaking to your boss. I think we have a common interest.'

CHAPTER 22

'**B**it wild and woolly around this area,' Shackleton commented as they drove down the main road towards Flinders Creek. 'Plenty of agricultural land, it's a likely place for fertiliser.'

Bramble didn't answer; he was studying the map on his lap. He traced his finger down the line of the main road they were on and marked the point with a pencil.

'We're nearly there,' he said. 'There must be an access road leading to it on the right.'

A road led off to the left, he noted the name and referred to the map again.

'I'd say it's between that road we just passed, and where the road goes into double track ...what's that? Over there, on the right!'

Shackleton drew in by the roadside, they examined the gate and driveway on the opposite side.

'Apsley Farm,' Bramble said. 'This must be the place.'

Shackleton did a three point turn and parked outside the gateway.

'The fertiliser purchase was made by someone named Bentley,' said Bramble.' I gather he recently purchased the place. How do you feel about creeping around in the dark tonight?'

'Just hope there's no snakes and they don't have dogs.'

'We'll find out in due course. There's a lane further on, we'll take a trip down it. We may be able to view the property from there.'

*

'Well?' Kelsey demanded when they reported in. 'Any joy?'

'Easier than we anticipated,' said Bramble. 'We approached from a country lane down the side of the property, it's a small place, a main building and two sheds.'

'Anything in the sheds?'

'Nothing, we managed to get into both of them, they weren't very well secured. The house was well away from them, there was a light in one of the rooms at the rear, but no activity and no dogs. We went through them both thoroughly, just rusted farming implements and a few old sacks with stuff in them, but not what we're looking for. The whole place looks run down. Whatever they're doing there, it's not farming nor any form of husbandry.'

'Are you sure of that?'

'We had a look around the general landscape in daylight, that particular stretch of land hasn't seen a plough in years.'

'Send a written report,' said Kelsey. 'I suggest you both stay tonight in that area. We'll be in touch.'

*

The next day a conference was held in the Police complex at St Kilda Road. Alan Kelsey had flown in from Canberra. It was headed by Superintendent Clucas. Also present were Chief Inspector Talintyre, David McKay, Ted Griffiths, Sam Stannington, Catherine Parkinson, Joseph Carter and John Edmonds.

'We've struck gold, I gather,' said Clucas.

'Apparently so,' Kelsey nodded. 'After a most frustrating exercise by Dave McKay and Catherine Parkinson. They had various leads, exhausted most of them and got precisely nowhere, but finally locked onto something.'

'We all did, sir,' said Talintyre, and turned to Griffiths. 'It seems we all struck the lode at the same time.'

'We approached this house in Prahran from three different directions, sir. All at the same time,' Griffiths turned to Clucas

'I don't follow,' Clucas looked bemused.

Griffiths dealt with the initial arrest of Taylor, the realisation he was innocent of murder, but his retention as a witness. He explained how ASIO were brought into the picture when Taylor's discs came to light. He continued on with the apparent release of Taylor, in reality Cope.

'Bit risky...for Cope,' commented Clucas.

'He was well covered, sir,' replied Griffiths.

'All right, what happened after that?'

Griffiths went through all aspects of the investigation, supplemented by Kelsey who dealt with the tracking of Asif after Alex Richardson had tipped them off that there was another computer in the chain.

'You say three lines of enquiry all converged at once?'

'We all met in a laundrette,' Griffiths said ironically. 'It was like a gathering of the clans.'

'One question,' said Clucas. 'How would the terrorists, or Asif in particular, know the computer hadn't been cleared?'

'The same point had occurred to us,' replied Kelsey.

'I can answer that?' John Edmonds spoke up. 'Simmerson made the computer exchange and transferred the data on the main C drive over to Asif's new computer, Roger Richardson's old one. What he didn't know, or maybe in his rush he forgot, was that Asif had a partitioned drive on his computer, which were designated 'C' and 'D' drive.'

'Why two drives?' asked Clucas.

'No idea, but that's how it was. Maybe Asif thought it more secure to keep everyday stuff on 'C' and undercover stuff separately on 'D'. But it appears Simmerson downloaded or transferred most of or all the 'C' drive data onto what became Asif's new computer, but omitted to transfer the "D" drive. I'm saying most of it, because some of Asif's engineering data still remained on the computer Taylor inherited,' said Edmonds.

'So when Asif booted up his new computer, he couldn't find the data relating to Melbourne Central or the bomb making, there was only university material, the engineering stuff,' Clucas concluded.

'He probably panicked when he realised all the compromising data could still be sitting on the computer Simmerson had taken away,' added Kelsey

'So they tracked Simmerson, easy enough, they knew where he worked. If he was doing this last job on his own account, he may even have given Asif his home address should there be any problems. When they realised what had happened, they contacted him and found where he'd offloaded it,' said Griffiths.

'Where's Simmerson now?' Clucas looked at Talintyre.

'We don't know, sir,' said Talintyre. 'He's vanished. That's why it took so long to exploit this lead, he's vanished without trace. I'd say it's not voluntary and we fear for his safety. His girl-friend has heard nothing and doesn't know where he is.'

'Where are we at now?' asked Clucas.

'We've posted surveillance outside the house at Prahran, also the house at Richmond where we tracked the first stalker who was watching Constable Cope,' said Talintyre. 'We've also investigated reports of purchases from various agricultural merchants in Victoria. We followed them up and most were valid. We had our doubts about one in Gippsland, a large consignment of ammonium nitrate was ordered for a farming property down there.'

'Two of our operatives had a look at the property; it's run down, mainly residential and certainly not under the plough,' said Kelsey. 'They had a look in the barn, but there's nothing there. This stuff has vanished into thin air.'

'Who owns the farm?' asked Clucas.

'Name of Bentley,' said Griffiths. 'We don't know much about him. He recently bought the property. We asked neighbours but they've never seen him, properties in that area are isolated from each other. The former owner was a fellow named Edwin Apsley, he'd been there for years and died a year or so back.'

'Have we got a watch on the place?'

'Two of our men are doing that,' said Kelsey. 'So far there's nothing!'

'We're running a check on Bentley,' said Talintyre. 'We've found the real estate agent responsible for the sale.'

'Leave that with us if that's OK with you,' said Kelsey. 'We've got two men down there already looking over the Bentley property. They may as well earn their keep.'

CHAPTER 23

Bramble and Shackleton paused outside the real estate agency in Traralgon and examined the placards and photographs in the window.

'Anything you fancy, Denis?' asked Bramble.

'That one looks good,' said Shackleton. 'In-ground swimming pool, tennis court, veranda and air conditioning throughout, standing in 5 acres.'

'A bit beyond an intelligence agent's pay,' sniffed Bramble. 'This old shack on the bottom row is more in your line.'

They entered and advanced to the counter. Bramble addressed the young receptionist.

'We need to speak with the manager, is it Mr...Ingram?' Bramble hesitated as he asked the question. He had seen the name on the facia outside but wanted to make sure.

'Yes,' the girl answered. 'Do you have an appointment?'

Bramble shook his head.

'No, but we'd like a word with him if possible.'

'Which property are we talking about?' she asked.

'It's about the small farm property off the Princes Highway, near Flynns Creek.'

'Oh, that one is already sold, but...!'

'We know, but we'd like to speak to Mr Ingram about it.'

She began to look quizzical and wary, Bramble realised with the two of them leaning over the counter they could appear intimidating; in addition, he was perhaps being a little abrupt. Bramble waved Shackleton away and adopted a winning smile.

'My name is Bramble, Robert Bramble,' he said. 'We are attached to the police. We need to speak to Mr Ingram about that property.'

'The police!' the girl's demeanour changed. 'Oh! I'll fetch Mr Ingram.'

She disappeared and returned within minutes.

'He'll be with you shortly. He's on the phone but I slipped a note in front of him. He won't be long.'

Presumably Ingram cut his phone call short when he read her note. He left his office and came around the counter.

'Rolf Ingram,' he extended his hand to Bramble.' You're Mr Bramble?'

'Yes, this is Denis Shackleton. We're making enquiries about a deal you transacted recently. Can we talk in private?'

Ingram led them to his office. He was fortyish, cropped dark hair and of athletic build. He wore cavalry twill trousers and a sports jacket, smart but casual, in keeping with the country town image.

'What's this about?' he asked.

'We're enquiring about the property at Flynns Creek, or near it. You sold it to a Mr Bentley.'

'Yes, I remember that one, strange business.'

'Why strange?'

'The Bentley family live locally at a small place called Glengarry. The purchase was made by their son.'

'Did he pay in full or by mortgage?'

'It was paid in full, which puzzled me. He and his family are not on good terms, a case of a son being a bit rebellious and I tend to believe he's got into some strange company.'

'Like who?' Shackleton enquired.

'I think you'd better ask them, his parents. What I've said, or know, could probably be hearsay. I'm fairly sure it's right but ...' he spread out his hands '...you should ask them. What I say could come into the sphere of gossip. I know the family, not well, but their family and mine have been living here for years.'

He moved to his computer and did some keying in.

'Here we are,' he said. 'We did another transaction for their daughter a couple of years back. She bought a property near Moondarra. No problems with that one, she married an accountant from Dandenong. I have the parents' address here.' He wrote on his pad and handed it to Bramble.

'You say the purchase of the Flinders Creek property was odd?' asked Bramble.

'Yes,' Ingram replied. 'What I do know is the son never appeared to hold down a job, yet he appeared here with the money when we put it on the market. I do know he had no help from his parents.'

'Why? Are they not on good terms?'

'Sometimes there is conflict between parents and offspring, it happens. But I think this one had something to do with religion. The Bentley family, the parents at any rate, are staunchly Catholic, the son rebelled, that's all I know.'

'I see,' Bramble began to have an inkling of what it could be. 'Very well, we'll go and see the Bentley family. Thanks for your help. Do you have a phone number for them?'

*

They reached the gateway of the Bentley small-holding, there was a five barred gate and the track wound away behind some trees. Shackleton climbed out and opened the gate, Bramble drove through while Shackleton closed the gate before re-entering the car.

'I see what Ingram meant,' Shackleton indicated a small shrine just off the track near the gate.

'What is it?' Bramble swivelled his head around. 'Oh, I see now, yes, you're right.'

They left the small statuette of the saint behind them as they motored slowly up the track. They rounded the bend, there was a house 100 metres further on. Bramble drove slowly through another gate, open this time, and they entered a short driveway.

'Impressive!' Bramble said approvingly as they left the car and looked around. The front part of the house looked to be of 1920s vintage with an impressive tiled porch. The front portion of the dwelling was single storey, what was clearly a subsequent two storey addition rose behind it. Another addition to the structure was tacked onto the right-hand side of the property, with a large window and veranda.

'Bloody hell!' said Shackleton. 'This is the sort of property my wife thought I owned when I married her!'

'You mean the sort of place your mother-in-law expected for her daughter!' added Bramble. 'I know the feeling!'

Mr Bentley appeared in the doorway and advanced towards them. He was bearded, about middle fifties, red faced and roughly 5' 10" in height. He wore working clothes and was wiping his hands on a piece of cloth; clearly in the middle of a job.

'Mr Bramble?' he extended his hand. 'Percy Bentley.'

'G'day!' said Bramble and introduced Shackleton.

'You wanted to see me about my son, I believe. Is he in trouble?'

'Not as far as we know, but we need to ask a few questions.'

'You'd better come in,' Bentley turned on his heel and waved an arm towards the house. 'You say you're from the police? Are you from the local station?'

'No,' said Bramble as they entered the hall, then a sitting room. 'We're not exactly from the police, certainly not the local police. They won't know we're here, but the police at St Kilda Road in Melbourne are aware of our presence here.'

He produced his identity.

'Intelligence from Canberra?' Bentley peered at it and looked quizzical. 'What's this, secret service?'

'ASIO,' corrected Bramble. 'We believe we may have a problem with your son.'

'With my son? Now why does that not surprise me?'

It was Bramble's turn to look quizzical, but he began to explain the situation as well as he could without giving away too much. He was obliged to mention they were pursuing a terrorist threat but didn't specify it. Bentley listened intently and then broke in.

'How is my son involved?'

'A considerable amount of ammonium nitrate was ordered by your son, or in his name, and delivered to the Flynns Creek property. It isn't there now and from what we've seen of the place it's very run down and certainly no fertiliser has been ploughed in there.'

'And ammonium nitrate is an ingredient for explosives,' Bentley commented.

'Ah, you know that?'

'I read the papers, wasn't that the stuff used in that bomb blast in Oklahoma City many years back?'

'Yes,' Bramble nodded. 'We heard that all is not...um...well between you and your son. Can we ask why?'

Bentley sat back and meshed his fingers together.

'Where is this questioning leading?' he began, then virtually answered it himself. 'You are saying you believe my son is involved in a possible bomb plot?'

'We think it's possible.'

'Oh God!

Bentley sat forward with his hands on his cheeks and began shaking his head.

'Let me explain,' he said. 'I have reason to believe my son Micah has allowed himself to be led astray, to be misled, that is my view. Let me start from the beginning.'

Bentley spoke at length, Shackleton and Bramble listened without interruption. As a story, it ran to a not unfamiliar pattern. Bentley and his wife were both brought up in strict Catholic homes. When they married and their children were born, they followed the same path as their parents and brought up their son and daughter very strictly in the Catholic faith.

As the two children entered teenage, conflict began with both of them. They both attended university, took science degrees and began to question Catholicism and all religious dogma generally which brought about dissension within the family. Finally, after protracted, furious differences of opinion, the daughter left home and entered into a de facto relationship with a young accountant from Dandenong who was running his own practice. Bentley and his wife had made overtures to suggest, firstly, that their daughter's partner, who subsequently became her husband, convert to Catholicism, which was pointedly rejected, and secondly that their grandchildren be brought up in the faith, which had a similar reaction.

The rift still persisted, the daughter lived in a small

settlement not too far distant but they were not on good terms and didn't see much of each other. She had not adopted any other faith. Her husband was nominally from a Protestant family but his beliefs were his own and tended towards the agnostic. The Bentley daughter tended to go the same way and shunned religion altogether.

The son presented more of a problem to the Bentleys, at university he had met a girl, a Protestant, and had been going out with her for months. The girl had finally broken it off, presumably weary of incessant probing from the Bentley parents as to when she was going to convert to Rome. After a fierce confrontation one day she never returned, and was apparently now in Sydney. Then Micah, resentful at the treatment and loss of his former girl-friend, had met a woman of the Muslim faith, also at the university, and after a lengthy period had defiantly announced his intention of marrying her. What made the situation worse than the dispute with their daughter, was that Micah stated his intention of converting to Islam, and had done so. Worse, it appeared the girl was from a particularly fanatical sect with connections that alarmed Mr and Mrs Bentley. Further, their son appeared to have enthusiastically embraced his new faith and to have adopted the fanatical stance of his partner's family.

During Mr Bentley's discourse his wife offered them refreshment, they accepted with grace offers of coffee, then Mrs Bentley joined them. It seemed from interjections she made that her religious fervour was even more pronounced than her husband's. Apparently, the son had left home in a huff and Bramble could understand why. The son had abandoned his studies, adopted his newfound religion with fervour and enthusiasm, then moved with his new wife to the property at Flynns Creek.

'Yes, we know about that property, we know where it is.' Bramble said as Mr Bentley paused, but didn't mention they'd already entered it and been snooping around.

'I don't know how they could afford it, it isn't a very grand property, but it must have been costly, I don't know where he got the money unless his...wife...!' he ground out the title through gritted teeth '...or her sect, had resources.'

'What's your son doing now?'

'I don't know, Micah seems to spend much of his time on the property as far as I know. We went there once, to try reconciliation, but there were several people there, mainly Asians, I didn't know who they were. We were not made welcome so we left.'

'He's not working?'

'If he is, I don't know where. He's abandoned his university career altogether, a damned shame, he is not unintelligent.'

'Where's your daughter now?'

'Living in a property at Moondarra. She works in Moe at an agricultural merchant.'

'We'd like to contact her if we may.'

'Why? You don't think she has anything to do with this?'

'No,' said Bramble. 'But she may have contact with him, we need background information. We have to find the stuff he and his friends have purchased.'

'I'll give you her phone number, but she'll be working during the day at Moe,' said Bentley. 'I'll give her a ring and tell her to expect you.'

He took a small pad from the coffee table and wrote down a couple of numbers.

'Thank you, we'll make contact,' Bramble stretched out his hand for the phone numbers. 'We'll be on our way and thanks for your help.'

'We are worried about our children because they have abandoned their faith, and we fear the consequences,' added Mrs Bentley. 'We pray for our son and daughter every night.'

As they drove down the drive, Bramble turned to Shackleton.

'I can see the problems; religious fanaticism must be difficult to live with.'

'Yet the son appears to have taken rebellion to another level by adopting another religion,' said Shackleton. 'Like a man whose house is falling down, when he abandons it, he has to seek shelter elsewhere.'

'You're full of bullshit, aren't you?' snorted Bramble. He waited as Shackleton opened and closed the gate, drove through and waited as Shackleton got back in. 'But bullshit or not, you're right. Converts can be the worst! One of the London Underground bombers was a convert, and convinced himself it was quite logical to blow up himself and many innocent fellow citizens with him.'

'It seems to me, if you have a problem, in this case religion, it won't be solved by taking on another,' mused Shackleton. 'You merely take on another but similar problem.'

'For once I don't disagree with you,' said Bramble.

'What do you reckon now?'

'I'm curious to see the daughter, but I reckon we'll need a warrant for the Flynns Creek property.'

'We've drawn a blank up to now. We had a good snoop around, we know the stuff was delivered there initially, but where the hell is it now?'

'Maybe the daughter has some idea; she could be on speaking terms with her brother.'

*

They arrived outside the agricultural merchant in Moe. Bramble found a small car park off the street and drove into it.

'Why didn't you park in the street?'

'Look!' Bramble pointed as he locked the doors. 'Country towns are the worst for drumming up revenue, there's two bloody traffic wardens just salivating. Put some dollars in this machine'

Shackleton grimaced, did so and they walked up the street.

'I'll do the talking,' said Bramble.

'Oh, you're in charge, are you? Carry on oh gracious leader.'

Bramble muttered under his breath as they entered. A bald-headed man behind the counter looked up.

'Good morning gents. Can I help you?'

'We'd like to speak to Mrs Lewin please.'

'Who shall I say?'

'Robert Bramble and Denis Shackleton, she should be expecting us, her father may have rung earlier on.'

'Hold on.'

When Mrs Lewin appeared, she didn't look too pleased, in fact she looked positively hostile. Bramble wasn't prepared for this, and wondered if her hostility emanated from her father's previous call to her.

'What does my father want now?' she asked which confirmed Bramble's assumption.

'He doesn't,' Bramble replied patiently. 'It's us who wish to see you, if we may.'

'Why? If this is to do with the church…!'

Bramble gathered the paternal conversation must have been very abrupt. He wondered if Bentley had got as far as explaining who they were, or whether he'd been tempted to touch on religion during the conversation. She obviously thought they were members of the church coming to save her soul. He decided to clarify their identity.

'We are nothing to do with any church. We're attached to law enforcement,' he said. 'Is there anywhere we can talk?'

'Law enforcement?' she looked startled. 'What sort of enforcement are we talking about?'

Again, Bramble was startled by the question. For the first time, he subjected her to a close examination. He thought her a very attractive young woman, dark-haired and stylishly dressed, well made up; her hair expertly coiffured. He thought back to Mrs Bentley, stern and forbidding with her hair drawn back in a severe bun. Mrs Lewin clearly still harboured suspicions they were the heavy squad from the church. He sighed, produced his ID and motioned to Shackleton to do the same.

'Intelligence?' some of her hostility evaporated and she said again. 'Intelligence? Why do you want to see me? Police intelligence...wait! You're not from the police?'

'Not exactly,' Bramble explained. 'We are from Canberra.'

'Canberra? You mean Secret service...ASIO?'

Bramble held up his hand, looked around and shook his head, not in a negative fashion but more as a request for discretion. He motioned her over to the shop front window, well away from the man behind the counter, who was on the phone.

'Yes, ASIO,' he said. 'We are pursuing enquiries relating to national security. We need to talk. Is there an interview room or should we go outside?'

She raised her eyebrows, then turned to the man at the counter, still on the phone, and waggled her fingers in front of him.

'Back in a few minutes, Eric,' she said, he nodded and waved a hand in response. She opened the main door into the street and preceded them around the side of the building into the nearby car park, where several cars, including their own, were parked. She led them to a parked Toyota and eased her posterior against the bonnet.

'Why me?' she asked. 'I know nothing about security or anything that can affect it.'

'You don't get on well with your parents, do you?"

'Is that a question?'

'No, it's an observation. You don't have to answer it, maybe you don't need to.'

That broke the ice. Her face creased into a smile and she broke into laughter.

'I guess you are detectives ...of a sort,' she said. 'Is it that obvious?'

'A little! They're praying for you every night,' Shackleton interceded and she laughed again.

'Why does that not surprise me?' she smiled. 'So what do you want from me?'

'Discretion first of all,' said Bramble. 'We need information, or rather, we shall be asking for information which you may or may not possess. It relates to your brother; we believe he may be on a course of action that could jeopardise national security.'

'How could Macca have anything to do with that?'

'Macca?'

'Mac...my brother!'

'Your parents referred to him as Micah.'

'Micah Abraham Christian, 'Mrs Lewin said bitterly. 'They christened me Rebecca Ruth but I prefer to be called Beckie. Macca always hated his names. They gave him hell at school so he insisted on being called Mac or Macca, a play on initials.'

Bramble nodded sympathetically. He began even more to understand why the two of them were estranged from their parents.

'You haven't answered my question,' she said.

'No, I haven't,' agreed Bramble. 'We need your assurance that anything we tell you goes no further.'

'All right, but just tell me what Macca has done...! Oh bloody hell! Is it anything to do with that damned wife of his, his conversion ...being a Muslim?'

'Regrettably yes, it is. We have reason to believe he's taken delivery of a large quantity of ammonium nitrate for his country property at Flynns Creek, and that he and the people with whom he is associating are not intending to use it as fertiliser.'

'Oh God! The stupid bloody prat!' She clapped her hands to her forehead. 'It's that bloody cow he married; I knew no good would come of it. That bitch is a fanatic and so are all her damned family.'

'Fanatic, what sort of fanatic?'

'Oh, wearing the burka, praying five times a day, attending a mosque which is run by some extreme imam or sheik. I've had many fights with Mac about that bloody woman. It was my parents' fault, some years back he started going out with a girl from Warragul named Celia. She was nice and I liked her. They objected to her because she was nominally Protestant, but she wasn't overtly religious! How stupid can you get? They are all supposed to be Christians. They were most unpleasant to her and finally she told Mac to forget it, she reckoned marriage would result in incessant sniping from my parents.'

'What happened to her?'

'She met someone else and married him. She lives in Sydney now.'

'How did your parents' religious fervour affect you? Did you marry a Catholic?'

'The hell I did! Bruce...my husband...is nothing. He belongs to no organised religion, and neither do I. I don't have contact with my parents, except a card at Christmas, and I won't have any regular contact until they modify a little. But Mac was embittered by the whole experience, he really loved Celia, I think he still does. I can't blame him for that, she was a really nice type, I got on well with her. Then he met some Muslim man at university and this...this woman is his sister. Mac converted to Islam and he's become extreme in his views, he's taking his lead from her. What you've told me is horrifying, but I can believe it, it's a form of pay back for Mum and Dad.'

'He bought that property at Flynns Creek, where would he have got the money?'

'From them, not the family necessarily, but the group he's mixed up with. I told him to get out, they were nothing but trouble. That caused a terrible row.'

'Group? What group?'

'Relatives and friends of his wife and other connections. He's very much under their spell...being led by the nose, bloody idiot!'

'Where? Are they at Flynns Creek as well?'

'No, they're at a place between Warragul and Drouin somewhere, they have a property out on a limb, her parents own it. There's a group of them living or working there.'

'You don't know where, do you or their names?'

'Razza or something like that, I'm trying to think, no it's Razzaq, with a Q on the end. It's near Drouin, bit off the beaten track.'

'Do you know them at all...have any contact?'

'No fear! I have enough trouble with radical Christi - bloody - anity without getting involved with Islamic fundamentalists, thank you very much!'

Bramble and Shackleton found themselves grinning at her forceful mode of speech.

'You referred to them as a group,' said Shackleton. 'Are they purely family or is it a political or religious grouping?'

'Well ...!' Mrs Lewin considered. 'I'd say more the latter. More a grouping than a family, but my sister-in-law's family...' she wrinkled her nose: '...are probably the central core, her parents and a younger sister. I don't know much about them, nor do I want to!'

'Is it a private house, on an estate or is it a farming property?'

'Bit of both, I'd say. It's off the beaten track, stands in its own grounds with a few sheds around it. I went there once, when Mac first got engaged to this cow. I can show it to you on a map if you like, but it's some time since I went there, for the first and last time.'

'Come to our car, it's in this car park, we've got a map in there,' said Bramble.

They walked to the car and Bramble produced the map. They pored over it; Mrs Lewin traced her finger along the main highway and finally pointed.

'That's about it, it's around that area there,' she said.

'We'll see if we can locate it,' said Bramble. 'You've been very helpful, Mrs Lewin.'

'Call me Beckie,' she said. 'I hope you find what you want.'

'OK Beckie,' said Bramble. 'But if we don't, we may need you to point it out to us, if you can remember where it is.'

'I'll remember it,' she said grimly. 'I can remember looking back at the place as we drove away from it and saying never a-bloody-gain!'

They were all grinning broadly as they solemnly shook hands, Bramble and Shackleton climbed into the car. They drove out and took off up the main street, as they overtook her, she raised an arm in salute and they gave her a toot in passing.

'Feisty young woman,' commented Bramble as they both

waved through their respective windows.

'She's certainly got personality,' agreed Shackleton.' I can't imagine her as a devout worshipper accepting everything without question.'

'Intriguing the way she fits swear words into the middle of words,' commented Bramble.

'Fasci - bloody – nating!' agreed Shackleton.

CHAPTER 24

Kelsey was occupying Joseph Carter's desk at South Melbourne when Bramble came through. He reached for a pen and pad and flicked the switch to record the conversation. He beckoned to McKay and Catherine Parkinson through the glass partition.

Kelsey completed his conversation with Bramble, and signed off with 'Hang on there and I'll get back to you. Have a look by all means, if you find it, but don't go up the track. Got that?'

He replaced the phone and sat back.

'That was Bob and Denis, as you probably guessed,' he said. 'We're getting more into the heart of things, I think. Apparently, Bentley is a Muslim convert and seems to be involved with a fundamentalist grouping. In addition, there's another property in the Drouin area where Bentley's wife's family and various other connections are based.'

'Why is Bentley a convert?'

Kelsey gave them a brief rundown of what Bramble and

Shackleton had discovered during their investigation

'Converts are often the most radical,' commented Catherine. 'Weren't some of the London bombers converts?'

'They were,' responded Kelsey. 'And so were David Hicks and Jihad Jack here in Australia. Seems converts need to prove themselves to the long standing faithful. I'm trying to arrange a flyover of the property, when Bob and Denis have pinpointed it but they may need assistance from Mrs Lewin. She's the Bentley's daughter and willing to help. Currently they're making enquiries in the town. We'll see what they come up with.'

'One aspect is puzzling me,' said McKay. 'What's happened to Adam Simmerson?'

'It seems they've removed him from the scene completely to prevent him contacting anyone. It's possible he was never aware of the dynamite left on that computer's hard drive, but I'd say they approached him first to find out where the computer was.'

'All they had to do was ask him.'

'Maybe, unless they just panicked and roughed him up,' suggested Kelsey.

'You reckon they've kidnapped him?'

'No doubt in my mind,' said Kelsey.

'I tend to agree in the main,' said McKay. 'But maybe the kidnapping wasn't inspired by the computer data itself. If he failed to fully download it onto Asif's new computer, that is, Roger's old one, he wouldn't have known what was on it.'

'What are you suggesting?'

'I reckon the kidnapping was inspired by Henderson's murder,' said McKay. 'If Simmerson heard about that, as inevitably he would from newspaper reports or television, and he'd already told them where the computer was, he'd put two and two together and implicate Asif and his friends. I reckon they hi-jacked him before he became a danger, worked it out and contacted police.'

'That could be,' Kelsey nodded. 'His comprehensive disappearance and that strange letter written to Gerry Parr... where is that letter by the way?'

'Ted Griffiths took control of it; they scanned it and e-mailed us a copy, John Edmonds has it on his computer somewhere,' said Carter. 'From what Parr told us; the writing was Simmerson's but the text and syntax definitely was not!'

'It seems the plan was for it to be written to stop anyone bothering to try to track him, but Simmerson was one step ahead and succeeded in passing a latent message by being erratic with spelling and grammar,' said Kelsey.

'Do you reckon he's still alive?' asked McKay.

'I hope so, he's an innocent party in this, although he landed himself in it by pulling a fast one with that trade-in computer,' Kelsey said. 'It's possible they've locked him up somewhere, until they've done what they've set out to do, then it doesn't matter if we find him or he finds us, it would be too late by then.'

'If he is being held by them, where could he be?' asked Catherine.

'We seem to have three possibilities right now, or maybe four,' Kelsey jotted notes on his pad. 'In order of discovery, we have Richmond, Prahran, Flynns Creek or now this latest address near Drouin, when Bob and Denis find out exactly where it is.'

'And this latest address may be where the ammonium nitrate is stored,' said McKay.

'Very possibly. When they find it, we'll arrange for a helicopter flyover,' said Kelsey. 'After that we'll decide what next.'

'Does Ted Griffiths know about Drouin yet?'

'No, he doesn't, thanks for reminding me. I'll ring him now,' Kelsey picked up the phone and commenced dialling.

*

'Oh...it's you two again,' Beckie Lewin gave a half smile as they stood before her shuffling their feet. 'I gather you can't find it.'

'We had two or three possibilities,' confessed Bramble. 'We need you after all to finger it for us.'

'All right, just let me have a word with Eric, how long will it take, you reckon?'

'Well...you tell us, you probably have a better idea of times and distances. If you lead us you can drive back here when you've pointed it out.'

'Makes sense,' Beckie Lewin smiled. 'Hang on while I speak to Eric, then I'll be with you.'

*

She drove ahead of them on the road to Melbourne and they kept a respectful distance behind her. They slowed down through the township of Warragul, then headed for nearby Drouin. After that she began to slow, ahead in the distance they saw two vans come out of a turning on the right which disappeared into the haze well ahead of them moving in the direction of Melbourne. Beckie Lewin drew to a halt, left her car and walked back towards them.

'Walks well,' commented Shackleton. 'She's certainly got class.'

'Keep your mind on the job...' Bramble reprimanded him. 'But you're right, she has!'

She came to their car, opened the rear door and climbed into the back seat. She pointed to a gate roughly 50 metres ahead on the righthand side of the road.

'That's the one,' she said. 'Is it one of the ones you'd earmarked?'

'One of them,' agreed Shackleton. 'We passed another one a few miles back and another one further on.'

'I know the ones you mean,' she said. 'They both look very similar now I think about it. Well...there you are, that's it.'

'Two vans just drove out of it,' commented Bramble. 'How far back is the house?'

'About half a mile, something like that, it's behind that line of bushes that starts near that bend. The house is just beyond that...and yes, two vans just came out from there.'

'Good. You've been very helpful,' said Bramble. 'Keep this under your hat for the time being, please Beckie, it's vital nothing leaks out, particularly to the press.'

'If you're going to bring that prat Mac to his senses, I'll do anything,' she said. 'All right, I'll love and leave you.'

She got out and started walking back to her own car.

'She *does* walk well, not a bad arse either!' observed Shackleton.

At this point she paused, looked fixedly over to the right, then swung around and came back, walking much faster this time.

'There! She's rumbled you. She probably sensed what you said,' commented Bramble. 'Now you're in trouble, Mr Shackleton! Deep trouble!'

'I doubt it,' Shackleton responded as they watched her progress. 'She'd take it as a compliment. I reckon she's well aware of the effect she has!'

She reached the car and leant through the passenger side window.

'Something odd going on,' she said. 'Over there, look! There's a fellow running towards the road, but he's not on the track.'

They looked. She was right.

'Yes, I see him. Bloody hell!' Bramble said tersely. 'What the hell's going on there?'

'A car's coming down from the house,' she said. 'Look, that fellow's running well away from the access track across that paddock.'

They saw the runner dive into roadside bushes and momentarily lost sight of him as a heavy truck roared past them heading for Melbourne. When he re-appeared on the roadside, he had a quick look along the road towards them, hesitated, then ran away from them westwards towards Melbourne. The car halted in a cloud of dust at the end of the drive, swung right and took off after him.

'What the hell...?'

The car caught up with the runner, who deviated from the road and plunged into the bushes, the occupants of the car got out and dived after him.

'Bloody hell, did you see that? Those two blokes were carrying side arms...!' Bramble spluttered. 'We'd better take a look at this.'

'I'll come with you,' Mrs Lewin opened the rear door and climbed into the rear seat.

'This could be dangerous,' protested Shackleton.

'We haven't time to argue,' snapped Bramble. 'They're catching up with him.'

He put his foot down and they took off like a drag racer. They roared up the highway, came to a halt alongside the stationary vehicle and piled out.

'Stay here...' Bramble rapped to Mrs Lewin: '...and I mean it, stay here!'

He and Shackleton headed into the undergrowth drawing guns, Beckie Lewin obediently stayed with the vehicle. They were just in time to see the runner caught and punched to the ground by two assailants, he fell heavily at their feet. One was an Asian, the other was European.

'The game's up, Mr Samson,' they heard him shout. 'Secure him, Naji.'

The European, his hand down by his side but holding a handgun, watched as the other man overpowered the hapless runner who looked utterly exhausted. Bramble and Shackleton approached and at this juncture the European caught sight of them for the first time. The change of expression on his face was wondrous to behold as Bramble and Shackleton, both with guns drawn, slowly emerged from the bushes and advanced towards him.

'Good afternoon,' said Bramble pleasantly. 'Would you mind dropping that gun please...*now!* Before we have a nasty accident!'

The other's eyes swivelled from side to side, obviously weighing up his chances, then realised the odds were two guns against one as his companion was still on his knees trying to secure the fugitive. The European dropped the gun, his companion still blissfully unaware they were not alone and in the act of securing the fugitive's wrists. He paused from his task, looked around in startled surprise, gave a curse and reached for his waistband. Shackleton swung and knocked him flat on his back. Shackleton turned to the European.

'Now lie down and put your hands behind your head, there's a good chap.'

He complied with bad grace and Bramble turned to the panting runner who was undoing the cords from his wrists.

'Who are you?'

'My name's Simmerson, Adam Simmerson.'

'By God!' said Bramble. 'So, we've found you at last. You've no idea how long we've been looking for you.'

'I think we've been looking for chummy here as well,' Shackleton remarked as he clipped handcuffs over the wrists of the European. 'G'day Macca Bentley.'

'How did you know my name,' snarled the other as Shackleton pulled him to his feet.

'Oh...we get around,' Shackleton secured the Asian with another set of cuffs that Bramble tossed over to him. 'Hallo Naji, just stand still will you.'

'You know his name too?'

'No mystery there, you told us that yourself a few minutes ago. Now head for the road and move over to our car. We've got another surprise for you, Mr Bentley.'

'Follow us, Mr Simmerson,' said Bramble. 'We have some questions to ask you.'

CHAPTER 25

Kelsey promptly asked for a helicopter flyover of the property, and requested it land at a point designated by Bramble, in a paddock on the Drouin-Melbourne Road. Bramble and Shackleton drove to the area with their two handcuffed prisoners, while Simmerson was driven by Mrs Lewin to Drouin, told to book into a motel and clean himself up.

Beckie Lewin's confrontation with her brother was hardly a family reunion nor an occasion for sibling affection. Her first comment was: 'Macca, you're a bloody prat!'

His response was on the lines of it being no place for a woman to criticise him or his actions, and that he'd be obliged if she addressed him as Youssef. Thereafter it became even more acrimonious as her response was 'Don't talk such bloody bullshit!' followed by acid comments about his religious conversion and his wife, who she referred to as 'that cow!'

At that stage, Bramble thought it politic to intervene and asked her to drive Adam Simmerson to Drouin, otherwise family pleasantries could continue indefinitely. Then he contacted Kelsey.

They drove to the area designated by Bramble and waited, the two men in the back sat in sullen silence, handcuffed together by wrist and ankle, which negated any possibilities of resistance. Their firearms were in the boot of the car. Conversation was at a minimum, Mac or Micah Bentley was presumably still smarting after the tongue lashing from his sister.

Simmerson had been in a state of euphoria, after being on a low for ten days or so, a high as he escaped, superseded by an even further low when he had been run to earth, followed by a higher zenith due to the unexpected intervention by Bramble and Shackleton. They supplied him with sufficient cash to hire a motel room at Drouin as he set off with Mrs Lewin.

Bramble got out of the vehicle with his phone to his ear. Kelsey gave him the latest position of the helicopter, which appeared in the distance and they homed it in.

It described a circle of the paddock and landed, four soldiers disembarked, a captain, sergeant and two troopers. They advanced to the car, with the helicopter whirring in the paddock behind them and Bramble greeted them.

'Bartlett,' announced the captain and looked keenly at Bramble. 'We've met before.'

'We have, in similar circumstances,' Bramble shook his hand and indicated Bentley and Naji. 'These two are for transportation. Alan Kelsey will want to speak with them.'

'He'll have to wait until he gets back to Canberra, that's where they'll be going,' said Bartlett. 'Alan's still in Melbourne but yes, he wants to question these two before some smartarse lawyer gets them bail. If they land in a police cell in Warragul or Drouin that's what will happen and some bloody fool magistrate will probably release them. We don't want them loose again. You've done a good job here.'

'All part of the service,' Shackleton commented modestly.

'Well, maybe,' Bartlett gave a brief chuckle, 'But well done! Right, let's get them aboard, come on you...move!'

The two prisoners were hustled aboard, Micah Bentley appeared to have lost much of his bounce, maybe the confrontation with and scorn of his sister had subdued him. Her acid references about his wife had been rife before Bramble had tactfully put an end to the family discussion and suggested she take Simmerson to Drouin.

Bramble called McKay and told him the good news, leaving him to ask Detective Sergeant Griffiths to pick up Adam Simmerson later from Drouin. He also added as an afterthought that McKay should inform Simmerson's girl-friend, Rhonda Muston, although he considered Simmerson would have been in touch with her via Beckie Lewin's mobile phone.

He placed another call to Kelsey regarding the farm property where Simmerson had been incarcerated, suggesting a search warrant but Kelsey had already set that in motion. He was in touch with Sergeant Griffiths on the subject and said he'd keep them informed.

'We've got to get in there before they realise anything is wrong - they already know Simmerson broke out, but they won't know yet that two of their men have been apprehended so we've got to take our finger out.'

*

Griffiths installed Simmerson in an interview room after picking him up from Drouin. At their initial meeting at the motel, he became aware that Simmerson, although having showered for the first time for ten days, still had problems in that he was wearing the same shirt. He had asked Simmerson for his measurements, ordered the police car into the main street and told the constable to purchase a 'T' shirt for him.

'Thanks,' Simmerson said as he pulled on the new one, bundled up the old shirt and placed it in the shopping bag. 'Much appreciated.'

'I was thinking of us as much as you,' Griffiths commented dryly, wrinkling his nose, which gave Simmerson cause to smile. Thereafter the journey had been uneventful. Griffiths refrained from questioning Simmerson as he wanted one or more ASIO people to be present. They took him into the St Kilda Road complex, supplied Simmerson with welcome refreshment and waited for McKay and Catherine Parkinson.

When they arrived, Griffiths put a tape into the recorder, sat and placed his elbows on the table.

'Now, Mr Simmerson, we need to know precisely what happened to you. I think a good starting point would be from the time you changed Roger Richardson's computer over and took his old one to Asif. We know you traded it in to Harold Henderson.'

Simmerson looked taken aback at that and bit his lip.

'You know about that?'

'We do. You also did that without the connivance or knowledge of your employer, Gerry Parr.'

'Oh bloody hell! Is there anything you don't know? Am I in trouble for that?'

'Not with us you're not, nor do I think you're in too much trouble with Gerry Parr, although he'll probably have words with you on the subject,' Griffiths said pointedly. 'While he wasn't too pleased at you trading on your own, I don't think he's too fussed about it, we're not talking big dollars here, are we?'

'How did you know I'd traded it in to Harold?' Simmerson asked. 'Did he get in touch with Gerry?'

There was a brief silence before Griffiths shook his head.

'I'm sorry. I forgot you probably wouldn't know yet. Harold Henderson is dead, he's been murdered.'

'What!' Simmerson jerked upright in his seat. 'Murdered? Harold? Why?'

'Hold it! I'll ask the questions; we'll answer yours later. All right? We must ascertain the sequence of events.'

'Yes, OK,' Simmerson nodded. 'But murdered...Harold?'

He looked around, then spread his hands in the air.

'OK! But I'm just worried on one score, have I got a job? Has Gerry sacked me? They made me write a letter of resignation.'

'Not to my knowledge, as far as we are aware, he is still employing you. Your ungrammatical resignation letter didn't fool Gerry Parr, he read between the lines and brought us into the picture.'

'So...he got the message! Thank God for that!'

'He was in full "agreeance" 'grinned McKay. 'He was onto that one straight away.'

Simmerson gave a dry chuckle.

'I didn't think he'd miss that,' he said. 'That distorted word was one of our pet aversions. It was a standing joke between us. We both shuddered every time anyone said it.'

'Now...' said Griffiths. '...tell us what happened to you from the moment you left that computer of Roger Richardson's at Asif's place.'

'Well I took Roger's old computer, which wasn't a bad piece of equipment, but he had the chance to upgrade when his father's firm put in new computers, they're not short of a bob or two, that family. Roger told me this fellow Asif was interested in his old one so I called into his place at Prahran and did the changeover. It was a place near Chapel Street, I can give you the address if you...!'

'We already know where it is, go on!' said Griffiths.

'You know that as well?' said Simmerson ruefully. 'All right, I did the changeover, I had already cleansed Roger's old computer so it was clear, then I downloaded all Asif's data onto Roger's old machine. That completed the transaction as far as I was concerned, and I took Asif's old computer home with me. I went out later that night for Rhonda's birthday and we had a meal at a restaurant. I remember I was in a bit of a hurry.'

'Then what?'

'I had an arrangement with Harold Henderson...Good God! You say he was murdered...? Why? Who by?'

'Never mind that for now, we'll fill you in later. What happened next?'

'I took it in to Henderson's shop in Balaclava the next day and negotiated a deal, he gave me a few dollars for it. It wasn't a big transaction but we were both happy. Then I went off to my next job.'

'What happened after that?'

'Nothing much, Gerry had a lot of work on and I was quite busy for that day, I was doing a fair bit of work around the traps.'

'Anything else?'

'No,' Simmerson pondered. 'Oh yes...I had a call from Asif next morning, he said something about some missing data, and asked me where his old computer was. I told him Harold Henderson had it and gave him the shop address. I couldn't do much about it myself right then as I had a job in Bacchus Marsh. I offered to contact Harold for him, but he said not to bother and rang off. From that I presumed it wasn't too important.'

'The understatement of the year,' was Catherine's cynical aside.

'What happened after that?'

'I arrived home late that night, it was a long job and Bacchus Marsh was a fair distance. I left home for work the next morning and was near our workshop when I was cut out by this vehicle, after that everything was a bit of a haze. I was set on by these blokes, dumped in their car and off we went. I had no idea where we were or who they were until I arrived at the house, which I know now was near Drouin.'

'And you managed to break out?'

'Took me long enough, but there were eight blokes there, plus an older couple and a younger woman. Six of them left in two vans yesterday. I had already taken the screws out of the lock, my main problem was getting out of the house.'

He sat back abruptly and placed his hands on each side of his head.

'Harold Henderson...was it Asif? He must have gone to see him that morning.'

'You've got it in one,' commented McKay dryly. 'That's why they kidnapped you. You've put two and two together now in a matter of minutes, a conclusion you would have reached days ago as soon as you heard about Henderson's murder. They knew that too, so they removed you from the equation.'

'My God!' Simmerson said. 'They could have killed me.'

'They could have,' said McKay. 'But I don't think they meant to kill Henderson initially. He'd hand passed that computer onto his assistant Donald Taylor, and was foolish enough to blurt out what Taylor had found on it. It had two drives, a 'C' and a 'D'. They wanted what was on the 'D' drive.'

'I knew there was a 'D' drive on there, I thought I'd downloaded it onto the new computer. Didn't I do that?'

'No, you didn't, and Asif realised it as soon as he switched on his new one. He would have found his 'D' drive files were missing when he booted it up.'

'Christ! I shouldn't have omitted that!'

'Damn good job you did, as it turned out,' McKay said pointedly. 'Not for Harold Henderson, but your omission may have saved hundreds of lives. All right...go on!'

'I was in a hurry because it was Rhonda's birthday and we were going out that night to a restaurant. What happened to that computer...you say Donald Taylor found something?'

'Donald Taylor was given that computer in lieu of wages by Henderson, he found what was on it, and told Henderson,' said Griffiths. 'Henderson blurted it out to Asif and his friends when they came for the computer, there was an argument and a scuffle and they killed him, but not before they'd got Taylor's address out of him.'

'Oh Hell! Don Taylor, he was the new bloke there. Is he all right?'

'Yes, he's OK, but they broke into his apartment and ransacked it. They would probably have killed him too the way things were.'

'Wait on, what the hell was on that drive?'

'A plan to plant bombs in a Melbourne underground railway station on Grand Final day. We're still working on that,' McKay said grimly.

'What? Bombs! In Melbourne?'

'Yes, in Melbourne, nowhere is safe now from these rat bags.'

'But why didn't they just kill me? Not that I'm complaining.'

'I've thought about that,' said McKay. 'That farm is in the name of an elderly couple, maybe parents or relatives of one of the plotters, who may know little or nothing about what's going on, so their presence made disposing of you difficult. Perhaps it was enough to just hold you until their task was done, then just drop you off miles from anywhere and either kill you or leave you to find your own way back to civilization.'

'Even then,' Griffiths added. 'You probably wouldn't have had much idea what had gone on or why you'd been imprisoned.'

'One question, were you able to see the registrations of these two vans?' McKay asked. 'We have descriptions of them, they were seen at a distance by two of our men as they pulled out into the main road to Melbourne, at the time we didn't realise what they were.'

'Both were Ford vans, one was silver, or grey, and the other light green. There was an N and a D in the rego of one, the silver one, it was ND something and...' Simmerson pressed the heels of his hands against his eyeballs '... the numbers were ...there was a seven in the numerals, it was the first number out of three...but the rest...I'm sorry.'

'That's a start,' Griffiths wrote it down. 'We've traced vehicles in the past with less than that. What colour were the plates, I mean were they Victorian or interstate?'

'Victorian,' said Simmerson. 'I'm sure about that, definitely Victorian.'

'Did you see what was being loaded into them?'

'Looked like backpacks to me.'

'Backpacks?'

'What people wear when they go hiking.'

McKay rose to his feet.

'We'll leave you with Detective Sergeant Griffiths to get it all in writing, then we've all got work to do. After that, you can sort things out with Gerry Parr.'

*

'Now it's falling into place,' McKay remarked to Catherine Parkinson as they exited the building. He nodded to Sergeant

Phillips, manning the main reception desk again, with a young constable. It wasn't Constable Cope and McKay wondered where he was. Was he still embedded in Taylor's apartment? Phillips gave him a surly nod. Plainly he hadn't forgiven McKay for having had a direct line through to the Commissioner and Superintendent Clucas.

'Where do you think the vans were headed?' asked Catherine. 'Do you think they would go to the Prahran or Richmond addresses?'

'That's what we'll have to find out, the days are creeping past now, if it is Grand Final day then it's getting close,' said McKay. 'Let's get back to South Melbourne, we need to talk to Alan Kelsey.'

CHAPTER 26

'**A** search warrant for the two farms isn't a good idea,' Joseph Carter commented.

'Why not?' asked Kelsey.

'We've lost the two vans, right?'

'Right!'

'We assume these two vans carried explosives, maybe in the form of backpacks from what Simmerson told us,' said Carter. 'They may not know they've been rumbled yet. Flynns Creek hasn't been approached, at least not openly, Bob and Denis hopefully left no trace and it's possible those at Drouin are no wiser either as the two we arrested left in a hurry, maybe without explanation. It's likely the only people still there are the smallholders, who Simmerson reckons are an elderly couple, and possibly a daughter, who may not be aware what's going on.'

'We don't know that,' objected McKay.

'No, we don't. But if we descend on both properties with search warrants and half the bloody Army, they'll know they've been outed, in which case the plan could be changed and we won't know where they intend to strike. Right now, we do.'

'So, you're suggesting we stake out Melbourne Central Station, catch them there and raid the locations later,' said Kelsey. 'Am I right?'

'That's about the size of it,' said Carter.

'Hmm!' McKay scratched his head. 'Either way we're taking a chance. If we do as you say we risk something being detonated in Melbourne Central, the other way we could have them blowing up another target we don't know about, and won't know about until the dust settles and people are killed. Bloody hell! What an alternative!'

'Joe may be right,' Kelsey mused. 'Maybe we should stake out the underground stations, all of them, and catch them in the act. Do we have a time of day on that disc Taylor downloaded?'

'Don't think so,' said Carter. 'But if they want to inflict maximum casualties the three or four hours prior to the game, or the two hours after it are most likely time slots.'

'We need to contact the Transport Authority; we need access to their operations room, so we can direct operations from there. We'll also need many undercover operatives in the underground stations ready to jump them.'

'We should have a look inside that shed at Drouin that Adam Simmerson mentioned,' said Catherine. 'We ought to know what's going on in there.'

'You're right,' agreed Kelsey. 'Opinions?'

'I agree with both points of view,' said Joe Carter. 'I'm itching to know what's in there, yet don't want them to know we're onto them.'

'Why not put Bramble and Shackleton onto it, let them creep around and have a look, they did well at Flynns Creek,' suggested Catherine.

'What if they're caught in the act?' said Kelsey.

'I don't see a problem with that,' said Carter. 'I don't think there are any activists left there, just the couple who own the place, who may or may not know what's going on.'

'If the small holders are parents or elderly relatives of one of the activists, it won't be the first time the older generation have been unaware what their offspring are up to, like the London bombers?' Catherine suggested.

'Precisely like the London Underground bombers,' Carter nodded vigorously. 'The parents of one of them, in Leeds, had no idea what their son was doing, they reported him as a missing person a week later.'

'Possibly suspecting what he'd done,' said Kelsey. 'But your point is taken; they had no idea.'

'That West Indian bomber's wife was completely ignorant of what he was planning,' Catherine said with a hint of anger. 'What a swine he was. Quite apart from the bombing and leaving his wife out on a limb; he clearly considered her a mere chattel he owned, of no consequence.'

'But if Bramble and Shackleton are caught it's an illegal entry, any defence lawyer could make a meal of that.'

'Isn't our primary aim to prevent a bomb explosion, not worry about what a defence lawyer may or may not do after the event?' queried McKay.

'Which may get the bombers off and release them into the streets again,' said Carter.

'I think it's worth the risk,' said McKay.

'Very well, we'll have a look,' Kelsey made his decision. 'Give Bob and Denis a call...and tell them to be discreet.'

'What about Ted Griffiths, should we tell him what we're doing?' asked Carter.

'I'll mention it to him. We're too close to the possible date of the attack to pussyfoot around, I think Ted will go along with it, and probably Nick Clucas as well.'

*

But Clucas disagreed when Kelsey rang him, although he agreed with the search.

'Alan, we may as well do it legally,' he said after Kelsey put the plan to him. 'They must know now that Simmerson has absconded, even if they don't know their colleagues have been arrested. Someone must have been in touch with the Drouin property if only to contact those two men. I say we descend on the place, take it apart and we may find an address where those vans are. We've had no joy with the registrations, so Detective Sergeant Griffiths tells me, although he's done some narrowing down. We may find something at Drouin.'

Kelsey thought it over, then agreed.

'You're probably right,' he said. 'But we need to go ASAP.'

'Then go now,' said Clucas. 'Get your blokes into that shed, we'll deal with the search warrant from here, and we can hit the house afterwards. We've no time to waste now, it's getting close.'

CHAPTER 27

After parking the car Bramble and Shackleton walked down the track towards the house and the nearby shed. There was a clump of trees between them and the house and the track curved around the trees to reach the house. They entered the trees and crept to the far edge to observe the house.

'Someone working up on the rise,' observed Bramble. 'Looks as if he's gardening.'

'Then his wife will probably be in the kitchen, which Simmerson said was at the rear,' said Shackleton. 'Didn't he say there was a young woman here as well?'

'She could be in the house,' suggested Bramble.

'Or, if she's involved in the plot with the younger men, she could be in the shed.'

'A possibility. Let's look at it. We'll go this way, behind that line of bushes.'

They kept an eye on the man in the grounds and crept around

to the rear end of the shed. After reaching a point where they could make a dash for the building, they headed for a window on the south side. Bramble scrambled onto a rain butt so he could peer with one eye through the window. He descended and dusted himself down.

'She's in there,' commented Bramble. 'Which stymies us right now. Give Alan a call. We need that warrant now plus the cavalry.'

'What's she doing?'

'I didn't have time to see...get down. She's coming out.'

They ducked down; the young woman emerged from the shed and headed for the house. She was dressed in a long robe down to her ankles, with a scarf over her head. As they watched her go Bramble dialled Kelsey.

'We're going into the shed,' he said when Kelsey answered. 'The daughter, or whoever she is, has just left it and entered the main house. We'll need that warrant quick.'

'It's being obtained through a local magistrate,' answered Kelsey. 'We're already in Drouin. It should be within the hour. In the meantime, if there's nobody around, get into that shed.'

They watched the woman enter the house about 100 metres away. They crept around the side of the building, reached the doorway and entered. They were unprepared for what they did see, rows of chairs facing a small platform, on which stood a whiteboard.

In front of the chairs was an expanse of carpet abutting the raised platform. Another doorway led into the rear of the building; the door had a key in its lock. Shackleton turned the key, inched the door open, peered inside and entered.

A bench ran along one of the walls, on it were trays and mixing bowls, a large vat, pipettes and burettes together with canisters and lengths of piping, a large box containing batteries and masses of electrical wiring. Sacks and a couple of backpacks were stacked against one of the walls. Bramble extracted a box from under one of the benches and Shackleton opened it.

'What the hell?'

'Detonators,' commented Shackleton. 'Plenty of them.'

'Look at this,' Bramble held up a sheet of paper.

'What's that?'

'A map of a railway station, Melbourne Central at a guess.'

Bramble dialled Kelsey again.

'I think we've found a bomb factory,' he said. 'There's a classroom which is possibly used for instruction on how to make them. We need experts.'

'We're on our way,' was Kelsey's reply. 'Just stay where you are for now.'

'We've also found another diagram of Melbourne Central railway station.'

"Hell! The buggers mean business!'

*

'She's coming back,' observed Shackleton. They had been sitting around the building now for nearly an hour. They had taken a few shots with their mobile phone cameras, but otherwise were consumed by boredom.

'What!' Bramble looked up. 'There's nowhere we can hide, too late to make a run through the door.'

'Stay in the back, if we're lucky she'll only go into that classroom area.'

They retired into the rear and heard her enter the front part of the building. She was armed with a broom and began sweeping up residue into a pile, which she scooped into a dust pan. She further busied herself around the room, they heard her moving around and cleaning, but considered their luck could not last forever.

They were right, the door into their sanctum opened and she entered. She had put down the dust pan and closed the door before she realised she wasn't alone.

She cried out, dropped the dust pan but held onto the broom, Bramble moved forward with a pacifying gesture, his hands in the air.

'Don't be alarmed, we are not here to harm you.'

'Who are you?'

She was about 25 to 30 years of age, dressed entirely in black with a head scarf over her head. She had large brown eyes, that in normal circumstances Bramble may have found alluring, but there was something about them that made him think of a tigress. He moved slightly to his left, thinking there was a chance she would try to hit him with the broom.

'Police,' answered Bramble, which was easier than explaining they were intelligence agents from Canberra.

'What do you want here?' she spat the words out.

'We are carrying out an investigation,' replied Bramble. He decided to keep it as vague as possible and make no mention of the bomb making aspect.

'Investigation?' she looked around, then darted out and slammed the door. The key grated in the lock but Shackleton was too quick, he wrenched the door open before it was secured. She dropped the broom and ran across the other room for the still open main door.

'Come on!' snapped Bramble. 'If she gets back to the house she'll warn the others, wherever they are. If she makes a phone call we're gone.'

As they ran out of the doorway after her, three vehicles

came roaring up the track and screamed to a halt outside the shed. They cut off the woman's escape route, she turned back to retrace her steps but found herself facing Bramble and Shackleton. Before she could take off again, Bramble had her by the arm.

'Calm down,' he cried as she struggled in his grasp. 'These are police, you won't be harmed.'

He turned as Kelsey and Griffiths disembarked from the first vehicle and came towards them, the second and third each had three men in them, the last vehicle personnel carrier, was carrying soldiers. Bramble indicated the shed.

'There's something odd in there, looks like they've been mixing explosives. There are several backpacks.'

'Who's this?' Griffiths indicated the woman, still struggling and spitting like a cat.

'She lives here, I don't know who she is, we haven't been introduced,' said Bramble.

Kelsey turned to the soldiers who had just disembarked.

'Captain, the suspected bomb making equipment is in there.'

'Right, come on lads,' said the captain, Bramble recognised Captain Bartlett who had earlier picked up Mac Bentley and Naji, the other man.

'Backroom,' added Shackleton. 'The first area is some sort of classroom.'

The soldiers entered the shed and Kelsey turned to Catherine Parkinson who had emerged from the first truck.

'Take care of this lady, Catherine, before we're accused of indecent assault,' he said. 'All right, let's head for the house.'

They drove to the house and disembarked. The gardener had realised something was amiss; left his work and returned to the house. Kelsey walked up to him.

'Are you the owner of this property?'

'I am,' said the other. He was Asian, about 5' 8", Kelsey assessed his age to be about late fifties. He had grey hair with occasional flecks that showed he had once had a head of black hair. His face was lined and he had a grey moustache. He was wearing a brightly coloured shirt and a pair of jeans.

'Who are you?' the man asked in bewilderment as the other two vehicles swung in through the gateway and parked before the house. 'What is happening?'

'Police,' said Griffiths shortly. 'We have a search warrant for these premises and that shed over there.'

'Search warrant!' the man looked startled. 'Why? What are you looking for?'

Kelsey experienced momentary unease. The property owner's reaction seemed genuine. Even though Kelsey was used to people professing indignation and innocence during interviews the other man's demeanour was too genuine for comfort. He momentarily wondered whether Bramble and Shackleton could have been mistaken about the contents of the shed.

'We have reason to believe there are dangerous substances on this property,' said Griffiths who was similarly discomforted.

'Dangerous substances!' the other man looked stupefied. 'What sort of dangerous substances?'

'Let's get on with it,' Kelsey said to Griffiths, his unease mounting. He issued orders to others in the following vehicles, they disembarked and headed for the front door of the premises. Griffiths handed the search warrant to the property owner.

'You are Mr Razzaq?' he asked.

'Yes,' the man's English was perfect, something Kelsey hadn't expected. 'Perhaps you can tell me exactly what you are looking for.'

'Please let us in,' ordered Griffiths, he wasn't in the mood for niceties and ignored the question. The houseowner reluctantly stood aside.

The search was entirely unsatisfactory, despite moving from one end of the house to the other, with the occupants, father, mother and daughter, huddled in the living room, the team found nothing that indicated anything to do with involvement with a plot for detonating devices in public places.

Kelsey might have deduced they had been given a false lead but for one item, the room where Simmerson said he had been incarcerated. Detective Constable Alec Oliver found it on the top floor and Kelsey was summoned to view it. It matched exactly the description Simmerson had given them when interviewed by police. For a start the lock was rendered inoperative, the striking plate or box Simmerson had removed was still sitting on the small table and the door was still in a locked mode but swung open easily since there was nothing for the locking bolt to engage on. The window had an uninterrupted view of the drive and the parking area at the front, also a clear view of the shed. Simmerson could easily have observed comings and goings between shed and vans.

'Look at this,' Oliver indicated a loose board near the foot of the bedstead. They eased it upwards. There was a small area beneath between the joist where Simmerson would have hidden his appropriated table knife.

Kelsey felt a flood of relief as he checked these items, and turned to Oliver.

'Carry on with the search and see if you can find anything up here. I'll have words with Mr Razzaq.'

He went below and re-entered the living room.

'We must apologise for this intrusion, Mr Razzaq, but we are acting on information received.'

The daughter jumped to her feet with her eyes blazing.

'You are harassing us because we are followers of Islam,' she shouted. 'We have done nothing, and you come into our homes to oppress us. We are not frightened by your harassment!'

Kelsey ignored her and directed his gaze at her father.

'Whilst on the subject of oppression, you had a young man imprisoned in an upstairs room for several days. Do you know anything about that, Mr Razzaq?'

'Imprisoned? He was not imprisoned!' Razzaq sat straight up and leant forward. 'Imprisoned! My nephew asked if he could stay here, he said he was a young man, a westerner, who needed temporary accommodation, we were pleased to help.'

'Do you normally lock up people who ask for accommodation?'

'He wasn't locked up, my nephew said he stayed up there because he...he wanted to be alone and devote his time to prayer while he was here.'

'He may well have done that,' Kelsey commented cynically. 'But to escape he had to break out and was then pursued out of the house and onto the main road by two armed men. Can you tell me why those two men needed to be armed?'

'Armed? You mean with guns? They were not armed! Why should they be armed?'

'Well ...' Kelsey was bemused, the interview wasn't going the way he had envisaged and again he was struck by the apparent genuineness of the man: '...perhaps you could tell *me* that. Two men from here were apprehended on the main road by two of my men, they were both carrying guns.'

'Guns! There must be some mistake.'

'There was no mistake, sir.'

'But they were all here conducting instruction, they had a special room set up in the building over there, they were carrying out religious studies, planning a new educational facility, and other matters.'

The other man spread out his hands, but Kelsey was eyeing the young woman. If looks could have killed, he would have dropped dead on the spot long ago, he couldn't recall ever having had such extreme venom directed at him. This made up his mind.

'Would you come with me please, sir?'

'Come with you, where?'

'Not far, just to your outbuilding over there. I want your opinion.'

'My opinion?'

'Yes, if you wish your wife may accompany you, but your daughter stays here.'

'She won't stay here alone, not with your men here. My wife must stay with her.'

'As you wish,' Kelsey nodded. He was aware of the Muslim penchant for having women chaperoned, but as far as he was concerned the daughter would be safe enough. He couldn't imagine any man wanting to get near that wild cat. 'If you come with me, it shouldn't take long and I assure you we'll bring you back to your family immediately.'

Razzaq looked at him quizzically and then nodded. He seemed to accept Kelsey could be trusted.

'Very well, what is it you wish me to see?'

CHAPTER 28

Kelsey stood aside to allow Razzaq to precede him to the door, into the hallway and out through the front door. They walked to the shed, where the first vehicle was still parked.

'Why are you harassing us?' Razzaq asked as they approached the barn. 'Is it a crime to allow people to use my own property to devote time to religious studies?'

'We're not saying *that's* a crime, but have you been in that shed since this group arrived?' asked Kelsey.

'No, my nephew requested use of the building for some months while he and his group engaged in studies. I saw no harm in that, the barn was empty and I was glad to have it used and occupied.'

'Did the young man in the house ever join them?'

'Not that I recall, I was told he preferred to study alone.'

Ye Gods! Kelsey thought. How naïve can you get? He entered the outhouse building and held the door open for Razzaq. They entered and Razzaq looked triumphantly at Kelsey.

'There, it's as I told you; they were using it for religious studies. See, the chairs, the prayer mats and whiteboard.'

Kelsey nodded but walked to the rear of the building, where Dean Hateley stood guard over the door to the backroom area. Kelsey opened the door, entered and gestured to Razzaq to follow.

'How long since you've been in here?' Kelsey asked.

'A long time,' answered Razzaq. 'Some months perhaps, but it's used for storing old farming implements. The previous owner left them behind, odd items like old shovels, rakes and an old sit-on mower. I just left them here. I rarely enter this part of the building and I've never used …used …I've never…!'

His voice trailed away as they entered the rear part of the building that housed rows of benches, chemical equipment and sacks of fertiliser stacked in the corner.

'What is that?' he asked faintly.

'In the sacks? That's ammonium nitrate,' answered Kelsey. 'It's a fertiliser but is also a constituent for bomb making. You may recall the bomb explosion in Oklahoma City years ago when the front of a building was completely wrecked by a car bomb; that was made with ammonium nitrate. We believe this is what has been manufactured here.'

'If it is a fertiliser, they must have been using it, for fertilising the soil.'

'What areas of your property did they fertilise? Can you show us where it's been ploughed in?' Kelsey asked acidly. 'Another point, would they use backpacks like these to spread it around? And this diagram we found here. Do you recognise it?'

'No, I don't.'

'Perhaps you don't travel to Melbourne very often, Mr Razzaq,' Kelsey said grimly. 'That is a diagram of a Melbourne underground railway station, these red markings are, we presume, where they plan to leave bombs, made here, which they intend to detonate.'

'There must be some simple explanation,' Razzaq spread out his hands in perplexity.

'There is,' said Kelsey impatiently. 'They are using a twisted interpretation of your holy book to justify blowing up installations and killing people. You now have a choice, either you condone what they are doing, or intend to do, or...you can assist us with our enquiries and help us stop them before they detonate these bombs and kill hundreds of people, which will probably include many of your own faith.'

'I...I must think about this. I don't understand how this can be.'

'Well don't think about it too long. We have ascertained they intend to commit these acts on Grand Final Day in Melbourne. We have only a few days left.'

'What ...what do you want from me?'

'Firstly, we want to know where those vans were headed that recently left your property. Secondly, we want names, addresses and descriptions, if you have them, of all the personnel who've been here over the last few months.'

'But I don't know who they were, my nephew brought them here, he said they were scholars who wanted a retreat.'

'If by retreat you mean somewhere quiet and off the beaten track...' Kelsey said grimly: '...that's precisely what they had. They wanted somewhere to manufacture these explosives without hindrance.'

'But...why should they do this?'

'Why indeed?' sighed Kelsey. He was becoming more and more convinced Razzaq was an innocent party. He also sensed he and Razzaq were forming the beginnings of a rapport. 'I was hoping you could tell us that.'

'I cannot, I do not understand.'

'Mr Razzaq, we're not hounding nor harassing your fellow Muslims for what they are, we are doing so for what they are doing or intend to do,' Kelsey said forcefully. 'This type of behaviour is, regrettably, not limited to your faith. We have had Protestant and Roman Catholic Christians fighting each other in similar fashion in Ireland for decades as you probably know. If Protestants and Catholics were fighting each other here, attacking the state government, setting off bombs or shooting people as they were in Belfast or London, we would be harassing them too!'

'I understand that,' Razzaq nodded, then looked Kelsey squarely in the eye as he clearly came to a decision and. 'I can give you the name of my nephew, but the others...I really don't know who they are.'

'Will your daughter know who they are?'

Razzaq shook his head, but it was more in resignation than of ignorance.

'I believe she will. Her behaviour pattern has been more aggressive over the last six months. She treats me and my wife with something approaching scorn or contempt. I knew she was becoming obsessed with the scriptures and although I welcomed an interest in our holy book, I did have concern about the direction her thoughts were taking. I wanted to believe it was just a phase and she would eventually study it for sheer love of the texts.'

'Well...I'd say she hasn't,' commented Kelsey. 'But she must now be our next stop, we must find exactly where these men are now.'

The attempted questioning by Kelsey wasn't a success. When they returned to the house Razzaq explained to his daughter what he had seen in the shed, and the purposes for which he believed it would be used. But she refused to listen. Kelsey was astonished such a beautiful young woman could exude so much venom and hatred.

'How can you believe these people?' she flashed angrily to her father. 'They are corrupting you with their lies. Don't believe them; the building was used for instruction.'

'It was being used for more than that, you knew that. Two of my men saw you cleaning out that laboratory at the rear.'

'I'll tell you nothing,' she shouted. 'We are only doing ...'

'We need the names of those people intending to blow up the railway station,' Kelsey interrupted her.

'Never!'

So saying she turned at Kelsey and spat, it landed on the lapel of his jacket and he started back in amazement. He maintained his self-control and confined himself to wiping it off with his handkerchief.

'Infidel!' she screamed at him.

'Be quiet!'

Kelsey was astonished; the interjection had come from Razzaq. He advanced towards her and seized her by the shoulders.

'You have been misled, badly misled, as have I. I blame myself; I should have known things were not as they seemed. These men are corrupted, what they are doing is against humanity. They are misguided, even your cousin Hamed...you must understand.'

He turned to Kelsey.

'Leave us,' he said.

'What!'

'Leave me with her,' Razzaq said. 'Please, let me speak with her.'

'Well, I don't know ...' Kelsey began.

'Go!'

Kelsey started upright in surprise, then acquiesced. He nodded to Jim Waters by the door, they both left the room.

'What now?' Waters asked.

'Leave it to him for the present,' replied Kelsey. 'I'm inclined to believe he genuinely knew nothing of what was going on, although he's been a bit bloody naïve when someone is locked in an upstairs room for days on end and he accepts that all he wants to do is contemplate his navel!'

Sergeant Griffiths was in the kitchen. He had boiled a kettle and made himself a cup of tea with a tea bag.

'Careful, they'll accuse you of theft or looting,' said Kelsey.

'The hell they will,' grunted Griffiths. 'I brought my own lemon tea bags with me, never without them,' he sipped at the cup and nodded approvingly. 'These are good, like some? I'll make you another cup. What's happening in there?'

'The daughter is up to her neck in it,' said Kelsey. 'She protested she knew nothing of any bomb making but Bob and Denis caught her cleaning out this morning. Nobody could be that bloody dense! I've left the father to deal with her, he's been a bit naïve to have no idea what was going on, but strikes me as being genuine.'

'Hope you're right.'

'So do I, I've been wrong before,' Kelsey grimaced.' But we'll try the soft approach first, we can't do that if we get tough beforehand. We must find where those blasted vans went. Found anything in the house?'

'Nothing of much interest, they must have spent most of their time in that outhouse or shed. We've been over the room where Simmerson was held, nothing new but we found the table knife he used to unscrew the lock from the door.'

'Where did these people sleep?'

'In the downstairs room, the one at the back next to here, through that door there,' Griffiths jerked his thumb at the door behind Kelsey. 'There are sleeping bags and mattresses lying about. Razzaq and his wife use an upstairs room, as does the daughter, at the opposite end of the house from where Simmerson was. He was at the front and they were at the back, there's a separate flight of stairs.'

'So…Simmerson was well away from them.'

'Which is why they accepted that ridiculous story…!' Griffiths laid his empty cup on the draining board. 'I'd say the back was added onto the house after the rest, there's no access from front to back except via the ground floor and separate staircases.'

'Well…the father knows the real story now,' said Kelsey. 'Let's hope he can persuade his daughter to talk. I reckon she knows where those vans went.'

'And if he can't?'

'Cross that when we come to it.'

Razzaq emerged from the sitting room, traversed the hallway and entered the kitchen where Kelsey, Waters and Griffiths were waiting. Griffiths had washed up the cups and stood them upside down on the draining board. Razzaq advanced towards Kelsey and handed him a piece of paper.

'That is where they went,' he said. 'I can't guarantee they are there now, but you may be lucky. I have also listed names of those she knew. I can't guarantee the spellings.'

'Thank you, sir,' said Kelsey. 'You've been a great help to us and to Australia.'

'These people do us no good,' Razzaq shook his head. 'Many of us come here to start a new life away from bigotry, oppression, overcrowding and poverty in our own lands, yet there are some who bring with them the very things from which they tried to escape. I have been living in this country for twenty years, I am an Australian citizen, I am also a Muslim, the two are not incompatible, but for some, they seem to be.'

'What of your daughter?'

'My fault, I failed to see the signs, or if I did, I failed to act when I should.'

'You have another daughter, I believe, she married an Australian.'

'Yes, she did. I have not seen her for some time. She lives at Flynns Creek. Her husband has been spending time here, he was here this morning but I haven't seen him for some hours now. He drove off in a hurry, I don't know where he is.'

Kelsey gave Griffiths a sidelong glance, best that Razzaq didn't know Bentley was probably now in Canberra in handcuffs.

'Has your elder daughter been contaminated by these extremists as well?'

'I …I don't know,' Razzaq bit his lip. 'I fear it's likely if her husband was one of them. My main responsibility now is my younger daughter. It is my responsibility to give her proper values. I trust I am not too late. Is she in trouble?'

'Not with me she isn't,' said Kelsey. 'But she will be if she warns these people that we know where and who some of them are. Does she have a mobile phone?'

'She does, that's it over there,' Razzaq indicated a mobile phone on one of the shelves. 'If it will make you feel easier, I suggest you take it with you…as long as we have it back eventually.'

'Thank you, yes I'll do that,' Kelsey reached up and pocketed it. 'Do you have any others?'

'I don't possess a mobile phone, nor does my wife, ordinary phones are enough for us,' Razzaq smiled. 'I have no wish to take photographs, play games or reach the internet while I'm out in the paddock.'

'Then we have something in common,' said Kelsey. 'We'll have to tap your land line; we can't risk her tipping these people off. It won't be for long, if we get hold of them quickly the line will be freed up again.'

'I hope you find them,' said Razzaq. 'If they do what you say, this will affect innocent people like me. Apart from being injured, many Muslims, innocent people, will be insulted and castigated as a result. I wish you success. I am happy living in this country and want it to stay that way.'

*

'What have you got?' Griffiths asked as he and Kelsey stood near the vehicles.

'Names and addresses where the vans might be,' Kelsey smoothed out the paper given to him by Razzaq and laid it on the vehicle's bonnet. 'Get your lads onto these quickly, we may strike lucky if you find the registered owners of these vans.'

'Do you normally teach your grandmother to suck eggs?'

'Pardon? Oh...sorry,' Kelsey gave a rueful smile. 'Guess I was... sorry! I'll leave this with you.'

'I'll be in touch, Alan...and thanks. How did you get the info from that wildcat?'

'I didn't, her father did. He is a moderate man, now he knows what they are and their aims, he is alarmed at what these fanatics are capable of and the damage that will result. He realises people like him will suffer from any backlash.'

'Regrettably they will. Leave it with me.'

'We need to tap that phone line,' said Kelsey. 'I'm worried about the daughter and she may try to tip people off. Her father can't watch her all the time.'

'I'll get onto it.' Griffiths gathered up the paper from the vehicle bonnet and took out his mobile phone.

*

When Kelsey and the others arrived back at the ASIO field office, Kelsey handed the Razzaq daughter's mobile phone to John Edmonds.

'Check all the numbers in the memory,' he said crisply. 'I want to know who they are and how often she's been ringing them and when. Right?'

'Will do,' Edmonds took the phone. 'Give me about an hour.'

CHAPTER 29

Kelsey's desk phone rang, it was Griffiths.

'Alan, we've found the silver-grey van, it's parked at the Carlton address Razzaq gave us. It's registered to Hamed Razzaq, same name.'

'That'll be the nephew,' replied Kelsey. 'The daughter seemed overawed and influenced by him.'

'A male of the same family,' commented Griffiths. 'In this culture brothers are dominant over female siblings, maybe the same applies to male cousins. But we haven't found the other van yet, it hasn't turned up at Richmond or Prahran.'

'Should we raid all three premises,' Kelsey rubbed his chin. 'What do you think?'

'Not yet, Alan,' responded Griffiths. 'We'll carry out surveillance for now. A raid may get some of them out of circulation as we haven't much time now, but if we hold off, we could scoop the whole pool.'

'I go along with that!' Kelsey agreed reluctantly. 'But we're dicing with lives here.'

'We're dicing with lives whichever course we take,' grunted Griffiths. 'We're between the devil and the deep blue sea.'

*

Jim Waters and Dean Hateley sat in a vehicle 50 metres down the road from the address in a Carlton side street. The silver-grey van was parked in the street, but there had been no movements. Hateley had his camera at the ready while Jim Waters was reading the sports pages.

'It's like watching grass grow,' grumbled Hateley. 'I reckon we ought to raid the place and have done with it.'

'Alan wants to find the other van before we do that,' Waters returned to the sports pages. 'If we arrest half of them, we've failed, they can still set bombs off!'

'Guess so,' replied Hateley. 'Hang on...what have we here?'

Three men had just left the house and entered the van. Jim Waters started the engine as the van drew away. Hateley reported to the field office the van was on the move. Waters followed 60 metres behind. The van turned onto a main road at traffic lights.

'Heading towards the city,' Hateley reported to John Edmonds on the other end of his line. 'We'll probably finish up heading south down Swanston Street!'

They did, but that was the problem, they reached the city centre and lost them in traffic. Waters cursed angrily as a delivery truck got in his way and there was insufficient room to pull around it in time. When they did, the silver-grey van had vanished.

Kelsey wasn't happy when Edmonds reported the van was lost.

'Get onto Sergeant Griffiths, ask him to circulate that

registration number, we need that damned van.'

But the van remained elusive, an hour passed with no trace of it, Kelsey and Griffiths paced up and down impatiently in their respective domains, but nothing turned up. It was a further hour before Hateley came through.

'We've found it again, but it's no help,' he said. 'It's back at the Carlton address, and so are we.'

'Bugger it!' Kelsey snapped angrily. 'That means it could have been delivering backpacks. We may have to raid the property now plus Prahran and Richmond. Stay where you are.'

He rang off and turned to Joseph Carter.

'Has John Edmonds had any joy with that mobile phone memory?'

'There are three land lines and two mobiles, the landlines are the properties we already know about, Richmond, Prahran and Carlton. One of the two mobiles belongs to Asif, nothing new there. We're still waiting on the other,' answered Carter.

'I'll tell Griffiths we may need to go in now,' said Kelsey. 'We could pick up a clue from the houses.'

*

'We need to draw up an action plan for the railway station,' Griffiths said when Kelsey contacted him. 'If we can't arrest them beforehand, we'll have to do it on the spot. If they are carrying backpacks they should stand out.'

'We should do that now,' said Kelsey. 'It's on the cards they'll hold a rehearsal to make sure they get it right on the day.'

'Agreed. I've already had our people studying surveillance tapes of the station forecourt and platforms, so far nothing untoward but that could change'

'If we raid these premises they may change plans, and go for one of the other underground stations, we need to check all three and maybe Southern Cross and Flinders Street Stations as well.'

At Carlton, Hateley and Waters were still maintaining surveillance.

'Apparently, we're conducting raids on the three places, and probably Flynns Creek as well,' said Hateley. 'We stay here until the cavalry arrives and then go in with them.'

'Anything is better than hanging around here,' growled Waters. 'How long do you reckon?'

'Alan said half an hour, so it won't be long.'

*

Kelsey co-ordinated the raids from South Melbourne and made sure they all coincided to prevent any warnings being transmitted one to another. Griffiths was with him and when the time came he gave the order 'Go, go go!' All teams went into action simultaneously.

Hateley and Waters didn't have long to wait, three vehicles drew up at the Carlton address and a squad of men jumped out wearing body armour and armed with a battering ram. They knocked at the door, but when the man who answered it saw what was outside, he promptly slammed it. It was smashed open and police piled in. Hateley and Waters sauntered across the street and arrived at what was left of the front door.

'Who are you?' asked a sergeant.

'ASIO,' Waters showed his identification. 'We'll have a look at the van, is it open?'

'Haven't tried it yet.' the sergeant peered closely at their ID. 'Go for your lives.'

Hateley and Waters checked the van, the sun was warm

and one of the windows was slightly open. Waters reached in, unlocked it and they looked inside. It was empty, Hateley checked the glove box but all he found was manuals for the vehicle.

'Nothing,' he said. 'Let's see if there's anything in the house.'

The three occupants of the house had been rounded up and were confined in one downstairs room while the police searched the rest of the house. Waters and Hateley went upstairs, where two police were examining a backpack. One of them looked up and grinned.

'Safe enough,' he said.' This one isn't primed, but keep away from that stuff over there. I don't know what it is but we're taking no chances.'

Hateley was inclined to agree, there were several canisters which didn't look as if they were for holding beer, with quantities of wire on one of the tables.

The rest of the premises were searched, but there were no more backpacks, the sergeant looked disconsolate.

'Looks as it they've removed them, there's nothing here.'

Hateley looked at Waters.

'They may have transported them elsewhere earlier today, when we lost them.'

'Let's go through that desk over there,' said Waters. 'There may be something.'

*

'What have you found?' asked Kelsey when Waters rang.

'A backpack which hadn't been packed with explosives, I'd say it was next in line when we battered down the front door,' explained Waters. 'There's nothing in the van; it must have been delivering when we lost them earlier today.'

'Anything else?'

'No, Dean's going through the desk in the front room. Any luck elsewhere?'

'Much the same at Richmond and Prahran, at Prahran they found two backpacks all ready to go, the bomb squad are defusing them now. They've arrested a couple at Richmond and one at Prahran.'

'Does that include that man Asif?'

'Don't think it does, which may be an advantage, if we have to look out for them at Melbourne Central that's someone we'll recognise,' said Kelsey. 'Keep us informed.'

'Hang on, Dean says he's just found something ...what is it, Dean?'

There was a muttered conversation at the other end before Waters came back on line.

'We've found reference to an address in Glenhuntly. I know the road; it's near the Glenhuntly Railway station. You ready?'

'Yes, fire away.'

Kelsey noted it and signalled to one of the girls to check it on her screen.

'What do they say about it?'

'Nothing much, it's written in a notebook, but so are Prahran and Richmond, plus the two country properties.'

'Bingo!' Kelsey gave a boxer's salute over his head. 'We may have found the missing van. Stick with it and we'll head for Glenhuntly.'

He phoned Griffiths and gave him details. They arranged to meet in the road near the Glenhuntly railway station.

'Looks hopeful,' commented Griffiths.

'Very!' Kelsey agreed. 'We'll need a warrant.'

'Leave that with me,' said Griffiths. 'We'll check the electoral register and see who's living there.'

*

They parked some distance up the road and examined the property, a weatherboard house, typical of many in the neighbourhood. It had a small front garden, a front veranda supported by concrete pillars and grilles on the side windows. They made a couple of passes but the house looked innocuous.

'All very innocent,' Griffiths mused as he and Kelsey sat in the car and examined the house. 'But then, I didn't expect to see machine gun emplacements all round it.'

'With the current burglary stats that should probably be the norm round here,' Kelsey retorted and Griffiths chuckled appreciatively.

'Maybe, maybe,' he said. 'But no van.'

'Could be round the back, there's a track leading up behind the rear fences, could be rear access.'

'How are you at peering through cracks in fences?'

'First rate! It's part of our training course,' replied Kelsey. 'Plus peering into bedroom windows!'

'Looks like it's up to you then.'

Kelsey sighed and opened the passenger door.

'Walked into that one, didn't I?' he said. 'I'll check it out.'

He ventured up the rear laneway and was back inside five minutes, shoes liberally encrusted with mud.

'They need to get their storm water drainage fixed,' he complained bitterly. 'But I couldn't see anything, nothing like a van. There's a garage in the backyard.'

'We may as well go,' commented Griffiths. 'Time is getting short. The Grand Final is nearly on us.'

'Who lives here?'

'Zyad Hasain appears to be the householder.'

'Well if everyone is ready, let's pay him a courtesy call.'

'The front drive leads around the side of the house,' said Griffiths. 'I noticed that when we passed by it, so the van, if it's here, could be somewhere around the side or rear.'

Griffiths hammered on the front door which was cautiously opened a fraction.

'Police!' Griffiths called out. 'We have a warrant to search these premises.'

'A warrant? Why do you have a warrant?'

'We have reason to believe there are explosive substances in these premises, will you let us in please.'

The householder tried to close the door but Griffiths placed his shoulder against it.

'Either you let us in peacefully, or we batter the door down. Either way we're in within seconds. One way you pay for a new door, the other way you don't.'

The householder hesitated, but Griffiths didn't feel disposed to argue. He pushed his shoulder against it and entered the hallway. A team of police went around the side of the house heading for the garage, while others followed Griffiths into the hall. Griffiths handed over the warrant papers to the owner, an Asian with a moustache.

'You are Mr. Hasain?'

'Yes.'

'If you have any dangerous substances in this house or anywhere on the premises, I suggest you tell us where they are now. Otherwise, we may have to take the place apart.'

'I don't know what you are talking about?' Hasain protested. 'How did you get this address? This is an ordinary residence.'

'We got it from a small holding in Drouin, and from a house in Prahran,' Griffiths was gratified to see the other exhibit some uncertainty. 'Do you have a light green van on the premises?'

The other man visibly deflated before their eyes. Griffiths

nodded to Kelsey and the Senior Constable behind him.

'Right lads,' he said. 'Let's get to work.'

*

They met together at the Police complex after the events. Superintendent Clucas attended with Kelsey and Griffiths. Others included Constable Stannington, McKay, Catherine Parkinson, Joseph Carter, Bramble, Shackleton, Waters and Hateley.

'So...at Glenhuntly we found the second van that left Drouin,' said Clucas. 'Any traces of explosive materials?'

'No sir,' Griffiths shook his head. 'All the birds seem to have flown together with the backpacks. We found one in the van so at least that one won't injure anyone, but the rest...!' he spread out his hands.

'And the other addresses?'

'Every one of them secured. That's Prahran, Richmond, Flynns Creek, Drouin, Carlton, and lastly Glenhuntly,' said Kelsey. 'We've found no new addresses. These people are now scattered, presumably they live within the Melbourne area somewhere, so they may all be at separate home bases, unless there's other places we don't know about.'

'How many in custody?'

'About a dozen, we've made much progress in the last week, a contrast to the previous two weeks when we couldn't find a damned thing,' Griffiths thumbed through a file before him. 'We've arrested fourteen in all from various places. We also went back to Drouin and the local police arrested the daughter. We explained to her father we didn't want her tipping anyone off, he protested but eventually accepted it. According to the local nick his protests weren't too emphatic; he just went through the motions.'

'Sounds as if he was relieved,' added Kelsey. 'I believe the father, Razzaq, is genuine. He was quite startled when he went into the back of the outbuilding. He thought they were using the place for religious instruction.'

'They were, of the worst kind!' McKay commented cynically.

'Plus, he extracted much needed information from his daughter,' said Griffiths. 'He persuaded her to grass on her co-conspirators, but she could revert and start warning people.'

'Is she in custody?' Clucas asked.

'Yes'

'Where?'

'Here,' said Griffiths. 'We thought initially of the local nick at Drouin, but decided to keep her where we could see her, although she's kept apart from the others. The other point was, if we left her at Drouin the local press would soon get wind of it.'

'Do we know how many backpacks there are likely to be?'

'No.'

'Well...we'd better ask her,' said Clucas.

'Who do you suggest, sir?' Griffiths enquired. 'I don't think I'll get very far with her.'

'I'd suggest Catherine Parkinson,' Kelsey broke in. 'She's expert at interrogation techniques, and bearing in mind the psyche we're dealing with, Razzaq's daughter should relate better to another woman.'

'That makes sense,' Clucas agreed. 'All right, let's do it. We must know what we're up against.'

CHAPTER 30

The constable departed as Catherine Parkinson entered the interview room. Kelsey and Griffiths had decided no other parties should be present.

'You know why I'm here?' Catherine asked.

The young woman ignored her. Catherine sighed and sat at the table.

'We know what your friends intend to do,' Catherine continued. 'They mean to kill many people by exploding bombs in railway stations. Do you know why they are going to kill innocent people, women and children?'

The other woman's eyes bored into Catherine's. Catherine returned the stare, and inclined her head.

'Why are they doing this?' she asked but still the young woman said nothing.

'Do you agree with the reason why they are doing these things?' Catherine persisted. 'Many of those they kill will be Muslims, have they thought of that?'

'They are not of the true faith.'

'Who are not?'

'The people who are being killed.'

'How do you know that? Do you know them all? And who *is* of the true faith?'

Again, there was silence but Catherine persisted.

'You consider yourself of the true faith, you and your cousin?'

The young woman made as if to answer, then said nothing.

'I would say those who work hard, observe their faith, bring up a family and provide a home for their children and treat people kindly, were of a true faith, somebody like your father.'

Again, silence. Catherine drew breath to speak again then thought better of it. She remembered her father, an insurance sales representative for many years, had told her there was a time to talk and a time to be silent. She had learnt the same when undergoing interrogation techniques training with ASIO. So, she said nothing and watched the girl.

She waited for what seemed an eternity, actually 12 minutes, as she noted from her watch, before she spoke again.

'Do you believe your father is not a good man?'

This elicited some response, she raised her eyes and looked at Catherine. Catherine thought she was about to say something, but again...silence. Nevertheless, Catherine considered it was progress.

'I liked your father, I am not of your faith, but he struck me as a good man.'

'He is.'

Catherine experienced satisfaction, she had elicited a response and an opinion.

'Do you believe what he stands for is good?'

Silence descended again. Catherine decided to follow it up.

'Does he believe it's right to kill innocent people, women and children, who are going about their daily business? Does he believe that?'

There was an almost imperceptible shake of the head. Catherine decided to continue, but not too strongly.

'Your cousin doesn't share your father's beliefs, does he?'

Silence again.

'He believes it's right to kill people, doesn't he?' Catherine persisted. 'Anyone who gets in his way or who doesn't believe exactly as he does, even young children.'

Silence again, Catherine allowed it to continue for two or three minutes.

'Who is right, your father or your cousin?'

The girl raised her eyes and looked at Catherine, was about to speak, but again subsided.

'Who would you follow? Your father or your cousin?'

*

'How did it go?' Kelsey asked Catherine after she had left the room. He was outside with Griffiths and Superintendent Clucas.

'Badly, she won't talk at all, apart from occasional responses that cast me as the epitome of evil,' said Catherine. 'How her father got that information from her beats me.'

'Maybe he can do so again,' suggested Griffiths. 'You are one of the enemy Catherine, you are a Christian.'

'I don't necessarily consider myself one. I haven't been to church for years,' protested Catherine.

'That isn't the criterion,' said Kelsey. 'To her you're a westernised Christian, a descendant of the wicked Crusaders. I think we need someone of her own faith to talk to her.'

'And if she doesn't respond?'

'We'll start flooding the underground stations with our

people, we'll want every bloody nook and cranny, every platform, every stairwell, to have a security operative on it.'

'What do you suggest we do now?' asked Clucas.

'Bring her father in, together with the local imam or sheik and make it plain they're not under arrest. Explain the situation to them, we need information, but get them here.'

'You want me to seek them out, Alan?' asked Catherine.

'Definitely not. At the risk of sounding chauvinistic, this is men's business. We're dealing with Muslims here and possibly Arabs. You keep on at the daughter, even if it's just sitting looking at her. She knows something for sure, I have full confidence in your interviewing techniques. I'll send Bramble and Shackleton.'

'We haven't overmuch time,' said Clucas. 'I'll get in touch with the local nick and have two plainclothes officers bring them in to Dandenong. Your two men can pick them up from there, time is getting short.'

'Sounds good.'

'We'll need to be in touch with the Transport Commission, we need access to the operations room and their video facilities.'

'Will that be a police operation?'

'Yes, but I'll suggest Captain Bartlett and his men be on hand around Melbourne Central, it's essential we have their bomb experts available.'

*

After the ASIO contingent returned to the ASIO field office, John Edmonds entered the room where Kelsey, Joseph Carter and Catherine Parkinson were drinking coffee.

'What is it, John?'

Edmonds indicated Catherine who was sitting at the table.

'Catherine's wanted,' he said. 'That young woman at St Kilda Road, she just asked for her, she won't talk to anyone else.'

Kelsey looked at Catherine.

'You may have got through to her, Catherine. Good luck!'

Initially there was silence, Catherine just sat and said nothing. She let the girl meditate but after five minutes she spoke.

'Where is my father?'

'I don't know exactly,' Catherine replied. 'We asked him to come in to see you.'

'You've arrested him.'

'No,' Catherine shook her head. 'We have no reason to; we know your father is a good man.'

'So where is he now?'

'I can only tell you he has been asked to come in, but I can't say exactly where he is now or when, it may not be today.'

'Is it true what you said...about bombs being set off in railway stations?'

'Yes,' said Catherine. 'We found a plan on Asif's computer that said they meant to detonate a bomb in a Melbourne underground railway station, with details of where the bombs were to be planted.'

She realised she had let drop something that hitherto the police and ASIO had kept to themselves, but consoled herself with the realisation it hardly mattered now. The girl was in custody, was unlikely to be released before the event, and Grand Final Day was imminent.

'I don't believe that. You are lying.'

'Where do *you* think they were going to explode them?'

'They said they were going to blow up military installations and blow holes in the fences of refugee camps so they could let our brothers and sisters escape.'

'They lied to you. We have proof where they intend to explode these bombs. It won't be soldiers they kill, or security camp guards, it will be people like your parents.'

'How do I know you are telling the truth?'

'You don't, but let me ask you this. Where are they secreting these explosives?'

'What do you mean?'

'They are placing them in backpacks, aren't they?'

The girl hesitated, then nodded.

'We found some of these backpacks in vans we captured, they are geared for suicide bombers.'

The girl looked up but said nothing.

'Which means they are hardly contemplating blowing a hole in a security fence. If they tried to enter a military installation they'd only get as far as the main gate and kill one or two sentries. Hardly worth it, is it?'

'What do you want from me?'

'We need to know who these people are, you've given us some of them and some addresses, but there are more. We need to stop these people before they kill and maim hundreds of people, your fellow Australians and other Muslims.'

'You are bringing my father in to see me?'

'Yes, but I don't know exactly when he will arrive.'

'I want to see him.'

'You will, when he arrives,' Catherine suddenly had an inspiration, a deviation that could bring about a result. 'He refused to come in by police car. He will be travelling in by train from Drouin and we'll pick him up from Melbourne Central.'

'Where?'

'Melbourne Central, the underground station.'

'When are you bringing him in?'

'He said he had work to do, he'll be coming in on Saturday.'

'Saturday?' the girl looked agitated. 'You mean this Saturday?'

'Yes, this Saturday coming,' said Catherine. 'The roads will be full that day so it will be easier by train.'

'Why?'

'It will be Grand Final Day and crowds will be coming in. The roads will be congested and there will be delays. The trains should be on time.'

'The Drouin train doesn't go to Melbourne Central.'

'No, it doesn't. He'll change trains at Caulfield so we can pick him up at Central Station, then from there we'll bring him down Swanston Street and St Kilda Road against the main stream traffic.'

'Why are you doing this?'

'Why are we doing what?'

'Why are you taking my father through Melbourne Central.'

'Why? Why shouldn't we?' Catherine enquired innocently. 'If we're bringing him here, St Kilda Road, then it's logical for him to get off the train there.'

'What you are doing is evil!'

'Evil? I don't follow you,' said Catherine. 'Your father requested it. He doesn't want to travel to Melbourne in a police car.'

'You said he is a good man, yet you are trying to kill my ...!' the girl broke off and Catherine raised her hand to scratch one of her eyebrows to mask the triumph in her eyes. Hitherto she had been inclined to believe the girl was sincere about refugee camps and military installations and knew nothing of the proposed bombing of Melbourne Central. Now she knew differently.

'Your father will come to Melbourne by train, we'll pick him up from Melbourne Central when he arrives and bring him here. What is wrong with that?'

There was clearly plenty wrong with that, the girl relapsed

into deep thought. Catherine decided to say nothing and let her mind work overtime. The silence continued; Catherine stood up, stretched, then left the room. Kelsey and Griffiths, on the other side of the one-way window looking in, turned to greet her as she emerged.

'Changing tack like that was brilliant, well done!' Griffiths said appreciatively. 'Now we know she's not entirely naïve or innocent and has knowledge of their intentions. Now she believes her father could be prejudiced it's given her something to think about.'

'Yes, she knows something,' said Kelsey. 'Probably exactly where and when, although we have a good idea of that already. I'd say she also knows more addresses where some of these people are hanging out.'

'All we have so far is Asif, he is one we can recognise if and when he turns up.'

'Agreed,' Kelsey nodded. 'And his cricketing friend, whatever his name was, the one who attended the cricket meeting with him.'

'Rafit Qadri,' announced Catherine. 'According to Roger Richardson he played for one of the lesser teams, 2nd or 3rd cricket eleven.'

'So that's two we know about, we took snap shots of them both before they entered that meeting so we should be able to pick them out if they appear anywhere near Melbourne Central,' said Kelsey.

'Where is Mr Razzaq?' asked Catherine. 'Is he on his way in?'

'Yes,' said Kelsey. 'But with the progress you made we'll see how we go here first before we allow them to get together. He may be able to get through to her if you fail.'

Griffiths turned to Catherine.

'We also have a problem now if we try to use him because

we've been guilty of being devious, she'll know that when he appears and tells her how he reached here, by police car all the way.'

'We'll cross that one when we come to it,' said Kelsey. 'Get a cup of coffee, Catherine, we'll keep her under observation.'

Catherine was drinking coffee in the canteen when Detective Constable Stannington appeared at her elbow.

'You're wanted,' he announced. 'She wants to speak to you again.'

Catherine joined Kelsey and Griffiths outside the interview room.

'What did she say?'

'She wants to see you again,' commented Kelsey. 'Maybe she has something to give us, or maybe not. Whatever...you seem to have made some progress.'

'When does her father get here?'

'Too soon for us, possibly,' grunted Detective Sergeant Griffiths. 'We'll just have to hold him off somehow. See what you can do anyway.'

Catherine re-entered the interview room, the policewoman who had been in the room acknowledged her and departed. Catherine sat at the table and looked at the girl.

'You wanted to see me,' she said.

Griffiths dialled a number on his mobile and raised it to his ear.

'DC Abbott?' he asked.

The reply was clearly in the affirmative.

'Where are you?'

Abbott gave his location and Griffiths checked the map of Victoria on the wall.

'I've got you!' Griffiths said. 'Drive to Pakenham Station

and one of you board a city bound train with Razzaq. Make sure it comes through the Rail Loop, if it doesn't then change at Caulfield, or Richmond onto one that does, then get off at Melbourne Central.'

D.C. Abbott was clearly asking the obvious…why?

'Never mind that now, I'll tell you when you get here,' Griffiths said impatiently. 'Give us a call when you're passing through Richmond station and we'll arrange for a police vehicle to collect you from Melbourne Central. Just do as I say, I'll explain later. Got that?'

He clicked off his mobile phone and looked at Kelsey.

'Done!' he said. 'We're keeping ourselves honest, after a fashion.'

Kelsey nodded with satisfaction and looked at Catherine Parkinson. She looked relieved. He looked at the sheet of paper she had handed to him.

'Your ploy clearly worked; now she's given us three addresses, but she's not sure whether anyone will be there. That's a chance we have to take,' said Kelsey.

'We've done well,' said Griffiths. 'Maybe we can stop some of them.'

'Ted, can you arrange for raiding parties at these addresses, Captain Bartlett's boys should be involved, being the bomb experts.'

'I've already done that,' said Griffiths.' I've alerted a squad for the first one in Kensington, Captain Bartlett and his men can deal with that one. Leave it with me, I'll arrange for the others if you can brief Captain Bartlett.'

Kelsey looked at Catherine.

'You've done well,' he said. 'I agree with you your stretching of the truth has to be legitimised; we may need more information from her if she has it. A transparent lie would have meant she'd never trust you again. Now she's given further information I consider she's bound to ask Razzaq how he got here.'

'I'm not sure if she has any more information,' said Catherine. 'She's struggling with her ethics, I'd say, if you could call it that.'

'Ethics! More like twisted logic!' Kelsey snorted irritably.

'She's been brainwashed into believing her cousin and his friends, who maintain they are the true believers,' continued Catherine. 'But she can't reconcile this with her father who is violently opposed to what they are planning now he's aware of what's going on.'

'It hasn't helped when they've had a firebrand cleric preaching to them, why we let these extreme fanatics into the country is beyond me,' Kelsey shook his head. 'Some politicians don't care what they do to secure votes. If there are considerable numbers of Muslim voters in their constituency, stupid politicians or government ministers will vote to let in more of them to attract votes. They don't seem to care what harm it may do the country if you let in people like that in large numbers with little or no security checks.'

'Tell that to the Spanish and the English!' Catherine said emphatically. 'Tell those people who lost relatives in the Madrid and London Tube bombings.'

CHAPTER 31

'There's the signal,' Captain Bartlett said to Sergeant Willoughby as they examined the rear of the Kensington address. 'They're going in the front so we go in the back.'

Willoughby nodded, waved at the two troopers and they crept to the rear door, accompanied by two police.

'Stand by!' Bartlett ordered brusquely. 'That's the front door being forced. Aston, do the necessary with this rear door...oh hold on! Somebody's doing it for us.'

They heard the back door being unbolted, it opened and two men spilled out onto the garden path but pulled up sharply when confronted by armed soldiers and police.

'Down!' Bartlett made a pushing movement with the flat of his hand. Whether they understood the word or not, his meaning was clear. They both dropped to the path, were seized by police and their arms pinioned. Both wore backpacks.

'Keep hold of their arms,' cautioned Bartlett. 'We don't want any accidents. Shine that torch over here, Aston?'

Sergeant Willoughby and his two men examined the backpacks, he gave an order, the men's arms were pulled back and the backpacks eased away from them. At this point police entered the kitchen from the hallway, one poked his head out of the back door.

'Great, you've got them!' he said. 'There's nobody else in here. That was the lot. What the hell have they got in those packs?'

'That's what we intend to find out,' Bartlett said grimly. 'Careful with those straps, Sergeant, ease them off slowly.'

The two men had been separated from their backpacks and escorted back into the house. Bartlett and Sergeant Willoughby examined the packs, Willoughby unfastened the straps while Bartlett indicated to everyone else to back off.

Bartlett held the torch while Willoughby worked at the two packs, it seemed like an eternity and he could feel perspiration running down the small of his back and under his arms.

'There must be a better way of earning a living,' Willoughby thought bitterly to himself. 'I should have stayed in Civvy Street and worked harder at my carpentry.'

He peered inside the first one as Captain Bartlett held the torch and reached in with his wire cutters.

'That one's fixed,' Willoughby looked up at Captain Bartlett. 'Can you shine the torch over here, sir.'

Bartlett did as Willoughby directed and cursed angrily when he realised the beam of the torch was shaking. Damn and blast, I'm losing my nerve, Bartlett thought, and slowly moved his hand up and down to minimise the shakes. Willoughby worked at the second backpack, there was a clicking noise as he severed wires and he straightened up.

'That's all sir.'

Bartlett felt some self-gratification to note Willoughby's

voice was strained and clipped. So...it had got to him as well!

'You right?' he asked.

'Yes sir, just glad the job's done,' Willoughby drew his sleeve across his brow.

'Better ways of earning a living, eh?' commented Bartlett and Willoughby grinned.

'Too damn right, sir,' he replied. 'I could do with a beer.'

'I'll buy you a bloody crate when this caper is over,' promised Bartlett. 'Let's see what they found in the house.'

*

'That was a job well done,' commented Kelsey when Bartlett reported progress via telephone. 'Another two bombs isolated and disarmed.'

'Not so good, we found a third man hiding in a cupboard at Kensington,' reported Captain Bartlett. 'He had a mobile phone with him. We tracked the last numbers dialled to two other mobiles, both untraceable.'

The desk phone rang and Kelsey snatched it up.

'Yes...good!' he said. 'How many there?'

The conversation was brief, Kelsey returned to his mobile phone.

'That was Abbotsford, Captain. We cleaned up there, two more arrested and three backpacks found. That just leaves the Fitzroy address. If you've finished there come on in.'

*

'The birds have flown!' Jim Waters reported to Kelsey on his mobile as he and Dean Hateley investigated the Fitzroy address and examined the ground floor rooms.

'Bugger it!' was Kelsey's response. 'That leaves two or three on the loose.'

'We're still searching,' said Waters. 'We may turn something up. They seem to have been here some time. There's a garden shed where they've possibly been mixing things'

'What?' Kelsey was all attention. 'What the hell is in there?'

'No idea, I'm going nowhere near it,' responded Waters. 'They've been making something, I had a quick look, there are drums and bags all over the place, it looks as if they've been brewing something in saucepans.'

'Then keep well away,' Kelsey replied. 'Let the experts sort it out. Look for paper work in the house.'

*

'We have a problem; we have a possible three men who will be trying to plant explosives, assuming they stick to their original plan,' Kelsey shuffled his notes and looked around. 'But we do have points in our favour. Although these blighters know we're after them, they may not be aware their plan has been completely compromised, although their safe houses have. Secondly, we haven't arrested this man Asif and his cricketer friend Rafit Qadri, so we can presume they are two of the three we're looking for. We got mug shots of them when we carried out surveillance at that cricket club meeting. We'll need Donald Taylor again, he may be able to recognise the third, or even a fourth or fifth depending on how many are left.'

'So...we have to stake-out the station,' said McKay.

'We had to do that anyway so we've lost nothing. We've drastically reduced the odds now, when I think back a week we'd got nowhere and everything we had turned into dead ends one after the other.'

'A break had to come some time,' said McKay.

'Sure, and it did. We'll need access to the railways control room now, to see who's on those station platforms, and have surveillance on all trains and stations leading to Melbourne Central.'

'The Grand Final is the day after tomorrow.'

'Yes, time is short.'

*

They met again to compare notes and procedures in the ASIO field office. Reporters were clustering around the entrance to the Police Complex; noting and trying to interview everyone who walked in, someone had clearly tipped them off. Something of this magnitude was bound to leak out, Clucas had already been waylaid outside the building and attempts had also been made to contact the Commissioner.

Consequently, it was decided to hold the meeting, courtesy of ASIO, commencing 6.30 am. Everyone attending came direct from their places of residence, so nobody could be followed from the police building. Clucas had not gone home the previous night, but stayed in an hotel near the city.

All members of the usually uniformed police contingent were in plain clothes. Those present included Kelsey, McKay, Catherine Parkinson, John Edmonds, Dean Hateley, Jim Waters, and from the police, Detective Sergeant Griffiths, Detective Constables Stannington, Alec Oliver and Bob Dempsey. Superintendent Clucas was in charge of the meeting, while Captain Bartlett and Sergeant Willoughby, the only uniformed representatives, were also present. John Edmonds, acting as doorman, closed the door.

'I've been creeping furtively around this morning to avoid

being waylaid by the press,' said Clucas. 'How the blazes did they get hold of this?'

'How do they get hold of anything?' grumbled Kelsey. 'My only fear is they could give the game away about Melbourne Central. If they do *that*...we're truly scuppered. The bombers could change plans and shift target anywhere.'

'We can only assume they don't know anything concrete; just that something's up,' said Clucas. 'I must congratulate you all on the footwork you've put in during past few weeks. I understand from Alan, until a week ago, you had nothing, then information and suspects turned up from various directions. All information came as a result of hard work, which was borne out when three lines of enquiry all converged at one point, the laundrette and the Prahran address.'

He paused to pour water from the jug on the table.

'One occurrence that could be termed fortunate, was the escape of Adam Simmerson, a very resourceful young man,' he continued. 'We had a lucky coincidence in that ASIO operatives Bramble and Shackleton were pursuing another line of enquiry and were on hand to intervene when he was run down by his gaolers. Alternatively, the line of enquiry Bramble and Shackleton were pursuing had an element of inevitability about it; it was leading to where Simmerson was being held.'

He paused to take a sip of water.

'We have possibly four or five of these people still at large of whom we know two, Asif and the other university student. We have people at hand who should recognise them if they show up, and we may be able identify other members of this organisation. Donald Taylor saw three men in Henderson's shop and Adam Simmerson reckons he saw about eight while incarcerated at Drouin. We've picked up the two who nearly recaptured Simmerson. Others at large he may recognise.'

Clucas turned to Kelsey.

'That's how we stand at present, where do we go from here?'

'Priorities are firstly to secure the Melbourne Central Underground Station,' said Kelsey. 'We must place as many operatives in there as we can, whether army, police or ASIO. We'll have an SAS officer supervising events at the Melbourne Control Centre, Major Collins, who has successfully overseen similar anti-terrorist emergencies in the past, is on his way from Canberra, he's well-known to us and to Captain Bartlett. We should be present at the Melbourne Metro Control Centre and need people viewing every CCTV to check people entering and leaving trains and stations. We should post contacts like Donald Taylor, Roger Richardson and Adam Simmerson where they can see people entering the station. Entrances are a block apart so they'll need to be in the control centre.'

He looked around.

'Any questions?'

There being none, he continued.

'We also need surveillance on the entrances. We have pictures of Asif and Rafit, it's likely they'll be two of the bomb carriers. Every man and woman on all the teams must study these pictures and know who they are. When we waylay the bombers Captain Bartlett and his men will be responsible for disarming them...Captain!'

Bartlett rose to his feet and cast his eye around.

'If or when we apprehend anyone carrying a suspicious package, for God's sake leave it alone. Send for Sergeant Willoughby or me or one of my men, if you touch the damned thing, you could easily set it off and kill yourself plus anyone else in the vicinity. If Sergeant Willoughby sets it off you have my permission to sue him afterwards for damages!'

There was some laughter and Sergeant Willoughby grimaced.

'The likelihood is, we'll have to disarm it on the spot,' added Captain Bartlett. 'The platform will have to be cleared. Further, if they are carrying any mobile phones make sure they are relieved of those immediately, the bombers in Madrid set off their explosives using mobile phones as triggers.'

He looked around and continued.

'We'll need personnel in the control centre, Major Collins will insist on that, and must make it clear to the railways staff on those monitors who or what we are looking for. In the main we're looking for people of Asian origin who are carrying backpacks. From recent investigation that seems most likely, but look out for suspicious cases or packages or anyone behaving suspiciously, which covers a lot of things. If you see anyone you have a bad feeling about, report them in and someone will deal with them.'

'Do we know for certain they'll be Asian?' asked Catherine Parkinson.

'Not necessarily, one European who was actively involved is currently under arrest in Canberra,' said Bartlett. 'Micah Bentley, known as Macca or Mac, according to his sister, who appears to have been a prime mover.'

'How do we ensure casualties are minimised if they manage to explode bombs down there?' asked John Edmonds.

'I'll take that one,' Kelsey rose to his feet. 'There will be traffic through Melbourne Central after the game is over, before the game the main stations in demand will be Richmond and Jolimont, both near the football ground. These two stations should be taking the bulk of the traffic afterwards, rail tracks that run through Richmond give access to virtually every suburb served by rail and some country railway lines.'

'Then why isn't Richmond the main target?' asked Stannington.

'There's an easy answer to that,' said Captain Bartlett. 'A bomb set off in an enclosed space can cause considerably more damage and casualties. Richmond station is not only in the open air, it is above ground level, so the effects of any explosions would be dissipated into the open air and above street level.'

'Jolimont is a much smaller station and in a deep cutting,' added Griffiths. 'The effects of any explosion would still dissipate upwards but towards grassy banks. In addition, Jolimont is a small station and less passengers would be using it. Melbourne Central, or any of the other underground stations, would confine the explosion to a limited and finite space, which would redouble the force.'

'I'm inclined to believe any attacks will be after the game, when they know the station will have an influx of people as they pour out of the football arena,' said Clucas. 'This influx may start early if the game becomes one sided, which has sometimes happened. Before the game, the crowding may not be so concentrated; nowadays with pre-match entertainment people will often get into the ground four or five hours beforehand.'

'So, we concentrate on the period after the game,' said McKay.

'I favour that as a more likely period,' said Clucas. 'I realise by saying that I'm sticking my neck out, but that's my considered opinion. But obviously we must be on our guard from 8 am. onwards.'

'Meaning we stake-out the station and the control centre from early morning?' asked McKay.

'We do.'

'What about Richmond and Jolimont?' McKay asked again.

'Stake them out,' said Clucas. 'The bulk of the homeward traffic will gravitate towards these stations. It's possible the bombers will be aware of that and if they suspect Melbourne Central is heavily guarded it may occur to them these two stations would make alternative targets. We know their main aim is to kill as many as possible, if London, Mumbai and Madrid are any guide. Melbourne Central has the advantage, to them, of a devastating explosion in a confined space which, being more open underground, will affect both sets of rail tracks at each level. At Parliament and Flagstaff stations the two platforms are separated ...but yes, security should also be concentrated on Richmond and Jolimont.'

'On the question of time of day ...' all heads turned to Catherine Parkinson. 'I'm trying to understand the mentality of these people, is their main object the killing of as many people as possible, or would it be the destruction of what is, to us, an annual festival?'

'Both I imagine,' said Clucas. 'What are you getting at?'

'I'm just thinking what, to them, would constitute the most satisfactory result, leave the Grand Final to run its course and then explode their bombs, or do the job early and destroy the Grand Final itself,' said Catherine. 'After all, who would enjoy watching a game after patrons have been killed in vast numbers before the event?'

There was silence, Clucas rubbed his chin, deep in thought, as were Kelsey and Captain Bartlett. Clucas finally spoke out.

'Shades of the 1972 Munich Olympics,' he said. 'A good point. However, it doesn't affect the issue very much for us, we shall be on high alert throughout the day. Nevertheless, Ms Parkinson has a valid point there, it makes sense to me and we must bear that in mind. We must ensure all squad cars are on their guard from early on.'

He turned to Captain Bartlett.

'Anything further, Captain?'

'I will just say that Major Collins has dealt with similar situations in the past, he tends to give instructions in an arbitrary manner, as though everyone is in uniform and below the rank of lance-corporal.' A ripple of laughter ran around the table. 'He can be abrupt at times, and impatient of people who don't jump to it straight away, but in a situation like this we can't have people questioning orders as the consequences could be serious. I've known the Major for years, an excellent officer who knows what he's doing.'

'I'll second that,' said Kelsey. 'I've seen Major Collins in action and he's nobody's fool. I've no objection to him treating me like a private if he saves lives, the last time I was exposed to him he did both!'

This caused more amusement, and Clucas looked around.

'We'll deal with the details at the next briefing. We've already worked out where everyone must be on the day and the means of communicating with each other. Major Collins will be in charge of the Melbourne Central Transport Control and Captain Bartlett will be in charge at Melbourne Central within the station itself. One further point, we have prevailed on the railway authorities to publicise alleged track work taking place which will divert several trains from the City Loop. There will be more traffic into Flinders Street Station direct, but that should not affect the fans greatly as most of them get out at Richmond.'

The duty senior police officer was Chief Inspector Talintyre, who held a preliminary briefing at Police HQ. He was an unsmiling and unpopular senior officer, shortly due for retirement, known to be very pernickety and critical of lesser ranks, forever poking his nose into matters that concerned him and others that didn't. It was thought he was trying to make his mark before he finally retired. He had held his present rank for some years, technically it no longer existed as the ranks of Chief Inspector and Chief Superintendent had both been phased out some years previously by Victorian Police, but anyone who held those ranks at the time of the phasing out retained them. Talintyre paused as a couple of late comers entered the briefing room.

'Nice of you to turn up,' he commented sarcastically, which caused both late arrivals to grit their teeth. 'Lucky for you we haven't really started so we won't have to repeat anything, but we have a difficult day ahead of us. I'll hand over to Detective Sergeant Griffiths, who's been very much involved with this... Sergeant!'

Griffiths advanced to the podium, a map of the Melbourne Central Business District was behind him and another which showed the two levels of Melbourne Central station.

'You all have details of what we believe has been planned by terrorists for today; these are in the folders before you. It's vital we all remain at a level of high alert. We are looking for men most likely of Asian appearance, carrying backpacks. But if you see anyone of any description carrying anything that looks dodgy, call it in, don't ignore possible suspicious characters because they are carrying something other than a backpack.'

He paused.

'There will be others on the ground you won't recognise, ASIO operatives, SAS personnel and Federal Police. It's possible you'll come across them during the course of the day, especially around the underground stations, Richmond and Jolimont. We have a password, the word is 'Lampoon'...a word quite unrelated to the operation we are conducting. Some of the others, especially the ASIO operatives, will not be obvious, and there will be some colleagues from the CIB from other nicks in Melbourne and Victoria who you may not recognise at first glance. Possibly you may mistake each other for suspects, be aware of that. So...if you do jump onto a suspect and start beating the living daylights out of him and he shouts 'Lampoon' you know what to do.'

'Thump him again!' said a burly constable in the front row and there were roars of laughter.

'Right!' Griffiths grinned and shuffled his notes. 'You got it in one …then his mates will sort you out later.'

He indicated the charts behind him.

'This is where we believe the attack may be attempted, where we need full coverage. Remember this is the main objective today and takes priority, if you see any drunkenness or disagreements between fans, I'm not saying ignore it completely, but remember not to lose sight of the main game;' he stopped and looked around.' It's no good successfully putting a drunk in the slammer if you miss one of our fanatical friends. Clear?'

'What if we see a bank robbery?'

'Don't spend too much time on it, give 'em a hand if necessary, then resume your patrol as quickly as possible.'

That went down well and Griffiths waited for the laughter to subside, then leant forward over the podium.

'I agree there are some situations we can't ignore, like that one, but what I'm emphasising is this. Forget the minor infractions we tend to experience on days of Grand Finals or games days, just pull 'em apart and move them on. If there's a fight, just apprehend one of the participants, dump him on the back seat and move him a couple of streets away. Just remember priorities. Now…' he reached behind him and produced several papers, took off the top sheets and indicated two constables in the front row. '…this is where you'll be, starting with you two!' He handed them the two top sheets.

Griffiths dealt with everyone at length then handed back to Talintyre. As he wound up, Superintendent Clucas hit the flat of one hand on the table and raised the other.

'This is one of the more important days of our lives,' he said. 'We are dealing with fanatics; some would say lunatics, who hate who we are and how we live. They probably don't care whether they kill themselves in the pursuit of their aims, past experience in London, Mumbai and Madrid indicates this is a possibility. Lastly, if you find what you suspect is one of their engines of destruction, don't mess around with it, send for the military. We don't want to lose any of you.'

CHAPTER 32

The squad car cruised through the Melbourne streets, with Constables Bright and Trollope keeping a watchful eye on busy pavements. Their beat was Latrobe Street from Melbourne Central up to Flagstaff Station, King Street, left into Little Lonsdale Street, Exhibition Street, then back to Melbourne Central, and so on ad infinitum. Many police colleagues were on their route, they recognised a few but none acknowledged the squad car.

'What do you reckon?' asked Trollope.

'Always thought this sort of thing happened overseas,' replied Bright. 'Bit unnerving when it's here.'

'Think we're over reacting?'

'Talintyre and Griffiths are no scaremongers. I used to be at Malvern with Ted Griffiths; he's no mug and doesn't panic,' Bright replied. 'Let's face it, we've been hearing rumours for days now, remember when they let out that young rookie - what was his name...?'

'Cope.'

'Aye...Cope, that's right,' Bright nodded. 'They let him out with a blaze of publicity instead of that murder suspect. That was weird, it was an open and shut case initially, then it turned out Taylor had just been a witness.'

'Sergeant Phillips said a spook came in from a federal agency and demanded to see him while they were grilling him; he had clearance from the top and Phillips wasn't too pleased!'

'Bloody spooks...now we have to do all the work.'

'Be fair, they're on the ground too, so Griffiths said, they could pop up anywhere ...' Trollope paused in mid-sentence '... hold on! That bloke over there, by the newsagents ...there...look!'

Bright drew the squad car into the kerb. They both had a second look at a man walking away from them up Latrobe Street, towards Flagstaff Station, sporting a backpack. In addition, as he walked, he looked across to his right and was plainly Asian.

'What you reckon?'

'The backpack looks suss to me,' grunted Bright. 'Call this one in.'

Trollope picked up his radio.

'IC 4 walking on Latrobe heading west, crossing Queen Street at the traffic lights, has a backpack. Heading west towards Flagstaff Station, away from Melbourne Central.'

*

Army vehicles drew up in front of the Transport Building and disgorged a squad of men including a major and a captain. They entered the building and were greeted by a supervisor, James Cardwell. The major advanced into the lobby and eyed Cardwell.

'I am Major Collins. I need access to your Control Centre immediately. You are expecting us?'

Cardwell nodded, and indicated the lifts. Some of them entered two available lifts, the remainder waited for others to arrive on the ground floor.

Collins and his men disembarked on the 6th floor where they were greeted by Kelsey. Cardwell indicated a conference room, they entered and Major Collins sat himself at the head of the table, his first move to establish his authority. He was 6' 5" in height, sported a military moustache, and possessed blue eyes that bored relentlessly into anyone he was looking at, or addressing.

'I have a direct line through to the Prime Minister; from this point of time, I am in charge. This must be made clear to everyone working in the operations room out there. All matters requiring a decision are to be channelled through me and/or Captain Roberts,' he indicated the officer accompanying him, also over six feet in height, in battle fatigues, with pronounced sunburn and also sporting a military moustache. 'As you can appreciate, we have several organisations represented here and with the gravity of the situation we can't afford clashes of authority or disputes resulting in delays. Understood?'

He looked around as everyone nodded or rumbled assent.

'Having said that, we have amongst us Alan Kelsey, with whom I have worked before on matters of Internal Security,' Collins continued. 'Alan knows as much as if not more about the background to this operation as I do, so don't hesitate, if you have a question, to approach Alan. Any questions?'

There were none.

'Right! Good! Everyone clear so far?'

It seemed everybody was.

'Then let's go upstairs. The Commissioner and Mr Cardwell will make matters clear to those in the control centre as soon as we leave this room. I'll need a desk, with a monitor from the CCTV and possibly a television set, I want to know at what stage the Grand Final is at any one time and no ...I am *not* a football fan! It's vital I know, and thus we all know, what stage the game has reached at all times as this could have a bearing on the final outcome.'

Major Collins marched into the Operations & Communications Centre with Captain Roberts, Kelsey and James Cardwell behind him. They fanned out so Cardwell, normally in charge of the centre until now, could call to attract everyone's attention.

'Attention everyone!' he shouted and the hubbub ceased. There were roughly twenty men and women in the room, many with headsets and facing monitor screens. There were three large flat screens on the wall which showed the full railway system. There was also a patchwork of monitor screens showing station scenes, passageways and platforms, in an array before which were five operators. The scenes they were watching flicked and changed to differing situations as they observed.

'This is Major Collins of the SAS,' announced Cardwell. 'Major Collins is assuming command of this complex until further notice.'

Collins advanced to the middle of the room and faced all the operators.

'All of you stop what you are doing and listen to me. If you are on a phone to anyone, if it is not operational, cease the call now and listen.'

There was a rumble of voices, heads popped up and turned in Collins' direction.

'Did you hear me?' he bellowed.

Most of them did. Some of his men wandered amongst the operators, tapping on the shoulder those still engaged on phones.

'We're dealing with a Category Red emergency which takes priority over everything,' said Collins. 'We are dealing with a situation where we suspect at least four men and possibly more will be trying to enter the system with explosives which they intend to detonate on the rail system. Everyone hear that?'

They did, there was a buzz of voices.

'Silence,' bellowed Collins. 'If you talk amongst yourselves whilst I am talking, you may miss something of importance. Listen! We don't know whether they are suicide bombers as per the London Underground or whether they intend to leave packages, bags or whatever on trains or in stations à la Madrid or Mumbai. We believe, from information gathered over recent days, they may be planning to enter the system via one of the underground stations and then disperse in four or more directions, as they did in London.'

'Is this for real?' a supervisor raised his hand. 'In Melbourne?'

'Yes, it is – and in Melbourne!' snapped Collins. 'Now, we want every CCTV camera in the system checked; particularly in Melbourne Central, Parliament and Flagstaff underground stations. These stations are likely targets for these people, better to target in the city centre if you're intent on making a statement. There's no point for them to hit a station in the outer suburbs, though I won't deny it could happen. All clear so far?'

Again, there was a rumble of assent.

'We are primarily looking for men of Middle Eastern appearance, Arabs, Persians Egyptians, call them what you will. They will either look bulky or be carrying bags, cases or backpacks.'

A girl seated at one of the first row of consoles spread her hands out in a protesting motion.

'We can't assume because they're Asian in appearance they have criminal intentions...?'

'Yes, we bloody well can, and we are,' snapped Collins. 'What's your name?'

'Julie Smythe.'

'Very well, Julie, have you any friends or relatives who'll be travelling or working on the rail system today?'

'Yes, I do, but...!'

'Then you could cause their deaths or injury if you have any reservations about looking for people of a particular ethnicity. If anyone has any politically correct emotions or reactions that will cloud their judgement and possibly cause disaster, I suggest you get out of here now. We have a serious situation and we don't have the time nor the inclination to horse around with political correctness. Does anyone have any problems with that?'

He looked around expectantly, Julie Smythe bit her lip but nobody moved.

'Good! We've been pursuing this situation full-time for the last few days and about a month overall. We know the types we're looking for and what motivates them. I'll certainly qualify what I am saying, look for anyone behaving suspiciously but pay attention to anyone of Middle Eastern or Asian appearance...' he turned with a grim smile '...anyone with a complexion like Captain Roberts here.'

There was a ripple of laughter, Captain Roberts smiled and raised one hand.

'Clear?'

It was this time.

'Remember, if these people carry out their intentions, somebody close to you or someone you know could be maimed or killed. We believe the time they have in mind is the rush, 4.30 to 5.00 onwards, after the game is over.'

He turned to James Cardwell.

'Mr Cardwell, can you contact every station master on the

underground system, and others, in particular Richmond and Jolimont. They have to be on the alert for anyone boarding trains who look suspicious, or behaving strangely, and report it here. That includes the main Flinders Street railway station and Spencer Street.'

At this juncture, the message from Constable Trollope came through on the air waves, the SAS operator passed it to his sergeant who took it to Major Collins and Captain Roberts who were collating information from various sources.

'Thank you, Sergeant,' Captain Roberts looked at it briefly and handed it to Major Collins, 'Maybe we should place Roger Richardson onto the CCTV from Flagstaff, sir, if this man enters the station, he may recognise him.'

'Maybe Donald Taylor as well,' Collins nodded. 'Where are they?'

'Over there by the door, sir,' said the sergeant.

'Very good!' Collins turned to the sergeant. 'Sergeant Cameron, can you guide those two young men over to Flagstaff Station CCTVs? They may capture the image of a man with a backpack who we think will shortly enter that station, probably via the entrance on the corner of Latrobe and William Streets.'

The sergeant went over to Roger Richardson and Donald Taylor, and briefly conversed with them before they were guided to a monitor which showed the William Street entrance to Flagstaff Station. They were introduced briefly to the operator, a dark-haired girl named Anna.

'What are we looking for?' asked Roger.

'This is a camera positioned outside Flagstaff Station,' explained Anna. 'It covers the intersection of William Street and Latrobe.'

'The person in question was walking up the slope in Latrobe Street between Queen and William Streets when he was spotted by a squad car,' explained Sergeant Cameron. 'Of Asian extraction and carrying a backpack. He should appear over there...' he pointed to a traffic light on the top right-hand corner of the screen '...assuming he's heading for Flagstaff. There are car parks in between plus a café, he could have gone into those... no hang on...who's that? That could be him.'

'I'll zoom in,' Anna manipulated her controls. 'There, how's that?'

Roger Richardson peered closely at the screen, and fingered his chin.

'Let me see, it could be...!' he said. 'Can you zoom in closer?'

'Not by much,' replied Anna. 'It can become fuzzy; we'll have to wait until he crosses the street when he's closer to the camera ...there...how about that?'

Roger leant forward, gazed fixedly at the monitor, then nodded.

'That's Rafit,' he said. 'Yes, that's him. His walk is distinctive, he seems to bend his arms forward from the elbows when he walks, see?'

'And you?' Sergeant Cameron turned to Donald Taylor.' Do you recognise him?'

'He was in Henderson's shop; he was the one who pulled the phone from the wall,' said Taylor.

'Right!' Sergeant Cameron moved back to Major Collins. 'We've identified one of them, sir, crossing William Street to enter Flagstaff. We believe his name is Rafit.'

'Put it on my monitor,' Collins glared at the screen when it flashed up. He turned to Captain Roberts. 'Inform Sergeant Gaston at Flagstaff, this man is entering Flagstaff Station from the William Street entrance, backpack, blue jeans, brown jacket. He's entering the station entrance now and heading for the escalator.'

CHAPTER 33

Sergeant Gaston had two men with him at Flagstaff Station, he was wearing fatigues while his men were both wearing denims and open necked shirts, others were posted at strategic intervals guarding escalators. Gaston seized his radio and spoke to his two men.

'Escalator from William Street,' he said tersely. 'Blue jeans, brown jacket, backpack, Asian appearance.'

'I have him, Sarge,' came the reply.

Gaston saw his second man leave his position and join the other at the foot of the escalator, where they ostensibly engaged each other in conversation.

'On his way to you,' he said. 'Jump him when he's in reach, pinion his arms...you know the drill,' Gaston switched channels and reported to Major Collins. 'We see him, sir. On the William Street escalator, man of Asian appearance, carrying a backpack.'

'Roger!' responded Major Collins. 'His name could be Rafit. Use his name just before you grab him, it may throw him off guard, he might think it's one of his off-siders. Don't worry whether he's an innocent traveller or not, I don't think he is, but we can't pussyfoot around. Better safe than sorry! Got that?'

'Rafit...right, sir!' Gaston responded and relayed the message to his two men at the foot of the escalator, still apparently engaged in perfunctory conversation. Rafit, if it was him, was now half way down the escalator, which was fairly full, and looking up at the ceiling as he descended.

'Probably asking for his 72 virgins to be lined up,' Gaston muttered to himself and, ever the philosopher, added. 'If sexual favours are ever offered to me to do a job, give me an experienced whore any day of the week...or night' he added as an afterthought. In a louder voice for the benefit of his minions. 'Stand-by lads.'

The man reached the foot of the escalator and briefly looked around. Gaston's two men were still engrossed in conversation, as he moved in their direction they turned and one of them went over to him.

'Rafit?' he called.

Rafit stopped as though he'd walked into a brick wall. He was still assimilating that he'd been addressed by name when they both advanced towards him and pounced. Too late he realised who they were, before he could take action his arms were seized and he was deposited violently face down onto the floor, before an assembly of astonished onlookers. Sergeant Gaston, in fatigues, arrived on the scene and made placatory gestures to onlookers.

'Just move along, this is a police matter,' he said. 'There is nothing to be alarmed about...' and added in an undertone only he could hear '...the hell there isn't!'

His soothing comments appeared to be having the opposite effect, but fortunately members of the Victorian Police arrived and began ushering the crowd along. Sergeant Gaston's two troopers subdued Rafit, his arms were pinioned behind his back and Sergeant Gaston was on his radio to Captain Bartlett. Rafit was pulled or dragged into a quiet corner well away from pedestrian traffic, later arrivals down the escalator did no more than give curious glances mainly at the little knot of spectators, Rafit and his captors were now well off the main thoroughfare. Captain Bartlett quickly raised Sergeant Willoughby at Melbourne Central.

'They've nabbed a backpacker at Flagstaff, Sergeant, get up to Flagstaff now.'

'No worries, sir,' responded Willoughby. 'No need for transport, a train's in the station now. I'll be there in about three minutes. I'll bring Aston with me.'

They had already relieved Rafit of his back pack by cutting through the shoulder straps when Sergeant Willoughby arrived, accompanied by Trooper Aston. Willoughby unslung his own pack and dumped it on the floor next to the backpack.

'Right!' Willoughby said. 'Get the hell out of here!'

He turned to Aston. 'Make sure nobody comes near, Aston, just move them away.'

The others needed no second bidding, they beat a hasty retreat and moved behind pillars while police went to the escalators and prevented any more passengers coming up or down. The concourse was empty and as silent as the tomb as Sergeant Willoughby carefully opened the backpack and laid it flat on the floor. He checked the positioning of the wires, gave it some thought, then took up a pair of pliers. They were demagnetised, to prevent them causing any slight variation that could trigger the bomb.

'Why did I take this lousy job?' Willoughby muttered as he settled on which wire to snip. He usually uttered the same platitude, it was almost a superstition to him now, he felt more secure if he muttered the sentence to himself before tackling explosive device.

'Aston, there's a green wire, a blue and a yellow. I'm cutting the yellow,' he called to Aston, who indicated he'd heard. Willoughby uttered a silent prayer and cut the wire. Nothing happened. He explored the innards of the backpack and found a wire leading to three canisters about the size of beer tins. He snipped three more wires, extracted the canisters and gave Aston a wave.

'All clear, Aston, all done!'

Aston radioed the news to Captain Bartlett. A message came back over the ether, Aston called to Willoughby.

'The captain is sending people to pick this up, Sarge. We're to return to Melbourne Central.'

'OK...!'' Willoughby re-packed his bag, ensuring all his tools were in their proper place '...let's go Aston!'

He directed police to keep anybody away from the defused device, before he and Aston went down the escalator to the platform.

*

Donald Taylor and Roger Richardson were on neighbouring monitors. They didn't have much time for conversation but had ascertained they were both computer enthusiasts.

'You knew this bloke, did you?' Taylor asked. 'The one we've just caught?'

'Not well,' answered Richardson. 'He bowled to me a few times in the nets, and we scored a few runs together in one match. I still can't believe it.'

'Neither can I.'

'With me it's different,' said Roger Richardson. 'I know this sounds silly, it isn't cricket and all that bulldust, but I just find it difficult to reconcile somebody you've played cricket with can be capable of something like this.'

'Anything to report?' asked a voice from behind them. Captain Roberts was on one of his periodic patrols behind the monitor operators.

'No,' replied Taylor. 'Nothing new. We were just talking about that bloke caught at Flagstaff, it seems incongruous he could play cricket, yet be capable of something like this.'

'That's how it struck the Poms when terrorists blew up Underground trains in London,' said Captain Roberts. 'Two of them were playing cricket the night before they left to do what they did. I know what you mean.'

'Guess it's the normal world becoming twisted into frightening reality,' said Roger. 'Not easy to grasp.'

'Let me know if you find anything, I won't be far away ...yes... what is it?'

Donald Taylor was jabbing his finger at his screen.

'I think I know that joker...that one there.'

Captain Roberts peered at the screen.

'The one with the briefcase?'

'He looks like one of the men I saw in the shop,' said Taylor. 'I reckon he's one of the bastards who killed Harold Henderson.'

Roberts radioed Major Collins at the other end of the room.

'Captain Roberts, sir. Can you key into Monitor 7,' he said. 'We have a suspect at Melbourne Central. This one's carrying a briefcase.'

Major Collins snapped an order to the lance-corporal on the keyboard who keyed in '7' to his monitor controller and the picture flashed on screen.

'Who identified him?'

'Taylor sir.'

Collins gestured to his radio operator.

'Get onto that ASIO man, what's his bloody name ...?'

'Bramble, sir.'

'Bramble...tell him this man is on the upper platform, heading for the escalator, looks as if he's making for the Glen Waverley platform. Tell him this man has been recognised and is carrying a briefcase.'

CHAPTER 34

Bramble and Shackleton were on the upper platform when the message came through. Bramble beckoned to Shackleton.

'Man descending escalator to the Glen Waverley platform, carrying briefcase, heading for down escalator at the eastern end.'

They reached and descended the western escalator, uttering apologies as they forced their way through passengers. They reached the platform and looked around.

'See anything?' asked Bramble.

'No!' Shackleton answered. 'I'll go down this side, you go that.'

'Some of our people are at the other end, I'll check with the Major.'

Major Collins took Bramble's call, he confirmed his men had been notified.

'They're onto him, approach with care.'

Bramble hastened towards the eastern end of the station, then sighted their quarry.

'He's heading behind the escalator,' he reported. 'He's being hemmed in; I don't think he's aware of it yet.'

Two casually dressed police were hovering at the far end of the platform; one picking up occasional cans from the platform and ditching them into bins, while the other sauntered along near the platform's edge with hands in pockets. Shackleton approached around the other side of the escalator and proceeded to its rear end.

'Nethercott! Where's bloody Willoughby?' Major Collins snapped as he gesticulated to his radio man.

'On a train heading back to Melbourne Central, should be there any minute, sir.'

'Raise him then, don't just sit there! Tell him what's going on, for Chrissake!'

'I've already told him, sir.'

'What! Oh! Very good! Well done, Nethercott.'

Nethercott, on the radio transmitter, smiled to himself. That was as near to an apology he'd ever receive from Major Collins. Whatever, it was better than nothing!

*

Bramble established contact with the two casually dressed constables, they recognised him and he received a brief nod from the man near the platform edge. A train drew in from Flagstaff as Bramble edged nearer the man with the briefcase. Bramble was near enough to make a direct move, especially as the incoming train was causing a diversion.

The Asian hesitated and appeared to be looking for somewhere to deposit the briefcase. This immediately registered with Bramble, he wasn't dealing with a suicide bomber; he was going to drop the bomb either after setting it or detonating it via remote control.

'I'm going in on the count of five!' he whispered into his radio. 'Tell your man, the one wearing the baseball hat.'

'Received, five, four three two...!'

They both launched themselves simultaneously at the Asian, while the platform stroller dashed to assist. Shackleton appeared from the rear end of the escalator. Their quarry never had a chance; he was thrust heavily onto the hard platform and submerged under Bramble, no lightweight, together with a brawny policeman. Shackleton wrested the briefcase from him.

'Where's Willoughby?' Shackleton snapped into his radio.

'Just got off that train, third carriage. I've been talking to him by radio and I have him on screen. He knows where you are, he and Aston are on their way,' Nethercott calmly responded as he viewed the scene on his monitor.

Shackleton looked up as Sergeant Willoughby and Aston pounded up from the escalator. Shackleton indicated the briefcase and Willoughby set down his bag. He didn't try to snap the briefcase open but cut the leather strap securing it and slowly eased it open.

'Jesus!' he exclaimed. Aston came over and held the bag open.

'He's set the clock, Sarge,' he said. 'The digits are clicking over.'

'You've just earned your pay for the week, Aston,' said Willoughby. 'Now piss off and take cover. I'm going to cut the blue wire, got it? The blue wire.'

Aston nodded and for the second time within twenty minutes retired behind a pillar. The struggling mass of Bramble and two police had vanished around the rear end of the escalator. Willoughby took out his pliers, uttered a silent prayer, again muttered 'Why did I take this lousy job'... before he snipped the blue wire. A thrill of fear run through him, he was sure he was right, but one never knew. He *was* right! Nothing happened, the clock continued to register but was now disconnected from the detonator.

'Aston!' he called.

'Sarge?' Aston's head appeared around the pillar.

'Tell them it's defused,' said Willoughby.

'Will do, Sarge.'

*

'Willoughby's disarmed it,' Collins said to Captain Roberts.

'Good!' Roberts inclined his head gravely. 'But we still have another one at least, sir. This man Asif hasn't surfaced yet.'

'Tell everyone to keep their eyes peeled,' commanded Collins. 'If only one of them gets through, we've failed!'

Midday arrived but still no sign of Asif, the preliminaries at the football ground were finally over and the time for the start of the game was imminent. Major Collins had had a television screen installed which faced him on his desk. As he had said, he was no football fan, it was purely to see what was going on and what stage the game had reached. The sound was turned down so no-one else would be distracted by it.

He looked up as Alan Kelsey came over to him, he too looked concerned.

'What do you reckon, Alan?' Collins asked.

'I've been thinking and have three scenarios regarding Asif. One: his bomb was a dud, a forlorn hope. Two: he's aware some of his playmates have been apprehended and isn't sure what to do next, or three: he's now on an independent limb and may be planning an attack elsewhere or at a different time,' said Kelsey.

'Two and three is virtually the same thing,' commented Major Collins. 'It's just the motivation that's different.'

'Just a thought, sir,' interjected Captain Roberts.

'Enlighten us,' responded Major Collins.

'It's possible he knows his friends have been arrested, the people we caught wouldn't have had time to warn anybody, but he could sense something is wrong. This could be either because he hasn't heard any explosions or because his friends failed to keep a rendezvous, more likely the latter. He may have been intending to explode a device shortly after one of the others, one of the tactics of the Irish was to let off a bomb, then detonate another shortly afterwards to kill approaching police, emergency and ambulance workers or bystanders running from the first explosion.'

Collins nodded thoughtfully, and pursed his lips.

'Go on!' he said.

'Is it possible sir, he saw one of the two we rumbled being rushed by our men? Could he have been present at the time, just standing nearby waiting to rendezvous with them?'

'At Flagstaff Station, you mean?'

'Primarily, yes, or maybe this last one at Melbourne Central. Flagstaff may be our best bet, he could have been there, somewhere in the concourse near the foot of the escalator with the intention of travelling onto Melbourne Central with the man we arrested. I understand the man we jumped on, Rafit, was the other cricketer from the university. Since they were friendly with each other, maybe they were teamed together.'

Collins considered, then looked at Kelsey.

'What do you think?'

'Captain Roberts has a likely scenario,' commented Kelsey. 'It's guesswork, and could be way off, but it could be on target. It's worth considering.'

'So Asif could have been nearby when we rushed that fellow at Flagstaff,' pondered Collins. 'It's worth following up.'

He picked up his phone and dialled.

'Mr Cardwell, can we obtain footage of the Flagstaff cameras from earlier on...we can? From when?'

Collins listened to the voice at the other end, then put down the phone.

'Yes, we can, I assume you'll have already gathered that. But there's a few of them, we may need assistance.'

'Shall I ask Victoria Barracks if they can spare a few men to assist us, sir?' suggested Roberts.

'Good idea, yes, do it,' Collins eyed the screen. 'The game's about to start,' he observed, 'What are the chances of him letting one off inside the ground?'

'Not good,' commented Kelsey. 'He's got to get in first, and everyone entering has been vetted closely, which caused quite a few grumbles and complaints. People are still waiting to get through the turnstiles. His best bet is to wait until the game's over and try to kill as many as he can coming out of the ground.'

'Or at the railway stations as people are going home, emphasis being on Richmond and Jolimont,' suggested Captain Roberts.

'We must have a look at these Flagstaff tapes, if he was there and we catch sight of him we'll know what he's wearing, that will help identify him if he turns up elsewhere. I don't think he'll be changing clothes now he's out and about.'

CHAPTER 35

The Grand Final ran its course, reaching quarter time then half-time. Major Collins relented to a degree and allowed occasional scoreline checks during the afternoon. He knew if he didn't, people may leave work stations to ascertain progressive scores and thus miss something or someone on their monitors.

But the elusive Asif didn't materialise on any monitor and at half-time Major Collins, Captain Roberts and Kelsey held a discussion as to what Asif may do.

'I'd say he knows things have gone wrong, he's either called it off, which I don't think likely, or he's going to conduct his own plan, something off the cuff. But where would he be likely to go?'

'I reckon he'll concentrate on the transport system; it's the plan he knows and relates to the Grand Final,' suggested Kelsey. 'That way he kills many people and also wrecks part of our infrastructure, the same pattern established at London, Madrid and Mumbai, all detonated during rush periods.'

'And the passenger influx after the game will be a rush period,' agreed Major Collins.

'He and his associates know the effect sporting events have on our culture,' Kelsey continued. 'They are striving for maximum publicity and casualties. He can't be planning to detonate inside the ground, I doubt if he's in there.'

'He knows Flagstaff and Melbourne Central will now be hard nuts to crack, my own preference is Richmond. Tens of thousands will congregate there and I don't see how we can close it down,' said Captain Roberts. 'It would be simple for him to join the crowds and merge in, I think a likely spot would be the underpass at Richmond Station, the explosion would be in a confined space and the force of the blast would go from end to end.'

'Agreed,' Major Collins nodded thoughtfully. 'I agree with all you've said and ...yes...it sounds plausible. Any other ideas?'

'Either that or he could plan to detonate close to a stadium exit,' said Kelsey. 'Maybe the footbridge across the railway tracks.'

'We have about an hour to prepare for any contingency we can think of. What about Roger Richardson, would he have any useful suggestions? He knows this man.'

'I don't think he knows him that well,' said Kelsey. 'They played in the same cricket eleven, but I don't think they had much in common off the cricket field.'

'Get him over here anyway,' grunted Major Collins. 'He may know something of the bloody man's likes and dislikes such as where he hangs out or who his mates are.'

Roger did his best after he was called over, he sat before Major Collins deep in thought but finally shook his head.

'Sorry, sir,' he said. 'I really can't assist, the only places where we had contact were connected to the cricket scene at Uni, either at the nets or on the field. Unless he's likely to gravitate to any of the cricket pavilions, pitches or practice nets I've nothing to suggest.'

Major Collins looked at Captain Roberts and Kelsey.

'Ideas?' queried Collins.

'That might be worth following up,' suggested Kelsey. 'If he's hiding up somewhere before making whatever assault he's planning, he's likely to select a place he knows, as long as it's not anywhere where he'd know we'd be waiting for him, such as his flat in Prahran, or any other houses they've been using.'

'A familiar location to hide, sounds feasible,' added Captain Roberts. 'I doubt if he'd be waiting at any of the stations right now, he'd stick out like a...sore thumb!'

'Well put Captain...or not put,' Major Collins gave a half-smile. 'But tell me. How far away are the university cricketing facilities from the city centre?'

'Not far,' said Roger. 'We played on an oval in Carlton, near the city. He'd know his way there, just a short tram ride, he could even walk there.'

Major Collins drummed his fingers on the desk top and reached a decision.

'Go there,' he said to Roger. 'Captain, select a detail to go with Mr Richardson and mosey around the cricket facilities. I'm inclined to agree with you, Captain,' he nodded at Roberts. 'If he's hiding out anywhere it will be in familiar surroundings, so we'll give it a try. Make the arrangements, Captain.'

As Captain Roberts left with Roger Richardson in tow, Major Collins' phone rang.

'Hallo!' he barked. 'Ah! Mr Cardwell...you have? Good! Where can they be viewed?'

He listened carefully, said 'OK!' and put down the phone. He thought for a moment and then dialled a number.

'Hello...this is Major Collins of SAS. Can I speak with Major Rawlinson, please?'

Kelsey heard clicking from the ear piece centred on Collins's ear followed by a crackling noise when a voice came on the line.

'Hello, Dick!' said Collins. 'I need some assistance...What? They've been in touch already, that's good. Glad somebody was using his loaf. The tapes in question are in the railways building at the Spencer Street end of Collins Street, can you get some of your lads up there quickly? We have some good photographs of the bloke we're looking for; we're transmitting those down there via internet now.'

There was a brief response from the other end.

'That's excellent, get them to give us a call when they've reached there, who's in charge ...Lieutenant Craig...OK! Get him to give me a call when he reaches there.'

He was about to hang up but stayed his hand.

'What's that? Oh yes, she's fine, how's Felicity? That's good news, Dick, we'll get together sometime. All the best.'

He sat back and looked at Kelsey.

'That was Major Rawlinson at Victoria Barracks. All we can do now is sit, hope and pray.'

*

Roger Richardson directed the army vehicle to the university cricket ground and it drew to a halt. There was a detail of five men with him, Sergeant Lumley and four troopers, all armed to the teeth, with Jim Waters and Gordon Anscombe from ASIO.

They piled out and Roger began casting around.

'That's the pavilion, guess I don't need to tell you that,' he said which caused Sergeant Lumley to smile. 'That hut over there is the groundsman's domain, where he keeps his mower and tins of whitewash for marking creases. The score-box is fairly obvious, that shutter at the front opens downwards and inwards, the hinges are at the bottom, the shutter itself acts as the bench where the scorers rest the scorebooks.'

'What's that building by the boundary?' asked Lumley.

'The back end of the tennis pavilion,' explained Roger. 'They put wire mesh across the rear windows to stop cricket balls going through them, it cost a fortune.'

'Are the places locked?'

'Should be, the groundsman will be around somewhere, I'll roust him out.'

'OK!' Lumley nodded. 'We'll check the pavilion first to look for any signs of forcible entry. Let's go.'

The troopers fanned out and made for the pavilion, Sergeant Lumley had a brief consultation with Jim Waters and the two ASIO men headed for the groundsman's hut. Both had guns at the ready, taking no chances. They reached the hut, one from each side, Waters headed for the door while Anscombe sidled up to one of the small windows. He edged around and peered in. Waters eyed the hut's construction and muttered under his breath, the timber was rotten in places, a bullet could go straight through.

'I'm going to open the door,' his voice crackled into Anscombe's ear piece.

'Ready,' said Anscombe. Waters kicked the door open and flung himself flat. The door swung open but nothing happened. From his recumbent position, Waters pushed at the door which swung back further, he could see a mower, a rake and several sacks containing whitewash. He applied his eye to the crack between door and post, then relaxed. He rose to his feet and entered in a rush, pistol at the ready but the hut was empty.

'Clear!' he called as Anscombe came around the corner and entered the small building.

'Groundsman's hut clear,' Waters reported to Sergeant Lumley who acknowledged.

'Someone's been in here,' said Anscombe as he ferreted around. 'There's chocolate bar papers and I can smell tobacco.'

'You're right,' agreed Waters. 'Put those papers in a bag and any nub ends you find. They may come in useful.'

'Unusual smell though,' commented Anscombe. 'Not one of the normal brands.'

'You're right,' Waters sniffed and nodded. 'I've smelt these before. I think they're French.'

'How far would the final have got?' asked Anscombe.

Waters peeled back his jacket sleeve and looked at his watch.

'Just past four o'clock,' he said. 'What do you think? Nearing three quarter time?'

Anscombe looked around for more evidence of occupation.

'Do we know what this bloke was wearing?'

'Not yet, they're looking for him on CCTV, that SAS Major reckoned he may have been in the vicinity when they pounced on that Flagstaff bomber.'

'There's a brown jacket here,' said Anscombe.

'Anything in the pockets?'

'Just looking ...no...nothing! Hang on, just a couple of lollies.'

'Lollies!' Waters looked up. 'Are they the same as these empty wrappings?'

'Yes,' answered Anscombe. 'The same.'

'I'll call it in,' said Waters. 'A brown jacket you say?'

'What do you reckon on colour? Have a look!'

Waters held it up to the light coming through the open door.

'Nearer mauve, or maroon, I'd say,' he pronounced. 'I'll call it in.'

*

An inspection of the pavilion, the groundsman's hut and the score-box came to naught, apart from the wrappings and the aroma of tobacco.

'Did your mate smoke?' Jim Waters asked Roger Richardson.

'He was *not* a mate,' Roger answered coldly. 'Acquaintance, yes, but a mate...no!'

'I thought you traded computers with him,' said Waters.

Roger swung around and regarded him even more coldly.

'Have you ever sold anything through the Trading Post or on the Internet?' he asked.

'No,' Waters answered.

'Have you ever bought anything second hand?' this time Waters nodded.

'OK, OK!' he said in a placatory tone. 'Point taken. There are acquaintances and friends. But I asked you a question about your frie... about this man Asif.'

'Yes,' answered Roger. 'About half a pack a day I'd say, about ten or so cigarettes.'

'What brand?'

'Brand!' Roger massaged his forehead. 'Good God! How on earth am I ...Oh hold on a minute! Yes, I do know. He has or had a fetish for French cigarettes, Gauloise I think. He often used to smoke those, if he couldn't get them locally, he went for another French brand called Gitanes. He couldn't always get them, thank God! They stank the place out.'

'That's what we could smell in that groundsman's hut,' said Waters. 'He's been in there for sure.'

'We'll have another look,' suggested Sergeant Lumley. 'If you smelt tobacco, he hasn't been gone too long. He must have been there today.'

'Probably after we nabbed his friend at Flagstaff,' said Anscombe.

'I'll call it in to Alan Kelsey,' Waters pressed numbers on his key pad. Kelsey answered on the first ring, Waters made his report.

'How long do you reckon he's been gone?' asked Kelsey.

'Possibly within hours,' suggested Waters. 'The tobacco smell was still pungent.'

'OK!' Kelsey replied. 'He's probably on his way now to either the ground itself or one of the stations. Hang on a sec while I have words with Major Collins.'

Kelsey returned in within seconds.

'No point in staying where you are, I can't see him returning there now. We need you near the centre of things. I suggest you go to Richmond Station and tell Sergeant Lumley to get himself and his men there as well, this is from Major Collins. I suggest you park the vehicle in the grounds of the football stadium. Have a good look around Richmond Station after the game finishes. We reckon Richmond is a possibility because most of the outgoing crowds will pass through it.'

'Will do,' replied Waters. 'But what about Roger Richardson, won't you need him on the monitors?'

'We've already got Donald Taylor and Adam Simmerson doing that, and virtually every cop on the beat has a photo of Asif now,' said Kelsey. 'I'm playing a hunch now. I reckon Richmond Station is probable as opposed to possible.'

'OK!' said Waters. 'Richmond it is.'

He went over to Sergeant Lumley to impart the good news.

CHAPTER 36

'They've found footage of someone who could be Asif,' Captain Roberts advised Major Collins. 'He's wearing dark trousers and a dark coloured jacket, could be black, blue or brown.'

'Where was he?'

'In Flagstaff Station concourse, he was waiting for the man we intercepted, as he came down the escalator. He was standing by one of the kiosks and was quite agitated when his mate was jumped on. Then he went up the escalator and out into the street, carrying a briefcase.'

'Are we sure it was him?'

'Donald Taylor had a good look at him, reckons he was also another of the three men in Henderson's shop.'

'You say he left the station altogether and went into the street?'

'Looks like it, sir.'

'Tell them to examine the footage more closely. What was he

wearing underneath his jacket?' said Major Collins. 'According to Sergeant Lumley he ditched the jacket in the groundsman's hut at Carlton.'

Captain Roberts spoke into his mobile.

'They're checking, sir.'

Major Collins fretted with impatience as Captain Roberts waited, his mobile phone to his ear.

'Tell them to take their bloody fingers out!' Collins snapped angrily. 'We've got a man wandering around the streets possibly carrying a bomb.'

'Still checking, sir,' Captain Roberts said patiently. 'They're trying to enhance the picture to isolate the 'V' at the front of his jacket, all they can say is, it's light in col ...yes? You're absolutely sure of that?' Captain Roberts broke the connection and turned to Major Collins. 'They reckon light blue, sir. The briefcase is light brown.'

'Good! Well done' snapped Collins. 'Get that circulated.'

*

Sergeant Lumley and two troopers alighted in the street outside the pedestrian underpass of Richmond Station in Swan Street, Richmond.

'Park the vehicle up there,' he ordered the driver. 'If any traffic warden starts whingeing about it tell him to get stuffed! Follow us in, but stay at this end. The rest of us will be at the Brunton Avenue end, if he comes in at all that's the most likely. What is it, Smollett?'

'Message from Control Centre, Captain Roberts, Sarge,' Smollett was cupping his hand to his earpiece. 'They reckon this guy Asif is wearing a light blue "T" shirt and carrying a light brown briefcase.'

'Guess that narrows it down,' said Lumley. 'In a football crowd a briefcase should stand out like dogs' balls. All right, let's go.'

He jerked his thumb; the two troopers and Roger Richardson followed him along the underground concourse. Roger had mixed feelings, aware he was placing himself in the firing line by staying with Sergeant Lumley, but his fears were balanced by a growing anger against Asif. That a man could apply to come to Australia, a country Roger had been born in and loved, to enjoy the benefits of what Roger believed was the best country in the world, and then abuse the hospitality offered him by attempting to kill, maim and destroy its citizens aroused extreme feelings of fury in Roger.

His emotions were enhanced by what he had recently witnessed first-hand in New York, the aftermath of the damage sustained after the attack on the World Trade Centre, now universally known as 9/11. He had also witnessed the grief of friends and relatives in New York who had lost loved ones. As he followed Sergeant Lumley his emotions ranged between fear and rage, but the latter began to supersede the former.

They climbed to the main platform level, walked to the exit at the western end of the station and headed for the underground passage that would be used by the bulk of the fans when they left the stadium. There were a couple of trains in the station and others were approaching from both east and west. Richmond was a busy junction as suburban lines entered it from the eastern and southern suburbs at one end, and Flinders Street Station and the Underground Loop in the other. Roger remembered reading once that it was the busiest junction in the Southern Hemisphere, true or not it was certainly active.

'OK!' said Lumley. 'Down we go. We'll stand at the far end

near the Brunton Avenue entrance. Remember, light blue shirt, light brown briefcase, Asian in origin.'

The passageway was relatively free with only a few entering and exiting.

'Pick a position that suits you,' ordered Lumley. 'The crowds will soon be coming out.'

'There's a few leaving now, Sarge,' Trooper Smollet commented and Lumley checked his watch.

'They're early, which indicates many have given up hope, one side must be well ahead,' he turned to Roger. 'What do you reckon?'

'I'd say you're right,' agreed Roger. 'We can check that when the first lot reach us.'

'All right, stand by lads,' ordered Lumley.

CHAPTER 37

'Where are Waters and Anscombe?' asked Major Collins.

'Heading for Richmond station,' answered Kelsey. 'They're travelling from that cricket ground at Carlton.'

'They won't be needed at Richmond station,' said Collins. 'I've arranged with Dick Rawlinson to send a detail there from Victoria Barracks. I suggest your two men park themselves on that pedestrian bridge over the railway tracks? If Asif decides it's too risky to go direct to the Station, assuming he's heading there, he may mix with crowds converging on the pedestrian bridge to approach it from the opposite direction, from Swan Street.'

'That makes sense,' Kelsey reached for his phone. 'I'll divert them.'

*

'Keep going,' said Anscombe.

'What! I was about to park next to that Army vehicle,' protested Waters.

'Change of plan, just over the wire.' said Anscombe. 'We're to head for the pedestrian bridge. Alan reckons Asif could use that to approach the station from the Swan Street end. Turn right here, looks as if we may have trouble finding a parking spot.'

'The hell we will, I'll dump it on the tram tracks if I have to.' Waters slotted the car between two parallel rows, they disembarked and headed for the near end of the pedestrian bridge.

'I'll go to the far end,' Waters said. 'You stay here. If he does come this way, he'd pick out two of us hanging around together, but one of us on his own would be less obvious. If I spot him, I'll give you a buzz, then follow him over. OK?'

Anscombe nodded and Waters began to cross the bridge. A trickle of people was crossing from the stadium end, Waters stopped a couple and had a short chat with them. He reached the other end and rang Anscombe.

'I'm here,' Waters announced. 'No sign of him...yet!'

'What did you say to those blokes?'

'Asked the score, one side is well ahead. They just gave up and left, there's a few others coming out now.'

'I guess it spreads the crowd out a bit,' commented Anscombe. 'I'll leave you to it.'

*

Bramble and Shackleton walked the full length of the platform at the lower level of Melbourne Central. By now they had identified some of Major Collins' men, Captain Bartlett's bomb squad and police operatives. Apart from brief nods nobody acknowledged anyone else's presence; they all had their eyes open for potential bomb carriers.

Bramble's phone rang.

'Bramble!'

'Kelsey,' replied the caller. 'Catherine has had some rapport with Razzaq's daughter and extracted some information, which we can only hope is accurate. She told Catherine how many bombs or bombers there were, and based on what she's told us it looks to me as if our friend Asif was the last one. Bear in mind she could have miscounted or is misleading us, I don't fully trust that bloody woman, too fanatical! Keep your eyes peeled.'

'What about Asif?'

'He was holed up in a cricket pavilion at Carlton, but he's left there. We've sent a detail to Richmond Station, always the busiest station on Grand Final Day, if he's been living in Melbourne a few years he'd know that.'

'Do you want us to go there?'

'No, stay where you are. There may be others...as I said, I don't trust that woman.'

*

'Stand by,' said Waters. 'They're starting to come out now.'

'The game isn't over yet!' Anscombe had his phone to his ear.

'For some it's a foregone conclusion, they're streaming out now.'

At the Melbourne Cricket Ground end Waters eyed the oncoming crowds keenly as he searched for a blue shirted man with a briefcase. He moved to one side, if he stood in the middle of the approach to the footbridge, he'd spend all his time dodging oncoming football fans, which could enable Asif to slip past.

The oncoming fans advanced towards the footbridge; further away large numbers moved across the green area towards

Richmond Railway Station. He registered the more distant crowds, but concentrated on those approaching the footbridge, if Asif was in the other moving crowds Sergeant Lumley's men would lock onto him. The numbers increased, Waters looked at his watch and realised the final siren must be imminent, if it hadn't sounded already. The exodus from the ground was increasing and Waters grimaced as he contemplated the difficulties of scanning all these people.

The exodus became more pronounced and turned into a torrent. Waters realised the game was now over. From flags being joyously waved he was able to gauge who had won.

'Ye Gods!' he muttered as the masses headed towards him, and another river of people made for the entrance guarded by Sergeant Lumley and his troopers. He cast his eyes desperately over the masses, standing on tiptoe as they approached and began to converge around the footbridge entry.

The task was wellnigh hopeless. He had to stand to one side, if he stood centrally, he would be roundly cursed by all and sundry as they tried to thread their way around him. His eyes flickered over the mob and he began to panic. It was impossible to ascertain who was wearing what and people were carrying a variety of items such as bags, eskies and football accoutrements.

At that point, he caught sight of a brown face, not surprising as there were a number of those, but this individual was wearing a blue shirt. Whether he was carrying anything Waters couldn't see but he decided to try for a closer look. He was swept to one side by the onrushing masses and was pushed hard and painfully against the parapet.

'Move on mate!' somebody said, and someone else also suggested he moved out of the way...or words to that effect! Waters tried desperately to move towards the Asian man he had spotted but could not. He fumbled for his radio, but his arms were pinioned as he was caught in the rush. He fought to raise his arm, nearly dropped his radio but continued being swept along surrounded by banners, flags streamers, gaily coloured hats and chattering fans.

'Gordon ...can you hear me?'

'What?'

There was considerable interference from the gaggle of voices of excited fans as Waters reached a quarter of the way across the bridge, the process wasn't assisted as a train passed underneath at the same time.

'Gordon!'

'I'm watching,' was the barely discernible reply and Waters relaxed to some extent. Anscombe would know he would only be calling if he had spotted something.

'I'm following, I'm coming over,' he called but couldn't make out Anscombe's reply. But a reply there had been; Waters hoped Anscombe had heard what he had said.

Waters was carried along by the chattering throng and avoided tripping over flags and eskies, it was all he could do to keep his radio to his ear.

'Can you hear me, Gordon?' he asked again desperately.

'I hear you...!' was the reply '...plus about a hundred others.'

'I'm nearly half way over, a man who looks like our friend is three quarters of the way across, bluish shirt, Asian appearance and ...!'

Gordon Anscombe had his radio pressed to his ear, missed the rest as two trains thundered under the footbridge in opposite directions, but got the gist of Waters' message. He scanned the crowds as they poured over the bridge and fanned out at his end. He eyed the centre of the bridge and wondered if he would be able to spot Jim Waters. He concentrated on the people spewing out into the car park at his end, then caught sight of an Asian in a blue shirt. As the throng around him spread out he was able to see he was carrying a light-coloured briefcase.

'Jim, I see him,' he said and heard Waters' acknowledgement. 'He's turned left after leaving the bridge, now heading east... towards Richmond Station.'

'Keep him in sight, I'm heading downhill now,' Waters indicated he had crossed the highest point of the bridge and now was over halfway.

'Roger and out,' Anscombe headed in the same direction as their quarry.

Asif maintained his direction, heading eastwards towards Richmond Station on Swan Street, in the middle of a mass of fans heading in the same direction. Some crossed the street and queued at the tram stops in the centre of the road. He looked back several times but Anscombe was well back in the throng and unnoticeable.

'Still heading for the station down Swan Street,' he radioed to Waters and heard the acknowledgment.

'I see you,' from Waters. 'Roughly forty metres behind you, can't see him yet.'

'I see him,' responded Anscombe. 'See you when you catch up.'

He refrained from looking behind to check Waters' whereabouts, he had lost people he was following before by glancing behind him, it only needed a second for one's quarry to vanish in a crowd.

'He's crossing Punt Road now,' Anscombe reported a few minutes later.

'I see him, I'm nearly up to you,' said Waters.

'Warn that Sergeant...what's his name?'

'Lumley,' said Waters. 'I've already reported in to Major Collins, Lumley should be aware by now. Don't look round, I'm with you, couple of metres.'

Anscombe didn't need telling, he could hear Waters' voice with his other ear as well as via radio. He raised his left hand in acknowledgment and continued to peer forward at Asif who was now halfway across Punt Road. Asif looked both ways before he crossed the second lane, landed on the footpath and commenced walking towards the station entrance.

Anscombe saw the lights had turned green for traffic, presently stopped on the south end of the Punt Road/Swan Street intersection. As he began to cross the first carriageway, he heard engines being revved up and vehicles began to move northwards in his direction.

Anscombe ran and paused on the centre bollard. He looked back, Waters was stranded on the side of the road he had just left, while Asif had crossed the road and was walking towards the station entrance. Waters had his radio to his ear, Anscombe assumed he was talking to Major Collins so he could warn Sergeant Lumley. Asif had vanished from view, Anscombe fretted and calculated his chances of sprinting across the roadway but traffic was too dense; he would never make it. No point getting run over now.

*

Sergeant Lumley clicked off his radio and signalled to his men.

'Swan Street entrance, now,' he snapped and they began to thread through the incoming passengers. Initially they were with the traffic flow but later, after they had ascended to and then descended from the platform, very much against it. Roger Richardson saw them going and attracted Lumley's attention.

'What is it?' he asked. 'Is he coming in from Swan Street?'

'Looks like it, you come with us, but stay in the booking office area,' commanded Lumley. 'Leave us to deal with him.'

Roger nodded and began to follow Lumley and his two men. Once more he could feel cold anger rising within him as he thought of Asif's intentions, he still couldn't fathom how a man granted admission to Australia to enjoy its educational and social benefits could contemplate actions to sabotage the country's infrastructure or kill its citizens. Again, his mind conjured up a vivid picture of the desolation and devastation in New York, and the continuing grief of many people he had encountered while he was there, those who had lost loved ones.

As Sergeant Lumley led the way into the booking hall, he answered a call on his radio.

'OK!' he responded and turned to his two men. 'He's entering from Swan Street now, keep your eyes peeled. Light blue "T" shirt, Asian appearance, carrying a light brown briefcase. Two spooks are tailing him, but in this crowd, we can't guarantee they can finger him...got that?'

They signified they had indeed 'got that' and went to each side of the passageway. People were flooding in. Many had deemed it easier to reach the station by crossing the line over the footbridge or alternatively crossing underneath the railway viaduct on Punt Road before turning left and approaching the station from the southern side. Having seen the pedestrian jam at the other end Lumley could sympathise with that.

He stood back and observed the influx, then sighted their quarry. The man was looking down, as though trying to make his dusky features less obvious, but Lumley spotted the light blue top. He caught the attention of the trooper on his side and jerked his head towards Asif. They began to move in.

But Asif perceived the danger. He cocked his head at Sergeant Lumley and began to push towards the right of the influx. Lumley tried to force his way after him, which brought forth complaints from many fans.

'Make way!' he shouted. 'Make way!' and forced his way into the centre of the throng. But Asif was well ahead, he also evaded the trooper approaching from the other side.

'Christ!' thought Lumley. 'The bugger might set the bloody thing off.'

This thought roused him to fresh efforts as he thrust his way through the throng, which brought forth shouts of 'Watch it, mate!' ... and ...' Excuse *me*!' ...but he was past worrying about them. Asif had reached a point where the crowd thinned, dodged into the concourse, ran to the far end, put his briefcase down and began fiddling with the clasp.

'Shit!' ejaculated Lumley which caused a young woman to look down her nose and say coldly: 'I *beg* your pardon?' He ignored her and thrust towards Asif, as he did so Asif straightened up, saw Lumley thrusting towards him and raised one hand. Lumley couldn't make out what was in it but assumed it could only be a detonator. Asif smiled triumphantly at Lumley, his hand raised, and began to utter words that Lumley couldn't understand although to him it sounded like Arabic.

Despair flooded through Lumley's system. He was ten or twelve metres short of Asif, he could never make the distance in time even if he had no football fans between them.

Lumley's nerves screamed at him as he realised this could be his last view of anything or anyone on this planet, he was about to be blasted or maybe dismembered by a devastating explosion and screams of fellow citizens within the Richmond station concourse would be the last sound he would ever hear.

CHAPTER 38

Roger Richardson had been tagging along behind Sergeant Lumley and his men, the uniforms assisted as people gave way to them, whereas he, Roger, met with resistance. Despite this he had reached the booking office concourse while Lumley and his men headed for the Swan Street entrance to station themselves on each side of the incoming flood. Then he lost sight of them, by this time Roger was facing the incoming tide, as opposed to travelling along with it whilst approaching from the Brunton Avenue entrance. He moved to one side and leant against the wall out of the traffic stream whilst he looked for Lumley and his men.

He caught sight of Lumley about thirty metres away, fighting to get into the middle of the crowd, with Trooper Smollett doing the same from the other side. Then Roger saw, unmistakeably, Asif thrusting his way through the incoming melee, he had passed Lumley and Smollett who had changed direction and were trying to intercept him. Asif was clearly aware they were trying to apprehend him. Asif reached the outer fringe of the crowd and, taking advantage of fewer people in that part of the concourse, gained on Sergeant Lumley and reached the booking area. With his back to the ticket windows, he put down his brief case and began fiddling with the clasp.

'Bloody hell!' Roger was aghast. 'He's priming it!'

His first urge was to turn and run, anywhere away from the blast that could turn this teeming mass of people into a scene of carnage. But where could he run to save himself? There was nowhere to go. Roger realised he was doomed, unless...!

Again, unreasoning anger surged through him, against Asif and his ilk who were prepared to kill indiscriminately... and for what? Simultaneously he knew he had nothing to lose and everything to gain. He couldn't run back, the press of the crowd prevented that, there was only one way to go...forwards. He adopted the fatalistic course, better to be blown up running towards it trying to do something, than running away from it which would only result in certain maiming or death.

Asif stood and raised one hand in the air, he was holding something and Roger saw him smile. At the time Roger was unaware Asif's triumphant smile was directed at Sergeant Lumley, but Roger knew a triumphant smile when he saw one. He also saw Asif intoning something which Roger couldn't understand but guessed what it was. He snapped into action and launched himself across the intervening space of roughly four to five metres.

As he propelled himself at Asif the one thought in his mind was Asif's right hand, holding what Roger assumed must be the detonator. His left shoulder slammed into Asif's legs from behind, his left arm encircled Asif's waist, his right hand and arm caught Asif's right elbow and the back of Asif's right hand hit the wall. Asif never saw him coming, he gasped as what he was holding in his hand was knocked out of alignment. He tried to seize hold of it again but, with a complete disregard for niceties, Roger hit him hard in the groin. Asif howled with pain, doubled up and Roger hit him again, Asif cried out again as Sergeant Lumley joined the fray, seized his right hand and prised the detonator from his fingers. It fell from Asif's grasp and skidded across to the wall. Asif tried to reach for it again but Trooper Smollett arrived and pushed it out of reach.

Asif struggled and for the first time realised the identity of his main opponent.

'You!' he snarled, then his head snapped back as Roger's clenched fist hit his jaw.

'Yes, it's me you bloody creep!' Roger ground out angrily. 'May you rot in hell!' He hit him again and Asif crumpled up. Sergeant Lumley forced the briefcase from Asif's grasp and pushed it against the wall.

'Hold him!' he snapped at Smollett and the other trooper who had come running up. 'Hold the bugger down while I call it in.'

A crowd of onlookers had formed, the incoming crowds were bunching up as people were rubber necking at the scuffle. Reinforcement arrived in the form of Waters and Anscombe who took over from the two troopers holding Asif.

'You two, clear the crowd out of the way, hold them back,' Waters shouted. 'They'll obey uniforms, just hold them back.'

*

Major Collins snatched up his radio as Lumley's call came through.

'Yes?'

'We've caught one of the bombers at Richmond station,' Lumley said tersely. 'We think it's safe but send the bloody bomb squad over quick, we need 'em here...now!'

Major Collins turned to Captain Roberts.

'Get Willoughby over to Richmond, pronto,' he snapped. 'They've got the bastard!'

As Captain Roberts communicated with Sergeant Willoughby, Major Collins acknowledged Lumley's message and sat back. He half smiled as he realised Lumley's impassioned call had not only omitted the use of the word 'sir' but had also presumed to give him, a Major, an order that included a swear word.

'Lucky for him I'm not a Second Lieutenant,' he mused and gave a dry chuckle.

*

Sergeant Willoughby and Trooper Aston disembarked at Richmond from the train they had boarded at Melbourne Central. They trotted up the rail platform along to the other end and down the flight of steps onto the concourse. Crowds of people were still milling around, but these were being diverted away from the pinioned Asif by Sergeant Lumley and his two men plus a couple of uniformed police who had arrived on the scene.

'Where is it?' demanded Willoughby.

Lumley pointed into the corner and Willoughby advanced towards the brief case.

'They told me he tried to detonate it with a handheld detonator,' said Willoughby. 'Where is that?'

'Over here,' answered Lumley. Willoughby examined it, and made a sucking noise between his teeth. He looked at the briefcase.

'Did he do that?' Willoughby indicated the loosened flap.

'Yes... but Roger here...' Lumley indicated Roger Richardson '... said all he appeared to do was take out the detonator.'

'OK!' Willoughby replied and knelt down by the brief case. He opened it cautiously and peered inside. He held it open under the nearest light, and pursed his lips.

'Harry!' he called out.

'Sarge?' Trooper Aston came over.

'Not sure about this one, we've got to get it out of here. I think he primed it, delayed action and then decided to use the detonator instead. I don't think we can stop it. Tell those bods to clear a way through, stop anyone coming in from Swan Street. Jump to it.'

'Sarge!' Aston needed no second bidding; he rushed over to the other soldiers and the police and shouted.

'Clear a way out, into Swan Street. We've got to get it out of here.'

The police and soldiers forced their way into the seething throng and formed a narrow passage. Willoughby and Aston ran down it with the briefcase and then outside onto the pavement.

Aston ran into the roadway with his arms held up and traffic screeched to a halt, there were angry shouts of '...what are you playing at, you silly sod?' ...and similar pleasantries but Aston ignored them as he cleared a path for Willoughby.

They weaved their way over the crossroads, to the accompaniment of horns, shouts, curses and screaming tyres. Willoughby was struck a glancing blow by a car, half fell and stumbled on the carriageway. Aston ran over, seized the briefcase and ran like the wind onto the parkland opposite. Aston ran and ran with Willoughby limping along behind and reached a deserted area of parkland. He whirled around in the fashion of a hammer thrower and hurled the briefcase from him as far as he could, and while it was still in mid-air, took cover behind the nearest tree.

'Here Sarge!' he shouted, Willoughby changed direction and

ran for the same tree but with it in line of the point where the briefcase had eventually landed.

Aston was lying flat on the ground behind the trunk which was about 2 feet in diameter and Willoughby flung himself on top of Aston.

'Hold your ears, open your mouth!' Willoughby screamed.

There was a vivid flash and a deafening concussion as the briefcase exploded. They lay with the heels of their hands pressing into their ears but could still feel the reverberations on their ear drums. There was a spattering sound as metal objects hit the tree trunk, Willoughby gasped with pain as one hit the toecap of his boot and penetrated it. Remnants of the briefcase landed a couple of metres away from them, the shower of metal objects continued and then ceased as they were spattered with grass and soil. Several leaves from the tree above floated down and covered them and the surrounding grass.

As the reverberations died away, Aston rubbed his ears, which were like cotton wool. Willoughby reached down and felt a metal spike or nail protruding through the toe cap of his boot.

'Bugger it!' he said feelingly.

'What's up?'

'I've been stabbed through the foot,' growled Willoughby. 'Can you pull it out, Harry?'

'I'm not touching it, Sarge,' said Aston. 'We need a medic.'

'I can't bloody well walk! Give me your shoulder, this damn thing hurts like hell!'

*

'What's happened?' Major Collins demanded as the call from Sergeant Lumley came through. 'What's that? It's exploded? For God's sake where?'

Lumley's voice crackled over the line, Captain Roberts and Kelsey could hear Lumley's agitated tones. Then Major Collins nodded.

'Well done, Sergeant,' he said. 'You say they're taking Asif to police headquarters. Where?'

He put down the phone and turned to Kelsey.

'They're taking Asif to St Kilda Road which makes sense, it's probably nearest. Chief Inspector Talintyre arrived on the scene with Detective Sergeant Griffiths and they claimed him. Sergeant Lumley was worried they may have people around the area who might try and lynch Asif before we're able to question him. Frankly, I doubt it, but I won't argue with the logic, better safe than sorry. I couldn't care less where he goes now, just so long as he's in custody.'

'What about the bomb, Major?' asked Kelsey. 'You say it's exploded. Was anyone hurt?'

'Oh...yes...sorry,' Collins waved a hand apologetically. 'One man slightly injured, Sergeant Willoughby copped a piece of metal through his foot and he's on his way to hospital. Looks as if Asif set a delayed action fuse into operation, clearly for all his fanaticism he hadn't initially planned to be a suicide bomber. Willoughby realised what it was and he and one of his men ran with it to parkland and it exploded there. Nobody else was hurt.'

'Thank God!' said Kelsey.

'In the meantime, we don't drop our guard,' snapped Major Collins. 'I wouldn't trust these bastards as far as I could throw them. Maintain security at all stations until 8 o'clock tonight, by which time the crowds should be at home, including late revellers who stay to celebrate at city bars.'

CHAPTER 39

Francis Burton looked around the conference table in the ASIO Canberra building. Present were Alan Kelsey and the ASIO personnel who had taken part in the operation. Also present were Captain Bartlett and Major Collins, plus Mike Duval, from the computer section, and Colin Attwood, who had taken the initial call from Donald Taylor.

'Happily, the whole operation was successful,' said Burton. 'But we can't rest on our laurels. We must analyse what did happen and learn from it, the war is not over yet.'

He sipped from a glass of water and resumed.

'The best outcome would have been to have rounded up all participants, well, we didn't. Some of the group escaped from the Melbourne area and we've reason to believe others got away from country properties in Gippsland. We won this round, but from the fanaticism encountered over past weeks we can expect more problems in future. We mustn't lower our guard. Consequently, we are forming a new squad which will deal with matters arising from this latest escapade, all the mistakes we made must be closely examined. Anything to add to that, Major?'

Collins shook his head.

'My operation went off satisfactorily, Captain Roberts and myself appeared late on while Captain Bartlett's men did an excellent job in dealing with the bombs after they had been discovered. How is Sergeant Willoughby by the way, Captain?'

'Fit and well, sir, and anxious to return to duty,' Captain Bartlett responded. 'His boot stopped most of the force of the bomb splinter, but it was still nasty and painful. He'll be on crutches for a few weeks. Further, I would commend the action of Trooper Aston. Aston risked his life to remove that primed bomb from Richmond Station. He saved countless lives by his action.'

'I agree with that,' said Major Collins. 'Both he and Willoughby deserve a bloody medal, leave that with me, Captain. I intend to make representations on that score,' he turned to Kelsey. 'Any comments, Alan?'

'A success, as Francis says, but we were lucky,' Kelsey looked around the room as he spoke. 'There were some appalling cock ups, the worst aspect was regarding Donald Taylor. When he was arrested as a murder suspect and told his story, nobody in Victorian Police believed him. We know from bitter experience there are numerous cranks around, and I realise many crims and other wrongdoers use outlandish stories to divert and confuse police after they've been arrested. I could understand their initial reaction but frankly, anything with terror connotations was worth a second look.'

'Amen to that,' commented Burton.

'Luckily Taylor managed to contact us before he was apprehended. Colin Attwood took the initial call and Bob Bramble handled it. Dave McKay attended the Police complex and made contact with Detective Sergeant Griffiths who fortunately was prepared to listen.'

Kelsey paused and sipped some water.

'We wasted precious days following leads that, although they led in the right direction, just fizzled out. Our biggest break came when Adam Simmerson escaped and Bob Bramble and Denis Shackleton, on a parallel line of enquiry, were on the spot just as his kidnappers recaptured him. But we can't rely on being that lucky again.'

He turned to Mike Duval.

'You were involved when Taylor came through on the phone, I know Colin Attwood took the call when you were both on the recruiting roster. You both took Taylor seriously despite numerous crank calls we get from jokers, activists and nuts. Bear in mind, we succeeded but we were assisted by luck, common sense, and persistence. We'll need all these attributes in the future.'

Kelsey gathered his papers together and was about to defer to Francis Burton when he paused.

'One further point, on a happier note. Adam Simmerson and his girl-friend Rhonda Muston are going to tie the knot in about a month. We have advised Adam Simmerson that Bob Bramble and Denis Shackleton will be attending the ceremony. They are the most appropriate representatives from here since they got him out of the mire and he knows them. This is not; repeat *not*, a social event for us, there's no need to buy any wedding presents!'

He paused as a ripple of laughter ran through the room.

'Our representatives will be armed and have a watching brief, Simmerson could be a retaliatory target since some of the Gippsland participants, perhaps his former gaolers, are still at large and may not forgive lightly. Detective Sergeant Griffiths of the Victorian Police will be present for the same reason. If we spot anyone, then we have a further line of enquiry.'

'What about Donald Taylor?'

'He's moved from his Melbourne apartment; fearing he could still be a target. He's moved back to Sydney and is presently unemployed,' said Kelsey. 'He has very advanced computer skills, maybe we could use him. We have a vacancy in Canberra and we have made him an offer.'

'So out of misfortune, cometh good!' murmured Bramble.

'Bob...you always were a sanctimonious bastard!'

T H E   E N D